ENEMIES AND ALLIES

LEGENDS OF NOLA

BOOK FOUR

Other Books by the Author

Published under the name Susan Elliston

Enemies and Allies

Legends of NOLA

Book Four

A Historical Time-travel Adventure

BY

D.S. Elliston

Elliston Entertainment • Florida

Enemies and Allies

Cover Image: Dylan Daniels
Cover and Book Layout/Design by The Book Team
ISBN 978-0-9854801-7-2 (Original Paperback)
First Paperback Edition: July 2022

Contact the author
On Facebook:
https://www.facebook.com/Author-DS-Elliston-287604241632452/

Book Series on Facebook:
https://www.facebook.com/Legends-of-NOLA-149136808530163/

Twitter: @Ldylstn

NOTE—ADULT CONTENT: Book contains profanities, harsh language, violence, and sexual abuse and is intended for adults.

THIS BOOK IS DEDICATED TO
MY HUSBAND, DANIEL POLCHINSKI.
WITHOUT HIS SUPPORT AND ENCOURAGEMENT,
THIS SAGA WOULD NEVER HAVE BEEN TOLD.

My Lady,

Time is as fluid as the sea I sailed upon. Its currents like the days washing you along on life's journey. The kindest, most beautiful gift time ever deposited upon my shore was you. The cruelest its waves ever became was the day it swept you from my life. And now it seems, in its grandest moment, I am to be put adrift in the mystery of its depths. Or rather, set free to sail upon heaven's ocean above.

Upon which star I wonder, will I wash ashore? Wherever time and tide take me, I go full of love and in peace. Let me no longer be an anchor to you. Instead, let the memory of us calm your soul, and set you free to sail the most glorious ocean of them all . . . the one called life.

Jean Laffite

❧ One ❧

T he muffled sounds that filled the night air drifted from within the house behind her. Tori had remained very still, staring at the stranger who had appeared from among the shadows. It was not so much how he looked or acted; it had been his question that had both stunned and confused her. She was standing there, holding her breath, while her mind raced to sort out what was real and what was her imagination. 'I had to have heard him wrong surely,' she thought. 'Just wait and let him talk first. Come on; you know you're upset; you simply imagined it. And you are about to panic. So, get a grip. Take a breath and…'

He spoke again. "I repeat, myself, don't you think a private jet would be better?" The man took another step closer; his head cocked to one side.

Tori did not move away; she just stood there looking at him. He had repeated it; he'd said, jet, and that was not a word of this age. There could be no doubt she had heard him correctly, but who was he, and what was his game? What the hell was going on?

The man smiled in a pleasant and kindly manner while watching her tormented face. "Right then, shall we start again? I shall repeat myself slowly, so there is no doubt. Look, I overheard all that nasty piece of work said. Unfortunately, every word the bitch had to impart is accurate." He became quiet once more, letting Laffite's wife take in what he'd just declared to be true. The information told to her moments ago had stung, no doubt like the slap to her face. The red mark left behind from Simone's assault was fading; however, Tori's strange reactions toward him were not. He could tell this by the expression behind her eyes and her continued silence; she was unsure what to believe. It was evident her fear and uncertainty were expanding because of him, and he wondered why? His

1

words were supposed to have caused happiness and offered her relief, not thrown her into a state of panic. He'd just told her in so many words that she was not alone and not the only time traveler around. Why, then, did she only continue to stare at him? He'd made himself clear, hadn't he? His mind raced through his actions and what he'd said. Had there been a mistake?

Cisco had come to this dinner to confirm his suspicions that Madame Laffite, like himself, came from another time. By over-hearing her mention a 747, he'd received his answer without a single doubt. No mistake there, and it could not have been a better way to confirm her origins to him. She'd talked about something that did not yet exist. No, he was right; it was her reaction to him that was wrong. The man took yet another step toward her. "Look, until just now, I've had my suspicions for some time that you came from the future, like me. I just returned from a long trip. Not to the future, please, don't misunderstand me. Got to admit, I do miss transportation like cars and planes. Could have saved me some long, lonely weeks on the road." He grinned. "Oh, don't look so shocked. Shit, say something. I'm going nuts here." He continued grinning at her as he shrugged his shoulders, waiting for a response that still wasn't forthcoming. Then his expression changed and was replaced by a look of concern. "Look, we are not the first, or will we be the last to travel through time. You have to know that. It's just until you mentioned the 747; I could not be entirely satisfied that I was right. Until I was, there was no need for me to come forward. You get that. I was going to introduce myself and have a little chat to see if I couldn't get you to slip up or reveal yourself somehow. Rather like me using the word jet, you might have used a word, also not of this era. Numbers even, like numbers that represent a certain model plane."

Tori continued to hold back. More so out of the sheer shock of what was happening, more than anything. Her initial surprise of suddenly seeing the stranger was wearing off, and because of his words, her excitement was building. 'Lord, if she were not careful, her emotions would take over, and thinking or acting in the right direction would evaporate,' she thought. In the past, she had always seemed to make the wrong move. Flashes of memories about her mistakes slipped by one after the other. Each one had taken her further away from her chance to return to the lake. The lake was her key to going home. Or maybe this stranger had another way for her to reach the future? This thought caused her to shudder and try as she might; it was getting harder to contain her excitement.

'I must remain in control this time,' she assured herself. Tori took a deep breath as the small voice in her head agreed and reminded her that she needed to have a firm grip on her emotions more than ever. After she'd told herself this, her mind raced on, and that voice of reason was fading. 'I need to think before I react. I need to remain calm and see what he's about?' Standing there and staying calm, however, was becoming increasingly difficult. Her mind continued to speed on with the what-ifs and why's. Her heart rate picked up, and her eyes began to fill with unspent tears as she willingly allowed herself to accept the man was real and not a figment of her imagination. Then out of nowhere, the realization of who and what this man represented started to sink in. Tori knew she'd heard him correctly, and that meant she was not alone; she had just met someone who, like herself, came from another time. He came from the time of jets and 747's.

He was dressed as a gentleman of this era; his appearance was that of a wealthy young man. To say he was good-looking was a bit of an understatement; the man was drop-dead gorgeous. With eyes a deep brown and wavey black hair, he had the look of a film star. His hair was styled, but not quite like the majority men wore these days. It was longer than some but shorter than Jeans. His complexion was olive, and his height was above average. He would stand taller than most she knew, and Tori wondered how he had explained his stature. Then there was his accent; it had a slight hint of Texas drawl. It was not strong, but it was there non the less. How did he explain that away to those who knew him?

3

Laffite's wife had continued to stand and stare at him. It was as if she was making her mind up as to what to say and do next, and then, there it was, the reaction he'd hoped to see. The woman had relaxed her fearful gaze and replaced it with one of hope. Now the time was right to explain himself, and trust she was ready to listen, he told himself. "Look, up until this moment, I was not going to do anything, just in case. You understand? Everything changed with that bitch's attitude. That's when I saw how you needed me. Let me help you. Like I said before, I can be your friend, and lady, by the sounds of that nasty creature that just left us, you need one." He held out his arms, and with no further hesitation, Tori moved into his embrace. Instantly he wrapped his arms around her and hugged her. "Much better. You're welcome, by the way."

There was something in his words and his mannerisms that made her feel safe. It was not that he was obviously from the future. No, it was far more than that. He was her instant friend, one Tori's gut told her she could trust. He had chosen to step forward to help, and in so doing, he'd become an answer to her prayers. To hell with stifling her emotions. She'd just met someone from her own time, a person who would understand her, who could indeed help her on so many levels. In her mind, he was proof that one day she could go home.

The dashing man pushed her back from his embrace and looked at her tear-stained face. "Now, none of that. Tears are not allowed on my watch. Look, it seems to me; you have two choices at the moment. Well, three actually, if you think about it. One, you could keep on hugging me, but as nice as it is, that won't get us anywhere. So that leaves us with the following; second, you can leave, or third, go back in, as if nothing is wrong, and blow them away. I opt for going back in. You can even be my partner. I love to watch their stuck-up, pompous ass ways; all fall apart when someone does something out of step." He wiped the last of her tears from her cheek with his thumb as he continued to whisper. "Look, I think you need a good stiff drink. What do you say? Are we on?"

His smile was infectious, and with it, somehow, things did not seem quite so bleak. Knowing this, Tori smiled brightly as a small chuckle escaped her. Tori had to admit; sheer happiness was all she felt at that moment. Then as fast as the glee had surrounded them, it slipped away. Once again, she was uncertain as to what to do. Was going back inside a good idea or not? Her hesitation showed clearly because a puzzled frown covered her brow. As great as meeting this stranger was, Jean desperately needed her help, and he came first. "I can't; I am sorry. I have to help my husband and..."

"Look," he interrupted, "you can't help Laffite tonight, but we will come up with something later, I promise. Let's go in, and at least have a drink, and ignore the dumbasses. At least that much will rattle a few cages. Far better not to give them an idea that you have hope, along with my undying attention, something I might add that Simone sought earlier. Talk about having the hots for me. That one was beyond horny."

Tori was laughing. God, it felt good to have someone to talk to without worrying about using the wrong terms or words. She had not remembered how much she genuinely missed her own time until right then. "You're on, but don't you think I should know your name, Sir? After all, I don't drink or dance with strangers," she purposely drawled.

"Shit, do not, I repeat, do not talk like that. These simpering, dumb Southern Belle's, bore me stupid. Well, almost... they are rather surprising in bed." He winked and took her by the hand. "Besides, dressed like you are, you look far from a Southern Belle. Fox is more like it." Chuckling to himself, he took a step toward the closed door and the party inside.

Tori pulled her hand free of his and looked directly into his grinning face. Her stern expression caught his attention. "You bet your sweet ass, I'm not or ever will be simpering, and if you think for one second, I'm about to be seduced into screwing you; if that's your plan, you're in for a shock. What I want to know is, who are you? How long have you known about me? Damn it, you have been watching me, and that's plain creepy if you get my drift."

The Spaniard chuckled. "Never looked at it as acting creepy, just cautious. One can't be too careful. Been here two years, and the name's Cisco to my friends. You won't believe what name I go by to everyone else, but then, that's for later. Since you first arrived in New Orleans with Laffite, I have known about you. Let's talk about that later too. The way I see it, we were meant to meet tonight. Look, I stepped out here rather than join those idiots in the smoking room. I much prefer to watch the ladies than sit and listen to boring political bullshit. Anyway, as I told you, I came out here to escape. A move that was lucky for you." He saw her frown and begin to chew on her bottom lip while a puzzled look filled her face. That would not do in his mind; he had to keep her from ditching him, and he offered help. "Ok, you got that, the part about being lucky I was here, more important, I offered my help remember. Now I tell you I am thirsty as hell, and you promised me a drink. I won't take no for an answer. After you," he bowed low, indicating the way with a swing of his hand.

Tori wasn't sure that he could help her, but she did feel that he was her only friend right then. Her expression changed once more, and a slight smile played on her lips. "I never said yes, nor did I offer you a drink, but having one sounds right up my alley." Smiling broadly, she nodded her head in agreement. Tori squared her shoulders and placed her hand over his arm, while turning to face the house. "Laffite's wife needs to show everyone, enemies, and allies alike, that she is not one to be ignored or shoved aside. If those inside assume I will do the so-called proper thing by quietly and shamefully leaving, well, they can guess again, right? No... better still, they can kiss my ass."

"Madame! Such language and, if I might add, nice ass too."

"And that's proper? Such a comment is just not spoken about to a lady's face." She was giggling, as was Cisco.

The man was enjoying himself, but he knew if he continued acting like he was, they'd blow it. "Come on, let's do this while I can stop laughing because much more, and I promise you, I will totally lose it."

Upon stepping back inside the room, escorted by Cisco, Tori noticed immediately how a hush fell around her. Then almost as fast as it had invaded her space, the sounds of softly whispered remarks began to fill the room. One or two couples moved away from her vicinity while others blatantly turned their backs toward her. A few more glared openly, almost daring her to respond, and Tori wanted to scream at them. She wanted to tell them what hypocrites they all were. But instead, she smiled and pretended that she noticed nothing odd about how she and her new companion were ostracized.

If Simone was shocked that her information had not devastated Tori, she did not openly show it. Only once did she shudder in anger, and that was when she saw who Tori's new escort was. Again, her hated rival had taken advantage of her situation and befriended the dashing rogue who she had wanted. Edward, far too pleased with himself, didn't notice Simone's jealous pout. All he knew was his lover wanted to depart shortly after Tori, and her male companion walked into the room.

Simone made her mind up that she'd deal with Laffite's wife soon enough. Right then, the jealous vixen had Edward Duval, and she reasoned, they had better depart because they were both so thrilled by the pirate's arrest; it was clear if they remained, it would be dangerous for them. Neither would be able to conceal the part they had played, she was sure. No, it was far better; they kept that to themselves. To allow any hint of Edward's involvement in Jean's arrest, as much as she wanted it to be common knowledge, would not be dignified or serve a purpose in their favor. Simone knew Claiborne needed to receive all the glory, thus assuring the strengthening of their friendship with the American. Her lip raised on one side as a smirk slid across her face. The man's ever-growing debt of appreciation would continue to expand, and soon the witless statesman would be accepting more involvement from her darling lover. "Come Edward," she clasped his hand, "it is time we left. I fear if we linger, I will not be able to contain how very proud of you I am, of your part in this wonderful outcome. That my dear must remain all Claiborne's"

Agreeing and giving in to her wise words, Edward and Simone said their goodbyes to their friends while seeming to ignore the spectacle Tori was making of herself. The stupid female should know that she was not wanted, and the proper action in her delicate position would be to depart. Instead, she had begun drinking, and the Spanish stranger was only too obliging. He even had his arm around her waist at one time and whatever he whispered into her ear had the bitch laughing; Simone looked away, she had seen enough.

Unable to help himself, just before he left the room, the dandy did turn to take one last victorious glance toward Laffite's wife. Seeing her on the arm of the stranger did not overly upset him. Edward had assumed that Tori had known Cisco before this night and let him escort her in her hour of despair. The man was a fool, Duval assured himself, for it would not do one well to be seen mixing with the likes of a pirate's wife. Jean's woman was, in his mind, as doomed as her husband. No one would associate with her after tonight. He had succeeded in her downfall at last, and it was exhilarating. After that brief moment of triumphant scrutiny, Edward looked away and dismissed any further thoughts on the matter. At that moment, he had only Simone on his mind, and she possessed such exciting ways in which to make the rest of their night one to remember. Oh, there was no doubt she would show her appreciation for all he had accomplished, and the dandy began to fantasize what delights he could ask for to add to their enjoyment and celebration.

AFTER the one drink, Tori decided she required another, and soon Cisco found himself filling her glass repeatedly. At first, he indulged her with no hesitation, but this poor decision rapidly caught up with him. In fact, by the time Tori decided that they had better leave, she was having a slight problem walking independently.

Rather than let her hostess or anyone else see her awkward condition, Tori asked her new friend to help her depart in a dignified manner. That consisted of walking calmly and not stumbling over herself before reaching the outside.

Cisco understood how rude slipping away without formally thanking their hosts was. Still, he had no choice because allowing Tori to fall flat on her ass would most certainly feed the gossiping mouths. They would have more slandering material to add to her now-disgraced position in society, something he would not allow. Wisely, Cisco ignored the required protocol of the day and escorted his charge from the house without further incident.

AFTER she had received her cape, and he, his coat, the old black slave opened the front door, and if he wondered why the woman was heading toward her carriage on the arm of a stranger, he said nothing. The black man didn't even wait to see what would happen; he just closed the door and faced the hallway to await the next departing guests.

When the front door closed, Cisco breathed a sigh of relief. However, it was short-lived because the mixture of too much alcohol combined with the fresh air, hit her hard. In seconds, it was all he could do to keep her upright and walking in the right direction.

The whole world was spinning, and as much as Tori wanted the pathway to stop its infernal up and down motion, it would not. Toward the end of the walkway, Jean's wife knew she was either going to throw up or pass out. Then to make matters worse, to her horror, Tori realized the step up into the carriage was too high. She could not keep her balance, or remain steady enough, to maneuver her foot. The now very inebriated female looked at her feet as a loud hiccup sounded in the quiet surrounding. "Oh, shit, guess I drank a tad too much. I just need to lift my foot like this." Tori's foot was on the first step, but it kept sliding precariously. "Sorry about this, the darn step-up is not cooperating, and Cisco, my friend, I don't feel so good."

Jean's wife had given up caring about who saw her in such a state and had closed her eyes to allow the blackness of unconsciousness to take over. She could feel the blanket of sleep blissfully sweeping her away from her problems and her spinning world. The last thought that crossed her mind was that there wouldn't be any aspirin to help her out with what was sure to be one hell of a hangover.

Cisco saw her slipping from the carriage step, and in his blurry state, he reached out and caught her before she could hurt herself. In a matter of seconds, the handsome stranger had in his arms a helpless, beautiful woman. He held Jean's lady close, as briefly, a wave of worry crossed his thoughts. Jean Laffite was the most respected and feared pirate of the day. Well, maybe not respected right then, but who would care. The pirate had connections, and if he ever learned his wife had been taken advantage of, well, that would be like shooting oneself. Tori's new friend looked down at the utterly venerable female and blamed himself. He was the reason for her inebriated state; hell, everyone would testify to that. Tongues were most likely wagging already that the lady in question had one too many glasses and left with him. Not that they had a clue how bad off she was. He'd gotten her out of the house before that, but they'd say Cisco had been the one to get Laffite's wife drunk. The worried man looked back toward the front entrance of the house. It would only be a matter of time before someone else departed, and when they did, what would they do? He was standing there, with his arms full of trouble, and he needed to make a move fast. "Decisions, decisions," he mumbled while trying to sort out what his next move should be.

Tori's escort had consumed more alcohol than he usually would at such functions but nowhere near as much as his lovely charge.

His drinking less had left him in a slightly better condition than the lady, and for that much, he was grateful. At least he could function and think somewhat more clearly, something he had to do for both of them, it seemed. After quickly evaluating their situation, he concluded that the only way he would make it home and see that Tori was taken care of was to hitch a ride with her. This action seemed to be the most practical idea and very logical too. After all, she had a carriage, and he did not. He kept looking from Tori to the house behind him and back again. Could he dare to be bold enough to use Laffite's carriage? Who was there that could stop him? If seen, the black doorman would never try to intervene, but he would most certainly gossip if he witnessed what was taking place or what was about to. If the Irish servant were to turn up, who the hell knew what would happen then? Unlike the slave, he had more guts to question what was going on, and no doubt he'd do just that. In the end, Cisco told himself, he had no other choice but to make his move and to hell with fearing the pirate. Laffite could be reasoned with at a later date if need be.

The sound of someone coughing drew Cisco's attention. The driver was looking down at his Mistress and the stranger, in whose arms she lay. His assessment of the situation was that it was not proper. He shook his head as if saying no and then ceased this action to rub his hands together while thinking.

Cisco was in a quandary as to his next move. A real friend and gentleman would see to it that the lady arrived home safely. Now, he'd have to trust her driver to do that, and how in the hell could he trust a man he did not know? Another good reason to use the carriage himself. Besides, Tori had many enemies now, thanks to Jean's arrest. Not to mention that sultry bitch Simone and her man. Something told him those two would love to get a hold of Tori. These thoughts and his situation sobered Cisco up enough to make his final decision. In seconds he acted with no further hesitation. Standing straight, he lifted Tori and placed her inside the carriage. When this awkward task was accomplished, he climbed into the

11

seat beside her and called out an order to the driver to take them to an address on Saint Anne Street, but nothing happened. Seeing Tori would not fall off the seat, Cisco leaned out the carriage door and firmly added to his directions. "Hurry up, get a move on; you have your orders."

His eyes glanced again toward the house. The last thing he wanted was to be seen leaving in Laffite's carriage. "Get a move on," he shouted in his most authoritative-sounding voice as his hand hit the roof of the carriage.

THE destination Cisco had given was well known by many. It was close to the edge of town, in an area of cottages where many white men of standing kept their Mistresses. Everyone in the city knew this and more; most knew the address he had given was to be avoided.

When at last, the driver obeyed, Cisco was thankful because their immediate departure had avoided anyone else seeing Tori leave with him. He could relax and think his next move through. At least there was time for him to consider his actions, unlike Laffite's slave, who sat guiding the horses to their destination while struggling with what he was doing. That man, unlike Cisco, had no choice; he had to do as was commanded, but he did not have to agree or like it.

SLOWLY, they had made their way through the darkened streets, passing by the grand homes of what would one day be called the heart of the French Quarter. The carriage driver looked from side to side, observing the many buildings as they proceeded, while Cisco spent his time watching his charge and forming a plan of action. The horses finally stopped, and when no one came to open the door, as was customary, he knew that the driver was wondering, even hoping for an explanation as to why their journey home had led them to this location first. A more determined and confident Cisco slipped from between Tori, and the cushioned seat, letting her lay gently down before he climbed out of the carriage to see what was happening. Standing on the step of the vehicle, he could look directly at the driver. The slave was seated, staring straight ahead, looking as if he had the weight of the world upon his shoulders.

"Is there a problem? Why have we stopped?" Cisco's voice sounded quite loud in the night air, so he lowered his tone. "I gave an order; maybe you misunderstood me. The address is 152 Rue Saint Anne. You do know where Saint Anne Street is, don't you?"

"Yes, Sir, I rightly, does. I know'd where da place is that you, want's ta go. I also know'd whose place that be. Da Boss, he'd not be happy with this here boy if'n I take his lady, da Miz Tori, over that way." The driver shook his head before turning to look at Cisco. Straightening up in the seat and squaring his shoulders, he continued talking, but with more authority in his voice this time. "I may be only da driver fo Master Laffite, but he be more'n Boss, ta me. Yes, Sir, an if" n you know'd, what be good fo you, taken Miz Tori in her condition, and all, over there... well da Master he goin' to kill us both. I sure don't want ta, go and die yet, and I think's you feel da same like."

A moan sounded from within the carriage, and Cisco checked on the lady's condition. While looking at her, his mind raced on. She was from his time, someone to talk to who would understand him and his actions. The woman was a liberated female from the future who would understand so much. Still, the driver was right; she was the wife of one of the most powerful men in New Orleans. He reminded himself Jean Laffite was no one to mess around with, and everything he knew about the Laffite's relationship led him to believe that they were very much in love. As he continued to look at Tori, he shivered with his subsequent realization. Any man in love was a dangerous man, especially one with the pirate's reputation.

Cisco knew he could become a friend to both of them, and the best way to do that would be to help Tori and assist her by getting Jean out of jail. Laffite's wife needed help real help, but first, he had to take care of her. Make sure she was safe, no matter the risk. The pirate would have to understand that much, surely? Besides, the idea appealed to his sense of adventure, regardless of the consequences. He could have fun while sealing his newfound friendship with his comrade from the future.

So, it was at this precise moment he realized he wanted more than the casual companionship of this beautiful lady. He didn't want a romantic relationship. He didn't even want to seduce her; what he wished for was a close and ever-lasting friendship and not only from her but her husband too.

Cisco looked the driver square in the eyes. "You have nothing to worry about, as far as Mr. Laffite is concerned. It is his orders I follow this night. He is not able to take care of his lady and has ordered me to do so. Why else, do you think Miss Tori departed this evening with me? Now, if I were you, I would be far more worried about the owner of the home we are to visit. For, if she were, to become upset with you, for any reason, well…" he hesitated, "need I say more?"

The driver, whose eyes seemed to bulge, and were as wide-open as they could get, nodded his head in agreement. He had been ready to question the right of this stranger further, especially to his so-called orders, but this stranger had scared him. He would do as he was asked, regardless. "Lord, protect us," he mumbled. He hoped this person knew what he was doing, for both of their sakes. A short time later, the carriage pulled up to the house on Saint Anne Street, and Cisco carried the passed-out Tori to the Creole cottage's door. The driver, upset by what he saw, called out to them softly, almost as if he did not want to be, heard. "What's, you want me ta, do now?"

Cisco turned and looked at the driver, knowing that the man was in turmoil. "You go back home and be sure to tell no one where

Miss Tori is. If you tell someone, and they tell, well, you know how things spread around this town. If you tell, it could ruin her reputation. Then, Boss, as you call him, he would kill us both. You can come to pick Miss Tori up tomorrow after you get word from me. Come carefully, and try not to draw attention to yourself. Do you understand me? You, do as I say, and everything will be alright, and Laffite will be pleased, I can assure you."

What else could the driver do? Here was a white man, giving him orders. True, it was not Laffite, but then he claimed he was a friend of both the Laffite's and said to come back the next day. Right or wrong, he just wanted to get away from the place, and the sooner, the better, as far as he was concerned. As for telling anyone where he'd been, well, no one had to worry about that, no Sir. He nodded his head, and without another word, he started off down the road.

Cisco watched him start off, and waited to make sure he was going to keep going. Once the carriage turned onto the street and disappeared from sight, he turned and faced the front door. Then he kicked the cottage door until it opened just wide enough for him to squeeze inside. "I thought you would never get here and open up. Give me a hand, will you? We need to get this woman to bed. I have to get her into the spare room before I drop her. I'm not exactly steady on my feet myself."

Marie Laveau looked at the bundle dressed in black and held the lamp close to the individual's face. The light illuminated Tori's features, and she recognized her immediately. Her eyes flashed sideways towards the man holding her. Marie's eyes were narrow slits, with their dark orbs reflecting sparks of light, holding his attention. "You do know who she is, don't you? Are you crazy? Her man will kill you for this."

"Her man, as you say, is in jail, and this lovely lady has had too much to drink and needs a friend right now. So come on, Marie, help me get her to the bedroom before I drop her, and then I will tell you the latest."

Cisco placed her down gently on the soft bed, and Tori, sensing that she was safe, turned and curled herself into a child-like sleeping position, oblivious to those who watched. Marie gazed into the face of the woman she had only, up until now, known as a client. Now, it seemed that she was destined to get to know her as a friend. So much pain she had seen Tori go through, but to have her man in jail, no wonder she got herself drunk; who would blame her? Tori was a strong woman and a fighter. She'd already proven that, but this had been one blow too much. Laffite in jail! Never in all the gossip among her followers was there a hint that it would happen. Sure, some wanted him finished and gone but put in jail; this was serious.

"You were right, Marie. Tori is what we suspected. She is from my time, or damn near it. That makes three of us now in this town, just as you predicted. I wonder how many more walk the streets?" Cisco watched Marie smile and nod her head but she didn't say a word. He was puzzled by this enigma of a girl, not yet a woman in years, by his standards. Eighteen was hardly old enough to qualify in that department, as far as he was concerned.

The black mulatto was feared and respected by all those who knew of her. Even those who had never met her feared her Ju-Ju. Marie had been studying for years; she'd started learning long before her association with Cisco. Voodoo and the old ways of healing had been her lessons until he had come along. Then, she learned things way beyond anyone in her time could have taught her, and she'd been a good student. Marie had learned from him so fast that it had amazed him and encouraged him to supply her with as much knowledge as she could absorb.

Standing there, looking at the dusky-skinned girl, Cisco nodded his head slightly. If it had not been for Marie, her understanding and complete acceptance, of how he had come to be in New Orleans, he feared he would have gone mad. He recalled how Marie had stumbled upon him after he had miraculously materialized out of nowhere, right before her eyes. She had told him he was running like his life depended on it, but instead of fear or shock, by what she had witnessed, she had instinctively chased after him, sensing the stranger was unique and going to be special. It had not taken her long to reach an accurate conclusion of what he was. Just by judging the strange way he'd dressed and the way he had popped up, even a fool had to admit, what their eyes told them, but then his Marie was no fool.

When she finally caught up with him that first night, he was wandering drunkenly around, mumbling to himself about the insanity of his situation. The young girl had taken him off the street and to her home, where she hid him until they understood what had happened, and then together, they devised a plan. Ever since that night, they had become close friends, and each one helped the other. They became lovers in the months that followed, but Marie was smart enough to know that no one woman would ever have this man's heart. Strange as it was, she had welcomed this, as she wanted no ties or permanent relationship, so young. At this stage of her life, she yearned for knowledge, not a husband.

Cisco had become her friend, teacher, lover, and protector. He did not tie her to him or question her about her life or Voodoo ways. Together, they made a perfect match, and there was just no denying that, and both of them felt safe in a relationship that only they would ever understand.

MARIE glanced at him and shook her head as she walked toward the door. "You will both require some pain reliever in the morning. I had best go to the kitchen and prepare some." She started to leave but then stopped, her body stiffening in the doorway; it was a posture he knew only too well. She saw something in that inner mind of hers. "Cisco," she whispered, "you had best sleep and prepare yourself for the days ahead. I feel they will be full of plans, trickery, and danger."

How she could know of such things, he did not understand. She was the genuine article, though, and he'd come to accept her and her visions of what would be. The fact that she was seldom wrong about anything was a regular occurrence. He frowned, feeling the beginning of a headache that Marie knew he'd have. That condition didn't take special foretelling; that was easy to tell because of the alcohol on his breath. Drinking too much was a guarantee of having a headache. It was other things; she predicted that had no root cause, that always surprised him. The young mulatto just knew everything at times. Hell, if she told him to stay home because the day held evil, he found that he would automatically do as she asked.

After his companion left, he turned to look at Tori and told himself, Marie had been right all along. Like when she had told him that he was not the only traveler and that she could foretell, of still another. She had laughed at him, and he had thought her crazy. That was in the beginning, but not anymore. He recalled the morning Marie had told him that soon he would meet a gentleman like himself, which came to be. Then the gifted female told him he'd meet the next traveler, and she'd be female. She could not tell him exactly when the third one would appear, just that it was their destiny to be part of a unique three, and now, right enough, there were three.

The number, to Marie, was a magic number. Many of her spells and formulas were created using three things, and her visions appeared in threes more often than not. One thing was for sure, he'd seen things happen that defied the laws of nature, and he knew that if she had been in his time, she would have been studied for her talent in ESP and the paranormal.

Cisco touched his jacket pocket and frowned slightly. Inside was a white feather, given to him for both protection and a weapon. Did he believe that Marie's spells worked, that a single white feather could do all she claimed? So far, he had remained safe from harm or discovery, and as of yet, he had not used it to curse anyone, like she said it would. At least now, he would have someone else to talk with, about all Marie did, and maybe he'd figure out how she did it.

The man had watched as the future Voodoo queen left the hallway beyond without another word and knew he'd do as she told him. Looking back at Laffite's woman, he now understood they had been destined to meet; he smiled. Why had he taken so long to make contact with her? He should have listened to Marie and approached Laffite's wife sooner. Maybe if he had, they would have become friends, and the pirate would never have ended up in jail. One thing was clear; he would never know now if their meeting sooner would have kept Laffite out of Claiborne's grasp. One thing he did know; it didn't pay to ponder on something that was over and done with when all you could do was move on and do your best with the cards dealt. Slowly, he tiptoed out of the room. Tori would sleep until morning, safe where she was. He would go down the hall to Marie's room, where he knew she would join him when she was ready.

THE light hurt Tori's eyes, and her head felt as if it would explode. Once again, she tried to open her heavy lids and focus on the bedside table. Maybe, if she tried to get some coffee into her, she might feel better, she told herself. Gingerly touching her temples, she swallowed hard as a wave of nausea enveloped her. Tori closed her eyes and breathed in and out through her mouth. Feeling better with or without coffee, seemed impossible because this was one of the worst hangovers she'd had in a long time. Sitting up, Laffite's wife reached for her robe and realized right away that she was not in her room, let alone in her house. Panicked, she wondered where she was and how she got there, wherever there was? Rapidly hundreds of questions flooded her foggy brain. "Slow down. One problem at a time," she told herself, mumbling as if to reinforce some much needed courage. Then, frustrated at herself, she whispered, "got to stop talking and do more thinking."

Her lips pressed closed as she intended to stop her infernal talking to herself. Instead, she began to think things through slowly. 'First thing I have to do is get dressed. Strange, I have no memory of undressing. So how the hell did I get out of my gown?' Looking down at the garment she wore, Tori saw it resembled a man's shirt more than a nightgown.

Panic started to grip her. Jean did not own such a shirt. No man she knew owned one, so who did it belong to? Try as she might, the confused female could remember very little of the night before. After meeting the man, Cisco, the rest of the night became somewhat a blur. Had she dreamed that he was from her time? Was it real, or was it just a drunken wish? Either way, Tori intended to find out, headache or not. Laffite's wife needed to get out of the room and see if she could at least figure out where she was and why?

The frightened female was mumbling softly again, as slowly and painfully, she climbed out of bed to make her way over to her clothes. "Come on, remember something, anything." Dread was haunting her as the memory of Simone's words came back to her. 'Edward was not finished with her.' What if that was the answer to her predicament? What if she was once again in his evil grip? Strangely, once she allowed herself to think of this horror, it pissed her off, more than frightened her. "Not again, you bastard, because if you are behind this, you're a dead son of a bitch," she said to the closed door. Tori picked up her gown and stood thinking. She had to help Jean, which meant nothing would prevent her from getting out of there. Once back home, nothing would stop her from reaching Laffite, and everyone else jailed with him. Grymes would help, and others would surely step up. Even this Cisco mystery man had offered to help. So, whoever held her right then, was in for the fight of their life. No house, no one person, was going to intimidate or keep her hostage ever again.

Laffite's wife knew she was not the same woman Edward had

held in the whorehouse. She was stronger and a fighter, the likes of which the dandy had no idea. Maybe, she'd get lucky and find a sword before confronting the bastard. Handling one could not be so different from what she'd been learning at Dominique's side. But she was jumping ahead of herself, and the last thing she needed was to act before thinking things through.

Tori looked around her and then towards the closed door. 'Let's just see if the door is locked first.' Tori put her gown back down and approached the closed-off entrance. Gingerly she took hold of the door handle and turned it. "Be quiet," she whispered and then bit her lip. 'Got to think more and talk less. Easy does it. Nice, and slow now, pull it a little and stay quiet.' Surprisingly, the door opened with ease and without making a sound, which was a good omen. It could mean she would have an easier time getting away undetected. Her trembling hand pulled the heavy door open a bit further, exposing a dim hallway beyond. In seconds Tori had to decide what her next move would be and how to best go about it before she was discovered, but before she could close the door, an old familiar odor filled her nostrils.

As nauseous as she felt, a distinct smell permeated the air and caused her stomach to grumble with hunger. The aroma was so very familiar, yet it was something she'd not detected in years. Crazy as it seemed, to her, it was as if she had woken up in her favorite fast-food restaurant, and there was just no way that was possible. Tori inhaled deeply to make sure that she was not imagining things. This time, there was no doubt in her mind that something she had not had in ages was cooking someplace close by, and curiosity overtook her modesty.

The unmistakable smell of hamburgers and fries convinced her to step forward to investigate. The hangover could wait; escaping could wait; besides, running down the street in a formal black gown would be stupid, and that was if she could even get to the road. First, she needed to know a bit more about what and who was in this house with her because her gut instinct was telling her they were friendly. Her reason for thinking this was finding her bedroom door unlocked. If she were being held against her will, then it most assuredly would have been the other way around. As to being dressed in a man's shirt, well, that indicated someone had taken care of her. The man called Cisco claimed he was from the future, and if true, not dreamed up, then it could be his shirt she had on. "Too many questions, not enough answers," she whispered under her breath.

Tori was just about to walk down the hallway when a frightening question filled her mind. What if she was no longer in the past? What if somehow, she was back in her day and age? What if the past was gone? What then? This thought had not occurred to her and now that it had, she was very nervous. What would it mean? How could she tell? She backed up and closed the bedroom door.

The night before was blank after leaving the party. The smell was most definitely that of modern-day fast food. "Shit! Where the hell am I, and what's going on?" The confused female turned to look around the room for a sign of her own time. A clock, a phone, a light switch would mean electricity. That would identify her time-line surely. Then she saw the small window and knew that it would prove to her one way or the other where she was. The past or future would reveal itself if she looked outside. Old New Orleans of the past or modern would be there, one way or another; the answer was right there for her to witness.

Her somewhat shaky hand reached out and pulled the curtain aside. The bright daylight sent a sharp pain into her head and made her eyes water. "Damn the hangover," she told herself as she placed her hand over her brow to shield her view and looked outside.

No cars, just people dressed as they should be, in the era she was stuck in. "Well, I got one answer, but now I need to learn who has me here, and what the hell are they eating that smells so much like fast food?" Without hesitating, Tori walked back to the door. "I am not being held here; I am not! So here goes nothing, open the door and go slow. You got this, especially if you shut up. Bad habit, talking to one's self." She closed her lips tightly together and continued with her thoughts. 'Too noisy and 'I need to listen, not make a fool of myself. Besides, I can't hear talking if I am speaking out loud. Could be I'd miss out on an important bit of information. No way will I make that mistake.'

Laffite's wife opened the door and took a few steps down the small hallway. Off in the distance, she could hear voices, and following their sound, she made her way toward what she figured to be a kitchen. The building she was in had many doors on both sides of the main hall, leading from the front entry behind her toward the back door at the far end. All the doors except hers and the one where someone was talking were open. So, it was to this doorway she quietly crept.

Peeking cautiously around the corner, Tori could see two people sitting at a table, and right before them, on that same table, was the biggest, most beautiful hamburger she'd ever seen, bun and all! The man from the night before, the one called Cisco, was about to take a bite out of one of the creations when he looked up.

It was then that she gasped in delight. "I'll be damned. How in the hell did you manage that? And are those real French fries, or am I dreaming?"

Cisco grinned, and Marie looked toward her, but neither seemed surprised by her entrance or questions. The man took a large bite of his burger, and wiping the juices that ran down his chin, he swallowed hungrily and spoke in a teasing tone.

"Well, good afternoon, to you too. How did you sleep? If you ask me, you look a little bit green, doesn't she, Marie? Better not show her the ketchup just yet, even though I'm sure that she's not seen any for a long time." He laughed and turned toward Marie. "Nothing like you make, that's for sure. It even beats the one back; I mean forward in time." He took another bite and began chewing."

Tori could not believe him. He acted as if the three of them were old friends who spent many mornings or afternoons like this, catching up. He was just so darn relaxed, and his partner in crime

23

seemed even more so. Seeing Cisco intended to fill his mouth with one bite after the next, Tori's attention was drawn toward Marie. She had a thousand questions to ask her but would start with learning more about Cisco.

"Who else knows about him? Have you...."

Cisco didn't let her finish her question; he interrupted her, as he intended to move the conversation along and not get bogged down with useless questions. "Tori, I know that you two females know each other, and before you say anything, might I add that this wonderful girl here has just what your headache needs. Pull up a chair. You'll be right as rain in a few minutes, and then, if you want, she will rustle you up, a Cisco burger, and yes, some fries. Just don't tell anyone. It's sort of a secret, if you know what I mean. Besides, this world is not ready for fast food yet, if you get my drift."

Tori sat down in the chair across from the carefree Cisco. She stared at the plate in front of him. "That is quite something. A sight for sore eyes, you might say. As long as I've been here, you know it never occurred to me to attempt to make a burger and fries. Best hangover food going." Looking up from the table at both of them, she was filled with curiosity. "You two are friends... and you, Marie... you, knew about Cisco? I mean she, does know, doesn't she? Stupid question, of course, she does."

"Yes, she knows Tori, and I must tell you, she has known about you for some time."

Tori turned toward Marie, who backed up Cisco's statement with a simple nod.

"But how?"

Cisco continued slowly. "Since Jean had the fever, and you lost your son..." He swallowed and shrugged his shoulders. The man was uncomfortable having brought up the child's death. "Look, I would have come sooner... to see you, but the time was not right, and I had to be certain. Surely, you can understand that? It's not easy, is it?"

Marie put a glass of yellow-looking liquid in front of Tori, and smiling at her; she pushed the glass closer. "You best drink it down, all of it. I warn you, it's bitter, but it does work. Go ahead. I'm not going to poison you."

Tori looked at the glass and continued talking to Cisco, ignoring Marie's statement. "Oh, I know it's not easy, that's for sure. It's just incredible, the two of you being friends like this, and here I thought that I was all by myself. You're not from another time, too, are you Marie?"

"Me? Lordy no! I was born here. Got folks thinking, born one year, and to some, I was born in another; Cisco's idea to plant such ideas. Says that in the future, they won't know which it is for sure; the year I was born will remain confusing. You know he had some papers made that had me born in 1801 and others with dates that... well, it, don't matter none to me. Seems that I was born at the wrong time, though. Your time sounds like more fun, and the foods far more interesting," she laughed. "Now, quit delaying and swallow," again, she pushed the small glass of liquid toward Tori.

As soon as the concoction slipped down her throat, Tori felt as if she would gag, and in fact, she nearly did. Cisco laughed at her and quickly gave her a cup of black coffee to wash down the bitter bile that kept trying to make its way up.

"It's not aspirin, but then it works just as well. I think a lot faster too. You will be right as rain, in a flash."

Tori looked at him, and with a grimacing look on her face, she spoke. "Well, I sure as hell hope so. Damn, that is the worst ever. I am going to need more than coffee to drown out that flavor."

"How about a burger and some good old-fashioned conversation? That should take your mind off it. Marie, grind up some more meat and make her one of your special burgers."

"You grind the meat? I thought you would chop it up. Guess I did not know a meat grinder had been invented yet. I have not seen one, but then I don't venture into many kitchens, and Bessy does not have one. She's our housekeeper, speaking of which, I bet she's worried silly."

25

"Bessy will be fine, and as to the grinder… yep, some dude in Germany invented it, and I bought it for us, so we can have burgers. It's hand grind, you turn the handle, and well, you get it. Surely you saw the old-fashioned things back home? I tried to explain a food processor to Marie, but she can't grab the gist. You still want a burger and fries?"

"Sounds good to me, but I have a question first about last night. How in God's name did I get here, and if I might add, into your shirt? I assume it's your shirt?"

He smiled. "God had nothing to do with your getting here; that was me. Your driver helped, but he won't go talking to anyone. Marie here is responsible in a way, too, I guess. As much as I would have loved to help you get ready for bed, I can assure you that nothing happened if that's what you're worried about. You are a lady who is safe, and always will be so, in my home." Marie made a jab at his side with her long wooden spoon, and the look he received sent a clear message. "Ah, that is Marie's home. That's where you are right now. If I had a home of my own, you would still be safe there, though." Marie giggled, and Tori found herself amused by Cisco and his playful nature. After frowning at Marie, he continued. "I want your friendship, Tori, both yours and Laffite's, that is. Seducing you would not be the way to gain that, now, would it?"

Tori looked at him, and she knew he meant what he said. He was the type that shot from the hip and was blunt and truthful. Just exactly why she felt this; she was not yet sure. She knew nothing about him other than the fact that they had one thing in common, and that was time travel. Before she could question him about where he came from, he spoke in a teasing tone of voice.

"You know, what would the grand ladies of New Orleans think of you now, sitting there dressed like that? God, it is good to see a woman who has no pretense or real hang-ups about her body." He bent down and looked under the table as he spoke, "Great legs there, lady."

Tori laughed. She had entirely forgotten how she must look and come to think of it; the modern-day woman did not feel one bit ashamed, sitting there, like she was. Laffite's lady made up her mind, right then, that just knowing Cisco would in the days ahead be like old times, talking with friends in her own time. He'd get her, and anything she said, any modern term would be understood at last. Looking at his beaming face, she realized Jean might not understand her new friend or accept his actions right away, but Jean would have no choice because this was one friendship she intended to keep.

A dark cloud covered her happy thoughts for a second as she remembered Jean and where he was. Tori knew she had to find a way to get him out of jail, and sitting there eating and talking with Cisco was not going to accomplish anything in that direction. Another dark thought hit her then, would she ever be able to get him out? This last thought was pushed aside with a determined affirmative motion of her head. Of course, she would get him out!

Laffite's wife knew she'd best make a move, so pushing her chair back away from the table, she began to get up. "I have a thousand questions to ask you, and I would love to sit and chat, but I have to get to John Grymes. I have to see what can be done to get Jean out."

Cisco grimaced. "Won't happen. Look, Tori, I hate to remind you of this, but this is not the nineties, with bail and due process. This is now, today, in this time, not ours, and you and I have to go along with their ways or stand out like a sore thumb, and worse, have people think we are bat shit crazy." Cisco saw the look in Tori's eyes and thought he had said something wrong. "You do get my point, right?" His mind raced over what he had just told her, and it hit him. "Oh shit! I just assumed you were from the nineties, like me. You are, aren't you?" Tori nodded her head, yes. "Oh, thank God. Thought I might have blown you away. You could have come from the seventies, for Christ's sake. They did have 747s then, you know." He laughed at her. "Look, trust me, Tori. We will do something, but it makes sense to me that we get to know each other before we do. How about those questions? I know that Marie and I have some of our own, don't we, babe?"

He seemed to know what he was talking about, and Marie nodded her head in agreement. She walked over to Cisco with a sense of pride on her face. Her admiration for him was quite evident. Gently but firmly, she started massaging his shoulders as she stood silently behind him. Tori watched as Cisco relaxed and leaned back against her; he took her hands off his shoulders and held them close to his chest. To Tori, it was evident the two of them were far more than just friends, and it did not surprise her at all.

Jean's wife sat back in her chair and smiled. "Well, if I'm to be your friend and you mine, I had better know your name. After all, I can't very well go around calling you Cisco, can I?"

"You could, but that would raise a few eyebrows, wouldn't it?" He was chuckling to himself as he leaned forward. "You're going to love this one. Bet it puts a smile on your face each time you hear it. How about this for a handle." He pulled Marie around and sat her on his lap, giving her a squeeze that made her squirm and giggle, as she wriggled free of his grasp. "Marie helped me, so don't put all the blame on me." Then, as if preparing himself for one of the most important speeches of the century, he arose and said, "I am, Señor Francisco Armando y de la Garcia de Vega, at your service." He bowed low, and his expression exploded with laughter as he stood up. "Do you get it? No? Well, let me explain. Francisco; that was after a certain town where I was born. Just left the San part off." Armando? Well, I needed a middle name. These people seem to have a ton of them, and I just had to have something easy to remember. Next came Garcia, Marie's choice, and then Vegas, but I dropped the s; it sounded better. Vega has a nicer ring. Don't you think? Well, you can guess where that came from."

Tori was laughing; it was impossible not to. Cisco's sense of humor was infectious. Still, she had to pull herself together. This was important. It was not a silly game they were playing. "That's what you go by here, but how about before?"

"Before, is not important. Before is gone, and thank God." He

28

saw her look of horror. "Don't look so shocked. I'm glad I found my way here. It saved my life. Okay, I'll put it in a nutshell for you, then enough of me, for a while. I was a first-year resident at Baylor in Houston. I'm a son of a prominent, overpowering, condescending doctor. I was trying to please dad; got the picture? I could not stand the pressure or live up to his expectations, so I left. I rebelled, went to Las Vegas, and did what I wanted. I worked backstage on one of the magic shows, building props and such. That led me to make-up, hair, and wardrobe-that sort of thing. Easy work, with no pressure, and it gave me time for the one other love of my life." He shot Marie a knowing glance. "I also loved the game of Poker, and well, one thing led to another, and before I knew what was happening, I was up to my neck in debts. I borrowed, and they wanted their money to make a long story short. So, rather than go to my dear old dad, I left town in a hurry and tried to hide in New Orleans." He sat back down at the table and picked up his cup.

He took a drink of his coffee and sat thinking for a minute, reliving what he saw in his mind. It was Marie's hug that seemed to help him continue his story. "Thought I could win back my losses. Stupid really. I'm sure that's how they traced me. It did not take them long to find me, and as I ran from them late one night... down a dark alley, I lost them. Sure did, and that's not all I lost. I also lost the nineties. One minute, I was running in one timeline, turned a corner, and bingo, I was running in another. Got to tell you, it was one hell of a shock. I thought I was on a movie set or something. Thank God I was too drunk to argue with Marie here. She caught up with me when I stopped running. On her part, that was quick thinking, what she did, and the fact that it was late at night helped. No one else was around. Before I could be seen, she whisked me here. Good thing too, or I would have stuck out like a sore thumb, the way I was dressed. You know, they don't have blue jeans, let alone sneakers."

Marie laughed at that, and Cisco looked at her, frowning as he continued. "Marie took me in, and we have been friends ever since, and you see before you, a man who is having himself one hell of a good time and thankful to be here." He sipped his coffee and winked at Marie. Then Cisco turned his attention back toward Tori. "But something tells me that you don't want to be here. Am I right?"

"It's not that I don't want to be here; it's more like I don't belong. Unlike you, I was not running away, and I left behind friends, a family, and a daughter."

THE next few hours spent in that kitchen were hours of discussion on what happened to them both. Tori told her tale, and as she did, it became evident to them all that she would try to go back one day, unlike Cisco, who had no intention of ever trying. Listening to Tori, he felt deep sorrow for her because he genuinely believed that she would have to accept that for her, like him, the future was dead.

"Listen to me, Tori. I hate to burst your bubble, but there can be no other way for us. After all, who has ever heard of anyone claiming to have traveled back and forth in time? True, we read books about such things but come on, you know, no one actually thinks it happens. No one has ever proved it, have they?"

Tori did not like the look on his face. She had seen his sad glance when she mentioned going to the lake and returning to her own time. "Seems to me that if I did succeed in going back, that I would have proof of sorts. After all, I've been gone some years now. I know that's no real proof; that's what you're going to say, right?" He didn't answer. She lowered her head and sadly continued. "Maybe, I would rather not talk about my… about this time travel thing once I got back. People would only think I was crazy. So maybe, it has happened to others, and they chose to remain silent. Think about it. People in history have always popped up now and then, people who seemed to be able to predict the future. People, like Nostradamus. If he did not time travel, then maybe he listened to someone who had. Or, Leonardo da Vinci, take a look at him. With all of his inventions, he was way before his time, let alone his knowledge of the human body. Then there is H.G. Wells and War of the Worlds. Captain Nemo and his adventure… am I crazy here?"

Cisco hated to shatter her hopes because she looked so helpless. It was as if she had to have something substantial to believe in, something that made some sense about what happened to them; he felt compelled to say something. "You do have a point about those folks and stories, but we might never know. If there is a way back, and you want it, I hope you find it. I mean that, but for John and me, well… we opt to make the best of it here."

Tori straightened up and leaned forward in her chair. "Did you say, John? You mean there is another person here, like us?" Tori was on the edge of her seat. Excitement was beyond what she was feeling at this point.

"Yes, and it's someone who you will be meeting. The sooner, the better, I think too. I have set it up already, as I figured you would want to say hi." Cisco was grinning from ear to ear, so pleased with himself and his little surprise. "You can't very well go in those clothes from last night, though, and even if John might like to see you as you are right now, well… we must be proper, mustn't we?" His expression was full of mischief.

"Cisco, I would love to meet this John friend of yours, but I can't. Not now, at least. I must find a way to help Jean and his men. I have to help them. This has been nice, great, really, but now is not the time for sitting around on my ass, talking about old times, or meeting new friends."

He broke in with a fake hurt look on his face. "How quickly you forget. I said that we would find a way, and I meant we, the three of us. That is why I have made arrangements for you and I to meet with John and see what can be done." Cisco lightened up and smiled again. After all, three heads together are far better than one, and if anyone can come up with an idea, it's going to be one of us, but not alone. You have information, I have some, and John has some. Don't you see? We can help each other, and believe me;

it will be my pleasure to help you." He smiled, then quickly added, "As I know, it will be John's pleasure if we twist his arm a bit. Now, your driver should be here soon to pick you up. I sent word for him to come and get you. How about I come by, say around eight, and pick you up to go out for some dinner? We will meet with my friend then."

Tori reluctantly agreed. "What choice do I have? You're all I have, and you're right; three heads are better than one. One thing's a given; I trust both you and Marie. I know that if you trust this John, well, whoever he is, I guess I'll have to trust him too. I'll meet this friend of yours. I only hope that he can help us because, trust me, one way or another, I'll get Jean out, with or without help, and you can take that to the bank. And Cisco, my new friend, believe you me, I get what I want."

THE driver arrived for her, putting an end to any further discussions. Feeling somewhat stupid, dressed in the same outfit she had worn the night before, Tori took her leave of Marie's house. She ran to the waiting carriage, hoping no one would see her, and if they did, that they would not care. Her driver asked no questions, not that he ever would have dared. The slave knew exactly why Tori had spent so much time at Marie's house. She was getting some mighty powerful gris-gris. Yes, Sir. His Master would be a-comin' home real soon. Ain't no one ever crossed Marie's gris-gris. No Sir. It always worked.

As he drove his Mistress home, he recalled all he could of Marie's Voodoo power. His brow wrinkled as he recalled the time, she used it on the white man's law court. Yes, everyone know'd how powerful she be and now his Mistress Tori, done gone and got herself some of the Voodoo women's help. Best he kept that bit of knowledge to himself, though, cause if he talked, he might find bad gris-gris heading his way.

Tori had no idea of what was wrong with her driver, the way he rolled his eyes and clucked his tongue against the roof of his mouth, making an awful sound as she pushed past him to climb into the carriage. She did not have the patience to bother with him either; all she wanted was to help Jean.

Instead of going straight home, as she had planned, she swung by the blacksmith shop to talk to Pierre or see if Dominique was there. Someone in Jean's circle had to know something or what could be done. She did not understand what Cisco and his friend could do to help, and if they could do something, they would need assistance. After all, they required a lot more than dreams and talk to get Jean and his men out of jail.

It was Thiac that informed Tori just how bad things were. She'd forgotten that Simone had told her that many of his men had been caught along with Jean. Of course, that included Dominique and Pierre.

Stunned and almost in tears, she listened as the large blacksmith told her all that he knew, and what he said frightened her further. He told her that he doubted anyone could do much of anything to help. Then, he added a bit more that unnerved her. He said that this time, they'd plum gone and got themselves into something that only a miracle could get them out of.

Laffite's wife hid her fears so as not to upset Thiac further. Cisco had been correct with his information, and right then, all her hopes now seemed to lay with her new friend. He did promise, after all, to help her and his other time traveling friend, whoever he was, might have a way to arrange Jean's freedom one way or another. There was still hope. Tori looked into the worried face of the blacksmith and spoke softly. "If I find a way to get them out, legal or not, will you help? Can I count on you, Thiac, and maybe some help, from a few of the men, at Barataria?"

"You can counts on me, and maybe a few men down there, but I ain't sure what you can do to help Boss, little Miss. I don't know how you can do anythin' at all. If you be a needin' me though, old

Thiac, I be here, ain't about to go nowhere's else." He had to admire this woman, who spoke with a look of sheer determination on her face and had the spirit of his forge fire, hot and wild-like. He'd seen her push back the tears and take hold of herself. She probably did not want to upset him any, and maybe instead of crying, she'd talk herself into thinking she could do something. Thiac knew a woman, who was fighting mad, was something to be reckoned with. He also knew that if she fought, and no doubt she was going to, he would stand by her, 'cause that's what Boss had done for him.

Tori knew the blacksmith would help her, but just how or when she'd need him, she did not know. Her face filled with worry, and for a second, it looked as if she was going to break down.

It was then Thiac remembered the strange new razor he had finished and smiled broadly. "I has somthin' that might make you smile and all. You just wait, and I will fetch it, right, quick-like. Sharp, it be too," he chuckled. "Was goin' to have it sent your ways, today anyhow's." He reached behind the small wooden table and found the small package. "Here, I hope I done made it like you drawed for me? I sure did try hard." He handed her the wrapped item.

Tori took the wrapping off and looked at the object in her hand. Happily, she realized that she held the small homemade razor, shaped just like she had told him, and true to his words, the edge was sharp as could be.

"No need to worry 'bout it stayin' sharp, none. You bring it here, any time, and I will have it sharp, just as it is now."

"I will most certainly do that." Tori turned the razor over and looked closely at the artistry. "It is just as I pictured it. Thank you, Thiac."

The smithy was pleased but puzzled too. The straight razor that most men of the day used seemed far more practical to Thiac. He felt that Boss would not like this new style. The object was, in his opinion, ridiculous. It had to be some sort of a joke between them, and he did not want to ask, as it was not his place. Seeing the smile on her face, though, that was enough for him. It told him he had done a fine job, and that was what counted.

Long after Tori left the shop, the blacksmith chuckled to himself. He hoped that she did indeed need his help to get Boss out of that there, jail. Thiac would enjoy doing anything that made her happy. He just loved to see the way she looked at him, with those big eyes, and genuinely meaning things, like when she thanked him. Not many white folks ever looked him in the eyes, let alone a fine white lady. He picked up the bellows and set to work while he waited to see what would happen next.

Tori spent the remaining hours dressing for her meeting with Cisco and his friend. She was already forming somewhat of a plan in her head. It occurred to her that the idea had first come to her at Thiac's. From there, the idea grew. It was a backup plan in case Grymes could not arrange bail or, better still, have all charges dropped. Yes, she had another workable plan, just like Jean had told her. Always have more than one option; that was the rule to live by. Her idea was straightforward. She would merely have to pull a good old-fashioned jailbreak. "I wonder if that's been done yet, at least in this town anyway?"

Bessy, who was used to Tori talking to herself out loud, ignored her Mistress. She was wise enough to allow certain actions, to pass as if unnoticed, like those of the night before. Even though the housekeeper had stayed awake for hours, waiting for Tori, who did not come home, Bessy was smart enough to understand; it was not her place to question. She could worry all she wanted, but that was her limit, and no way was Bessy going to go past what was expected of her. The housekeeper knew she'd keep an eye on Laffite's wife and help if asked, but that was all she could do if she wanted to remain in the house.

FINALLY, Tori was ready. She went down to the study, and lit up one of Jean's thin cigars, and poured herself a glass of white wine while she waited for Cisco. The curious female wondered about his friend, John. So many questions were swirling around in her mind; the most important one of all was, would he help them? Tori remembered the bit about twisting his arm. It could be that Cisco's friend was not willing to mess with history like herself and might need a bit of persuading to join them in their cause.

She looked up at the small mantle clock and let out a long sigh. Time seemed to be dragging by. Why was it that when you waited for something, it always seemed to take such a blasted long time? Sitting down and taking another sip of her drink, Tori reminded herself not to consume too much this evening, as she needed to keep a clear head. Then she made herself a mental note to ask Marie for some of that liquid aspirin or whatever it was. The stuff worked, and headaches were something else she didn't need.

Her hand ran up and down her leg unconsciously as she sat thinking. Her eyes glanced at the clock again but were drawn away as her fingers caught on her gown. It was then that she realized what she'd been doing and more, the reason why. The smoothness of her skin beneath her hand was an old familiar sensation. Looking at her bare leg with a smile, she had to admit; the razor had worked like a dream. For the first time in ages, her legs and underarms were hairless, and she felt human again. Oh sure, she learned that some women used hot wax, but she was not into pain, and using a straight razor was, to her, nothing short of lethal. Shaving, up until now, had been taboo for her. But, at last, her hairy days were over, smooth as silk, soft, and scented, was how Jean would find her. Now that could be exciting, seeing his reaction to this new hairless condition, and she looked forward to it.

Tori continued to daydream about that event. She was sat in a chair, with her legs propped up on the side table, with her skirt pulled up over her knees, admiring her latest achievement. A cigar was hanging from her lips, and the glass of wine in her hand rotated slowly. This is the view that first greeted Cisco, as he was, shown into the room by a very confounded Bessy.

Standing just inside the doorway, he raised one eyebrow before he let out a soft whistle of admiration. On the other hand, Bessy was more to the point as she grunted her disapproval loudly. The cook turned sharply to leave, tossing her head in the air and almost knocking Cisco down; as she pushed by him.

The housekeeper headed back toward the kitchen, mumbling and carrying on, loud enough for everyone to hear. "Miss Tori must have taken the news of Massa so bad that she has done gone outta her head. And, who that Vega man? Never seen the likes of him afore." She entered the kitchen and closed the door, none too softly. Bessy was at a loss as to what to do when she sat down and looked back at the closed entry. "Whoever he is, he, smell of trouble, dressed up fancy, like a Christmas turkey, and callin' on my Mistress, knowin' the Massa ain't home. Whistlin' like that… like she be from down the market way. It is not proper at all." She shook her head. 'Lordy, this was a-goin' to be somethin', she had best be keepin' to herself,' she thought. 'As for the Massa, he didn't need to be a knowin' about it either. If she kept quiet, chances were, he'd not know nothin' about any of it. She'd be sure to wait up again, just in case Miss Tori needed her and to make sure none them others in the house started seeing or gossiping like. If the Massa learned his wife was seeing a stranger while he was in jail, that would not go good for the stranger or Miss Tori.' Bessy told herself that she best pray for help 'cause Massa was going to need it and Miss Tori, she be needing too, 'cause she sure was a heading in the wrong direction.

Tori felt a pang of concern for Bessy and almost went after the poor woman to explain, but what could she say that would put her mind at ease? She felt it safer, at this point to, ignore her and pretend she had not heard her housekeeper at all. With that in mind, she turned her attention toward her guest. "Pour yourself a drink. I'll finish mine and this cigar if you don't mind. I deserve it."

He did not move. Instead, he spoke with a husky voice as he openly let his eyes travel the length of the woman's body. "You know, I think you were better suited as a Southern lady. Keep this nineties lady thing up, and it's going to be hard to keep my hands off you."

Tori looked up at him, wondering if he was kidding or not? She lowered her legs to the floor and pulled her gown down to cover up. Next, she reached over and extinguished the remainder of the cigar before looking back at Cisco. "I do hope that was a joke?"

"Let's just say that you can stir a man's blood, and it might be a lot easier if we kept our friendship platonic." He looked away from her as he spoke, pouring himself a drink.

Tori would have taken him seriously if she had not seen that his shoulders were shaking. The man was laughing at her. He was teasing her, and she'd fallen for it. Well, she'd put an end to his smug attitude. Walking up behind him, she took her glass, and with the remaining wine in it, and poured it down his neck. "Let's hope this cools you off." He reacted instantly, and Tori could not help but fall back in the chair hysterically, laughing as she watched him.

Cisco jumped about the room, looking at her, with an expression of complete shock, on his face. They were acting like kids, not adults, and he loved it, almost as much as he enjoyed a good joke. In seconds, the two of them were both reeling with laughter, and why not? It felt good to be able to communicate on an entirely different level, one that was as foreign and strange to this time, and place, as they were.

Tori loved her new ally and knew that a special bond between them would always be there, no matter what the days ahead brought their way, and there was only one way to see what that might be. "Let's go meet this John friend of yours. You have not told me very much about him, you know, and I am dying of curiosity. Who is he? Where does he come from? How did you meet him?"

"Slow down! One question at a time, please. How about I tell you everything on the way over to his place? It will give us something to talk about, and maybe by the time we arrive; I'll be dried out a bit. Good thing, it was a white wine and not red. It won't stand out even if it remains damp. Might smell a bit." Cisco grinned and offered his hand. "Shall we?"

"We shall." Tori was smiling because his fun-loving mood was infectious.

"Best step back into our rolls, though," he added. "This era is not quite ready for us to act so 'rashly,' as they say." He took Tori by the arm and escorted her outside to the waiting carriage. Once there, he graciously helped the lady inside his carriage, then climbed up beside her. Cisco didn't need to give directions; he only tapped the vehicle's roof to indicate they were ready to start their journey.

〜⊰ Two ⊱〜

Tori looked at the man sitting beside her as he began to explain where they were going. While he spoke, for the first time, she pondered the idea that perhaps, they had been brought back in time to be together. Maybe to accomplish something, and it could be that something was to get Jean and his men out of jail. Whatever the reason, Laffite's wife, found herself thinking that the events which were happening were more than mere coincidence. It was more like fate. She was always telling Jean everything happened for a reason, and now she was telling herself the same thing. Right then, it seemed, it was time to learn if that old saying held any truth. Tori turned her attention to Cisco and what he was saying.

Her new friend looked directly at her as he began to explain to Tori just who it was, they were going to see. "His name is John Davis, and he came over to this time in 1801. Like you and me, he got himself a name to use here. Realizing he had a chance to be happy, he began by using certain knowledge he brought with him. He's built himself quite a life, as you will see. I can tell by the look on your face that you've heard of him?"

"Who hasn't? He is the owner of what some call the John Davis Hotel. Before purchasing the place, it used to be the Tremoulets, and he renamed it the United States Hotel for a while. I laughed at that one. What a name. It just never dawned on me that he was like us. Mr. Davis is well known to Jean and his brother. I have eaten in the famous dining room on many occasions but never met the man myself. I do know he has a gambling parlor on the other side of the hotel. It's where Jean used to play cards. Shit, Cisco, even Jean's attorney, John Grymes, lost fifty thousand dollars last year at poker and dice; that's what he claims anyway. Why is it that I'm getting the feeling there is more to this..." she stumbled for the

41

right words, "than a plain gambling house? It's fair, isn't it?"

"Oh, John runs a good place. It's the first of its kind in this time-line anyway, and that makes it both popular and profitable. If you ask anyone about John himself, they will tell you that he comes from Cuba or Paris; they do not know for sure. He is a gentleman and respected by many. He plans to use most of his profits in the near future to subsidize the nation's first opera house. Man, digs music, not my style, but hey, different strokes for different folks. He helps out with the Theater D'Orleans, right now. He also plans on running the Orleans Ballroom. Did you know that the famous Quadroon balls are held there? And there is more. It's not by acci-dent that all this has come about. John, you see, was a dealer in Vegas. He ah, used to see me quite a lot back then, and watched me lose a fortune, come to think of it… anyway, he was in New Orleans, on a working vacation. John was the dealer in a big game. Claims he loved New Orleans more than any other place. Maybe, that's why the man intends to remain here. He knows a bit more about American history than I do. I don't know too much about this time and area myself. How about you?"

Tori frowned and chewed on her lower lip but said nothing.

"Ah, I see by that enterprising look that you are just like myself!" He jabbed her in her side and laughed. "Anyhow, back to the main subject here. He had been in a big game in one of the hotels on Bourbon Street. After playing most of the night, he excused himself from the party and made his way to his own smaller bed and breakfast down a dark street. Sound familiar? He took a shortcut, or what he thought was a shortcut. Best we can figure out is that he walked back in time, just as smooth as you like." Cisco looked at Tori and gingerly asked, "Do you think this kind of thing happens more often than we'd like to admit? I mean, think of all the missing persons in our time?" Cisco fell silent while both of them sat pondering what he'd said. The coach hit a bump, and it broke his daydream and silence. "Anyway, back to John. He was different from you or me because he saw a great opportunity; once he realized what had happened to the twentieth century, that is. He sold his gold chains and rings down the riverfront, bought some clothes, and started building his small empire. I'll tell you that his knowledge of casinos and gambling helped him a lot. He started by playing and gambling down at the docks, both here and along the coast. Upriver and down, anyplace he could until he had enough to start his very own round-the-clock gambling place. At his first attempt, he did so well that it was easy for him to get investors in what is now known as 'The Palace.' He has bought his investors out, by the way. The Palace is all his now. If you take a good look at it, it's just the same as a Vegas casino. It runs the same, has all the traits of one, and well, it should, as that's just what it is modeled after. The Palace is making him a very wealthy man."

Tori nodded. "I bet it is, no pun intended," she giggled. Then seeing he was serious, she apologized. "Sorry. Please go on."

"He loves music, all kinds, especially country, but that had to go. It's not exactly invented yet, you know! That was John's one big disappointment about this time, I think, no Country-Western. He sings some now and then when we are together. He's not too bad either, come to think of it. Anyway, he has replaced his country music with a new love, opera. So hence his plans for the opera house." Cisco grinned. He could see that Tori was very impressed and intrigued so far.

"Shall I continue?" He knew she would say yes; how could she not?

"By all means, don't let me stop you."

"Right then. Fine food and this lifestyle are right up John's alley. John has fine dining in his hotel for both the gamblers and guests staying in the hotel. That went so well that he opened his dining room up for the public. Only the very well-off can afford it, so he has no worries of the wrong sorts turning up. Only the top citizens of this fair city come in to eat and be seen. The food is renowned in town and beyond."

"As I have heard and agree. The food that is."

Cisco briefly chuckled, then continued. "Wines and liquor are the best from all over Europe, thanks to your husband. The rooms are the most luxurious, and for a reasonable price, you can have whatever you need. He can afford to give the gamblers free food and drinks because he's making so much profit from the winnings. Did you know there is no limit to the bets? Why, it's not uncommon to see a man lose twenty thousand dollars, or more at one time, or even in one game, and that, Tori, is a hell of an amount in this day and age. It's Las Vegas-style all the way, right down to his croupiers and dealers, who work four-hour shifts around the clock. He has transformed the game of Brag into Poker. A smooth move if you ask me and one of his best. He's even using a larger deck than the brag game requires, and he intends to introduce the fifty-two deck of cards as soon as he can. That was a stroke of genius, introducing poker. The fools think the Americans invented the game, a game that is still so new they don't play it too well yet. So, you see, he can run it fair, and as far as I know, it is all on the up and up. That is, for the most part. I think he sometimes fudges, you know, rigs the game when he needs extra, but he would never admit it."

"How did the two of you meet here?"

"Now, that was a hell of a shock, I tell you. Shit, I almost thought I was seeing through a damn time warp or something. Thought I was going crazy or about to be flung back to the future!" He tried to look horrified at the thought, and then, laughing, he went on. "I was doing all right. The ladies and I… we get along fine, and with my knowledge of gambling and counting cards, something that I seem to be quite good at, the money was easy enough. I was able to make a comfortable lifestyle for myself. I helped Marie out with some things. I got her going on hair, you know. That's how she gets most of the knowledge about what's going on. When she styles hair, people talk, and she listens, and it comes in handy if one knows when and how to use such information. Also, I explained if she were to gift certain spells or potions to the slaves and house-hold, they would be more willing to spill the goods on what's going on under their roof. On more than one occasion, I have shown her how to, shall we say, make the most of the information she's been able to glean. I would never exactly call what she sometimes does as blackmail, but it does come in handy. Like a certain judge a while back. She got him to find a kid, not guilty."

Tori's mouth dropped open with both surprise at this last statement and also excitement. "How did she do that? Hey, if Jean goes to trial…"

"Slow up there, one thing at a time. Now, do you want to hear the rest of the story?

"Ok, if it explains the how she did it part."

Cisco grinned. "Come on; I'm serious here. Marie had the goods on the old judge. Gentleman or not, he had a secret, like most men, but unlike most, he would die if it got out. Blackmail, at its best, I tell you."

"She blackmailed the judge? You just told me…"

"That she did. Look, the guy on trial came from a rich family, one that did not want a dark mark, so to speak, on their upstanding and very proper name. It's all about honor with the Creoles, but you know that by now. Anyway, the kid's dad thought Marie's Voodoo got his son off. It was common knowledge that a gris-gris pouch was found under his chair. Disposed of quickly, so no proof could be used to upset the verdict. Anyway, the father did not care how or why, but he was so grateful that he gave her the house on Rue St. Anne Street. The one she has now. She caught on how to manipulate situations quickly after that. I hardly have to advise her any longer. I have taught her some basic medical skills and shown her a few herbs to make her potions. The headache potion was my invention for her. It's the bark of the willow tree, boiled down. Did you know that it has the same properties as aspirin? Yep, I learned some of where our modern drugs came from when I was in med school. Anyway, with my knowledge and her uncanny ability to know things… well… bingo, there you have it. Some powerful Voodoo," he smiled.

Tori nodded her head and smiled. She had guessed someone was behind the girl from the start but never dreamed it could be someone from the future. "So, because of you, history has the Voodoo Queen of New Orleans, Marie Laveau."

"Well, I don't want to take all the credit, but someone had to help her, so why not me? Besides, as you get to know her, you will undoubtedly witness what I know now to be true. The girl has an uncanny ability to know things ahead of time, and other strange things happen." He fell silent for a few seconds, "but back to John. I do seem to wander somewhat, don't I? Anyway, I went to gamble one night, at the Palace. As I sat at the table, who walked into the room? You guessed it, the owner, my old friend John. One look, and we recognized each other. Blew us away at first—real trippy kind of feeling. Now, we help each other out and have had some damn good times together. We checked around for about a year and found no one else like us, so we gave up looking. That was until Marie told me about you."

He shifted in his seat and looked directly into his new friend's face. Tori had the strangest expression. Her lower lip curled and twitched nervously as if she wanted to talk but was holding back. Then it hit him; he realized that the woman had no idea how Marie had found out about her. How could she? So, Cisco rushed on to make it all clear. "It was nothing you did or said; you can relax there. You have done a most excellent job of hiding the truth. It was Jean; he talked in his delirium when he had the fever. Marie understood more than you could have imagined. After all, I had been talking to her about the future for some time. Telling her all sorts of things Jean was. That girl has a thousand questions, and once she gets going, there is no stopping her. At any rate, we thought it might be Jean, that was the traveler, but it soon became apparent, it was you." Cisco became quiet, letting her absorb the information. "Enough for now. We are here at the hotel, and a meal of a lifetime awaits you. Let's go on in and enjoy ourselves, shall we? I, for one, can't wait until we three get together later and see what the outcome of all this is going to be. One thing is for certain; something's going on that's weird. I mean you, John and me, all from the same time, and here now, at the same place. What are the odds of that do you think? I don't know about you, but it gives me that 'twilight zone' feeling. I need a stiff drink." He saw the strange expression on Tori's face, a look that told him the woman felt very much along the same lines as him. "Come on; you look as if you can use one too."

THE hotel was one of a kind for its day. The atmosphere was one of wealth and prominence. It was common to find the plantation owners alongside the high rollers on any given night. Even though gambling was outlawed, nothing was done to interrupt the proceedings under this establishment's roof, and Tori made a mental note to find out why. Gambling and gamblers had not smeared the reputation of splendor surrounding her. The hotel was considered an upstanding place and not a mere gambling hole. The casino was on the opposite side of the hotel where they were to dine. This prestigious restaurant was where many young ladies of society often dined under their chaperones' watchful eye during the day. In the evenings, many older ladies of society, accompanied by their husbands, would arrive. They would ask to be seated where they were most likely to be seen by all who entered the building. Thus establishing, having been there, without saying a word. After all, none dare brag openly about such matters themselves, as it was deemed unbefitting to do so. Let the gossip mill deal with such delicate details, they would tell themselves.

From the moment Tori entered the dining room, she felt the eyes of quite a few of the patrons upon her. Her husband and his men's arrest, was now common knowledge in town. Judging by the expressions on many faces, she also could see that the gossip mongers were having a heyday with the news even then. How could they not? Especially with her out on the town, with the handsome

Spaniard. Tori realized that she had added more fuel for tall tales and innuendoes by being there, not that she cared too much about that right then.

The light from the chandeliers was soft, and the music that played was soothing and romantic. However, Tori felt far from calm, let alone romantic, as she allowed Cisco to escort her to their reserved table in a far more secluded area.

The thought kept crossing her mind, that she should be doing more to help Jean, instead of chasing down this John Davis, in hopes of him being able to do something. Tori was here only because Cisco had been so insistent, and now Jean's wife began to question her wisdom in listening to him. What would he think if Jean learned that she was out dining with a handsome stranger? Maybe, however, she just had to believe in Cisco and trust that fate was playing a more significant role than they knew instead of worrying. 'Everything happens for a reason,' she kept thinking.

They had just received a glass of wine each, compliments of the house when Tori's attention was drawn across the room. "To our success," said Cisco raising his glass and bringing her eyes back to his. The waiter placed the bottle on the table and was about to leave when Cisco stopped him. "Sir, if I may be as bold to add that I wish for our evening's expenses to be placed on John's account as usual."

"Yes, Sir, it is already taken care of, as usual. Will there be anything else?"

"Maybe, let Mr. Davis know I am here."

Cisco had told their waiter to put the entire bill on Mr. Davis's account. There had been no argument, no hesitation at all, and not even the slightest hint of surprise on the server's face. Tori noticed little things such as this. Her regard for detail was becoming acute; that's why she'd spotted the older woman, who was staring at them both, and none too kindly.

"Cisco, can I ask you something personal?"

"You may, but I may not choose to answer. It depends on how personal you get."

There it was again, his wicked sense of humor. The whole world and everything in it was a game filled with fun for him. He was sitting there looking as if butter would not melt in his mouth and that nothing he could do or say would be interpreted any other way but innocent. His face, with his dark eyes, was straight, too straight, Tori told herself. It was as if a mask was hiding his real emotions. However, the corner of his mouth was twisting mischievously, backing up her theory, while his whole body seemed ready to spring up, like a jack-in-the-box.

"Cisco, I'm serious!"

"And, so am I. What makes you think that I'm not?"

"It's just that lady over there… she is looking our way, and none too happily, I might add. Have you any reason to be the object of her anger? It can't be me; I don't know her."

He flashed a quick look in the general direction but did not see the woman.

Tori looked puzzled. "At least I don't think I have ever met her before."

Cisco slowly turned in his seat to take a closer look. He was searching the room for the individual Tori spoke of when his eyes locked with the hostile stare of the only person looking their way.

Tori thought that the lady, whoever she was, would leave her seat, and walk toward him, that very second. She positively looked as if she could kill him, but then, to Tori's utter surprise, she watched as the lady's face softened, and her glare turned to a slight blush, somewhat like that of a young un-experienced, schoolgirl. Tori looked at her dinner companion and saw he was openly flirting and mouthing something to the older woman. Jean's wife would have loved to understand what he was saying, but damn him, he was speaking in Spanish.

Just then, a deep male voice from behind Tori's back spoke with a hint of concern. "Might I add that her husband has already killed three on the field of honor, and if you value your life, you had best desist at once, my old friend, that or be ready to duel."

John Davis had joined them, and for the first time, Tori was about to meet the mystery man. On many occasions, she had seen him when they stopped in for dinner, but Jean had never introduced her. She had assumed that Laffite liked to keep his business and pleasure separate, and Mr. Davis had been nothing more than that, a business acquaintance. Now, he stood before her, a natural showman in his glory. She was sure that his light-colored hair was well-groomed and styled by Cisco or Marie. He was dressed immaculately, right down to the gold chain, shining in the light hanging from his pocket watch. John was tall and distinguished-looking. His elegant appearance and smooth-talking charm only added to his masculinity. He had the friendliest blue eyes that sparkled as he gazed knowingly upon her, and in no way did his scrutiny disturb her like she thought it should. To think that this man, who fit so well into these times, and with the people around him, was nothing more than an impostor was amazing. No one could ever guess where he was from and had Tori not been informed by Cisco, she would never have had a clue.

Mr. Davis smiled brightly and took a step her way, placing him right by her side. "So, we meet again, and on a far different level than I had ever thought that we would," he said, bending forward to kiss her lightly on both cheeks. Then lowering his voice, he whispered into her ear. "I think it best, before we carry on any further conversation, that we move to a more private location." Switching to a voice that could easily be overheard by those close by, he added, "Let me escort you both to my office. You are here to pay a debt that you owe; are you not, Francisco, my friend? And, it would be my pleasure if you accompanied us, Madame Laffite. To leave you sitting here by one's self would be extremely rude on my part." He pulled her chair away from the table and offered his arm. Tori stood up and gladly slipped her arm around his."

"It would be my pleasure. My husband has often spoken so highly of you, and I am most grateful for the invite."

"Then, by all means, come right this way."

Cisco was more than willing to depart right then as the woman who had been the focus of his attention was again glaring at him, and the last thing he needed was any kind of confrontation, verbal or otherwise.

Tori and John followed Cisco, who was hastily walking ahead of them. He began the climb up the grand stairs toward Davis's office on the upper floor, without even looking back. If anyone watched the three of them leave, they obviously would think nothing of it, as it was common knowledge that many paid their debts in private. When Cisco reached the first landing, he turned and looked at John, who had conducted himself most splendidly. To those below, it would not seem strange to see Jean's wife join them, as it was apparent by Davis's informal greeting, he was a close friend of both Laffite and his wife.

Grinning, the young Spanish gambler couldn't help but express his admiration. "Hand well played John never expected to see you so soon."

"I gathered that by the predicament you were placing yourself in, outwardly flirting with the woman. An action, I might add, that a gentleman of today would never think of doing. Let's get out of sight before you go and blow our cover."

"I would not!"

Davis ignored his younger counterpart. "Tori this way, please." John opened the large door and stepped aside. "Let us get him away from prying eyes, shall we?"

Once inside the large room that looked more like a sitting room than an office, John began filling crystal glasses with fine wine. Softly, he spoke and without a hint of his dismay at Cisco's reckless actions. "Your husband has been a good customer over the last few years, and might I add, a good friend. It's because of his ability to acquire, ah, certain furnishings for me, at a very reasonable price, that I was able to build all this. Everything you see, I have purchased from your husband." John handed her the glass of wine and smiled knowingly.

51

Tori hadn't realized that Jean's business dealings with John had been on such a large scale and was genuinely stunned. "You mean you bought all this from Jean? Even the paintings, everything?"

"This, and much more. Your husband's ability to always have what I need, on a scale that is economical to both of us, has been very beneficial to him and me. I always told Jean that if I could ever do anything in return to help him, all he had to do was ask. It seems to me that the time has arrived, has it not?"

Tori sat down and took a sip of her wine. She smiled over the rim of her glass and nodded her head. "I believe you could say that. This is going to shock the shit out of him, you know. It's going to be quite something to see his face when he finds out that you and Cisco are… well, you know, like me."

Immediately Davis's face turned deadly serious, and his tone was stern as he spoke. "When, and if the time comes that I tell him at all." His eyes had a look of concern and sent a shiver of doubt through Tori's body.

"What, do you mean, if?"

"Just that. I'm not too sure that I want anyone else to know of our little secret." He shot a strange look at Cisco, who, in return, took a large gulp of his wine but said nothing. "I will help you get Jean out of jail, on one condition, and that is, if I decide to let anyone else know about my origins, then it will be my decision, and mine alone. You have to give me your word on that." He held his hand up to stop her protest. "Hear me out, please. I have my reasons. It's not that I don't trust you or Jean; I do. We understand each other very well. It's just that the more people that know, the bigger the chance of it all coming undone. I'm happy here with what I have built, and I would like to keep it that way. Look around you. Not only here, look at the whole street." He escorted her to the balcony and pointed. "Everything you see on this side of the block is mine, and I built it. The largest building is this, my hotel. Granted, the idea is not exactly new, but here and now, it is all very new. Call it ego, or call it whatever you want," he grinned, "I wish to go down

52

in history as the creator of all this." He raised his hands above his head and made a grand arch, slowly encompassing the whole area as he continued. "I'm the man who had the vision to create this place, way before Las Vegas or Atlantic City was ever born. I want history to say they copied me, not the other way around. I have gone to great lengths to assure that I get full credit, I might add."

Cisco joined in the conversation. "You can say that again. John goes over the top if you ask me."

"No one is asking you," snapped John. He took a sip of his wine and smiled slightly as he continued talking while escorting Tori back inside to a seat next to Cisco. "You see, in the nineties, I was no one. Here I am, the biggest and the best. Me, Mr. John Davis, I've pulled the greatest con. I will have the last laugh on all of those that put me down, and they will never know." He grabbed the air and made a fist as if snatching something invisible. "I took it from them," he laughed.

Then, he looked at Tori with an earnest face. "Did you know that I will not have a portrait of myself done, not even a sketch if I can help it? I can't have my face popping up in the future, now can I? It has happened, you know. There are photos of certain people who have lived in the past like me, like both of you. Old photos have shown up of them, years before they could have been taken. True, they are called look-alikes, and only a few dare suggest they traveled in time, but that will not be me. So you see, if anyone else is to know who I am, it has to be my decision, you understand?"

Tori was stunned, both at his wanting to remain anonymous and implying that others had lived in the past. "Excuse me, but are you telling me that they found a way to return back to the future?"

Cisco burst out laughing. "I'm sorry, Tori, really I am. It's just that was one of my favorite movies."

"What was?"

"Back to the future." He chuckled again. "Look, I know what John is talking about, well, some of it anyway."

John shot Cisco a stern look; it was so threatening that it

silenced him right away. It seemed the subject was not going to be, discussed any further. Sipping her glass of wine, Tori decided that she would ask him more about the matter later. Right then, she did not want to interrupt John by demanding; he explain himself and his statement when she needed to befriend the man, not alienate him. John was eccentric and utterly obsessed with his gambling legacy. The man was also very talented, to have built so much and in such a short amount of time. Talent, skill, and cunning were traits Tori needed a lot of if she were to succeed in the days ahead. If he wanted to remain, John Davis of this time, then that was his choice, and Tori had no problem with that. "I understand how you feel. If, however, you do tell Jean, I can assure you that your secret will be safe. He has, after all, known about me for years. I have told him so much, explaining and describing as much as I can. His understanding of it all has been commendable, and he is not the only one that knows. His first lieutenant, Dominique, his brother Pierre, and John Grymes, they all know. It has been kept a safe secret among us."

"That's just my point! Don't you see? First Jean, then his brother, then this Dominique and John Grymes, who's next, I ask? No, I have to have your word that you will not reveal what you know to anyone! That is the only way I can get involved and help you."

He meant what he said, and she knew that he would indeed walk away from this meeting if she did not comply. Fearing that, Tori spoke, sounding very sincere. "You have my word. I may not agree with you; still, it's your life, and I respect that. What I need is all the help I can get, and I see no real harm in keeping your secret, that is, if you keep mine." She grinned, trying to lighten the mood in the room. "So, yes, you can rest easy. I will not tell Jean or anyone else. After all, I have no reason to, now do I?"

Relief immediately spread across John's face. The lines on his brow seemed to vanish as the muscles around his neck relaxed. He breathed an audible sigh, and spontaneously he began to introduce an idea he and Cisco had, concerning how to get Jean and his men out of jail. In seconds, it was as if the previous conversation had never taken place.

OVER dinner, which was served in his private dining room, Tori learned that her new friends had been very busy and had done their homework. After exhausting all other options and avenues open to them, they were left with only one line of operation. It was going to have to be a good old-fashioned jailbreak, just like she had thought. However, there was another piece to their plan that she would never have come up with.

Davis explained that stealing all the evidence back was crucial to keep the Laffite and his men out of jail. Evidence, some of which John was only too proud to admit, was rightfully his, as he had already paid for it. "Most of the goods were being unloaded and headed for my establishment when that nosy, good-for-nothing Governor, got his sticky fingers involved," John grumbled.

"No evidence, no crime," Cisco added excitedly. "No crime, no charges. All we need is a plan, and some extra men, who can be trusted, and bingo, your Jean is free, and everyone gets what they want. You get him back. I get to be friends with both of you, not to mention the adventure of a lifetime, Hollywood-style, and John here," he slapped his friends back hard, causing him to take two steps forward, which Cisco ignored, "he gets to pay off a debt, one that John feels he owes Jean, for all his past help. Isn't that right?"

John looked at the younger man with a blank expression. Cisco was enjoying every moment of the evening, and it showed, unlike John, who was the calm hard-to-read poker type. Tori could tell the hotel owner was the one who would do all the worrying. They may be from the same time and cut from the same cloth, both gambling men and all, but they were as different as chalk and cheese as her nanna would say.

John took a seat and spoke sternly. "Look, until we do a lot more research into the problem of breaking them out, we can't do anything. I hate to burst any bubbles here. It's just that we can't go rushing into anything. Unlike you, Cisco," he shot him a dirty look, "I don't make a move until I feel the odds are in my favor. This is not a game! This is very real. I, unlike you, do not have the luxury of fantasying or going off half-cocked. Neither will I have you acting like Rambo. You can't just rush in and win the day. That kind of action and your careless attitude will get us nowhere but caught and thrown in jail, right next to Jean and his men."

"Well, I know that," snapped Cisco. "I'm not stupid, you know. So, give me some credit here."

John nodded his head and turned to face Tori. "Then, there is a small matter of which I am very concerned. Have either of you asked yourself if by doing this, by getting Laffite and his men out of jail, we will change history?"

Cisco looked at Tori, who once again was chewing on her bottom lip. She shrugged her shoulders and spoke up, sounding a bit concerned. "I have to admit to you that did not cross my mind. Maybe, he and his men were placed in jail and broke out. They could have been, right?"

John nodded his head. "Correct in that assumption. Historically speaking, I do know that they do go to jail; well, some of them do. Also, I can tell you that the particular event won't happen for a while yet. So, what I am asking is, are you willing to go ahead knowing this?"

Immediately Cisco spoke up. "Hell, yes, I am, and she is too, right, Tori?"

Tori didn't speak because part of her wanted to agree, and the other was concerned, so she just nodded her head slightly.

Cisco grinned. "There you have it; we are going ahead."

John raised his glass in a toast. "If you are sure, then. We will have to make airtight plans…"

Tori was not surprised when John was interrupted before he could finish what was on his mind. What did cause her to sit up and take notice was that Cisco spoke seriously for what seemed to be the first time that night. He sat down across the table from his friend and displayed a far different demeanor than she had ever witnessed before. "John, it just seems to me that the element of surprise is going to have to play a big part in this, and we do need help. The three of us can't do it alone, that's for sure. Any ideas?"

Tori's face lit up. "Gentlemen, maybe I can be of help in that area. First of all, I do have some extra help. How many, I'm not sure. If I were to go to Grand Terre with Jean's blacksmith Thiac, I could rustle up a few good men, so to speak."

"You mean, go into the heart of the pirate's den," beamed Cisco? "You, by yourself? That's crazy. I hear that Gambi and others would love to run the place their way. They did for a while; you know, before Jean took over." He was genuinely worried, and it showed for a few seconds. However, he quickly brightened and leaned forward, ever the optimist, seizing the opportunity of a lifetime. "No, it's just too crazy for you to go alone. You'll need someone to go with you, and I would love to accompany you. In fact, I insist."

"I don't know about that. Getting you into Grand Terre might not be so simple. They know Thiac and me, while they don't know you, and they don't take kindly to strangers."

"Wow!" Cisco sat bolt upright at the mention of Grand Terre. He was so eager to get her to agree to his suggestion that John and Tori looked at each other and laughed out loud.

John poured his younger counterpart another drink and spoke to him in a joking tone. "I think I'd best keep an eye on you, you, crazy fool. Keeping you out of trouble is going to be one hell of a job, let alone pulling off the jailbreak. What have I let myself in for?"

"John, what have we started?" said Tori, trying to keep a serious tone. "Look at him. You would think he is actually enjoying all this." She was trying hard not to laugh again as she looked at them both. "Cisco, this is nothing to take lightly. I don't know if I should take you with me. I don't even know if it's safe for me to go without Jean."

"Exactly, and you will need a man along. It's etiquette, you know, a female has to have an escort; she can't just go off on her own, especially with a black man. Female escort, maybe, but you need a man, and I intend to be him. I'm sure this Thiac dude won't care. It's settled, and if you don't mind, I would like to talk about other things for a while. We will finish with all this espionage shit later. Much more talk like this, and I will start to introduce myself to the beautiful women around here, as Bond, James Bond!"

They all had a good laugh at that, and for the first time that night, the three friends felt as if they could relax for a bit. Cisco downed his glass of wine in one big gulp and handed it to a stunned John to refill. "I would like to enjoy each other's company for a short while. It's been a long time since I've had anyone to talk to and have some good old-fashioned fun with. Old stuck-in-the-mud here, never let's go. What do you say, Tori? Shall we get him to loosen up and get another fine bottle while he's at it?"

He was impossible and lovable at the same time. With nothing left for them to do that night and realizing that the next few days could very well change their lives, and history, they did what Cisco advised. They just let go and enjoyed each other's company.

Little did the men know that Tori's mind was racing ahead and trying to sort through the dangers of what they were facing. It was vital for her to get Laffite and his men out of jail and that they carried it out so that it would not have a significant effect on the timeline that already existed. It seemed that the only way she would know if it changed anything would be if Jean and his men didn't end up back in jail sometime in the future, as John said they were destined to do. If they didn't go back into jail, they would have screwed up royally, which would mean that her future would be affected. If she did find a way back home, what would home be like? It was all one big twisted, tangled timeline of events. Pull one thread out of place, and it all changed everything and everyone, but she had no other choice, and Tori knew it. She had to take the risk and pay the price, whatever it was, because she owed Jean that much. Jean and his men had to break out. Besides, she loved Laffite, and if there was no way back, well, she'd never know if they changed things or not, so what did it matter in the grand scheme of things? The trouble was, everything they did mattered, she thought.

"What a mess, and what a shit load of responsibility, why the hell me?" Tori had spoken this thought out loud but softly and glad she had because John and Cisco, who were talking about which wine to open, had not overheard her. She wished more than anything, right then, that she had more historical details to go on. One thing was sure, Jean Laffite and his men fought in the Battle of New Orleans, and if she didn't break him out now, maybe that would change things, and he'd never get to fight. Jackson would lose, and the British would have a foothold in this new nation. The United States, as she knew it, would never be built. Either way, she was damned if she did and damned if she didn't. It was then that Tori knew her best bet was getting Jean and his men out regardless of her worry over the future. She, Cisco, John, and Jean's pirates, from Grand Terre, would make history one way or the other, and if lucky, more than once in this era.

TORI, John, and Cisco enjoyed another exquisite bottle of wine while listening to more of Cisco's antics. All of his adventures were described between the country music songs that John loved to sing. Like Cisco had told her, the man sounded professional and very much like a country music star from their own time. After he finished each song, Tori encouraged him to continue, which he gladly agreed to several more times. He ended the night's entertainment with his favorite tune by Kenny Rogers, a song that suited him and Cisco well. The title was 'The Gambler,' and the words had both men and even Tori grinning by the time the last key played.

Tori clapped her hands and raised her glass in a toast. "That was amazing, John; you even sound like him, you know? Kenny Rogers, that is."

Cisco laughed while pouring the last of the wine into his glass. "I told you he was good, and even if I detest country, that one song does make me grin. I can run rings around these idiots."

"Cisco, I have warned you. Those idiots are learning faster than you know, and I feel the time is almost here to make things a bit more interesting and difficult for you." John was enjoying himself. He took the empty bottle from the younger man's hand and began to open another.

Laffite's wife frowned. "John, no more for me." Tori was not sure she was ready for another hangover, and as much as she enjoyed the wines they had consumed so far, she thought it best to end the evening while she could still think clearly.

"Oh, come on, Tori. If it's a headache you don't want; I will stop over with some of Marie's cure-all. Come to think of it, John here can send you home with his stash, right old man?"

John grinned. "One more glass while we chat, a bit, won't hurt."

"Well said," added Cisco. "Besides, you're not even buzzed yet and most certainly nothing close to last night. You really tied one on, but Marie fixed you up, didn't she?"

John cleared his throat loudly. "Cisco, can you please be quiet and stop interrupting me. Tori, I would be most happy to send you on your way with my stash, as this idiot calls it. Now, pass me your glass and let me tell you what I think we need to do. I have been mulling it over while you two have been entertaining yourselves and listening to me, of course."

Once again, the three of them settled down and discussed what had to be accomplished according to John's estimation. Cisco had sat and listened and then added his ideas, which were very sound and shocked both Tori and the hotel owner. John had nodded his head and smiled to himself before winking at Tori. "It seems that our young, 'lady's man' here is taking this serious at last."

"Well, of course, I am. Contrary to your continued unfair evaluation of me, I am not a complete fool, or am I stupid."

John laughed and looked up at the heavens. "Thank God because what we are about to try and accomplish is not without peril. Should it work out, we will either make history or change it. So, yes, Cisco, I need you to be just as serious about this as Tori and I. Just glad to see you are, that's all."

Tori was watching them and nodded her agreement back to John, who at last seemed more than relieved and indeed pleased by this new responsible-sounding Cisco. It was still quite something to know that the man who she now called a friend was like herself. He was a time traveler, but more than that, Laffite's wife guessed that when she got back to her own time if she got back, he would be in the history books. That would mean she was now good friends with yet another historical character. This thought sent shivers up her back. If she did not return to her own time, would her daughter read about her in some book or text and not even realize she was learning about her mother?

The sound of Cisco's voice interrupted her thoughts. "Tori, are you with John and me on this? Is it a go or not? It's up to you. What do you think?"

Their plans had come together rapidly, and so did her decision on the subject. "Well, as you are asking me, and as we all agreed upon the plan, without any doubts, I might add, then it's a go. Bottoms up, gentlemen." Tori emptied her glass and stood up. "John, if you don't mind, I will take that liquid, whatever you call it, of Marie's. Just in case I have a headache later when riding. Cisco, you know what to do. John, there is no time better than right now to get going. Time is crucial, and we do not need to go back over anything again. What say you, my friends? Agreed or not?"

Cisco burst out laughing. "Like you have to ask. Oh, John, my friend, hang on to the potion. Plenty more," he swallowed a mouthful of wine, "where that comes from, for sure. I will pick some up for our use, trust me. I may need it myself after this." Cisco put his empty glass down and held out his hand toward his friend, and John took hold of it firmly and shook it, sealing the deal.

"Good luck then. Tori, keep an eye on him." He walked to Laffite's wife and hugged her briefly. "Take care, and let's make history together. May the outcome be what we want and what is needed for us all."

WHEN Tori arrived back at the townhouse, she'd sent word to Thiac to expect her and a friend within the hour. She also told him to have three horses ready to ride, as he was going to be joining them. It had been decided that Cisco would meet Tori at Laffite's Blacksmith Shop after returning from Marie Laveau's cottage with what he needed for his trip. From there, with the help of Thiac, they planned to go on to Grand Terre and hopefully persuade some of Laffite's men to join them in their plans. They knew that this task had to be accomplished if the jail breakout was to succeed.

"OH, Miz Tori, you be plumb out of your head, like I done told you. I know you think it be best to go down to that there, place, I ain't' never seen, but knows of. Yes, I do; I know it ain't no place for a lady like you to go. It ain't safe like."

"Bessy, I told you, I am not going alone, and besides, everyone down there knows who I am. I am Boss's wife, and they would never touch me. I have to go, don't you see? Because if I don't, my husband could very well hang."

"I understands that. You could wait until tomorrow an all. It been so late now and dark, plum dark as can be, 'specially down the bayous way."

Tori took a hold of Bessy's hand. "We can't wait, and the sooner we go, the faster we can come back. It's all been sorted out and decided on."

Bessy put on her best pouting face, hoping it would add weight to her opinions. "I don't like you taking that there, Master Cisco man. He ain't proper either, but if'n you has too and seems to me, you done made your mind up, you has too, then it be better you go with him. Better than going by yourself an all." She stood there, shaking her head. Then she looked at Tori and spoke up. "One problem comes to my head; what I going to tell folks that come calling?"

Tori stopped cold in her tracks. She let go of Bessy's hand and walked to the side of her bed. Laffite's wife had not thought about this situation. Slowly, the puzzled woman sat down on the bed to think it out. "Well, I don't think too many people will be calling anytime soon. Like I told you, people don't like me much right now."

"There be fine folk who do. You know there be Master Grymes and your friends from the plantation, the Destrehan's Mistress and her man. What I done goin' to tell them if they come's here asking for you?"

"Well, if the Destrehans come by, you tell them to go and talk to Mr. Grymes. Mr. Grymes won't' come calling, so you don't have to worry about him. He will be told all he needs by morning. If anyone else comes calling or sends an invite, which I don't think will happen, but if it does, you tell them I am indisposed and not seeing anyone. I am to be left alone. In fact, after I leave, you tell the girls to stay out of the house. Keep them in their quarters or outside working the garden. Tell the driver to keep everyone away; only you are allowed to take care of me. That is what you will say and do until I return. If I need to send word, Mr. Grymes will come and talk to you. No one, and I mean this, Bessy, no one else must know I am gone. No one else will you trust, no one but Mr. Grymes. Do you understand me?"

"Sure does. Don't like it none, but I will do as you say. You just take care of yourself and bring the Massa back home." Bessy dabbed at her eyes with a small handkerchief and blinked several times, trying to stop herself from crying. "Lord Miss Tori dis be hard on my heart, you and the Massa gone and ain't no tellin' when I goin' to see you again."

Tori stood up and hugged her tightly. She knew how upset the woman was by the way she had slipped back to her old way of talking without realizing it. There was nothing to do about it but hurry up and leave. Then she turned and picked up her tiny bundle of clothes wrapped up in a blanket.

Bessy handed her a pair of leather boots that sat at the end of the bed and shook her head as Tori took them. "Those ain't fit for your feet, not meant for no lady of any kind, that I kin reckon on."

Tori smiled as she looked at the boots in her hand and then looked at Bessy's worried face. "Jean gave these to me just before I came here the first time. I have not had the chance to wear them often. I wore them maybe once when we went away… that was then, and this is now. Don't you worry yourself any; these are just what I need until I reach Grand Terre. Now, remember everything I told you, and God willing, you will get word that Jean is safe, and I am with him very soon."

The black woman took a deep breath and spoke softly. "Still don't got to like it none, but you be smarter than me and has to know what's to do. I will pray every day, lots like, until I get word what's it is you has to do, is done. You best go now. The carriage is waiting, and I will call them girls to the kitchen and sends them to their rooms after you is gone. You just come back safe like," her words trembled as she spoke.

Bessy was trying so hard not to cry that Tori felt sure, if she didn't depart right away, the poor slave would begin to wail, as only she could, and there would be no stopping her once that happened. So hastily, she left the room, calling out as she went toward the stairs. "Clear the house after I am gone, and once the carriage returns close, and lock the gate."

"Yes, Miss Tori. You stay safe now, you hear?" The only response was the sound of the downstairs door closing. Her Mistress was gone, and suddenly, the house felt empty. Bessy dropped to her knees and began to pray. She had time for a quick prayer before she had to clear the house of everyone else, and lord knows, Miss Tori needed all the prayers she could get.

❧

THE Laffite carriage pulled to a stop behind the small cottage. It was out of sight of any prying eyes on the side street. When they passed the front of Pierre's cottage, Tori had looked to see if they had been seen by anyone inside. She need not have worried; the place was dark, indicating that all those inside, were sleeping. Nervously Jean's wife looked both ways along the streets and saw that they were desolate and just as dark as Pierre's cottage's interior. This was a relief and helped her tremendously. It was imperative that she, of all people, not be seen leaving town.

It didn't pay to be careless, and it always paid to be overly cautious in her estimation. Had she seen anyone, Tori would have remained inside her carriage until the coast was clear. Her mind was racing, and yet her thoughts were clear. 'Always have a backup plan; that's what you taught me, my love. I'm coming for you, Jean, and you taught me well. This is it then, time to make my move.'

Through the open doors of the building, Tori could see the interior of the forge. It was cloaked in deep shadows, with no sign of life, except for the amber glow of Thiac's fire. It was a fire that always seemed to be burning, and she wondered briefly how long the embers would burn unattended? Laffite's wife looked around her and listened intently to the sounds of the night. The outcome of the following week depended solely on the elements of secrecy and surprise. If anyone saw her and recognized her, that element could very well be compromised. "Won't happen," she whispered before biting her lip to make herself stop talking. 'Time to go. Stop delaying.' Once she stepped out of the carriage, she spoke softly to her driver. "You go back now, and don't you dare tell anyone you brought me here. I am at home, and Bessy has all the instructions. You listen to her, you here?"

"I, sure enough, will do so. I ain't never come here tonight." He shook his head from side to side. "You be in the house, and anyone asks about you; they has to talk to Bessy. Yes, I got it right. You take care, Mistress. If you need me, you send word." With that, he backed the horses up and pulled the carriage onto the street. He did not even look back once he started off down the road. The slave had his instructions, and that was good enough for him. Tori waited for a few more seconds to make sure that she could slip into Thiac's shop without detection, and then she made her move.

One set of eyes had been waiting and watching anxiously from the shadows, unseen, and as the coach pulled away from the small area, footsteps echoed in the night air. Thiac's giant strides covered the distance rapidly between them, and in a flash, the man was standing in front of her. Tori had not seen him coming, and it stunned her, for it seemed to her that he had appeared out of nowhere and if he could do so, who else might be lurking in the vicinity? The stunned woman quickly looked over her shoulder before facing the blacksmith's grim expression. The large smithy stood silently, waiting for her next move and instructions. "It's alright, Thiac, I am fairly certain that I was not followed, but I best come inside before anyone comes along. Don't look so worried; everything is under control, I assure you."

"Not worried, none. Just needed to let you know there's someone here, Mizz Tori. Says he's waitin' for you. Claims to be a friend. You want me to be rid of him? I can; you say the word." Thiac continued while looking up and down the road. "I ain't never seen him around before and thought maybe, he be a lying or causing you trouble like. But then I asked myself, how'd he know you was comin'? He had to be a friend to know that, right? He could be the one you told me was coming, so I let him be."

"Thiac, it's fine. He's telling the truth." Tori reached out and took hold of the blacksmith's arm. Her small hand gripped his forearm as she spoke. "I would like you to meet him and hear what we have to say together. Can you close up the shop, by that, I mean for a few days or longer? Can you do that without anyone caring?"

"Anythin' you want, Mizz Tori. All you has to do is ask. Let's get inside cause it's a way warmer and fewer eyes to be worrying about."

Without waiting, Thiac left Tori's side and walked to the side of his building, where he pulled the large door toward a closing position. He stood aside when the entrance was narrow. Tori didn't have to ask or hesitate, she hurried past him, and as they entered the confines of the small establishment, the large hands quietly pushed the shop's doors closed.

Once inside, with the doors firmly shut, the fire was the only source of light illuminating their surroundings. The soft orange glow lit up Cisco's grinning face as he stepped forward out of the dark recesses. The fire's embers were dim in places and comprised of shades that ran from deep reds to golden yellow. Gone were the tall crackling flames that Tori had witnessed on her last visit. The wood in this fire lay undisturbed and silent until Thiac took up the bellows with his powerful arms. Then, along with the sound of large amounts of air blowing under the wood, the fire sprang to life and lit up the room. Once again, Tori witnessed the white-hot flames leaping upward. To her, it looked as if the flames danced. It was like they were trying to reclaim the sparks that jumped ahead of them. The wood crackled and snapped as the dormant inferno awoke and grew larger. With each blast of the bellows, the new flames expanded, and a wave of heat came with them. The wall of hot air shot out into the area, on a curtain of golden light, cloaking the room in its warmth, and it felt good to her.

"Is this the man," the protective voice of Thiac asked? He was holding a poker when he questioned her, something that did not escape Cisco's eyes.

"The one and the same," snapped Cisco. May I suggest you put that down and stop worrying so damn much. By the way, let that fire die down before someone sees it. Miss Tori here can't be seen, so dim it, right?"

"Sure, will do so, but we need some light. Even these old black eyes can't do much without any," he chuckled. Thiac sounded more relaxed, now that he knew for sure his visitor was a friend and not a foe.

The blacksmith took an old oil lamp and lit the small wick, which he raised until the light was bright enough for his liking. He placed the lamp on the small wooden table and stood back, waiting for whatever it was that these two had to say. The blacksmith could almost bet it had something to do with Boss, but he was not so clear where that dandy fit in. He would keep a close watch on that one, he told himself. God help him if he tried anything, anything at all, toward his Mizz Tori. One wrong move and he would snap him in two, just like a stick. Thiac looked away and took in a deep breath as he did so. "Down temper," he mumbled to himself, "no needs to get all worked up over nothin'. No need to invite trouble into whatever this here is."

The slave was a large and powerfully built individual. He towered over all that came into his shop, standing a good six feet five. His body rippled with muscles, and his voice rumbled in a low tone when he spoke. His skin was the darkest of ebony, and a sizeable protruding brow shadowed his deep-set shifting eyes. His large head seemed to sit right on top of his shoulders; his thick neck was so wide and short that it did not seem to exist. The man's overall appearance was enough to frighten even the bravest of souls. Many said that he was nothing short of a savage beast that could never be trusted and was surely untamable. It was also whispered that such an animal belonged in the cane fields, out of harm's way, and not left unsupervised in the city, but none were brave enough to voice their concerns to either of the Laffite brothers.

In truth, Thiac was a big old teddy bear most of the time. He hated violence of any kind and had such a gentle manner about him that even the stray cats would visit to eat out of his hand. This gentle giant, who fed stray cats and dogs, who could sit and play with the children, was a stark contrast with the image he presented to most adults.

There was never any denying that he was very good at his job. In his large hands, pieces of wrought iron would twist and bend easily into designs that were so intricate that they were indeed works of art. Out of this blacksmith shop came a significant percentage of fancy grills. Many were surrounding balconies, overlooking the Creole part of town. Of late, some were even turning up and gracing the American's elegant homes in what would become known as the Garden District in Tori's time. The forge was the perfect front for Jean, as many citizens had assumed this was Laffite's primary source of income. Things were changing, though, and Tori knew that soon, there would be no denying the truth behind the cover.

What Thiac sold went toward the rent for the cottage, and what was left over, and there was plenty, became a secure cash flow for the Laffite's. This allowed them time to utilize their fleet of ships and operate them out of Grand Terre. By using both the cottage and the blacksmiths, they were also able to have the perfect meeting places in town for the select few, such as John Davis and other citizens of exceptional standing. For always, there were those who were quietly looking for a bargain and could be trusted to remain silent on how they came about such merchandise.

Still, most of the pirated goods were sold openly along what would be called Pirate's Alley in the future. This was the small area between the Cathedral and what Tori knew as the Cabildo. In her time, it was a museum in this time; it was a building that was utilized and expanding. Jean and his men were incarcerated in a secure area one block behind the Cathedral. It was the jail of the day, one that would burn to the ground, causing the jail cells to be added to the Cabildo. The same area toward the rear of the Cathedral was a small graveyard, and it was utilized to set up shop by Laffite's men. In the years to come, the graves would be forgotten and covered over, and by Tori's time, not many would ever guess, they walked over an old forgotten graveyard when walking to Jackson Square via the famous Pirate Alley.

More substantial merchandise sales were dispersed in the outer regions of the city. These other locations were for those that did not need to know the truth behind Thiac's blacksmith shop or Pierre's Mistress's cottage. Besides being the perfect cover, the locations allowed more. Thiac ran a close operation and was always Jean's ears and eyes about the comings and goings-on around town. He was trusted by all of the blacks, free or slave; thus, most of what went on in the city would sooner or later end up being whispered to Jean or Pierre. There were very few secrets that he would not become aware of via the slave wave, as Tori liked to call it. The black man was forever on the job and always in command of his situation, be it as a smithy or spy.

However, there had been times when Thiac could not control himself as he was doing at that very moment. Only once, since working in the blacksmith shop, had he become that uncontrollable beast many thought him to be. Wiser now, he let no one see his fits of temper. Instead, he would go out back and let off steam unobserved. He would have loved to take a step outside at that moment but feared leaving the Boss's wife alone. So, he stood with his fists clenching and unclenching while watching and waiting. He would do nothing unless he absolutely had to.

The last time he had lost complete control had almost cost him his life, and if it had not been for Jean stepping in and purchasing him when he did, Thiac knew that he would have suffered much. It had happened quite a few years back before he had come to New Orleans. He had lost his temper and done the unthinkable and hit a white man. This unfortunate event occurred in the islands, and as far as slave owners were concerned, this gravest offense was always met with deadly consequences. Thiac, however, had been lucky. His size and ability to carry large workloads had made him a valuable slave and one that his owner hated to see destroyed. He had instead given the order for a public whipping. Lashes were to be administered. Loathed, as he was to damage and scar this beast, for Thiac's value would decline sharply after such a whipping, the owner had no choice; the law had to be obeyed. It did not matter that he understood the slave had been fully justified in his actions; he had accosted a white man; therefore, his owner's hands were tied; the sentence was set.

That's when Jean stepped in and had saved the slave. He had bought him outright for a considerable amount, a deal that the former owner was only too glad to take. To be rid of the problem and make a profit while doing so was very agreeable indeed. By the time Jean and Thiac arrived in New Orleans, Thiac owed Jean Laffite his undying loyalty. He worked long, hard hours in the smithy, and the blacksmith gave both his reliability and service to Jean out of both gratitude and friendship.

The slave slipped his fists behind his back and shifted his massive body weight from foot to foot. The smithy made sure he was seen by the dandy and that this new friend of his Mizz Tori saw in return, he was not happy. When the blacksmith was sure the man knew he was closely watching him, Thiac resumed his statue-like stance. He was keeping his temper in check. No white man was worth a beating or death, he told himself. Even though he was no longer just any slave, nothing had changed with the law, here or in the islands. He was still black and therefore had fewer rights as a man, but Mizz Tori and her safety and honor; was another matter. He would not hesitate to break the law for her if need be.

Tori looked away from the fire and directly at the smithy. "Thiac, you told me that you would help Jean and me, any way you could. I know you are aware of where Jean and his men are. What you don't know is, I intended to get Boss and his men out of those cells. I need your help, and if you are still willing, then Cisco and I would be very grateful."

"Yes, Mizz Tori, I meant it, that's for sure. You just tell old Thiac what you need, and I will find a way to get it done. But, Mizz Tori, you know, that no one has just walked outta that there, place? I reckon they will be tryin' to make sure no one ever does too."

"Let me worry about that. I just need your assistance. I knew you would keep your word to help me. I only wanted Cisco to hear you say so. Now, the first thing we need is more men to put our plan into action. To get them, I have to go to Grand Terre with Cisco. It would be a big help to us if you could come along, as you might know, which men we could trust. You did work and live down there for a while, didn't you?" Giving him no time to answer, she went right on explaining her plans as she warmed her hands by the fire. "You did tell me you could close up shop here without causing too many questions? The last thing we need is to raise any suspicions that something is amiss."

"I can at that, close up is no problem. The fire will die by itself, left unattended. Boss, he, close the place, all the time. People, they don't ask no questions. But, Mizz Tori, I be thinkin'. I mean, should you go to Grand Terre by yourself, without Boss? I know'd, it's his house, that be down there and all, but it be so close to trouble. I mean, you bein' a genteel lady and all. The roads this time of the year, they be a hard travelin', and once there…" he rubbed his forehead as if trying to erase his wrinkled brow. Worry was written clearly across his face and sounded in his concerned tone as he added more to his opinion. "I know'd you been there afore. You know'd it's not safe fo you, that be sure. Old Thiac here, be glad to go fo you. I could brin' back all the men's, you need."

"No, that won't work. I thank you for your concern, but I have to go along. With Jean and his brother and his second in command, Dominique, all arrested, well, I have to show who is still Boss. I fear if I don't act fast and strongly, well, some might take the chance to try and take over. I don't know if Gambi, Nez Coupe, or Beluche are in port; those first two are my biggest fear. Beluche, I can deal with and trust, but the other two, I don't trust those roughnecks at all. I would not put it past one of them to try to take over as the new boss. Some men will stay loyal to Jean, but even those will be looking out for themselves. I thought this through; we both did," she looked toward Cisco. He did not speak or move other than nod his head in agreement. Tori looked back towards the concerned smithy. It's the right thing to do. I am going, with or without your help, so are you still coming?"

"Like I done said, I will be with you. Boss, would kill me if he learned you asked, and I didn't do nothin'. But, that ain't why I'm goin'. No sur. I goin' cause, you asked for my help, and that is that. 'Sides, I reckon, if you, has it in your head to go, Boss, he'd want me to watch over you, not try to stop you and get you all riled up like, till you goes an does somethin' by yourself like."

Tori grinned at his last statement. "Thank you. I knew I could count on you. Now, we have to be careful. We can't let anyone see us head out; I mean, leave." She looked toward the closed door. "Once there, if all goes according to plan, Cisco here will be able to explain our attentions to the men far better than me. Knowing their type as I do, they would never listen to you, Thiac." Tori tried to smile to show she disagreed with what had been implied. "No offense, it's just the truth. I also realize that they would never listen to a woman, even if that woman is Laffite's wife. No, it has to come from, forgive me, a white man, with me backing him." Tori walked over to the smithy and put her hand on his massive shoulder. "You understand, don't you?" He nodded his head, accompanied by a grunting sound. "Once that is done, Cisco also will need to meet with our contact from here in town. He will have to gather the rest of the information that is crucial to our success. We have so much to do and such little time in which to do it. Everything has to be ready to go in the next seven or eight days."

The area fell silent. It was as if she'd spilled her emotions with her words and was left exhausted. Looking into the men's faces and taking a deep breath, she spoke with determination. "So, my friends, if you are ready, let's go."

Thiac looked from Cisco to Tori and nodded his head. "Mizz Tori, can I asks you just one bit of a puzzlin' question?"

"Of course."

"What is it you, has planned, that you needs you some of those men we set on goin' to fetch?"

"We need them because I intend to break Jean and all his men out of jail. By that, I mean we intend to march in and take them out. Do you understand?"

"Yes, um, I, git the idea. Just don't like it much."

"That's alright. As we travel, I will explain more, and you will understand the plan and not worry as much."

Thiac just nodded his head again and turned to Cisco. "Can you saddle a horse? Seem's Mizz Tori is in a hurry and ain't about to change her mind. It took some doing, but I got three of the best mares I could find. I need help getting the last two saddled up."

"That I can do," Cisco answered. He then faced Tori with a puzzled expression. "And, don't you think you had best find a more suitable riding garment, Madame? I mean, riding in a dress like you are wearing may present somewhat of a problem, wouldn't you say? You can't tell me you are going to ride sissy sidesaddle; that's just not right."

"Agreed, I am not ridding, sissy sidesaddle, Mr. Wise ass. I am way ahead of you. I have my outfit right here. She bent down and picked up her small bundle and her pair of boots. So, if you two gentlemen will excuse me, I'll be right back. Just get the animals ready to go, will you?"

Cisco rubbed his chin in amusement. 'This should be interesting, seeing what she comes up with,' he thought. 'The look on her face was a dead giveaway that something was up; after all, Levies for ladies were not available. Just what she intended to wear could be worth a great deal of laughter. Pantaloons, no doubt, trimmed in lace, with small pink ribbons.' This image in his head had him chuckling to himself as he walked to the back of the shop to help Thiac.

The blacksmith was looking very upset and worried as he faced Cisco. "I don't have no riding saddle, fo Mizz Tori. How she going to ride?"

"Just like us, old man, just like us, and I assure you, she would have it no other way. So, wipe that worried look off your face, and let's get to work."

Tori hurriedly walked to a darkened corner not far from the warm fire. She hung a blanket over the stacked wrought iron, making a changing room of sorts, and stepped behind it.

"If you two don't mind, I will trust you to keep your backs turned while I change."

"Yes, Mizz Tori. We will, and I's see to it that this here dandy keeps his face and eyes, all a pointin' the right way." Thiac placed his big black hand on the back of Cisco's head and physically turned it away from Tori's direction.

"Ah, you ruin all the fun, Thiac, my man, and if we are to be friends, will you please call me Cisco and stop referring to me as a dandy? You will wreck my image."

The big black man just grinned as he cocked his head to one side.

"Well, now, I might enjoy callin' you by your name. Ain't never had no white man offer that before. Not even Boss." He scratched his head, puzzling over this latest predicament. "You and this here, Mizz Tori, you don't seem to care much about the color of my skin. It, be, real black, you know. You sure nothin' is wrong with them eyes of yours?"

Cisco laughed and shook his head, and Thiac let another huge grin fill his face. "You treat me as a man, and I like that. Yes, Sir, I like that a whole lot. So's Cisco, we be friends. That is when it's only us and ain't no one else around. Now, you keep your eyes forward like, all the same." As he propelled Cisco forward, he made a growling sound, someplace between a grunt and a laugh. "You just come on out with me and help with them horses. The saddles ain't a-goin' to put themselves on."

Tori smiled to herself as she felt a wave of confidence and safety flood over her. She no longer feared going to Barataria. The pirate's wife knew that she was far safer than she could ever have hoped. Moreover, it was doubtful anyone would try to get past them to harm her with the two men traveling with her. Besides, Thiac would help keep Cisco in line, and she had a feeling that was not going to be an easy task.

By the time the horses were ready, Tori was dressed and ready to ride. When she walked outside to join the men, what they saw before them, was nothing short of a miraculous transformation. Where before a beautiful lady had been standing in their company, they were now stunned to see, a handsome young man had replaced her. That was if one did not know what to look for.

Her hair was pushed up under a bandanna, and her white blouse, which was open from just above her bust line, to the top of her neck, was slowly being laced closed by long strips of thin leather. Satisfied, she smiled with the results as she finished tying them together. The shirt was baggy enough to conceal her breasts and their bindings. Tori had bound herself tightly around the bust, partly for support and somewhat to help hide her curves. Everything she wore, she did so to help keep her identity safe. Her pants fit tightly, and her long black leather boots rode high, stopping just below her knees. The matching soft strip of leather tied around her waist was supposed to hold the pants up, but it looked totally unnecessary to Cisco's trained eye.

She put the last two articles of her outfit on while walking toward the horses. First came a man's calf-length brown jacket. When it was buttoned shut, she pulled the large collar up around her neck. Last was a soft brown hat that she pulled down low over her forehead.

Thiac was shocked and started to laugh, slapping the sides of his thighs with his hands. To go out in public dressed like this was indeed the act of a woman full of courage.

Cisco couldn't help focusing on how well her pants outlined her figure, and he had to keep reminding himself that she was to be left alone. 'That's one hell of an ass filling those pants,' he thought to himself. Then he grinned because, despite his own enforced 'hands-off' oath of loyalty, looking was allowed in his books. "Very impressive. Could not have done better myself. But, what did you do with your boobs? They seem to have vanished into thin air, more's the pity." This last statement he had whispered into her ear, in a mischievous tone of voice, that reminded her somewhat of Jean.

Laughing, she jabbed her elbow into his ribs. "That, my friend, is my secret. One for me to know and not one for you to worry over."

Pretending that her jab had hurt him, he playfully continued. "Ouch! I was only asking in case you needed help concealing any other part of your feminine charms in the future." His eyes were full of mischief, and his voice was on the verge of laughter. "I would be more than willing to come to your aid and as a doctor…"

"Resident doctor, you mean. One that is still in training… oh, but then you did say you ditched that position, right? So, that makes you not quite a doctor in my books." She poked him again in the ribs. "I bet you would like to help, you, dirty old man—enough of this. We had best get going. I would like to be out of town before too many people are around. Disguise or no disguise, no one must see me leave. As far as this city is concerned, I am at home, indisposed. I want no visitors, as I am distraught over my husband's arrest, and that's the cover that has to stay intact. So, let's get going now!"

THE three of them mounted up and headed out of town, using the back alleys and empty roads. From the cottage to the cemetery was a distance of about a mile or less. The surrounding land on the outskirts of town was rural and cloaked in thick vegetation. Along a narrow road to the right of the cemetery was the only cleared and open area. It was known as Congo Square and was primarily occupied during the daylight hours by the black population, both free and slave. That was their area, and knowing when and how it was used, Thiac didn't worry about being seen as they rode near by.

The few homes that dotted the sparsely populated vicinity, just past the city of the dead, were dark and showed no signs of inhabitance. They had chosen well to depart when they did, and by the time they were beyond the outskirts of town, the slow pace of the horses picked up. They'd spurred their mounts into a full gallop with the break of dawn and did not look back.

Thiac had noticed right away that Tori was seating a horse like a man and felt ill at ease, never having seen a woman handle an animal in this fashion. He could never even recall a woman handling a horse of this size and power at all. Seeing her now, riding like the wind with ease and with no sign of fear, the black man concluded that this lady seemed to be able to do anything she put her mind to. As the hours passed and he continued to observe the determination on Tori's face, his admiration grew. During these first hours of travel, Thiac came to a firm conclusion. He told himself, they really did have a chance at getting Boss free after all. The signs were there to see, and he was big on signs, big on believing.

❧ Three ❧

While Tori, Cisco, and Thiac rode toward Grand Terre, Simone and Edward lay in bed celebrating. "I told you, Edward, William is ecstatic, and did you hear him tonight? He has only had Jean in custody two nights, and already he is itching to get the man to trial. He was even saying that hanging would be too good for some of those sitting in those cells. Do you suppose he meant both the Laffites?"

"My dear," Edward stroked her arm and handed her another glass of wine. "I think maybe, with a bit of encouragement, we can sway the man's position on that subject. At least get him to agree to hang Jean. Indeed, I am quite certain it is you and I that shall determine that swine's fate." The dandy leaned forward and kissed her passionately. "Laffite can rot in jail or swing; it's up to you in the end. I shall endeavor to see your wishes carried out."

"How deliciously wonderful." She sipped her drink and then placed the glass on the bedside table. "There is one small favor I am dying to ask you, though."

"And, that is?"

"Tori, what are we going to do about her? I mean, you heard the Governor; he said she is not receiving any visitors and has had herself locked away in that pitifully small place she calls home. I understand what I want, and you, my darling, should have what you want. Tell me, what is it you have planned now that her husband is out of the way?"

"I am not sure about that; I think I shall enjoy her suffering. See how long she remains in seclusion, and we will hear if and when she receives any callers. I will have some men watch the house to see if she leaves or who comes and goes. I might even get William to pay the men instead of me. After all, those who pay her a call

79

will prove themselves to be sympathetic towards Laffite. Thereby, an enemy of not only the Governor but the city."

"Oh, I just love the way you think, but do tell, how long are you going to allow her to remain free of your grasp?"

"I think that shall be up until the pirate's trial. Then, I will allow her to see her love convicted and maybe hung or if it pleases you, placed in a rotting jail for life. Once that happens, I will make my move. I shall have her and if the pirate lives, I will make certain he knows of her fate, and trust me; I intend to make her fate as interesting as possible."

He reached up and twisted Simone's nipple until she squirmed. "I think you have my intentions clearly pictured in that pretty little head of yours. Tori is not one for such delightful pain, and her pain, that which I shall enjoy inflicting, will be not so enjoyable, especially if you are witnessing it. You would enjoy that, would you not? Watching the bitch, suffer by my hands. Taken, like the whore she is. Seeing you watch us and laugh at her predicament will be pure hell for her, don't you imagine?"

"My dear Edward, how delightfully decedent. I will indeed enjoy watching and maybe, just maybe, join in the fun. I hear tell that three in bed can be quite entertaining."

"My little minx. What a sinister mind you have, my dear." Edward dropped his empty glass onto the floor and rolled on top of Simone. He took both nipples in his fingers and twisted lightly. Then he lowered his head close to her ear and whispered. "All this talk has driven my excitement to the lower parts, the part you so enjoy." He took her hand and placed it around his erection. "This is going to be what, the third time tonight? Ah, but this time, we will both talk of things we will enjoy with our soon-to-be plaything. Maybe, show each other what we will do. I know I am ready, are you?"

"Edward, I am always ready, and you, Sir, are going to enjoy what I have planned." Simone squeezed his erection in her hand and then let it go when he moaned in delight. "Not so fast, my darling, you need to show me how you will take her the first time. I will play Tori, I will fight you, and you will show me, hurt me and make me yours."

THE trip to Grand Terre was a long one. They had to stop and rest the animals as well as themselves several times that morning. The little food and drink they had brought with them was soon consumed, and stopping for more before dark, was out of the question. Not only was there no place along their route, and even if there had been, Tori could not have run the risk of being discovered. Once, late in the afternoon, Cisco had ventured to a small farm on Thiac's insistence and bought back some bread and cheese and filled their flasks with fresh water. However, this sidetrack would not be the last time they broke from their plan.

When at last they stopped to make camp for a few hours, they were going to sleep in shifts under the night sky. Tori lay close to the small fire that helped take the chill off. If she'd had her way, they would have kept on going, but seeing how dark it was and not wanting to run the risk of injury to animal or herself, she had grudgingly agreed to the stop. At first, she was sure she would not sleep at all, but seeing how easy Cisco had drifted off, she allowed herself to trust Thiac to keep first watch and closed her eyes to rest, confident they would ride at first light.

TORI was surprised to find Cisco waking her up, and observed Thiac kicking dirt onto the fire, to put it out. She looked back at her younger companion's flustered expression and tried to make sense of what was going on. He spoke with an edge of unease in his voice. "You ready to go? Thiac has some news that should help speed things up."

"What news and how?" She was still trying to wake up, let alone understand what was happening. It was cold, and it was still night,

81

so riding in the pitch-dark seemed still to be a bad idea. "You said earlier that riding at night was dangerous, and I tend to agree with you."

Tori heard laughter by the horses and looked to see Thiac, who was enjoying himself and their situation. He was laughing at them while holding the reins out toward her. "It will be fine, Mizz Tori; you wait and see if it won't. Got to leave now, though." He moved forward, bringing the animals their way. He still had not answered her questions, though, and she looked toward Cisco for answers.

The upset man let her take hold of his hand, and as she squeezed his fingers, he realized that she was concerned. "Seems to me, it's a good idea. Old Thiac knows where we can catch a boat and make the trip in half the time, but we have to get there before they leave. Something about the tides or such. Didn't know bayous had tides. Thought they were simply made up of swamps and small rivers. Seems the closer you get to the Gulf, the more the tides affect the surrounding waterways. I knew we had to cross the river some-place, but I assumed it would not be so soon. So, it's off to the boats, if you will move your ass along, that is."

Now it was Tori's turn to laugh out loud as Cisco pulled her toward the horses. "Is this true, Thiac? This is great news, so why is our friend here acting so piss… upset?" She was brushing the dirt off her pants when a more critical question entered her mind. "Who are they, and more importantly, can we trust them to know the way?"

"Sure, can Mizz Tori. They be Boss's men, and I made a deal with them while you rested. Took myself a small ride to a place I know'd the boats stop at. Made 'um a deal. Now, if you will follow me, they are less than half a mile from here. I had hoped that they would be camped there. Know'd it was a place that they rest at. Been there myself, I, has. Would have told you sooner about it, but I did not want to get your hopes up, what with Boss in jail and all." He was rambling on and repeating himself because he was nervous. He'd taken the liberty to leave them when he was supposed to stand guard. On top of that, he had made a deal without asking. Could be, Mizz Tori would be upset some, and who know'd what that Cisco man would say? To him, it seemed that Cisco liked the idea, but he, weren't in charge; Mizz Tori was.

Cisco had to admit he saw the good side to this news but silently vowed to sleep with one eye open from then on. He frowned at the blacksmith. Thiac had left them alone and made arrangements while they slept. Hell, he could have been gone hours, and he had slept like a baby, all the time thinking the black brute was standing guard. Cisco knew the man could have, at the very least, told him of his plans. If he had thought to do so, he could have kept watch while the smithy was off getting them passage on some boat. Yes, he would have words with him but not right then and not in front of Tori, on account he did not want to upset her.

"Well, what are you waiting for?" Tori mounted her horse, and pulling her collar up around her neck, she excitedly spoke. "Come on, you two; we don't want to keep the boats waiting, do we?"

"No, Mizz, we aint a-goin' to do that." He handed the reins of the last mount to Cisco and wasted no time in climbing up onto his mare. "I ain't the one who be slowing you up any," he growled.

Cisco hurriedly settled on his horse and started forward. "Who's slowing who, Thiac, my man? It seems you could use a faster nag or me a slower mare." He was teasing, and Tori knew it, but by Thiac's thunderous glare, she guessed he took Cisco's words to heart. Good God, she thought, if she made it to the boats before they killed each other, she'd be lucky. At least whatever had been eating at Cisco had disappeared. Maybe he was a grumpy riser, or perhaps he was put out because Thiac had outshone him with the new arrangements? Whichever, Tori did not care so long as they both kept level heads.

TRUE to his word, three pirogues were waiting for them on the shoreline. Cisco took one look at the small craft and turned to the blacksmith. "I thought you said boat; I mean, those are not boats. Hell, they don't even look safe enough for a man your size, let alone me. You are serious, right, that's it?" He looked up and down the waterway in hopes of spying a real rowboat or some such craft.

Tori giggled, "I know just how you feel, remind me to tell you about my first time in one of these with Jean. I mean, this is easy compared to how my adventure began. Come on, we have to push off, and if you don't get in, they will leave without you. I will even let you ride with me; there is room trust me." She was off her horse and walking toward the largest of the crafts. "They are called pirogues."

"I know what they are called Tori; I am not stupid. Just never seen one up close, let alone thought of riding in one."

Tori turned and faced him. "Cisco, trust me on this. They are quite safe, and as you see, come in different sizes too. I have chosen this one. It is, after all, the largest. Now, stop your bitching and come on."

Thiac chuckled and took a seat in one of the smaller vessels while Tori and Cisco sat in another. The two men, whose places, the three took, said they would take care of the horses and wait for further word. Neither man asked about Jean or the reason why his wife was traveling to Grand Terre. After all, Thiac had said it was on Jean's command they were going, and what Boss said, they obeyed.

Tori watched as they pushed out into the waterway and observed the men left behind as they started to make a more permanent camp. Having Thiac along had already proved to be helpful; she just prayed her luck would continue to pan out. She looked up at the dark sky and shivered slightly. The moon had long ago set, and it was pitch black and cold. 'Always the coldest right before dawn,' she thought.

The camp soon vanished from sight, and she was wondering how anyone could find their way without daylight or flashlights? Then as if answering her unspoken question, she turned to see lanterns being lit and placed on the front of each pirogue. After this was done, they slid rapidly across the water, and within an hour, left the small bayou they traveled on to emerge onto the Mississippi River. This they crossed quickly, and somehow the men miraculously paddled their small crafts into the opening of one of the larger canals on the opposite side. How they had found it in the dark, Tori could not imagine, but they had gained her trust in their skills to get them safely to Grand Terre.

Tori and Cisco would whisper as Thiac rode in the second pirogue close behind and listened, but more often than not, he lost himself in his own thoughts. These two people with him were very different in many ways. At times he did not even understand them. It was as if they were talking a strange and new language. They used terms and sayings that he had never heard before, and it sounded like they were serious, but how could they be? Then he told himself, that was as it should be; after all, he was nothing but a dumb nigger boy; at least, that's what he had been told enough times. He knew he was not stupid, but he sure was dumb about a lot of things. Trouble was, most white folk, they just thought the two to be the same thing, he reckoned. Dumb was not stupid, 'cause if you was dumb, you could learn. If you was stupid, you couldn't unlearn that any. Thiac did know one thing to be true. He told himself he was seldom wrong about folks. The good ones was as clear to him as the bad ones, and he knew that Cisco and Tori, well… they was in the good group.

As time wore on, he found that he was beginning to consider both Cisco and Tori his very own personal friends. This was something that caused him intense emotional feelings. Feelings he had never experienced before. His shying away from talking to them as friends was also wearing off with each passing mile they covered. Laffite was his friend, but the man never acted or spoke to him as an equal. Sure, Boss was his friend, he was the man who had given him his freedom from the whip, and he could never forget that, but these two, on the other hand, just plain liked him. They had no real reason to treat him the way they did, and he would never forget them for it either. Maybe someday, all the people of New Orleans would be this way, he thought.

LONG before they arrived close to the Barataria stronghold, the pirates were aware of their presence. Word had gone on ahead of them that they were headed for the settlement. Not much happened on this route that the men who lived and worked there did not know about. They did nothing to stop the three, as one was well known to them as Boss's blacksmith Thiac. As long as the other two men stayed in his company, they could wait to see who they were and what they wanted.

THE sun had just set when the three of them finally reached their destination. Exhausted, Tori knocked on the door and waited instead of just walking in. After all, it felt strange to barge in unannounced, even if it was her home.

Cisco watched as the Spanish woman took Tori into her arms, despite Tori's disguise. She acted like a mother, welcoming home her child. Laffite's wife took her hat off and shook her hair free as they entered the hall, and once inside, he saw she was very much at home. She tossed the cap onto a nearby chair and headed directly for a room toward the rear of the house. Cisco and Thiac followed her into a large sitting room. When Tori turned to face the pair, she couldn't help notice the look of uncertainly on Thiac's face, and thinking it might make things better; Tori invited him to have a drink with them. Thiac, however, felt this was more than he could handle at the moment.

He turned to the Spanish woman, who did not show any sign that anything was amiss. "It has been a long journey, and Boss would want me to settle in now that Mizz Tori is here. Would you be showing me where it is? That be, where am I to stay? I have no need of drinking…

not my place if you understand?" It seemed to him the whole world had gone crazy the past few days, and right now, all he wanted was to get outside to sort things out in his mind. This day had been one he would think about for a long time. Treated as an equal and now asked to drink with them? It just did not seem possible.

Seeing his troubled face, Tori realized that she had not thought one bit about how uncomfortable Thiac must be. She then told herself that she had perhaps overstepped the bounds between what was expected and what was custom. The new relationship between them could prove to make things difficult, and the last thing Tori needed was for the smithy to feel awkward. Jean had tried, again and again, to warn her against following through with rash actions. Interactions such as treating slaves or even free blacks as equals was not wise, yet she'd done just that. Stupid was not the word for how she felt at that moment. Still, what was done was done, and they would live with it. Thiac just needed time; they all did to get comfortable with their new forged friendship. He would feel better about himself and his new standing once he had more time, but she understood to go slower until then.

Tori knew that if she were not careful, their friendship could be misunderstood and land the blacksmith in a heap of trouble, and she would never do that to him. Here and now, he was safe, and when they were alone, it would be fine, but from now on, she would have to watch her step more carefully. Without hesitation, Tori instructed Carlotta to place Thiac outback and then explained to him what that meant. "You shall stay in the little house, as we call it. It's not much more than a small shack, but you will have everything you need, and you will be warm." She walked over to him and, wanting to hug him but daring not to, she smiled into his large brown eyes and spoke softly. "Goodnight, Thiac, and thank you. We will see you in the morning, right after breakfast."

As always, Carlotta took over. She had lit many candles and two oil lamps before turning to hustle the smithy from the room, but not before giving instructions to a young boy. You use your hands the way I showed you and light a nice warm fire for Boss's wife and guest. I shall be in the kitchen if you need me, which I doubt. Then, you come to me once you have that fire blazing, and I will have you help bring in a light supper. When that is finished, you and Thiac will have more than enough to eat."

"Oh, Carlotta, don't go to all that trouble. Cisco and I can eat in here, and we have plenty of wine. It's not like I don't know my way around. Knowing you, if I allowed it, the dining room would be filled with food…"

Cisco laughed and faced Tori. "Nothing wrong with that. I am starving, and trust me, my belly is thinking my throat is cut."

"Your teasing is not going to win you any points tonight, my friend. Carlotta will see to it that we have what we need, isn't that right?" Tori faced the Spanish woman who was beaming.

"Leave everything to me. You sit and rest. I will make sure to have some food in here as fast as I can. So, sit and have that drink. I see by the flames the boy has the fire started. My word, you need to relax, because you both look like you need to if you ask me. Plain as the looks on your faces. Come, boy, we have a meal to fetch." Carlotta hurried the young lad from the room with that proclamation and motioned for Thiac to follow her.

NOT much time seemed to pass before they were both served a beautiful dinner, which they consumed slowly while they talked. The house was quiet, and because she needed privacy, Tori had instructed Carlotta to fill them each a bath of hot water and then take the rest of the evening off. She and Cisco had many things to discuss, and most assuredly, there would be details talked off that didn't need to be overheard.

THE logs on the fire crackled, and the warmth of the fire filled the room. All the candles had been lit, and the soft light illuminated Tori's face, which Cisco saw had a sadness about it. She was sitting looking toward the fire yet not seeing it. The woman was daydreaming about something or someone, and Cisco had an idea just what her thoughts were about. "You still miss the nineties, Tori? I don't know why. After all, it seems to me that you have it made here. I mean, look around you, girl. This place, for instance, is quite a cabin in the woods. Your lifestyle must be something."

Tori sat back for a moment and considered Cisco's question. True, despite the lack of electricity and air conditioning, she did have it made. She missed technology, automobiles, and simple pleasures, like running water and hot showers. There again, one could say that her lifestyle was better here than in her own time. Look at the luxury that always surrounded her; she always had the best of everything. Yet, it didn't feel right because deep down inside, she did not feel a part of any of it, and she doubted that she ever would.

"Cisco, can I ask you a hypothetical question?"

"Sure, go ahead."

"Well, say you had a girl back in Las Vegas, and she had a child who you cared about; then, one day, the girlfriend vanished, and then some years later, she just turned up with a tale of time travel. Let's say you believed her, but then she went on and told you everything that had happened, knowing that some of it would hurt you. Do you think that she would have been better off staying in the past? Or, do you think that she did right by going back and telling all?"

"I would say that this question is about you, and if I might add, what makes you think that there is a way back at all? You seem so certain that there is."

"It's Tom, that young black boy; I told you about his story. If he made it that way, to the future, I mean, then the way back must happen every so often."

"True, I get that. There is a possible way, but when and for how long is the doorway open? You could spend the rest of your life waiting for it to happen. Then, who knows what? You could turn up in another time, you know? It could be before you were born or even after you should have died. Have you thought of that? And, if you did make it back, who would believe you? After all, it would sound sort of… like, forgive me here, well like you were on something, or crazy. Look, no matter how much your boyfriend and child loved you and no matter how much they wanted to believe you, without proof, beyond a shadow of a doubt, they would always wonder. Even if you could prove it, don't you think to tell your boyfriend that you lived and loved another man, had his child and all… don't you think that would be asking a little too much?"

"First off, I don't have a boyfriend back there, just family and Linni." Her voice broke up with emotion, and she fell silent, thinking about Dan. 'He could have become my boyfriend, should have. Maybe I have it wrong.' Tori was very still, and as she sat there looking into the fire, she could feel her eyes cloud over with tears. Cisco was right. She knew he was. Yet, she could not let go of wanting to return to her own time. Why was that, she wondered? If John and Cisco could accept what had happened to them, then why couldn't she? Could it have something to do with the fact that they didn't leave anyone behind? That both of them had been running from something and happy to have escaped? No one here knew their past or much about them at all. They didn't lie; they just didn't talk about their former lives. She looked into her friend's eyes and spoke softly. "Maybe, if I did go back and I could prove what happened, maybe I wouldn't have to tell everything that occurred in my life here."

"True, but what if you did get back and found your daughter had moved on with her life. Grown-up and fallen in love with someone? What if you found that you did not fit in anymore? What if you found that you belonged here with Jean in this time, and you wanted to get back to him? Think about it, Tori. What you are doing now shows you care about the man…" he briefly hesitated, "you are trying to get Jean out of jail, risking so much.

Doesn't that tell you something? Like how much you love the man? I would have to ask myself how much he really meant to me before I tried to leave. It might be only a one-round trip ticket, and if you made the wrong move, you might not be able to forgive yourself. You could live the rest of your life, in the wrong time, and with the wrong people, and really be alone!"

Tori stared at him. She had never thought of it like that, but then what if she never tried and this was the wrong time that she got stuck in? Did she actually believe that she could ever sit back here in this era and not always have a pull to the future? It was just too much to deal with. Her head was spinning. So, as she often did, she pushed the problem to the back of her mind. Tori raised the wine glass to her lips and looked back into the fire as she sipped her drink and tried not to think about things that upset her.

Cisco knew he had upset her and needed to fix things. An idea came to him, and he lightly touched her arm as he spoke. "Look, Tori, this might help you. I live here by a saying. I quote Voltaire. 'Unhappy is he who trusts only to time for his happiness.' You get it?"

"Wow, I must say you are well-read. Something I would never have guessed about you in a lifetime." She smiled at him and patted his hand. "I will have to think about that later. Right now, I don't have the luxury or the time to continue worrying about time travel. We both have bigger problems to think about. Jean and his men have to come first and foremost. Tomorrow, we have to get some good men to help us and then head back into the city. I wonder if John has had any luck getting the information we need?"

A chuckle filled the room; her friend could not help himself. "Knowing him as I do, you can count on it. Let's just do our part and let him do his. It will all come together; you'll see."

"Right now, all I want is a bath and some sleep. I feel as if every muscle in my body has locked up, and if I sit here any longer, I won't be able to move for a year." She got up slowly and walked toward the door.

Cisco stood and smiled at her. He knew that she was still deeply troubled about her life here, and he wished he could help. That, however, was something she was going to have to sort out for herself. He could try and lighten the moment, though, a little before she went to bed. "I take it that I'm to sleep in the house somewhere? I hope on a bed and not here on what they call a couch, or am I to go out back?"

"Picky, picky. What if I told you that you were to sleep on the couch or outside?"

"I would have to say you're kidding. You are, aren't you?" His face looked like a crushed schoolboy's, similar to the look he used to practice in front of the mirror for hours when he was young. It had always worked with his teachers.

The corner of his mouth was twitching again, and Tori wondered how he ever won at poker. In her opinion, he couldn't keep a straight face if it killed him. "Of course, I'm kidding, and you know it," she laughed. "You can stay in the guest room. I'm sure Carlotta has a hot bath waiting for you by now, and knowing her, some of Jean's clean clothes to borrow until she can wash yours, that is. If you need anything else, you only have to ask, and you'll have it."

"Really? How about a blond, about this big," he said, creating the shape of a large-breasted woman with his hands, "and, maybe she could have a friend so that the evening could be twice as much fun?"

Frowning, Tori snapped her retort. "This is not a plantation, where the guest can expect a bed warmer, or any such thing, and if you think for one moment that you can have your way with any of my help, think again, my friend."

Cisco burst out laughing. "Madame," he bowed, "I only jest. Why such an angry reaction? Tut, tut." He was wagging his finger at her while making faces of pain again. "Maybe you are far more uncomfortable than I thought, all bound up like you are. Must have made you touchy, touchy, touchy!" He grabbed himself, dramatically, in all the places that she must have been feeling uncomfortable.

Tori laughed, despite the fact, that she was exhausted and really in no mood to horse around. All she wanted was to go to her room, have a hot bath, and fall asleep. She walked up to Cisco, put her arms around him, and gave him a hug and a sisterly kiss on his cheek. "Thank you, my friend, for being so understanding and for listening to me. You have to forgive me. Sometimes, I don't know what comes over me… really, I don't."

He didn't say anything, just drew her into his arms and returned the hug as his hand stroked the back of her head. It was a comforting action that his mother had done to him as a child.

"Cisco, please don't ever take your friendship away. I need you. You have become very important to me, you know?" He could feel her heart beating against his chest as she clung to him with her head resting on his shoulder. Were those tears he could feel on his neck? He was sure they were. So now, what was he supposed to do? Quickly he decided, doing nothing seemed the best move for him at this point, so that's what he did.

The pair stood there, letting Tori's emotions drain while he sorted out what it was that he was feeling, toward this very vulnerable individual, because something was tugging at his heartstrings. Cisco had to admit that for the first time in his life, he was feeling something he had never felt for any other woman before. For one thing, here he stood, Cisco, the self-centered carefree gigolo, worrying about another human before himself. That alone was way off. Then there was this new caring feeling, which was totally out of character for him. It was different, all right, this emotion that filled him; because it was one of protector, friend, and more. He was feeling an overpowering emotion of brotherly love, and this new brotherly thing was strange, to say the least. This new emotion came with no burning deSire; there was nothing sexual to it at all. It had nothing to do with Jean or his fear of what the man would do to him if he did try to seduce his wife. It had nothing to do with his sex drive either. Somehow, somewhere along the way, in the past few days, he had grown to think of Laffite's wife as a sister.

<header>D.S. ELLISTON</header>

How that had happened, he was not sure, but there it was, loud and clear. He loved her as his sister. Upon realizing this to be true, Cisco pulled Tori very close and squeezed her tightly. Then before he could change his mind, he pushed her back a step so that he could look her in the eyes.

"Tori, I want you to know now and forever that I am and always will be your friend. You mean so much to me. Wait, do not say anything; let me finish." He stopped for a moment, cleared his throat, and went on. "My feelings go deeper than just friendship. If you can bring yourself to think of me as a brother, I would like that. I think you would feel so much better, knowing that our bond is that strong. That, my attraction, is honorable. You are family to me. I'm not making any sense, am I?"

"Oh, yes, you are. Perfect sense. You just got yourself, one little sister," she sobbed. "Just what the doctor ordered I think." Tori released herself from his grasp, wiped her tear-stained face, and smiled softly toward him. "Now, I have to go to bed. I am so exhausted, physically and emotionally, but I do feel happy. Thanks, Cisco… my brother. Sleep well."

"Goodnight, sis. Sleep well yourself. Oh, and if you don't mind, I'll stay here for one more drink before I go up. I'll find my way, don't worry."

TORI lay in bed, looking at Jean's side. She had soaked in the bath until the water went lukewarm and would have remained longer, but the soft bed, with its enticing feather mattress, had called to her weary bones. Her hand went to his pillow. "Lord, I miss you, and I will find a way to get you out. I promise you that. Stupid tears," she brushed her hand against her cheeks to dry the wet skin. "Can't cry now. I have to be strong. I will cry when you hold me in your arms; then, I will cry because you will be home with me." With that statement said and knowing it to be accurate, Tori turned onto her back and looked around the room.

<footer>94</footer>

With the lamp turned down low, the room had corners that remained in the dark. Laffite's wife did not mind. Tori was not afraid to be alone in the bedroom or the house. She was, however, just a bit fearful of being on the island without Jean or Dominique. What was the morning going to bring? Would she find men to help, or would she find trouble? Everyone knew where Jean was and that he would not be returning anytime soon. Was that pirate Chez Nez away at sea or waiting ready to take Jean's place? He was a despicable man with a hot temper, and he scared the hell out of her. There again, she reminded herself, that his demeanor was a cover for his face. Her hand touched her nose, and she scowled. 'Nope, he's, mean for sure. Look how he treats his wife. Trying to keep the gold for himself, even the thimble.' She looked at her thumb and wondered briefly what a solid gold thimble would feel like? Her mind wandered. 'There again, I have never been to the other side of the inlet and seen for myself, how he treats her. I mean, could be, he is a good man to her when he doesn't have anybody to see that side of him. God, I hope so because if he is in port, I need him to join me and not become my enemy. I am glad I have Thiac and Cisco, glad they will be with me.' Her eyelids were heavy, and thinking was becoming too much of an effort. Seconds after this thought registered, the worn-out female gave in and closed her eyes. Tori fell asleep before she could continue to worry or wonder what would happen next.

MORNING arrived all too soon. The bright light outside had woken Cisco, but that was not the only thing that aroused him. Something else had stirred his sleep, and that something had set his stomach growling loudly as different aromas hit his nostrils. Someone had been frying up ham, he just knew it, and that was one dish that could pull him from the grip of death itself. Wide awake and more than ready to greet the day, he hurriedly dressed so he could make his way downstairs and find the source of such savory fragrances.

On the stairs and long before he found the dining room, the adventurous man added the aroma of freshly brewed coffee to his senses. The strong hickory scent permeated the air and was, in his mind, just what the doctor ordered for his slight headache. Marie's tonic could wait, as its bitter taste was not desirable when coffee could do the trick.

The dining room table was set for two, and on the table was a fresh pot of coffee. The plates on the sideboard were full of fruit and freshly baked bread. Carlotta had a platter of ham, fried eggs, and what looked like the fluffiest, fullest omelet he had ever seen. Now, this was living, he told himself. Cisco very seldom ate much for breakfast, let alone had one of such variety presented to him. In Vegas, the all you could eat buffets would entice him when he was not too hungover, but this here was far more enticing than those ever were, and he was trying to decide what to eat first when a female voice welcomed him.

"Good morning, brother. I trust you slept well?" Tori had joined him and was smiling brightly. "Go ahead, take what you want. I'm going to eat until I can't move. Might as well. I can hardly move as it is, damn horses." She awkwardly walked toward him, her stride emphasizing her aching thighs as she entered the room.

Cisco laughed at the sight of her cowboy-like strut and rushed forward to help her to a chair. "Allow me, please," he said, pulling the chair out for her. "Your butt must be so sore. Do you think a cushion might help? Or maybe, I can give it a rubdown," he said playfully, patting her on her rear.

"You will do no such thing, brother." Tori had laughed but also emphasized the word 'brother.'

"Just brotherly love, my dear, I swear it." It was his turn to chuckle and let her realize he had only been teasing. The jester winked and then strolled around the table to take his place. She looked good today. Even if the shirt she had on was one of Jeans and a bit too large, it fit her like those tops women wore in their time, the kind they wore with leggings. Instead of the shirt hanging loose, though, Tori had it belted with a soft brown leather strip. The belt gathered the white linen about her slim waist, and the tunic effect suited her far better than she could have guessed. The rest of her outfit was hand-made to fit her, not borrowed from someone else's wardrobe like his. The pants' soft blue material went very well with the brown boots, which were far shorter than the pair she wore the day before. Her hair was pulled back and fastened in a ponytail with a piece of blue ribbon. She had not managed to catch all the hair, though, for some had fallen free around her face.

Cisco nodded his head slightly as if approving of what he saw. "I see that you have not bound yourself in this morning," he said, grinning from ear to ear. "I would even venture to say you fill that shirt and those britches, a damn sight better than Jean does. His men, no doubt, will think the same. Don't you think it wiser to go about dressed like a lady?"

"The men, as you were saying, have seen me this way before. Granted, I was always with Jean or Dominique, but maybe, if I dressed as a lady, it would cause us more trouble. Who knows? Let's eat and then go and see, shall we? Besides, with you and Thiac by my side, I think that I will be in safe hands. That is if you can keep yours to yourself?" she scolded jokingly.

"Well, I can, and I will. Have to give it to you; your life here seems darn fantastic. I mean, look at this spread and the house and all slam dab in the middle of the pirate stronghold. God, I can't believe it. I don't know what has me more excited, all this grub or walking out there among honest to goodness cutthroats and swashbuckling buccaneers."

"Oh, stop it. You may not like what you see today. I am deadly serious here. It would be best if you stopped kidding around; this is no game. Remember, any one of the men or women, for that matter, can slit your throat, stab you in the back or shoot you. Those would be the best and quickest ways to dispose of you."

"You mean they have other ways. Do tell… they will take me out to sea and make me walk the plank?"

"You are impossible; you know that? Aren't you just a tiny bit nervous about what we are about to do? You should be, you know."

"Nope, just hungry. Pass the eggs and my God oranges, oh, and some of the bread. I'll top the coffee up. Do you suppose Thiac is eating this good? I hope so; damn shame if he's not."

"I am certain that he is eating good and most likely finished a while ago and is waiting for us. So, don't dawdle and hurry up, ok? We have a lot to do."

"That we do. I have to tell you, walking behind you today will be a delight. The way you are decked out is sure to raise some eyebrows and maybe a few other parts of the male anatomy."

They both laughed. Tori couldn't help herself; Cisco was just too darn funny, and he was not about to stop; she could tell that. The man was having way too much of a good time. Besides, many a truth was said in jest, and she did look hot, as they said back home, and she knew it.

THIAC, on the other hand, shook his head and had his doubts when he saw Tori come out of the house with Cisco. He almost felt as if his heart would stop completely. How could she dress so? It was not right, yet the most confusing thing was that she still looked every part a lady. How could that be, he pondered? Maybe a gown did not a lady make?

Tori decided to ignore the puzzled expression on Thiac's face and pressed onward. "Morning Thiac, how about we take a walk around and see what we can find out. I have a few places in mind to rustle up some support, and please don't look so worried. After all, these are Jean's men, or most of them anyway. They know better than to mess with me. To step out of place, I mean."

She was already walking ahead of him, and as he watched her, his face filled with worry. Damn, he hoped she was right. His eyes rolled upward to the sky. Lord, it was far too beautiful a day to fight, even if it was for the lady's honor.

By mid-morning, word had spread like wildfire that Laffite's wife was in the small village at Grand Terre, looking for some men to help her get Jean out of jail. Most shook their heads and laughed. What could she hope to do except get more men arrested? Hell, she was a crazy wench, they told themselves. Others admired her and her spirit, yet they were not about to step forward and offer help for fear of being laughed at. Anyway, some were already saying that it was useless to do anything. After all, the Governor had it in for all of them, not just Boss. If they wanted to stay free, maybe it was time to lay low for a while. Besides, with Boss, his brother, and Dominique in jail, and Beluche not yet in port, that left no one in charge, telling them what to do. True, Gambi and Chez Nez were rumored to be talking about taking control, but no one knew for sure. Chez Nez had also sailed out, just as the sun was coming up the day before, so maybe the rumors were just that, words with nothing behind them. They would just have to wait to see what Boss's lady could or could not do.

Every place the trio went, all agreed to this tactic behind their backs. Some even refused to stand long enough to engage in a civil conversation at all and would walk away, ignoring Tori's invite to join her and listen to what she had to impart. More often than not, Tori was met with strange looks, shaking heads, and low mumbles of apologies but nothing more. Because of this, she found her temper rising as she talked to these so-called brave pirates. These were men who Jean had treated fairly and often went out of his way to help. Therefore, it seemed to her way of thinking that they owed him. Still, every time she tried, she got the same cold shoulder, along with a good many lusty looks and a few lewd remarks, spoken loud enough for her to overhear. It was after experiencing more than a few of these innuendos that Tori realized; if not for Cisco and Thiac, she would have, no doubt, found herself the object of far more than mere dirty words directed her way.

In the end, after several hours of talking and walking all over the area, Laffite's wife just exploded. "What in the hell is wrong with these dumb sons of bitches!" she shouted. "You would think they would jump at a chance to help Jean, but all we get is a bunch of chicken shits. God damn it, I am so damn mad. I wish I could kick some sense into their thick skulls and make them see what idiots they are. They need Jean. Cisco, why won't they help me?"

"Hell, I don't know, but then maybe we have been going about this all wrong. Follow me and stay close. Keep an eye out, Thiac, my old friend, this could backfire, and we all might have to run like hell." Then before either of them could ask any questions, Cisco had pulled Tori by the hand and disappeared inside a small tavern. This tavern just so happened to be the very same building that Jean had never allowed her to go near. Laffite had told her once that this place was even unsafe for him at times. Of course, Dominique had boasted, he had friends who would watch out for him, but it was also his insistence that she never step inside the place that rang in her mind as she looked around. The moods of a drunken cutthroat can never be trusted, he had explained, and thereby best avoided at all costs. That or be ready to fight!

The interior was dank and dark. Even in the middle of the day, the place had an unearthly gloom about it. It smelled of body odor, old booze, and tobacco. The floor consisted of solidly packed dirt and, at the far side, stood what looked to be the bar. There were no barstools, just tables, chairs, and a wooden shelf-like contraption, that ran around the entire interior wall. Some rough-looking men stood, leaning their backs against the distant wall, with their drinks sitting on the lower wooden shelf, by their sides. There were no windows, so small candles sat on each table, and at a few, there were oil lamps. Every chair around the tables was occupied, and a hazy, light-colored cloud hung in the space directly above them from the numerous pipes the men smoked. There was no escape for this smoke like there was no escape for Tori and her friends because, as far as she could tell, the bar had but one entrance, which was thereby the only exit, and onlookers now blocked it. Feeling vulnerable, she slowly walked forward, followed closely by Thiac.

Glancing around as they entered, Cisco could see that even at this hour, the tavern had a good size crowd, all of whom had fallen silent when they boldly stepped inside. A few burly types, who had been loitering around outside when the three had dared to enter the tavern, now stood crowding the doorway behind them, watching and listening intently. It was evident that they all wanted to see what would happen next, and any form of entertainment that helped with the day's boredom was well appreciated, also hungrily anticipated. Still, this situation they were all witnessing now could go way beyond the average bar brawl. Unknown to Cisco, no one dared enter the Devil's Den, as it was known, unless they were willing to fight or die for the honor. All those by the door and inside knew that going into the tavern uninvited meant things would get interesting quickly. Especially dressed as Laffite's woman was, the men would go crazy over that alone.

Cisco marched up to the bar and demanded three rums. Also, he announced to make sure Boss's wife's drink went into a clean mug. He then slowly turned around, making eyeing contact with every man he could; without giving away, he'd begun to regret his move of entering the establishment. Tori's new companion was looking into the grimy faces of some of the roughest sea-going males he had ever seen. Also, he noticed that more than one man had their hands on their weapons. His eyes were drawn to a particular pirate as this individual took out his long knife and placed it on the table in front of him. It was as if he was daring him to react or make a move. More importantly, the ivory-handled knife never left the pirate's grip, and his eyes never left Cisco. The atmosphere was tense, and as far as Tori's friend was concerned, right then, he needed to make a firm stand or run the risk of exposing his doubts and raw nerves. According to his assessment of all those glaring his way, it would be a move that could have deadly consequences, but he had no choice if they were going to get out of there without a brawl or worse.

The stillness that hung in the room was almost deafening in its silence. The only sound filling the air came from the pouring of rum as it splashed and gurgled from one container to another. When that sound ended and the mugs scraped their way across the bar top, Cisco made his move. "Before I talk to the lot of you, the three of us here," he waved his hand toward Thiac and Tori, who were slowly making their way toward the bar, "we need to quench our thirst and wash down the bitter taste of chicken shit. Seems we came here to find men and found ourselves a pack of cowardly boys instead. Boys, who can't seem to get up off their fat ass's and help out the fine lady there." Again, he pointed to Tori without taking his eyes off the crowd.

A few men turned to look where Cisco was pointing, while others growled a few obscenities, quieting down, only when the intruder carried on with his speech in a louder voice. "To help her, with her fight, to get you yellow bellies back, your friend and Boss, that is."

In that instant, it was as if a bomb had exploded. Two men rose to their feet so fast their chairs fell over. Another shouted out in Spanish, words that Tori knew would make whatever Cisco had just said pale in comparison. Still more joined in, and the whole room became involved in an uproar, which quickly got out of hand. One, somewhat besotted ruffian, intent on doing far more than just screaming, angrily pushed forward from the recesses of the tavern. The look of thunder on his face made it clear that he had every intention of bashing Cisco and anyone else who got in his way. What was worse was that many of the men got out of this angry pirate's way and let him proceed. There were even those that physically pushed him forward, anxious to goad him on.

One man in the room, though, decided to intervene, and he did so immediately. Thiac stepped between the on-coming thug and his intended victim and slammed his fist down onto a table in front of him; he crushed it with one blow. It smashed into splinters as if it was constructed of nothing more than matchsticks. Cisco watched as the table's legs went spinning out in all directions while other pieces of wood went flying upward before showering over the patrons who were closest to this thunderous uproar. It was such a raging sound of anger that escaped Thiac's mouth as he hit the table that for a second, it dwarfed the rioting noises, filling the place. In later years, some would swear that the earth-shaking sound from that black beast had destroyed the table, not his fist, and many would agree.

Then, amongst the angry cries and yelling pirates, came a roar of one word that stilled the entire crowd. "Parley!" Once again, the room came to a complete and utter standstill. Cisco was not sure if no one dared to move or speak because of the call for 'parley' or because the crowd feared that the black giant would not hesitate to do to them what he had just done to that table. In the end, he decided it was more likely they feared the Italian Captain, Chez Nez, as he was the man who had called for 'parley.' All eyes went to the back of the dimly lit room and toward the man who stood up slowly. The pirate looked directly at Tori and even dared to wink before making a move. He grinned broadly and satisfied by what he saw; the Captain turned his attention to the tabletop before him.

Chez Nez took a swig from his bottle before he continued. Meanwhile, not a soul dared make a sound; even those standing in the doorway to the tavern stood holding their breath, and Tori found herself wondering what the Italian hoped to gain by calling for a parley? This wasn't his fight; it was hers, so she should have been the one to call it, surely? Tori knew very well what it meant and wondered what the ugly pirate was planning? Then she wondered if the idea of calling for a parley would have ever crossed her mind? She looked at the Italian and briefly nodded her head, appreciating his attempt to calm things down.

Satisfied he had the entire room's, undying attention, the Italian pirate began in a far calmer tone but one that never less demanded obedience. "As was written down many years gone by, written in their own hand, Captain Morgan and Bartholomew set forth the 'Code of the Brethren,' and we all know that code." He looked around the room and watched as more than a few nodded their heads. "Now, I am sure that Boss's wife may not know of our code, but Boss does."

Suddenly he was interrupted by the shout of an angry voice. "You can't' call 'parley' for her; she ain't one of us!"

Before anyone could react to the man's outburst, all watched as Chez Nez drew his pistol and calmly shot the pirate dead. Then, casually, he placed the pistol back in his belt as if nothing had occurred. He was a master of control and proved it as slowly and deliberately; he looked around the room. "She is as good as one of our own," he roared. Then in a normal tone of voice, he continued. "She is Boss's wife and has sailed with him, fought alongside him. Saved Captain You's life and his bloody arm, mores the pity. I had my eye on his ship. A fine vessel he has, and you can be sure, should the man have lost his arm or his life, it would have been mine."

There were a few heartfelt laughs, and one or two yelled support of the Italian's statement. "You all have heard the stories, and they be true, as I am standing here. I have called 'parley,' and we will listen to her, her man, and Boss's black bastard. After, we will decide if we should cut their throats. I myself will decide what to do with the lady there; no one touches her but me." He briefly chuckled and then looked at the three who had dared to enter his tavern. No one moved or said anything, as all eyes were on Tori. Then, in the silence, another gruff voice spoke up.

"Well, you can do as you please," said the man sitting next to Chez Nez. Do as you see fit with her, but that one you shot, he was one of mine, and as such, I claim all he has on him. Someone, drag the stupid bastard out of here. Do it now, 'cause he is bleeding all over the floor, and it stinks in here enough, without adding the smell of blood and death." Gambi looked at his Italian friend and grinned. "You have a problem with that? I mean, if you are going to follow the bloody code, then you know I am right. What was his; is now mine."

"It is, you are right, but may I suggest in the future, you crew your ship with men who have respect for the two of us. He should have listened and not acted like a stupid land lover. No one moves or acts when 'parley' has been called. If they do, they end up like him, don't they?"

Gambi grinned. "All but you and me, that's for sure."

Chez Nez laughed, took another swig of his drink, and then coughed as the liquid went down the wrong way. Tori watched in disgust as some of his drink sprayed from his nostrils and fell onto the table. Still, more of the liquid ran down from his destroyed nose and over his top lip, which he licked away, snot and all, before taking another swallow from his bottle. The two Captains toasted each other and then refilled their mugs. Both were having a grand time, it seemed, while all those around the room watched nervously as two men began to drag the body of their comrade from the tavern. Chez Nez sat down, but Gambi remained standing, watching as one of the crew carried what he had taken off the body towards him. The contents of the dead man's pockets were handed over, and without any feeling, the greedy pirate placed the coins into his pocket before angrily calling out. "His pistol too, damn you! I said all of his is mine and put the word out; Gambi is looking for a man to join his crew. Now, where were we before the idiot interrupted you?" Gambi looked at Chez Nez with a puzzled expression.

"I was saying that we would listen to them," he pointed toward Tori and Cisco, and so we shall." The Captain spoke directly to Gambi, but all knew his words weren't meant for him alone. "I have no fear they won't be heard, as 'parley' has been called." The Italian looked at Cisco. "Please proceed, but make it fast. Gambi is running out of men!" All laughed before settling down and turning toward the stranger, who had started all the trouble, to begin with.

Cisco picked up from where he had been interrupted as if nothing had happened and addressed the crowd in a firm and calm voice. "The lady has not had her drink yet, or her say, and until then, I suggest that you all stay where you are, or Thiac there might have to break a few skulls, 'parley' or not." Cisco kicked at a piece of the broken table; then he walked to where the rest of the remains piled up. He stood pushing what remained of the top apart with his foot. "And, for those of you who think you can stop him, think again. Good call, by the way, Captain, and we will abide by the rules you go by unless you intend to do us harm."

Tori did not know where or when it appeared, but Cisco suddenly brandished a pistol for all to see. She hadn't realized that he even carried such a weapon but found herself thanking the Gods he did.

"Now, it might be small, but gentlemen, it does kill, and I don't think that any of you is foolish enough to die just because he wouldn't listen to the lady."

Tori, who had been watching all this, pulled herself together. To anyone observing her, she seemed in no way upset or unnerved about the situation they were in. However, unbeknownst to anyone, she was thankful that she remained damn angry inwardly because that emotion gave her the courage to continue to act out her charade and not turn to run out and away from the bar.

What had just occurred had only served to fire her up more. She joined Cisco at the bar and reached for her tankard of rum. A good stiff shot of liquor was what she needed to give her even more courage, she assured herself, and so without thinking, Tori raised the mug to her lips. The nervous female swallowed several long gulps, feeling it burn down her throat. Her eyes began to water when her breath was sucked out of both her lungs in one big rush. To her surprise, her body refused to let any air back in, and all Tori wanted to do was cough and splutter. Maybe she'd even beg for a glass of water if she could utter a word clearly, which she doubted was possible at that moment. However, to falter now, in any way, to show the slightest sign of weakness, would be a big mistake. If she obeyed the urge to cough, they would all laugh at her, and that would mean losing her standing as a tough bitch, one who was not to be messed with. What she needed was time. Time to catch her breath and get her voice back, which she was sure, had been burned clean away. Tori was desperate to hide her watering eyes as she tried to control her physical conditions; therefore, she turned her back to the room. To cover her ploy of hiding her uncomfortable state, she slowly poured herself another rum. Deliberately Jean's wife made these actions visible, so all those close by could see what she was doing. To the pirates, it would look like she was going to have another drink and nothing more. It was a great stalling tactic that was causing a significant amount of anticipation in the tavern. However, she could stall only so long, and time was running short.

The Boss's wife spun around and faced the crowd, not daring to look at either Cisco or Thiac, who she knew would be wondering what in the world she was up to. Instead, Tori slowly and deliberately raised the mug to her lips and then stopped. "On second thought, I had better say my piece before I get drunk." Thank you, God, she thought; at least my voice did not come out all squeaky; it was a little shaky but not so much as to be noticed. Now, buck it up, buttercup, and show them what you are made of. You got this. Slow and easy, but sound like you mean every word, regardless of the consequences.

Tori faced the room. "Yes, I did say drunk, and why? Because you all disgust me, that's why. I thought of you as a brave and loyal lot." She looked around the dim area. "Not men who would give up a chance at a good old-fashioned fight. Jean has always told me only the toughest, and the best came here to be with him. But, unfortunately, what I have found is a bunch of cowards, who are willing to let me go alone to get him out of jail."

One man started to move forward, his anger at her statement clearly expressed on his face and in his actions. He did not like what he was hearing and was not willing to put up with a mere female, speaking to him like she was, 'parley' or not. Calling him a coward was just too much.

Thiac began to growl at the man while Cisco looked the offender straight in the eye and shook his head no while motioning the same with his pistol. It did the trick as the man had second thoughts and stopped dead in his tracks.

Laughter shook the back of the room, and Chez Nez added his words to Cisco's actions. "Wise move there, you stopping him like you has. If I shoot another of Gambi's men today, I think maybe, even though he gets richer from the action, I'd place our friendship on the line. Now, not another one move, until this here parley is finished or by God, you will join the other dead bastard."

Ignoring the little drama, Tori continued as if the slight commotion did not phase her one bit. "Now, I could be wrong. Maybe you are smart and just needed to know that I have a plan that I assure you will work. I have spies working for me right now, finding out the last of the information I need to make this a success, and, have no doubt, a success it will be." She sipped on her drink, letting the men absorb what she'd said so far. "Let me end with this thought. You all know Boss. Do you think he would sit around if you ended up in jail? Hell no! He would find a way to get you out. I would bet my life on it. I intend to get him out, and all I need is a few good men to help me. I'm telling you this because I wish to make it clear. With or without you, I will succeed."

One of the men close to Tori spoke up. "Pretty talk, lady, seeing how it would not be your neck, you be risking. I, for one, say we lay low until it blows over. Boss will get out. He's got his-self money to buy him lawyers, which is more'n a lot of us has if we gets caught." There was murmuring of agreement all around.

Then someone else dared to shout out, "Why risk our necks so that she can have her man to fuck sooner? I bet that's what she's missin', a good man between her legs." The laughter was loud, mixed in with whoops and whistles. Someone else yelled out that he would volunteer to take Boss's place for a while, and the bar exploded with even more hilarity.

The situation was not what Jean's wife had expected or wanted, and if not dealt with immediately, she ran the risk of losing control, along with what little respect she'd gained so far. Tori was fuming mad as she walked toward a man who was laughing at her and licking his lips rudely. Cisco tried to grab her arm and drag her back, but she shook his hand away and ignored him. All her attention was on the dirty scoundrel before her as he continued his taunting. The sailor rubbed his crotch openly with his hands and made a gesture that he was more than ready for her.

Gambi grabbed Chez Nez's arm and whispered something into his friend's ear, to which they both grinned and sat back to watch what would happen next.

Tori moved forward until she stood right before the rude pirate, who was enjoying his lewd actions. Then, before he knew what had happened, she slapped his face with all her might, with one hand, and tossed her rum at him with the other. The room went wild. Laughter filled the air; it was laughter that was not directed at her but in support of her actions. Even the two who held their rum-soaked mate back were laughing.

Tori stood her ground and held up her hand for silence, not expecting anyone to pay attention, let alone obey her. So, it came as a surprise when her request was immediately heeded. The pirates fell quiet, and more than one leaned forward to hear what she was going to say next. "It seems to me," she told the rum-soaked sailor, "that it is you, who has his brain between his legs, not me, and a small one at that." The tavern went wild again. Men laughed harder than before and openly pointed at their friend to make sure he knew it was him who they were laughing at. Some others standing close by were motioning to their own crotch's as if to agree his cock was small, and theirs were larger. The tavern was in an uproar, and try as she might to calm things down; Tori could not make them stop their continued lude antics.

Suddenly, and with no warning, Thiac hit another table nearby, just hard enough to make a sound and to gain the attention of the crowd, who once again fell silent. Tori smiled at the black man and mouthed the words, 'thank you.' Then she faced the randy pirate and began to make her plea. "Now, for the rest of you and especially you, you little shit. I will declare right now that I have no intention of sitting at home while the rest of you risk your necks to get Boss. Hell, I would not ask you to do anything that I would not do myself. Is that not what Boss says? That he would never ask anyone to do anything, that he himself would not do? Well, I am the same. So, are there any men here? Or am I the only one who has the right to wear breeches? Maybe, the rest of you should be in gowns!"

Those who were still snickering over their friends' dowsing in rum stopped as they waited to see what would happen. In their opinion, she was asking for trouble. Who did she think she was, talking to them like that? The room was buzzing with low growls and whispers, but what happened then was a surprise even to Tori, who thought her words had not moved anyone into her court. The rum-soaked sailor spoke up.

"I ain't no lady, and I ain't no coward either. But, I ain't no fool. It can't be done, I tell you. No one ain't ever got out of where they are keeping Boss. No one! So just how in the hell do you intend to do it? Tell us that, why don't you?"

"All right then, I will," Tori answered quickly. "We are going to do more than get Boss out of jail. We are going to get back all of them; every single man caught with him." She waited a few seconds before adding, "every single one of them will get out of jail. And, on top of that, we intend to get all the goods back too. If there's no proof of any crime, well, without the merchandise, can't you see it? Think about it. The Governor will not be able to do a damn thing without any proof!"

Someone in the back growled a response, "She's got a bloody good point. I agree with her." Everyone turned to see who had spoken. A few recognized the voice and pushed their chairs back to make a pathway through the crowd for the Italian pirate as he made his way forward. Tori and Cisco looked too, as they also wanted to see who had interrupted the conversation. Upon seeing who was making his way toward them, Tori froze and then looked at Cisco, praying he remembered everything she had told him about this particular man.

Cisco couldn't believe it. Walking toward him, and staring at him, was the most repugnant man he had ever seen. His face was like something out of a horror movie, and he knew the pirate was just as deadly as he was ugly. Sure, he'd watched his actions earlier, watched as the man shot and killed another, but the Italian had been in the back, and the light was not good, so he'd not had a good look like he was now. He recalled Tori telling him about Chez Nez and thank God she had because he was able to mask the terror he was feeling and hold a blank sort of expression on his face. The last thing he needed was to let this Italian know how repulsive he looked.

"Thought you took off for the islands?" One of the men near the Italian Captain had spoken up. "You did; I saw you sail. I know the drink has me…"

Chez Nez shot him a dirty look. "Aye, and how drunk are you? Did you not see what I did just now? Shot your mate because he spoke when he should have kept his trap shut. So shut up, or I will have to shoot you too, and that will make Gambi extremely upset. So, upset he might up and shoot someone else for all the trouble his crew is making." The ugly pirate looked around, and seeing that he was back in control, he spoke in a calmer tone to the men. "Now, true, as you said, I had sailed, I give you that. Then I got word that Boss was in a spot of trouble and thought it best to take a gander for myself. Thought I might be needed, to take my place as Boss, just while the man is gone, mind you." He turned and looked at the woman before him. "A pleasure to see you again," he said to Tori before bowing. "Looks like I made the right choice. I was having a drink before heading to my wife empty-handed." There was chuckling in the room, but it quickly dispersed as the ugly pirate took a step forward, looking fiercely around.

Once he was satisfied, he had everyone's attention; he addressed the interior of the establishment. "Imagine my surprise to hear this pretty little thing calling you all cowards." He tossed back his head and roared with laughter. "This 'parley' has been very informative if nothing else. I tend to agree with her because I tell you all, no bloody wench, sept maybe my own, would ever dare call me such as she has. Come to think of it, she knows better 'cause I am far from a coward. Never walked away from a fight. This here," he tapped what remained of his nose, "shows I am a fighter."

Slowly, the Italian walked toward Tori, and Cisco's heart rate picked up. He knew he had Thiac and his gun, but he had only one shot in his pistol, and after that, if he missed, old Chez Nez would tear him apart, Thiac or not.

The Italian looked at Thiac and smiled. "No need to worry yourself, or you pretty boy here. You," he looked at Cisco, "just keep that little pistol under control, both of them if you get my meaning," he grabbed his crotch and tossed back his head, and laughed. "And, you Thiac, keep them big bloody hands under control, like the rest of your huge appendages." This time he did not laugh alone, and he roared even louder. He bent over belly laughing, showing he was enjoying himself and was not concerned about either man before him. Then, just as suddenly as he'd begun laughing, he stopped and strolled the rest of the way across the small tavern to stand in arms reach of Laffite's lady. "I listened to all you had to say, and I happen to agree with you. Just think of the look on bloody Claiborne's face as he sits eating his fancy breakfast." The pirate turned and walked a few steps away and then back again while acting out his speech. Every eye in the place was on him. "Governor Sir, Jean Laffite is gone, and so's his bloody booty. What we going to do, Sir?" The Italian lifted a mug off the table next to him and held it with his pinky finger sticking out. The man was mimicking how the so-called finer ladies and gentlemen acted. He looked ridiculous, but his point was made.

This time the entire building rocked with laughter. Everyone loved it. This was something the pirates could all relate to, one of their own explaining how it would be. Besides, if the crazy Italian pirate thought it was a good idea, then that's all they needed to convince themselves. Even the rum-soaked sailor had forgotten his anger. He stood by Tori, and with a wink, along with a smile, he picked her up and placed her on top of one of the tables. Thiac stepped forward to protect her, but Cisco shouted at him to wait. He was a gambling man, and he was willing to gamble that Tori had just won the day.

The drunken man smiled at Tori, who, in his mind, had placed her up on a pedestal. "I say that we follow this little lady of Boss's. Like Chez Nez said, she has a bloody good idea. The wench just might pull it off. Hell, I bet she's right, and I, for one, am tired of sitting around here with nothing to do, 'sept dry off." More laughter filled the air. "I don't mind cracking a few skulls. If nothing else, it sure sounds like it's going to be bloody fun."

"My sentiment exactly," Cisco murmured under his breath. 'They had done it. They would have their men and their chance at making the jailbreak, but now he had another problem to solve. How was he going to keep Tori out of danger during the jailbreak? He doubted he should even try, as the men would expect her to be there because she had declared she would. Damn it to hell; this was a complication he'd not seen coming.' Cisco knew that he'd have to keep her out of the thick of things; and miss some of the fun, but not all. He would make sure he got to see some of the action.

Cisco put away his pistol, and Thiac walked over to Tori. He pushed by the Italian without so much as a word. When he reached the table, Tori stood on he reached out for her. Laffite's wife smiled triumphantly at the blacksmith and let him take her hand.

Tori thought he would only assist her down, but the gentle giant picked her up as if she were a small child. Carefully he lifted her off the table, and once the lady was safely in his arms, he carried her toward the doorway. Realizing the smithy was going to take her outside and away from the tavern before she was finished, Tori shouted back over Thiac's shoulder. "Captain, Chez Nez, may I suggest you call the 'parley' finished. I will get word to you all when I need you."

The men quieted down to listen to her. A few were jabbing each other and telling all to shut up, so they could hear the rest of what she was saying.

"I promise you, it will be soon, so get ready and…"

The Italian pirate broke into her speech. "Hell lady, we are ready. We could leave now if you want." Chez Nez meant it too, and everyone knew it.

Tori rapidly called out. "No, not until I send for you. Cisco will be back to go over the plan of attack when it is finalized. Until then, be ready to go and not drunk. Anyone drunk stays behind."

"Bloody hell, who's ever sober?" cried out Gambi. The response of which was a rousing applause.

TORI knew they would have to act fast. Keeping something like this under wraps was going to be difficult. What they needed now was the information from John, and they needed it soon. "Cisco, I've been thinking. I'll stay here at the house. You'd better leave right away and alone. It's better than taking the men with us to the outskirts of the city to sit and wait. We're not ready yet, and the chance of so many being seen; well, if that happened, it would blow it. You have to bring John back with you. He'll tell us what he's found out, and then we'll leave from here, totally prepared and not going off half-cocked, don't you see?" Noticing his doubting expression, she added, "We need him and his information as soon as possible. I could use his help too. His authority and his demeanor alone, screams leadership. It's the only way."

"I get it; I do. But should I leave you here? Are you safe?"

"You know I am. You saw those men, I won them over, and besides, with Thiac by my side, I will be just fine until you return. Come to think of it; I had better send you with a couple of Jean's men so that you can get back in here, in one piece. After all, you will be bringing another outsider with you. Besides, they know the quickest way, and I don't need you getting lost."

"Lost? Me? Are you kidding? I do like the idea of the company, and maybe a faster horse and a shorter trip. I'll show them how to ride," he was grinning at the thought of traveling with some of Jean's men. "Beats a trip in those itty bitty…."

"Do you ever take anything seriously?"

"I do, and you can count on that. You know me, always looking for the lighter side to calm my nerves."

"Well then, having cleared that up, I must assume that you are more than ready and calm enough to leave right away."

Cisco agreed with her, and even though he hated to leave her, he knew he must. Before the hour was up, he was riding for New Orleans with two of Jean's men, who knew the fastest and safest way to town. He'd still have to cross the Mississippi when they reached it, but they assured him it would be on a barge and not in a small pirogue, making him happy and relieved at the same time.

To his surprise, his trip had begun in Grand Isle and not Grand Terre, as that was the side where land offered more opportunities to transverse. Grand Isle's side of the pirate's encampment meant more waterway travel, and Cisco was not a fan of that mode; it was too slow for his liking, and Tori had agreed he needed to reach John as soon as possible.

As he headed out, Cisco started thinking more and more about what was about to occur. Shit, this was going to be great, he'd told himself. He couldn't wait to see how some of those guards at the jail reacted to his karate. His black belt had been wasted until now, but soon it would be put to the test. Not once did the idea that they would fail even enter his mind. For Cisco, life was what you made it, and he was making it the grandest of all adventures one could imagine.

꧁ Four ꧂

Cisco had been gone for two days, and for Tori, that meant he had safely made it to the city. She hoped that her fun-loving friend was with John, and both were ready to enact their plans. The pirate's network had remained silent since Cisco left, and in a way, Tori was glad. After all, no news was good news, and as it was still too soon for Cisco to return, the silence had to mean everything was going according to plan. Therefore, all that was left for her to do was pray for Cisco's quick return with the details. That and for the time to pass faster. Pirates, she learned, especially Chez Nez were not the kind to sit around and wait for action. That was why she had called for another meeting.

"Carlotta, please make our guest and myself some lunch. Also, add a bottle of wine."

The housekeeper frowned and then left Tori and the despicable Italian talking. She would never have left them alone, but knowing Thiac remained in the room with the pair; the housekeeper decided that Boss's wife was safe enough.

When the door closed, Tori sat back and smiled at her guest. "So, let us sit and talk about our situation at present."

The man coughed, which created a squeaking noise through his nostrils. "I am not the kind to sit and do nothing. Unlike Boss, I act, and I take that which I want. You have done nothing but send Thiac to the tavern for two days and tell us we will hear the plans soon. Some of us say there is no plan. That you have lost your nerve to go get Boss. Not your fault you being of the female breed. We need to know, 'cause if you have lost your nerve, we will act and go get him for you."

"I can assure you, Captain, I have not lost my nerve, and Cisco will return as soon as he is able. Like I have told you, he is with our

117

acquaintance, someone I might add who Jean trusts. I can assure you they are placing things in order. We will get Boss out and do so without being caught or killing anyone. After all, we don't need the Governor putting up warrants for our arrest for murder, now do we?"

"I see your point in that." The Italian walked to a chair and took a seat. "How long do you suppose we have to wait for food?" He coughed again, and then after gaining control of himself, he looked at Thiac and then back at Tori. "A man could cough himself to death in this house. How about something of Boss's to drink, to soothe my parched and very much, in need, self?"

Tori smiled politely. "Thiac, if you wouldn't mind, the bottles are over there," she pointed to a side table. "Open the cupboard, and you will see a rather tall glass container. Please, if you would be so kind as to pour our companion here, a glass full. That should do the trick," she looked at the pirate, "especially if you don't swallow it in one gulp, Captain." Tori continued to stare at Nez Coupe. She preferred calling him Chez Nez, not that she would venture to tell him in person. The man might take it as a slight and then blow his temper to kingdom come. Chez Nez, Nez Coupe… it didn't matter what his name was or which he liked or not. It was better to keep such thoughts all to herself. So, she'd stick to calling him Captain; for now, no need to rock the boat.

Unfazed by the suggestion of properly consuming his liquor, Chez Nez nodded his head slightly her way. "I can assure you that I am quite capable of partaking of the finer things in life." He licked his lips and winked. "I shall endeavor to sip all dainty like." The pirate took the half-full glass from Thiac, and while holding his pinky finger away from the glass, he took a sip of the contents. Upon finding it was far too tasty, the rouge couldn't help himself. Manners or not, there was only one way for a man to enjoy such quality booze. He faced Tori, and with an over-the-top sad expression, he spoke in a saddened tone. "I am sorry, but this is just too damn good to partake of slowly." Without waiting for her answer, he opened his mouth and, in two gulps, downed the contents of the glass and then smiled brightly. "Now, that's how a man takes his liquor, ain't that right, Thiac?"

The blacksmith just stood looking from the pirate to Tori and back again, unsure what to do or say. "I'm not too sure as to how a man drinks Boss's liquor, but I think maybe, taking his time, not all ladylike, but slow like would…"

"Hell, I was only fooling with you, Thiac. Like you would ever know how to drink. Most likely, never tried the stuff yourself." He looked at Tori then and frowned. "I suppose if we have to wait, then having a mid-day meal with you and drinking Boss's stash will keep me from marching with the men. I will do this a few more days, I think, just to be sure to keep abreast of any information you may impart."

At that moment, Carlotta entered the room. "I have put the dining room in order, and your meal awaits. Thiac can join me in the kitchen. If you need anything, Tori, we are only a room away; call out." With that, she turned and left.

"Bloody hell, the woman thinks I am going to accost you, or steal, or some such action. Maybe all of them," he laughed. "I assure you, Miss Tori, I know my place, and I am in Boss's house and will conduct myself as required by his standards. Why would I do otherwise? Why would I cut my nose off to spite my face? Oh, wait, I have had my nose cut off, well half of it." He laughed, and again his nose made the strange sound. "I only have to have half manners, 'cause I only have one half left to cut off. No, that's wrong. I need to be on my very best behavior, or Boss may cut more'n the other half off." He tapped his nose. "May I escort you to the dining room? I give my word; you have nothing to worry over, not yet anyway. Maybe in a few days, if that dandy isn't back with news, well, then things may change. Come, I do so enjoy Carlotta's cooking, as you know." The Italian Captain stood up and offered his arm. Tori politely smiled and allowed herself to be escorted to the dining room.

IN the days that followed, Tori and Thiac kept a watchful eye on Jean's men and spent many hours explaining that the waiting would not be much longer. Indeed, the wait ended sooner than Tori herself had thought possible.

John Davis had gathered the needed information long before Cisco's arrival and was thankful for the extra time he had while he waited for news. It allowed him to put his affairs in order in preparation for a few days' absences. He told everyone that an urgent business matter had come up, which required him to travel out of town. It was not far from the truth.

As he packed a small bag, he allowed himself to consider what would come of his action? What would the populace think if they knew the truth behind his short trip? That he was about to travel to Grand Terre on behalf of his dear friend and supplier of goods. A fleeting smile crossed his worried face. With the facts he had to give Tori and a touch of lady luck, the raid had better than even odds of success. His part, in what would happen, would go unnoticed. Should they fail, he was in the clear. Every detail had been considered, and all loopholes were taken care of to his liking. The plan was damn near full proof, and the odds were on his side; they always were. He was ready to explain all to Tori, and then it would be up to her and Jean's men. Within hours of Cisco arriving at the hotel, John was ready to depart.

ONCE at Grand Terre, John spent a day going over every aspect of the complicated plan. A meticulous person such as himself could see no other way. Nothing was going to be left to chance. Time, however, was running out. He could not afford to be away from the hotel much longer without raising questions, and going over the plan once again, seemed futile. If they were not prepared now, they never would be. The only problem that remained was when to put things into action? Laffite's men would not wait much longer; they were all fired up and ready to go, threatening every hour to do so, with or without Tori and Cisco. The fuse had been lit to a powder keg of emotions, and John knew Tori and Cisco needed control over those they had chosen to join them. Without it, they would surely fail in the attempt to free Jean and his men.

John's worried frown seemed somehow to creep into his voice, giving it an anxious edge as he spoke. "You know the longer we delay, the harder it's going to be to keep this matter under wraps. You need to act on this as soon as you can."

Cisco nodded in complete agreement. If he had his way, they would have left right then and there. Like John, he could see no need to delay the mission. Strangely the Italian Captain had remained silent, only observing up to this point. The man was wise enough and cunning enough to listen and sort out what was going on. More importantly, he considered what his options were if they succeeded or lost. He wanted to know how best to arrange the outcome of this questionable endeavor in his favor no matter what happened.

They had sat there the whole day and gone over every detail, and now they had just repeated the same thing, leading him to think that maybe Laffite's wife was stalling, or worse yet, doubting the plans which had been presented to her. John Davis had been thorough in his estimation. His ideas, well, his and the wench's opinions, their goals, could work out if they made a move now. To delay would be deadly, not by him, no, but by those in the tavern who were rearing to go. Still, he kept his silence and waited for the right time to add his opinion, knowing it would present itself soon enough.

All eyes fell on Tori. Each person in the room was looking directly toward her, waiting for her to give the go-ahead. She could see that what John said was right, but on the other hand, they would only have one chance at pulling the plan off. "You all have to let me have a few minutes to think. Just give me a second, all right?" Tori's mind was racing, chasing one thought after another at random. One, in particular, seemed to overshadow everything else. If they were to go now, in a hurry, it could bumble the operation, and that would end all hope of Jean and his men ever getting rescued. She just had to be dead sure that every angle had been taken care of before making her move.

Tori found herself reflecting on the hours of conversations; they had had in the past few days. She and Cisco had asked John before this meeting what he knew about the history of this time. His answer had been simple. He knew nothing more than they did. His fascination had been with the actual Battle of New Orleans. The only fact that he could add about that event was he knew beyond a shadow of a doubt that Jean and his men had a big hand in helping the city to a victory. The battle was still some time off, and his knowledge about how it came to be, well, his understanding of that was not much better either. He explained he'd just begun his research into that timeline when his crossover had taken place—knowing these few facts served to raise more questions than answers for him and the others.

Were they making or changing history, or were they a part of history all along? Tori squeezed her eyes shut and opened them. She had pushed all thoughts about the future to the back of her mind. Tori needed to concentrate on what was happening right then. Her thoughts subsided, till once again, she became aware she was sitting in the room and fully appraised of her situation at that moment. Tori continued to focus on Cisco and the famous Italian pirate. They were still silently watching and waiting for a response, but by the looks on their faces, doing nothing while waiting for her to say something, was wearing thin. Her time was up, and Tori knew it. "I agree, John; we have done our part here. What we need to do is clear. The only thing delaying us moving forward is you. How much time do you feel you will need to hold up your end of the plan? Without you playing your part, we could still go ahead and attempt it, but I would feel a lot better if I knew Governor Claiborne and a few of his supporters were out of harm's way."

"You have my word. My guests will be so busy having a grand time that they won't even realize they are being held out of harm's way, as you put it. Besides, it will be fun to see their faces when they get the news. Think about it. I will be the only one of us that has that pleasure, and it will be worth every bit of money I allow them to win."

"Are you sure that's the only way to handle this? It could cost you quite a lot, you know. You have to keep them there until word reaches you that Jean is long gone. Can you do that?"

John frowned. "Tori, we have been over and over this. I can assure you that I know just how to keep them hanging on. It will be a challenge of sorts to let them think they are winning at the table." His face went grim before he spun around for them to see the laughter in his eyes as he continued. "Yet, I can't let them know or guess the game is fixed. I told you they are like everyone else. If those invited think their luck is holding and they are winning more than folding, then the gambler in them will want more and more. In truth, I could most likely keep them all damn night if I wanted. So, don't you worry your pretty little head."

The sound of the Italian laughing to himself caught everyone off guard, and they all looked his way. The scrutiny made the man feel somewhat uncomfortable, a feeling that he hid well. "What? I can't help it. Remind me never to gamble at his place. But him saying Boss's wife had a pretty little head and all. Seems to me, she has a head large enough to hold a brain that has plenty of good ideas." Chez Nez drank from his glass and then lowered it slowly and placed his finger on his lips. Somewhat unsteadily, he put the empty glass on the table next to him, without so much as looking to see what he was doing. It was evident that he was intoxicated, and knowing such, everyone in the room had to tread carefully. The pirate lowered his finger and spoke in a growling tone. "You just be sure to hold up your end," he slurred.

"I'll have the easy job, trust me," replied John. His voice lowered as he sat down, whispering to himself, "the hard part will be getting them there, not keeping them there."

Tori was wringing her hands. So much had to go just right. If one bit of timing was off or one person was out of place, it could all come down like a house of cards.

Cisco smiled and spoke up. I have an idea, John. "It's Edward, who is your best bet. He could never turn down a good game. He seems so buddy-buddy with Claiborne, to boot. Maybe you could use him as the bait. Use him to get to the others."

John's sly smile and narrowing eyes was a poker-face expression that Cisco had seen often at the table and knew it to be one that told of a winning hand.

"Way ahead of you there, Cisco, my man. Now, how about both of you just relax and leave the fun for me?"

"Done," said Tori in a determined voice.

The Italian slapped his knee and spoke up in a loud response. "About goddamn time. Thought you were backing out, all this talk and no action." Chez Nez stood up. "I will be in the tavern with the men. Just come and fetch us soon, 'cause that's what I will tell 'em. That you are about ready." With that said, he stormed out of the room, and everyone heard the front door slamming.

Tori let out a huge sigh. "I suppose we had best make a start then. Keeping him in a good mood is not easy, and that, gentlemen, was his good mood if you get my point."

"Can he be trusted?" Cisco asked Tori while still looking toward the empty doorway.

"I am not sure about that, but right now, he is the leader around here, and he seems to have his own code of honor. So, I suppose we have no choice but to go along with him. Trust him, but keep a close eye on him." Tori faced John. "You still have not answered the question: How much time will it take you to arrange this little game? When can we make our move?"

John sat so still and in such deep thought; that Tori found she had to leave her seat and walk around while he pondered the problem.

On the other hand, Cisco looked toward John and, seeing that he needed a little prodding on the matter, leaned over to his friend, and jabbed him playfully in the ribs with his elbow as he spoke. "How about a little wager on this one? I'll bet you that you can't pull it off three nights from now. If you win, I'll work for you for one year." Cisco rolled his eyes toward the heavens with a look of mock agony on his face. Then he looked toward John, and with just a hint of despair in his voice, he added the bait. "Just room and board. That's all the pay I will take. If, however, I win, then a one-year free go of the Palace is mine, no hole's barred." The whole room had fallen silent as this new drama played out. "How about it, old friend. Is it a bet?"

John could see just what Cisco was up to, and his first reaction was not to give in to this childish blackmail. Still, at the same time, he thought it would be great to take some of the wind out of Cisco's sails. A broad grin followed as a low chuckle of pleasure escaped from the gambler. It did not quite match the intense voice that answered, but he spoke, still grinning. To John, any wager that he undertook was never to be taken lightly, no matter the circumstances, and this was no different. "You're on; you have yourself a wager."

The two of them sat there, shaking hands, sealing the bet, and looking as if they were enjoying themselves. Relief spread across the room, and the tension of moments ago evaporated. It was a go. Everyone seemed pleased, everyone except their leader.

Tori thought they were acting like children. How could they possibly put all that was riding on this plan in jeopardy with something as trivial as a stupid bet? "Stop it, the two of you. I'm not about to let either one of you jeopardize the outcome of this whole ordeal simply because you want to win a stupid personal bet. How could you, Cisco? And, you John, I would have thought you knew better."

The two men looked up at the angry woman that stood glaring at them, and for just a second, Cisco felt like a child getting scolded by his mother. His spirit quickly bounced in the opposite direction, though, as he told himself that all would be forgiven and forgotten as soon as he smoothed Tori's ruffled feathers. Nothing ever kept him down for long, he told himself. "Look, Tori," Cisco said in a calm voice. "Our bet has nothing to do with you. Besides, we are risking just as much, maybe more, on the outcome of this. Don't you think you should give us credit for wanting to make it work also? For one, I happen to know that John here works better if he's under a little pressure. And, I just gave it to him, that little-added pressure, that is. So, I say we act and act fast. What better time than three nights from now? After all, we're ready. There is nothing left to stop us, is there?"

Thiac, who had been silently standing in the corner of the room the whole time, caught Tori's eye and nodded. It was clear that he was ready. It was this gentle giant's nod that pushed her to agree. Once that was accomplished, the plan sprang into action, almost with a life of its own.

It was as if their plan was now a living, breathing entity that could no longer be detained. Once it started, and it had done just that, it would be impossible to stop. The death of this plan would be its outcome. God help them, Tori thought. She prayed that she had given birth to an angel and not a monster, ready to devour them alive.

John stood up and looked around the room as he spoke. "Well then, I had best depart this very second. I have much to arrange, and you still have to do your part down here. If I may have one of your men to escort me back to the city." He walked toward her, and once by her side, the gambler placed his arms around her. He gave a quick hug before releasing her. "Next time we meet, let us hope it is for you and your husband to join me for dinner and to watch my new employee." John laughed as he looked back toward Cisco. "I shall depart with your blessings." He bowed and turned to begin his journey.

Cisco frowned, and then realizing he'd been lured into his own idea, he chuckled. "You knew you would leave today, didn't you? I would never have guessed you were so certain of the outcome. Our meeting might have fallen apart, you know? You gambled and won this hand, it seems."

"In more ways than one." John looked back at Cisco. "I have no need of a horse. The Italian has made arrangements for me to sail on the tide and travel up the Mississippi. I will be home long before you fall asleep tonight. I would say I out bluffed you." John was in high spirits, and it showed.

Laffite's wife frowned knowingly. "So that's why old Chez Nez kept quiet. He'd already made a deal, and a good one, it seems. You never so much as hinted that a bargain had been reached between you. Remind me never to play poker with you." Tori laughed out loud and then turned to the smithy, who was grinning and nodding his head. "Thiac, see that Mr. Davis has a man accompany him to his ship and tell those on board who are a part of this that they are to meet us, in two days, at the rendezvous point. The men are to make sure they are not seen or followed. John, you can send your information via one of these men. On your word, we will move. Good luck and safe travels."

Cisco stood up, smiling brightly, and held his right hand up to form a V shape in the middle with his fingers spreading apart. "Live long and prosper."

Tori laughed. "Cisco! Really, can't you be serious at a time like this?"

"But I am. It fits, right? Spock's, saying. I have always wanted to say it and mean it."

"You are impossible. Safe travels, John. See you soon."

"That you will. I do pity you. Your job is going to be harder than mine. Keeping this idiot under control is sure to be a chore. Good luck."

SEVERAL hours later, she wouldn't have been able to call back the troops even if she wanted. John was on his way to New Orleans to play his part. Jean's men had received the go-ahead news, and Cisco had gathered up items for their journey. Monster or angel, she could no longer control it. Tori could only hope that she had the power to guide it and somehow, step by step, make it turn out the way it was planned. Still, she had to make sure of each step along the way.

STANDING by the barges and trying to remember everything had Tori a bit on edge. "Cisco, has Thiac got the men ready to go?"

"Yep, and Chez Nez has already sent word ahead to prepare our camp and keep watch. I have us some extra goodies from Carlotta and took the liberty of helping myself to another bottle. All packed and ready. Everything is going to plan; you have to trust us."

"It's not a matter of trust. It's just that we have so much riding on this. Tell me; we will pull it off?"

"We will if you are ready and rested. It would help if you slept, and I need to also. Can't be sleep-deprived on the biggest adventure of my life. Guess we can catnap on the barge, right? I mean, that will be the boring part of all this, no action there, unless we get attacked by a gator. Now, that could be interesting, a real adventure."

"What am I going to do with you? Adventure indeed."

Cisco could not help how he felt, but he also knew that Tori did get him; he'd make sure to be safe. "For me, it is wanted, the adventure that is. I will let you and the others do all the worrying. I'm around for the thrill of the ride and the biggest jailbreak in the South." He chuckled and then hugged Tori. "Don't worry, I may be kidding around now, but I get it. This is serious. It's just my way of dealing. You get me, right? I know John has planned this all out, but I do worry."

Tori chewed her bottom lip and thought for a few seconds before responding. "I hope John is ready. Once we get up there, keeping

Jean's men together and waiting will not be easy. You see how old Nez is. Hell, if he says go, they will follow. It worries me that he's coming along."

"I wouldn't worry too much. Thiac and I will be with you. We will keep them under control."

Feeling somewhat better after seeing Cisco was more serious than she'd thought, Tori wanted to lighten the moment. "I did see to it that Carlotta put two small mattresses on one of the barges. That will help us sleep a bit. Sleep tight, and don't let the bugs bite, right?"

Cisco frowned. "I hate that saying. I have slept in a few beds, more than a few, come to think of it, that had my skin crawling."

"Well, that's where the saying comes from. The ropes that lash the bed together; they hold the headboard and footboard upright. Those ropes support the mattresses. It's those ropes that have to get tightened now and then. You know when to do that because the bed begins to sink, and the headboard and footboard lean toward each other. Besides that, the mattress is filled with who knows what and often has bugs, as you said. Thus, the saying, sleep tight and don't' let the bed bugs bite. Don't worry, our beds in this house are good to go. No ropes, and the mattresses are filled with feathers and moss, that's been debugged."

"Well, aren't you an encyclopedia. Never knew that, but won't forget it. Shame we can't bring one of your beds along."

"Impossible, I'm sad to say. Would have been nice. Think about the look on the men's faces if we turned up with a full bed." Tori was laughing, and she was glad to be feeling less worried and more carefree. "Are you ready, even without a bed onboard?"

"Hell, Tori, I was ready yesterday. Let's go, but there is one other thing I have to ask you. I can put up with one Italian pirate, but please tell me, the rumor that Gambi is not joining us is true. There is something evil about him."

Tori laughed. "Like Chez Nez is not evil? As far as Gambi joining us or not, we shall have to see. As you said, we have to keep an eye on them, and I don't trust any of these pirates, let alone trust the rumors they spread. My take is he will remain here in case we get caught, and then he will be in charge. That is his game plan, I am sure. What his buddy's plan is, I don't know, but one thing is a given, he's in this for himself and not just to set Jean free."

THE two groups had set out right away to get into position. It was a monumental task but attainable because of the number of men pushing and guiding the two large barges along the waterways. Tori only hoped that they would get the word from John that the coast was clear soon. Once they reached the campsite, she knew that the point of turning back would have vanished. They were all so wound up and ready that nothing was going to stop them from releasing Jean and their friends, with or without the go-ahead from John.

It was well after the sun had set when they arrived at the designated point. The first part of the trip had gone without a hitch. The journey had even been somewhat of a mini-adventure. The time the journey took; temporarily allowed her mind to escape from all the worries and pressures that surrounded her. They had traveled by barge and then, to her surprise, by pirogues. These small and often swift-moving boats carried them the rest of the way through the bayous. Many of the routes they used were known only to Laffite's men and used exclusively by them. They traveled along these various narrow channels like modern-day highways, and as Jean had told her, there were a great many small canals twisting their way through the underbrush.

TORI sat for hours in one of the smaller crafts and quietly watched as the world floated by her. The trip was one of speckled shadows and dancing lights, of calling birds and insects, of splashing sounds made by jumping fish, and of plopping turtles, who slid from their Cypress logs into the murky depths of the water. Now and then, the whispers of men's voices would drift on the wind, then pick up and die just as fast.

It was the last of the long trip, the point where the small crafts crossed the Mississippi that blew her mind. She had not realized that they were taking an entirely different route than the one she knew about.

Tori realized something was up, as not one of the men talked or called from boat to boat, as they had along the way. No one said to be quiet, and no one told her anything. It was just assumed that she was aware of what was about to occur.

It was dark when the small pirogues slipped quietly out of the mouth of one of the small bayous to cross the vast expanse of murky flowing water. At first, Tori was nervous, but upon seeing the lantern's light on the opposite side of the river, she relaxed. Jean's men knew what they were about and had made this trip often, she assured herself. It didn't take her long either to realize this part of the journey seemed to be the trickiest part. They were, after all, out in the open and, knowing this, kept the men's ever-increasing excitement temporarily in check, as well as keeping them silent, both of which, she was sure, was difficult for some. These were men of action, not of taking pleasure cruises. They were men who led rough and often violent lives. Their lives were governed by the law of doing what they wanted and when they wanted it. These were men who were not used to taking orders from a woman. Oh yes, they were silent and thinking about their situation as they closed the gap between themselves and New Orleans, but what they really thought of her, she had no idea.

ONCE on shore, the pirates quietly waited for the time that they would receive the message to proceed. Some slept, and others sat in small groups talking amongst themselves. The anticipation of what they were about to attempt hung in the air. It was as tangible as the very breeze that moved amongst them. A group would laugh softly every so often, and all heads would turn to look at Tori. She felt uncomfortable under such scrutiny and could only imagine what they were talking about under their breath. Up until now, only she, Cisco, and Davis knew all the details of the plans, and Laffite's wife knew that many of the men were restless and more than just a tiny bit curious as to what their roles would be and when. Davis had decided this was how the operation needed to go, just in case there was a chance of their plans getting out. After all, one man could sell the information and then disappear, with his pockets full of gold.

Cisco had found it an excellent opportunity to brush up on his game of chance and line his pockets with a little extra cash. He was always careful to lose just enough when the situation seemed to call for it, such as when an angry, suspicious brute was about to call him out for cheating. Not that Cisco ever looked at it quite like cheating. No, he liked to call it creative card counting, with player, beware. Ever the crafty one, he was good enough that they never suspected what was going on.

Thiac could see that Tori was impatient to be on her way. He also knew that she needed a little comfort and a friendly face to talk with. Sitting there, looking more like a man than a woman, with her face frozen in a stern glare, she did not fool him. Her eyes were dulled but able to drill right through those who dared to stare at her too long. She was a formidable woman to reckon with, that was for sure. Yet, he knew all the acting in the world could never hide the vulnerable, caring individual that she was, at least not from those who knew and loved her.

Tori had smeared some dirt on her face to help hide her soft complexion and the exact color of her skin tone. The hat that hid her long hair sat on the ground next to her, and tucked into her belt was Cisco's small pistol that he insisted she might need.

Thiac approached her cautiously. Standing behind her, he cleared his throat to let her know that he was there. "Sorry, Thiac. I didn't hear you. I was thinking about everything that is about to happen. Did you say something?"

"Sort of; I ain't good with words like you or other white folks. But I can use my head, and it seems to me that you should not be going with us tonight and all. It ain't no place for a fine lady such as yourself. I, knows that Boss, he's not going to be none too happy when he finds out you come along."

"You let me worry about Jean and about this being no place for a lady. I can assure you that I can take care of myself when I have to, and that part of me is about as far away from a lady as you are from being white." She laughed, trying to cover her doubts and lighten poor old Thiac's mood. "I promise that I will be very careful, and Cisco will be with me each step of the way, as will the other men."

"Yes, Mizz Tori, I, knows that. It's just if something should go wrong. Well, the others might not be worrying about you any. They all will be a trying to save their own skins. If Cisco gets parted from you… then you would be all by yourself. Maybe I should come with you?"

"Thiac, we have you in the other group because you are needed there. You are the only one I can trust to see that the shipment arrives at the warehouses back on Grand Terre, and you know that the men will depend on your sheer strength to get them through. You have to go with them, as much as I have to go with Cisco."

"That's what I was afraid you'd say. So… well… here, this is for you." He brought his hand around from his back and held out a small but beautifully crafted sword; the blade was so polished that it caught the slightest beam of light and reflected it a thousand times brighter. The hilt was engraved with such intricate designs that one could sit for hours, picking out shapes and images from within the filigree design.

The blacksmith saw her shocked expression and decided he'd best explain how it was the weapon was in his possession. "I was walking around with nothing else to do a few days past, and I met up with a man who said that Dominique had him making this for you. I thought it must be right because of the size of the top here. See, my hand, don't fit in here to hold the sword right, and I don't think there is a man here whose hand could fit in the way yours could. You havin' such small hands like. Anyway, this man said that he's seen you and Dominique and that he thought maybe you should have it now." As he handed her the weapon with one hand, his other was scratching his head. His face had a look of disbelief and questioning about it. "He also told me that you know'd how to use it and really good too if you needed. Sure, hope you don't have no need."

Tori stood up, taking the sword in hand and slipping her fingers through the golden loop that made up the hilt. Once in her hand, she could feel that indeed it had been made for her and her alone. The balance was excellent. Moving it through the air, it cut smoothly and without much effort. Her fingers fit so precisely that only a fraction of an inch was between her flesh and the cold, smooth metal that surrounded her fist. As she held it, the sword seemed to become an extension of her arm, of her very soul, just how Dominique told her it should. The weapon's hilt had been fashioned to not only protect her hand but to make it almost impossible for anyone to dislodge the weapon from her grip. Every detail had been mastered and carefully crafted into this gift, and she loved Dominique for caring so much. He had designed it for her, with her protection in mind. He had built into it every advantage he could. It was so like him to pay close attention to detail, and a part of her considered that he had created this weapon, with her using it in mind. Maybe he had an inkling that one day, she may have to use it in a fight to protect herself, regardless of how many times he had told her the to the contrary. Or maybe he just wanted to give her every advantage when she showed Jean what she'd learned and challenged him to fence.

The gift had lifted her spirits, and joy radiated from her smile. Gone was the scornful face, replaced by one of excitement. "Indeed,

I can use this. It's wonderful. I will feel a lot better having this by my side. Don't look so worried, Thiac. I will only use it if I have to, and my teacher was, and is, one of the best."

"I'm going to slide it under my belt, and if I have to, I will use it, and not you, nor anyone else is going to take it away from me."

Cisco, who had watched the smithy give Tori the weapon, spoke up. "Are you crazy? Do you know how dangerous those things are? With that tucked in your belt, you might very well get hurt. By simply falling, you could seriously cut yourself, let alone using the damn thing as a weapon. No, I can't allow that." He walked quickly up to her. "You hand it to me right now." Cisco stood there with his hand out, expecting to be obeyed.

His insinuations and demands infuriated Tori. How dare he? How arrogant of him to assume that she couldn't handle such a sword, and only because she was a woman. "I damn well will not do any such thing, and you can't make me. As for not knowing what I'm doing, I'll prove you wrong, Mr."

There was laughter all around and none louder than from Chez Nez. "I'd be real careful there, lad; she might prick you with that fine little weapon. Let her have her little ladylike sword."

More laughter erupted, and Tori was forced to reply to the arrogant Italian. "For your information, it is a foil, or you may refer to it as a rapier."

Chez Nez burst into a fit of laughter, and those around him were also amused. "Did you say rape-he-her? Not sure I understand you. If you wish to partake of my charms and are hinting such…"

"You bloody well know I am not. For your information, this weapon is quite deadly in the right hands."

"Is it by God? Nice little scratch if you can get near any bloke willing, I bet."

"I will take on any one of you. Come on, be brave; who wants to try?" Tori stood up and began looking around.

The Italian saw a few of his men poke each other, and one tried to push his mate into having a go, but in the end, it was the Chez

Nez who pointed to a younger man. "You there, I have seen your swordplay many a day, or night, can't quite recall which. But you are fair enough; give her a go."

The man stood up, not wishing to try his hand at taking on Boss's wife, but his fear of telling the older pirate no, well, that was worse right then. "Ma'am, if you want, I will go easy." He walked into the area where most of the men now stood around. In fact, a complete circle had quickly formed around the pair. Then, before Cisco could utter a word of caution or even try to talk her out of such a rash action, their swords raised. To the Spaniard's horror, they were really about to put on a demonstration, and it was too late to step in and prevent it.

Her sharp voice rang clear in the evening air. "en garde!" There was a short hoot and hollering before a deadly silence enveloped the area. It began slowly at first, with only the occasional clash of blades, as each one felt out the other's ability. If Tori had shocked Cisco with her skill, she could not tell. However, she had most certainly surprised her opponent, as recognition of her talent registered on his face.

Right away, he realized she did indeed know what she was doing. The man found that she was excellent; he could maneuver and try all he might; but she was always there, ready and thrusting, keeping up with his every move.

"Stop!" yelled Cisco. "You've made your point, and there is no need to go on with this display. Did you hear me? Stop!" The young man backed up several quick steps and lowered his sword.

Tori slowly stepped forward and let her sword drop to her side as she wiped her brow and tucked back a strand of hair that had fallen over her eye. She thanked the man for his help and turned to face Cisco. "You forget, my friend, that I am not the Southern belle but a liberated lady."

Chez Nez clapped his hands loudly. "Bloody hell mates, Boss better never return home with an empty hand. I can handle my wife and her tongue but face that," he pointed to Tori, "well now, I'd think twice. My apologies to the lady," the pirate bowed her way, "but be glad the lad went easy. If it had been me, I…"

Tori spun around and grinned at the pirate. "If it had been you, I'd have drawn blood before stopping. Now, I think it's time to get ready to move. It looks like you, Cisco, might have won your bet after all. No news from John, and we can't afford to wait much longer. With or without his help, we will have to try tonight." Turning to face Chez Nez, she smiled. "No hard feelings? You do agree with me, don't you? We can't wait much longer."

"Takes a lot to hurt my feelings, and I agree with you. It is time to go and get Boss. Someone has to keep watch over you with that thing in your possession. Bloody dangerous, if you ask me. Why, in all the saints above, Boss would give you such as that, I will never understand. Better a darning needle, less chance of killing yourself."

"Well, Captain, Boss did not give it to me; Dominique did, so I would take it up with him if you dare. Now that's settled, let's make plans to go and get Jean." Cisco's face dropped, as did Thiac's. "Oh, Thiac, don't look so down. You have just given me one of the best gifts I have ever received. Dominique will be so pleased that I have it." She patted the hilt of her sword and smiled softly. "Don't you worry, we will all be together tomorrow celebrating. Dominique trained me, and thank God because if a certain Italian had, bets would be off."

Suddenly Thiac began laughing. The look on old Chez Nez's face was one of mixed emotions, but the best was the color of his puffed-up cheeks; they were burning red. Everyone around him was having fun at his expense, and the irritated man was unsure how to react.

Knowing the pirate's temper, Thiac calmed down. Finally, he was able to control himself and speak what was on his mind. He faced Tori and, sounding very serious, added his feelings on the matter. "You know, I think you are right. It's, sure enough, a good gift from Dominique. I ain't-a gonna worry none about you, no more. I's sure be worried about the man who is a-goin' to come up against you, though. He's a-goin' to be in mighty big trouble. Yes, Sir, mighty big. 'Cause, he ain't a thinking a little bitty thing like you, is a match at all. No Sir, no trouble." Most of the men joined Thiac in his chuckling, whooping and hollering their support and praise toward their female leader and her newfound talent.

A lone messenger walked into this noisy crowd, quieting down the group as he approached Tori. Everyone wanted to hear the news he had brought because this was what they had been waiting for. Instead of going to Tori, though, he walked up to Cisco, who was standing next to her. "Monsieur Vega, I have a message for you. Monsieur Davis, he told me to tell you that you now work for him, and he wants to congratulate you himself on your first day of employment, and that be on this coming Monday."

Tori tried hard to hide her amusement. Cisco had placed a bet to get John to act and had done so without thinking of the outcome. "Hey Cisco, you and John can settle up later, she laughed." Tori turned to the man who had given his message and stepped closer to him. "You have more information for us, right?"

"I do, indeed. Not too much, but all you need to know before we head out. Mr. Davis said I had to tell Mr. Vega first, as he needed to know he lost. Don't rightly know what he lost but don't care much either."

Thiac found himself chuckling. How much more could his sides take, he wondered? They were already sore from the last round of laughter. Only one person amongst this happy crowd had a sad-looking face now, and that was Cisco. Even old grumpy Chez Nez looked somewhat pleased.

Cisco was far from pleased. On the one hand, he had not wanted to lose the bet, so things would go well for them. Right then, however, he realized that he might not like the result of his little wager. He was a man of his word and would honor it. He was, though, always the opportunist, and an idea quickly gave him hope of a way to escape his upcoming doom. After all, he'd never said that he wouldn't try to get fired, thus ending his working days. His look of gloom turned to a more hopeful expression, having quite possibly discovered a way out of his yearlong commitment of 'free' labor.

He smiled at Tori, who noticed that he looked like he had something up his sleeve. Just what it was, she didn't know, but she'd get it out of him later. There were other things to focus on at the moment. The female looked back at the man who had delivered the news. "I think you had best finish telling us the rest of your information before time gets away from us, don't you?"

"Indeed, yes, Mr. Davis said I needed to be fast. Here is what I know. The guards change every hour. Those are the ones on the outside of the Calobozo."

Cisco laughed. "The what?"

"That's the Spanish Colonial prison, you idiot, snapped Tori." She was not happy with his attitude and shot him a stern look before turning her attention back to Davis's man. "Please continue."

"Right then. Once inside, you will have to be quick and quiet. He was not too sure how often they rotate the guards inside the jail section. John said those that change on the perimeter replace two on the inside. And them that are replaced go and sleep in their quarters. Next, he thinks there will be around eight soldiers walking the halls. There will be two or more sitting at the cells, and those should be easy, as they are the fat and happy kind. Those were his words, Miss. He said you talked about it all."

She could not help but smile. "We did, so then, I suggest we make our way to the jail." Tori faced the men and spoke with conviction. "You heard his news, and you all know who does what. Let's go and get the Boss."

Chez Nez took a step forward. "And, which way would that be?" The Captain was standing with a smirk on his face, knowing only too well that Laffite's woman didn't have a clue. The Italian continued. "Seems to me, it's lucky for us that one of my men was a former river rat and just happens to know the quickest way and easier too, I might add."

Tori was not about to be put down, and she also knew that right then was the turning point. If she faulted, she would lose her standing as the leader, and the Italian would take over, and in her estimation, the raid would become a blood bath. "Well then, Captain, I suggest you have your man guide us, or I most likely would have us walking all the way to the gulf before we knew what was what. Oh, no, wait a second. If we walk keeping the river on our left, we should reach the square, right?" She did not wait for an answer. "I am certain the walk would take longer and be rougher should we go my way, so your man is most welcome to guide us, and I thank you for your offer."

Chez Nez was not pleased, and it showed on his face. "Did I offer him?"

"Yes," were the cries from the men, who were itching to get going. Even Cisco and Thiac were making ready, as both were kicking dirt onto the fire to put it out. The smithy finished extinguishing the last ember and turned toward the Italian. "No need chancing a scrub fire. Could make them, in these here parts, madder than a hornet nest if that happened." He chuckled briefly before continuing. He faced Tori and added the rest of his statement. "Besides, the Italian Captain is in one of his moods." Again, there was laughter, and this time, even Chez Nez saw he meant no harm. Still, he had to give a response and make it sound like he meant it.

"I shall let that one by, but be careful, Thiac; Boss is not here to keep me from slitting your black hide wide open." He looked at the small woman standing in front of him, and his admiration grew. "For you, at this time, I am in your full command."

There was a brief outburst of cheering, and then before she could say more, they were moving quickly away from their camp and toward what would, in the future, be called Jackson Square.

The night was just perfect for what they needed. The moon was full and shone down brightly, lighting the rest of their way through the swampy surroundings. There were just enough clouds that, now and then, one would slip across the bright orb, granting them cover and protection from being seen. Tori had realized this and passed her thoughts on to Chez Nez. "If we use the cloud cover to our advantage, we can make our entrance into the 'Place d'Armes' unseen."

"Smart wench. I see more and more why Boss went soft and got you by his side. Me, I got my wife so she could take care of me, not the other way around. I thought Boss was taking care of you; now I think that got all turned around—last thing I will say on the matter. I only want the goods back and money in my pocket. If Boss doesn't make it, then someone will step into his position."

Tori stopped walking and looked the man in the eyes. "And, that someone would be you, I suppose."

The pirate grinned and winked at her. "Could be. Best stop your jabbering; we will be getting close soon."

Tori snapped back. "I, Sir, was not the one jabbering away. You were, so shut your gob and watch where you walk. I don't need to go picking your ugly piece of ass up out of the mud."

There was general chucking up and down the line of men, while others could be heard asking what she had said to the Italian. It was Thiac's hissing to shut up that silenced them.

Cisco looked behind him and could not make out how far behind him the last man was. True, it was bright enough to see your way clearly, but he also realized that if he had walked the route by himself, he was sure he'd have gotten lost. He was glad the former river rat did his best to slow down, now and then, to allow the men to catch up, but every time he did, the Italian was right there to hurry him along.

They were less than a quarter of a mile from their destination when Tori called a break. "I know we are close, so let's take a break."

This order angered the older pirate. "And how do you know we are close, I ask? You sure the break is for the men, or does the little lady need to rest?"

"For your information, Captain, if you look ahead instead of looking at your feet, you would see the lights of the city. And on the waterfront are a few more vessels anchored, indicating our position."

"She's got you there, Captain," one of the men chuckled.

The Italian laughed. "I suppose she has, but her being of the female kind, I thought it best if I did not trip over my own bloody feet and fall into her arms all cozy like. I mean, the small thing could not hope to keep me upright; we'd fall to the ground and roll around something awful to see." He was leering at her and licking his bottom lip, which turned up in a huge smile.

"Captain, could you just shut the hell up for once and stop trying to be so pompous or tough. I mean, we all know your reputation, so zip it."

The man looked at her closely. 'Had she just insulted him in front of witnesses? And what in the hell did zip it mean?' He was about to respond when Tori turned to face the group.

"I trust you all know what has to be accomplished and fast. The men destined for the warehouse better head that way now. Make sure you are not seen and that no one, I mean no one, gets killed. Thiac, I place you in charge of making certain that everything goes to plan."

"Mizz Tori, I just a simple man. I think maybe one of these men is best suited for that there, responsibility."

Tori let a smile curl her lips. "I don't think anyone minds. Anyone have a problem?" Not one man spoke up, and seeing they were itching to get going, she added, "Right then, you best be off. Good luck. We will see you back at Grand Terre." So, without another word, the large group of burly men departed. Left behind were those that Chez Nez and Tori had handpicked. This small group was chosen to go and rescue Laffite and his men. Some feared the Italian had a different plan in mind, but most said he would do nothing to risk freeing Laffite. After all, he did not want to get caught himself. If he or any of them failed tonight, they would swing right next to the so-called gentleman pirate. This fact they assured themselves would keep the crazy Italian under control.

Tori tapped Chez Nez on his shoulder. "Captain, lead the way. Next stop is the Place d' Armes."

TORI wished she had a watch to keep track of time. How long they'd been walking, she did not know, but it seemed to her as if they had been going forever. The lights of the city seemed so close, but distance at night was a tricky thing. It was when they started to scurry along the dockside that she realized they were almost there.

The two groups had split up some time ago, as each had a different destination and task to accomplish. The other group was probably already removing the stolen goods from the dockside warehouses, where Claiborne had seen fit to store them. He had not left them in Jean's storage building, something Davis had learned about and passed on. They had been taken to a more secure location but not safe enough. Tori estimated that if all had gone to plan by this time, the men would be loading the merchandise onto the barges and getting ready for the long trip back to Grand Terre. She was so deep in thought, thinking about them, that she didn't realize her group had reached their destination.

It was Cisco who gained her attention, as he whispered in a low voice. "There it is. The square, the church, and the streets beyond. All looks quiet, does it not?" He spoke low, and the tone of his voice sounded subdued. It was his fingers that kept tapping his side, which showed Tori he was full of excitement.

Laffite's wife knew that each of them was more than ready for the task that lay ahead, and realizing this, she felt a surge of excitement herself. Speaking slightly louder so all could hear her, she commanded, "We might as well get going. You all know what to do. Good luck to you all." She hesitated, and with a slight crack in her voice, added, "and thank you." She saw the nods from some of the men and heard a few soft "ayes." Some smiled in their roguish way, offering her support. Still, others were boosting her bravery as she felt the odd slap on her back in a team-inspired spirit. One of the larger men stepped forward and stood before her, dwarfing her in his presence.

"Before we go, well, the men and I, we want you to know that we ain't doin' this for Boss. We was in the beginin' like, but now… we be a breaking him out of there, on a count of you. You are one hell of a lady, beggin' your pardon Miss, but that's how we feel, and we want you to know that."

Tori did not know what to say; one thing was clear his statement had deeply touched her. She could feel the tears springing to the corners of her eyes and thanked God; it was dark enough that no one could see she was about to cry. The woman hid her emotional condition by keeping herself busy. She pushed her ponytail up and under her hat and then pulled the front of it down on her forehead. As long as it sat tightly on her brow, her long hair would remain hidden. As she planned, the cap obscured much of her face. Once again, her appearance denoted that of a young lad. With nothing left to do, Tori realized she was very nervous and maybe frightened too. Now that she had admitted this to herself, it gave her the courage to overcome both emotions. Then for a fleeting moment, she wondered if they could pull it off. Could they get Jean and his men out as planned?

Cisco saw her staring at the church. Tori looked far more than worried to him, and he knew that maybe she needed some encouragement. He pushed the men in front of him off to the side and gave an order, which they obeyed. "Give the lady and me a few moments. I think she wishes to pray. An idea that maybe you all should take part in."

"Aint prayed in years," said an older pirate as he passed him.

"I'm with him; a swig of drink is what I need," grumbled the Italian. The Captain pulled a pewter flask out and began to open it.

"Whatever you need to do before we begin, then do it. Just keep down and quiet," snapped Cisco." He crouched down by Tori and pulled her with him. "Let them think you are praying. Give you a bit of time before all hell breaks out."

Tori whispered into Cisco's ear. "Thank you. I only need to pull myself together."

"No problem. Hey, the square doesn't look a bit like our time, does it? I mean, the church is not the same, and old Jackson's statue is not there. The two large buildings that sit on both sides of the square haven't even been built yet. You know, the Pontabla buildings or some such name? All expensive apartments in our time. It's an open, plain old space, just waiting for us to cross. Hell, do you realize where we are couching right now?"

"Yes, in front of Jackson Square."

"Nope, we are on the very spot where 'Café du Monde' will be. God, I loved that place; miss it sometimes."

Tori looked away from the open area and spoke even softer to Cisco. "I don't care right now; what we left behind is not here, and I think it best if we stop talking about it. All we need is for one of them to overhear and wonder what we are about. They would think us crazy."

"Got you. But the men are far enough away, and they think we are praying. Hey, did you ever take the tour inside that building, the museum part? I looked at the cells they had in the back. Did you see those? There was a courtyard on the lower level and then all those cells up higher."

"I did. You know, it's a break for us that those jail cells have not been constructed yet. I can't imagine trying to get them out of there. It's hard enough breaking them out of the place they are holding them now. Better for us as they are all on the same floor too. If I recall, the jails that will occupy the Cablido will be on two, or is it three floors? Hell, that alone would complicate things. As it is, even with all the info on the guards and such, it's going to be close."

"Have to agree with you, but having them held out of sight of the garrison over there and in a building that is easier to crack gives me hope. So, do you feel ready to go? It would be best if you got things rolling, you know. Those that are securing the barracks have it easy. Over there, that's the building the garrison is in. All tucked up in their beds." Cisco had pointed to a building on his right.

"Yes, I know. We better get started. If not, and please don't take this wrong, but I think I will back out if I delay a second longer." Tori stood up and Cisco with her.

He frowned and then broke into a grin. "You know you won't, but we best make a dash soon. The man over by the barracks is waving to go. See him? John's man is there too."

She saw the man in question and knew it was the signal she'd been waiting for. While facing the church, Tori said as firmly as she could, the one order that would begin the action. "Let's stop talking, and let's do it!"

All at once, the men went into action. They were so precise; it was as if they had done this many times before. The first four were over the low stone wall before she could check if the timing was right. They had to cross the square's open grounds and then get onto the side street, which would be called Pirate's alley in Tori's day. Once there, they had to get to the building behind the church and its grounds. That was where the Calabozo stood and where they were holding Jean and his men.

Once across the square, the small group ran along the church's side, and as they ran, Tori realized that they were going to succeed with this first step of the plan. Once again, she was glad that they did not have to break into the Cabildo to rescue Jean and his men. She also hoped that any soldiers left inside the building were asleep and unaware of her and the men she had by her side.

Ahead of her, she could see the building they had to get inside of, and at the same time, she witnessed two guards as they came around the corner of the Calabozo. If her group's timing had been off, they would have been spotted, but lady luck held. Before the guards realized what was happening, they were quickly brought down and knocked unconscious. Tori had stopped running and stood watching the events unfold. Now, it was time for those chosen to make their move back toward the barracks. Cisco waved the signal and watched as their small group split into two. Knowing what to do, the other half headed off toward their goal without breaking their pace or making a sound. Cisco turned to look at Tori. He spoke just above a whisper. "Are you ready to go? It's our turn, and I am more than ready." His voice sounded wound up with excitement.

Sounding just as excited, Tori responded. "I'm as ready as I ever will be." She gasped, trying to catch her breath before adding her order. "Let's do it."

Her small group stepped out of the shadows and quickly made their way to the building's front entrance. Upon arriving, they passed the fallen guards, whose uniforms were being hastily removed. While watching this action, Tori witnessed that anything of value, or other personal items, found its way into the pirate's pockets. One man even took a pair of boots for himself, and the coveted guard's weapons were now the property of the men who had knocked the soldiers out. After they'd been stripped of their uniforms, the two men were dragged out of sight. Next, they were bound and gagged. All accomplished under the watchful eye of Chez Nez.

Tori helped Cisco remove his jacket and started dressing him in one of the fallen guard's uniforms. She even held the soldier's pants for him to step into. "You know, I didn't think men wore bloomers," she giggled.

"I will have you know they are not bloomers; they are winter underpants, made for me by Marie's seamstress. Nice piece of ass, that one. The seamstress I'm talking about."

"Oh my god, is there ever a time you don't have women on your mind?"

"Well, yes, there is, actually."

"Step into this leg and then the other. You can pull them up your-self."

"I don't think of women when I play cards, or when I am with you, or when I am with Marie. Well, maybe when I am with her, and she's got a headache." He was pulling up his pants and buttoning the front. "These are damn tight; if I bend over, I will split them for sure. Hell, I do miss zippers and belts. There… all done up and like I said, real tight."

"Then, don't bend. Here, button the sides; you missed two and put the coat on. Now, let me look at you."

The transformation happened in minutes; he stood up for her inspection, chuckling to himself.

"Now, what's so funny?"

"Do me a favor and don't tell Jean that you stripped me and dressed me," he said, winking at her. "He might get the wrong idea. I quite enjoyed the process, though. Could we do it again, slower next time, perhaps?"

"Oh, you are incorrigible, you rogue. Come on and quit clowning around. We have to get on the other side of that door, and we can't do that until you and your companion have taken care of the guards. Hurry up before they open up." Tori glanced at the locked doors. "It's got to be about time. Your hat, don't forget the hat."

It was Chez Nez who handed him the last part of the guard's uniform. "Right then, now you look the part."

"It's too big."

The pirate laughed. "Who cares? By the time they notice, you should have taken care of them."

Cisco and one of the other men, both now dressed in the guard's uniforms, immediately marched up to the door. There they stood as if they were the original soldiers on duty, and Tori held her breath as she continued to watch from the shadows. If John Davis was correct, then it was time for the guards to change at any moment.

Proving he had been correct with his knowledge of the guards' changing routine, the large wooden door began to open, and Tori realized that they had just made it. Laffite's wife stood in the shadows and watched as the new jail guards stepped outside. It was then that Cisco and the sailor turned to face the open door and walked right by the unsuspecting soldiers. Then, as planned and before the guards knew what hit them, it began. It was great to see

Cisco turn and take the two of them out with swift karate moves. It all happened so fast. He had spun around; about the same time, one of the soldiers realized they were not who they should be. The man from the future flew up and off the ground as he swung his leg outward, allowing his foot to connect with the soldier's head. Upon landing, he spun again, and his karate chop connected with the second surprised guard. Both had been knocked out cold in a matter of seconds, leaving a very proud of himself, Cisco. The pirate, who had accompanied him, had stood for a second with his mouth open and his fists held up, ready to fight. In his disbelief and with nothing left to do, he dropped his hands by his side. He was supposed to have taken out one of the soldiers. Cisco was to handle the other, but this dandy had taken care of both silently and far faster than anything he had ever seen before. It didn't matter that they had acted before getting inside; what mattered to the pirate right then; was how this dandy had handled himself.

Looking at Cisco, he laughed softly. "Blimey never saw a man fight using his legs as his arms. Bloody hell, never seen anything like that. You going to have to show me how you did it, 'cause crikey, I could use those bloody moves for my own advantage."

"Well, I can show you, but it took me years to learn how to apply the moves. It's not that simple; it takes skill and training."

Tori was proud of him, but here they were again, dilly-dallying around. "Will you two stop your talking and feeling so proud of yourselves and get those two guards out of sight. You were supposed to have done this after they got inside, not before," she hissed at him. Then, the anxious female looked up and down the street to see if anyone was watching them. The area was empty, and upon seeing that, she faced Cisco once more. "Still, good job, but let's get a move on. Quickly, come on. We have to close the door. Let's hope that John's information is correct and that the place is not heavily guarded, from here on, and that the rest of the soldiers are in their barracks sleeping."

The remaining men in their small group hurriedly joined them, and once they were all inside and out of sight, Cisco and his new admirer pushed the wooden doors closed. For better or worse, they were inside.

The moment the doors were shut, the men began to move swiftly and without making a noise. Only Chez Nez, held back to travel by Tori's side. She was not sure if he was doing so because he feared she would blow things, or he was there to protect her. Either way, it made her uncomfortable because she in no way trusted the man.

Sensing her discomfort, the Italian grabbed her by the arm and held her back. "You know, I have never seen the likes of you before, and I believe I owe you an apology of sorts. You are doing all you said you would, and if I was not seeing it with my own eyes, I'd never believed it. An, so that you know, I will keep by your side till you are with Boss. Besides, if we get caught, I will have a barging chip, you see." He cocked his head knowingly and grinned.

There it was; she had been right. The man would use her to save his own skin. The pirate was just as awful as he looked. Still, if he helped her and they got out of this without any trouble, he'd have done his job. What got her wound up was Tori knew Chez Nez was sure to try and take all the credit, something she'd have to deal with later. Right then, she just wanted to be rid of the cold, calculating pirate. "I don't think I need you or anyone to aid me. Besides, I have Cisco. So, if you don't mind, let's keep to the plan, shall we?" Tori pulled her arm free, and without another word, followed the route through the building toward the hallway they needed to find.

By the time Tori and the Captain, followed closely by Cisco, caught up with the other pirates, all was quiet. It was too quiet for her, and Tori looked around nervously, trying to figure out why? "What have you done with the guards that were on the inside here? I don't see any sign of them. There were supposed to be some, that's what John said."

One of the pirates gave her a sizeable toothless grin. He turned and spat a mouthful of dark fluid before he spoke. "Well now, that's because you ain't looking in the right place, Ma'am. But, if you look over by the wall in the shadow, you'll just about see what you be looking for."

Indeed, she did. Some bodies were lying out on the ground, while others were sitting up. These men had their backs against the wall, with their chins resting upon their chests.

"Just like you wanted. Not one of them hurt bad—just sort of taking a nap like. I always say that there is nothing like a little bump on the noggin to send you off to dreamland. Sides, my mother, God, rest her soul, used to tell me, when I was a wee one, the little folk was about when you slept. You know, like the ones that bring's you something for being brave when you lost a tooth. And I bloody well went and lost me last tooth! One of them buggers knocked it cleanout. Least I could do was knock his out. See if them, wee folk, leave him anything but a bloody headache." Everyone around them chuckled softly.

Now Tori understood. The spit had been blood, not chewing tobacco as she had assumed. She looked at the dark stain on the floor not far from her feet, and her stomach turned over slowly. Tori was about to ask him if he was all right when she realized by the expression on his face that he was having the time of his life. He didn't care one damn bit about the pain he was in. Instead, he was chuckling away to himself. "How many men would you say are taking a... nap?" she asked. "John didn't know for sure how many there would be. He said maybe eight."

"Eight, to be exact. Not one more or less. Just like you said, and right you were. You said the guards would be there, and there they were. Hell, it was so damn easy. Just thump and dump is what we did. Had that one spot of trouble, with that there, bastard that took me tooth. Lucky shot, if you ask me. Had that one tooth nigh on ten years or more. Been in fights too, never lost it till now. Lucky for him, that one shot with his fist, and there again, unlucky. He got far worse than just bump and dump." Again, the sailor was chucking; his wheezy chest gave out a sort of whistle with each exhale. "He ain't dead like, but when he wakes up, my bets, he wishes he was.

His head took a bashing." The man chuckled some more and spat another mouth full of blood and saliva toward his victim.

So far, all of John's information had been correct. The times and the number of guards were exact. From here on in, though, it would be tricky. Grymes and Davis had not been too sure of how many remaining guards would be on duty, and at all costs, they had to remain silent. To wake up the garrison on the other side of the Place d'Armes, would be suicide.

Tori knew that some of the men had stayed to keep watch just outside the building, while others went to barricade the garrison's quarters so that anyone inside would be delayed getting out if aroused for some reason. That should have already happened if the small group who had split off from them had followed the plan. It would be about this time that two others from that group would make their way to the armory to secure all the weapons. It had been difficult convincing them not to steal any of the guns, but in the end, Cisco had reasoned with them, and they saw sense in leaving everything intact.

She also knew that Thiac, by now, was hopefully finishing emptying the warehouse. The barges they'd traveled on at the start of the journey should have docked where Laffite had been caught in the first place. Unlike the night Jean had been seen, the pirates would keep a close watch out. Obviously, they had not posted men to do so on the fateful night of their capture, or they would never have been discovered, she told herself. Tori could think of no other reason for what had happened. A chill ran through her. All she wanted was for the men to steal the merchandise and depart into the night as if they had never been there.

It had been hard to convince the pirates that this all had to be accomplished without killing; Cisco again had succeeded where Tori could not. He'd explained to them that to leave as if there had been no big fight would be to their advantage. Easy in and out is how they had to make it appear. Cisco had continued and explained that this action would embarrass and humiliate the soldiers along with Governor Claiborne, far more than if there had been a bloody battle. Besides, if the silenced individuals were left with a few cuts, bumps, and bruises to accompany their slight headache, people would have a good laugh at the guard's expense, but killing guards, or anyone for that matter, could make things quite difficult for them. They all would be wanted for murder, for one thing, and murder was a far more severe crime than roughing someone up, and killing anyone would not go unnoticed or forgotten. The men had listened to Cisco and his reasoning and, in the end, agreed that they would do it all without causing any deaths. At least they would try, they had laughed, and as for now, it looked to Tori as if they intended to do their best to keep their word.

It was Chez Nez who got Tori's attention. "It's only a bloody tooth, and they don't hang anyone for that." He chuckled. "If they did, half my men would have swung on the end of a rope by now. So, why are you standing here worrying your head over his sore one, might I ask? It is time to move on." His hand reached out, and he pushed her lightly on the shoulder. "Let's be off; time is wasting here."

Tori nodded her head and, without a word spoken, moved ahead. With confidence, she walked directly toward where the small passageway ended. It was at the 't' intersection that she stopped. Hesitantly looking around, Tori stood thinking. At this point, it would take up too much precious time to go in the wrong direction, and she knew it. Tori stood looking first one way and then the other. A mistake now could ruin all their plans, and the choice, the next order, was all up to her. Her legs suddenly felt weak, and one began to tremble as she pivoted one way and then the other.

Seeing her dilemma, Cisco pushed in front of her and quickly appraised the situation. Before him was only one choice, as far as he was concerned. The passage was pitch black and silent down one way, the other way was dimly lit, and voices could be heard mumbling and occasionally laughing. This was the way to go, he reasoned. Putting his finger to his lips, he signaled for the small group to follow him.

The passage had come to another intersection, and again they halted. Slowly, Cisco peered around the corner in the direction of the men's voices and quickly observed the surroundings before making his move. Things did not look good to him. Everything so far had seemed to be going too easy, and this proved it. He motioned for them to move back down the passage, away from the guards, where he could tell Tori what they were up against without being overheard. "There are just two of them sitting at a small table playing cards," he whispered. "And you do know how I like a game of cards, don't you?" The famous Cisco grin filled his face, but before she had a chance to question him about what he had up his sleeve this time, to her horror, he was gone. He had turned and boldly walked back down the hall, none too quietly either and around the corner, right into plain sight of the soldiers.

The two men, engrossed in their game, jumped at the sound of footsteps heading their way and quickly tried to hide the evidence of their gambling. While on guard duty, caught in such an activity was a serious offense and one with severe consequences.

By the time Cisco was standing in front of the soldiers, they were anxious and quite rattled, just how he needed them to be. Both of them were also a bit angry and on the defensive, though. He would have to deal with these emotions rapidly if he were to diffuse the situation and win them over.

A red-faced, furious individual barked at Cisco, "It's not time for a guard change. Just who are you, and what are you doing here?" Spit flew, along with his words as he spoke. "Besides, you are not supposed to be in here."

"And you are not supposed to be playing at a game of chance," replied Cisco, nodding his head in the direction of the table. "Look, I'm bored. I have to go on duty outside in another hour. I was looking for something to do, and I think I've found it. How about letting me play until I have to go? Come on; it can't hurt, can it?"

The two looked at each other, and one shrugged his shoulders. "Don't see why not. Come on, then, sit down." The guard who had spoken kicked a small stool in Cisco's direction. The other guard looked as though he was about to add more to the conversation when he noticed Cisco's shoes. They were certainly not military issue and a dead giveaway that something was wrong. "What the hell? You're no guard. Who are you?"

Realizing he had only seconds to act, Cisco went into action. His movements were swift and silent. Just his exhaling breath, with a whistling sound, accompanied each blow. A leg kicked in one direction as his arm swiveled in the other—both connected with a cracking sound, followed by a soft thudding as the soldiers hit the floor. The result of Cisco's actions had two guards down but not out. One got to his feet rapidly and came at him from behind, while the other started to get up off the floor to help his comrade. Hearing the commotion, Tori and the small group burst into the room to help.

It was immediately evident that Cisco knew what he was doing, but Tori also saw that the second soldier was going for his gun. To have that go off would be like an alarm sounding, one that would wake up the whole place. "Cisco, stop him, behind you, look!"

Cisco was way ahead of her, and before she could move, his foot lashed out once more and rendered the man unconscious before he even knew what had happened. Turning to face the first soldier and do the same, Cisco felt the man's blow connect to his chin. It was a blow that caused him to take a few steps backward. Then, just as fast as the first blow had hit, the angry guard now aimed his other fist for Cisco's middle. Sadly, it connected also, and the pain was instant. He buckled over, trying to gasp for air, as the guard came forward to hit him once more. It looked as if the soldier had the better of the fight, but then he had never heard of self-defense or martial arts. In a sudden blur of action and a twist of his body, Cisco turned, bringing his arm above his head, and let his hand hit its mark full force. The soldier fell to the ground and did not move.

Tori ran forward, flinging her arms around Cisco's neck while asking him, "Are you all right?" Her hands turned his head, so he was facing her. She was examining his face, knowing he had taken a hard blow to his face. "You're bleeding. Here, let me see."

Cisco shook his head free of her grasp and touched his chin gingerly. His adrenaline was still high from the fight, and he found it hard to stand still. It was action that he craved, not a female fussing over him. His gut hurt, but his pride hurt more, and having gained his breath back, he spoke, sounding very serious. "Look, we don't have time to worry about a split lip, do we? That was too close, though; I'll give you that. Let's get the keys and get into those cells and do what we came here to do, okay? We can worry about me later."

Tori frowned but knew he was right. His lip could wait. "If you say so."

"I do." Cisco reached up for the keys that were hanging on the wall.

Lightly touching her hero's shoulder, Tori asked, "Is he all right? I mean... he's not dead, is he? You did wallop the man."

"He's not dead, but he's going to have one big headache in the morning, not to mention a good case of whiplash."

Chez Nez, who was right behind Tori, had overheard this expression and laughed. "Whip what? I saw no lashing from a whip, nice kicking and swinging of fists, though." Again, he laughed. "Now what?"

Cisco handed Tori the large metal ring that had about twenty keys or more hanging from it. She took it, but the joy of having the keys in her possession was soon overcome. What Tori saw before her made her heart fall. There was a long line of closed wooden doors on both sides of the hallway and still more down another hall. "How are we going to get them out? Which doors do we open? There are so many cells, and time is running out." Tori looked to Cisco as if he had the answer, but he did not. Instead, the Italian stepped forward and took the ring that held the keys.

He pulled on it until it opened, and the keys came off one by one. "Here you go, men, a key each." No one waited; instead, everyone took a key and started trying them on the locks, going door-by-door.

A few doors matched right off and were flung open. Then to Tori's surprise, some of the released men began helping while others stood to watch. All the time, Tori could hear men whispering directions. Every man understood the need to be quiet, and not one of them even looked her way. Not wishing to be left out and wanting to find Jean, Tori took one of the keys for herself. Then before attempting to find the cell it fit, she called out to Cisco softly. "I have to try. If you find him, let me know."

Chez Nez laughed. "Hurry up; you blasted slowpokes; we got plenty of cells to open, you know. Anyone find Boss yet?" Then he was gone from view, and Tori was left looking at the key in her hand.

THE open cells were damp and smelled of human waste and rotting food. Looking down inside one of the open jails, Tori could see the remains of what had been someone's meal slopped on the floor, and a bucket of waste sat in the back, with flies hovering over it. She frowned, held her breath, and wasted no time but moved on to the first locked cell she saw. Quickly, she pushed her key into the lock and turned her key. By sheer luck, it worked. Immediately she pulled the door open, and a man who she did not recognize pushed past her. "Thanks, lad. God… never thought I'd get out of that one. Here, someone hand me a key." He took a key from a man holding two and moved off to help. Tori smiled, as did Cisco from across the way. The man had thought she was a boy and never questioned his assumption, and that's what she wanted, wasn't it? No one was supposed to know she was Laffite's lady right then.

Several cells were open now, but there was still no sign of Jean, which caused her to worry. Had he been moved, she wondered? There was only one way to find out, and that was to open all the doors, every single one of them. As fast as she could, Tori began going door to door. She'd stop and call in the small slot-like opening used to hand the plates of food through to the occupants.

It was Jean's cell; Tori wanted to be found and opened as soon as possible. If the men had their Boss, they would listen to him, and then they would have a better chance if anything went wrong.

The second small window she called in located a response from one other she wanted to be found. It was her dear friend, Dominique, who called back at her. Tori lowered her head and looked through the small opening. "It's you!"

Dominique stepped forward, and for a brief second, the older pirate could not trust what he saw. Finally, shaking his head, he spoke as a father would to a child he loved, but had to reprimand. "Ah, Mon Cherie, why does it not surprise me that it is you? But you are taking such a risk, no?" He had a stern sound in his tone of voice, yet his beaming smile told another story. "I, for one, could think of no one I would rather have here to let me out of this stinking hole. So, open up and allow me to help find Boss."

"I don't have the right key. So, you have to wait a second."

Dominique always seemed to find humor in any situation, no matter how grim. He continued teasingly in French, "Pardon, Mademoiselle. Avez-vous un guide de Calabozo?" Then, for the first time that night, Tori found herself laughing softly as she replied, "Oui Monsieur. J'ai un bon guide de Calabozo. And you are going to get the hell out of here as soon as we get this damn door open." It was then she heard Jean's voice, and she turned to look at him. He was out, standing at the other end of the now-crowded hall.

Once again, their leader was giving orders and helping open the few remaining cells. Someone pushed Tori aside as they tried another key on Dominique's cell, and hearing the critical click; Tori turned to look again at the man she loved like a grandfather.

Cisco reached Jean before the Italian Captain or Tori and took him by the arm. "Monsieur, you and I have not met; still, that does not matter at this time. What does matter is that I must inform you that up until now, the plan to free you has worked because it is just that, a damn good plan. We will get to know one another soon, but until then, trust me and let me be the one to give the orders and get us all to safety. After all, I do know the plan, and you do not. For it to be successful, you have to listen to me. Oui?"

Jean looked at this man, who stood before him in a soldier's uniform, and disdain filled his expression. "I do not trust traitors, Monsieur. Even those who are helping me."

Cisco laughed at him. "No, Monsieur. Neither do I. I am not what it seems. Take a look around and ask some of your men if you do not believe me. I'm no soldier." He took off his coat and threw it to the floor. "Now, we have no time left to argue the point. You will have to do as you're told."

Jean could not believe the audacity of this stranger. Just who the hell did he think he was to give him orders? The privateer's aggravation not only showed clearly on his scowling face but also sounded in his growling. That this fool should assume he was not capable of escaping without his help was preposterous. He was about to hit Cisco when one of his men broke in between them.

"The changing of the guards. It'll be time soon, and we have to be gone before then because it won't happen; on account, Cisco here took care of them. They are sleeping off his blows and in no condition to show up to change anything. That said, if they don't show up, someone might notice. Remember that we all gave our word; we would try to get away without a fight. And if that's what we have to do, let's do it."

Cisco nodded his agreement. "Look, there is no more time left. We have to leave now—everyone for themselves once we get outside. Run for the river and the barges. The front door should be open, and all you have to do is run and be damn quiet. Once you are past the church, run like hell and don't stop. It's open ground there, and no time to take your sweet ass about it. Boats are waiting; now go!"

Quickly the jail area emptied. Men ran down the hall past the fallen guards and followed the directions of those waiting to show them which way to go next. First, they ran down one gallery and then turned to go down another, and finally through the open front doorway, and out into the night air. Once there, they ran for the cover of the shadows and the river.

Jean waited with Cisco to see all his men out of the cell area and to keep an eye, on the stranger, just in case he proved to be a problem. As the last four men raced by them, his eye caught sight of a young lad standing at the far end of the courtyard. He seemed to be looking around to make sure all the cells were open, something there was no time left to do.

The pirate was heading toward the lad when Cisco called softly to them both to hurry. Quickly he took account of the situation unraveling. A love reunion was not advisable at this point, and unless the anxious man acted, that is just what was going to occur. He pushed past the gentleman pirate and took hold of Tori's hand. Then, with no hesitation, he shoved her past Jean before either of them had a chance to speak, let alone get a good look at each other. Time was running out, and even though they were making their way to freedom, Cisco had a dreadful feeling, and in seconds, his feelings were confirmed.

They ran out into the night and immediately realized that they would not be so lucky as to escape without a fight. From down the darkened side of the wall, three soldiers appeared. Somehow, they had avoided being locked in with the rest of their platoon. How that had happened, Cisco could not imagine. He knew it was too late to run, and fear gripped his guts as a flash of everything coming undone took hold.

If not silenced in just seconds, the three soldiers would alert the rest of the camp, and who knew how many would heed their call. True, most should be locked in, but if these three weren't, then that meant others might be close. Cisco turned without thinking; he ran with all his speed and took down the first soldier like a modern-day football player. He hit him full force and, in seconds, was on top of him. While his fight ensued, Jean took on the second soldier, just as he reached for his sword. Not having a weapon himself, Laffite was glad he reached the soldier before he had a chance to use his.

Jean's first blow to the man's midsection sent him flying backward, and this gave the pirate time to look toward Tori, who he still assumed was one of his men. The younger pirate had pulled a small weapon from his belt and was about to take on a much older and far more experienced opponent. This was the third soldier who seemed to have appeared out of nowhere. For Laffite, there was a nagging in the back of his fast-moving thoughts as he helplessly watched the beginning of the fight ensue. Something about that rapier was familiar, but he had no time to worry about it just then. He needed to finish what he had begun and bring down the man who was once again trying to pull his sword.

"Remember," shouted Cisco as he faced his enemy, "do not kill him. At all costs, we have to leave with no one dead."

"Then I shall make short haste of this bastard; Jean called back. Then help you with yours, or the boy, he will need help, by the looks of things." Laffite stepped up; and knocked the first soldier to the ground with a mighty blow to the chin. Then before the man could stand, the pirate swiftly kicked his side, and while the guard was buckling, he raised the man's head and delivered the last punch that rendered him unconscious.

Quickly Jean turned and faced his two companions to see which was in need more. The young boy was fighting as he himself would have and showed skill enough, but apparently, the lad was inexperienced. He was making mistakes that an experienced pirate would never do. However, the Spanish stranger was doing just the opposite. The man was spinning around like he was dancing and motioning for the soldier to advance toward him. It could be this Cisco person did not know how to fight, and he did not understand how to disable the guard without killing him. Then to Jean's utter amazement, he watched as the Spaniard not only disabled but knocked his victim clean out with three swift actions. The last strange blows coming from his hands were not in a punch-like motion. It was more of a chopping kind of hit, and he used the sides of his hands, a thoroughly unorthodox method but one that worked.

"Laffite," shouted the stranger, you need to help her now. Don't worry about me, man. I only let this one up to have a bit of fun. He's down for the count now."

One word registered for Jean; the word 'her,' and as he looked on, he witnessed the boy's cap falling off and long chestnut-colored hair cascading down. This left no doubt that the boy was none other than Tori. She did not look his way but continued to battle with swift moves, and even though she was doing an excellent job, Jean could see she was tiring. One thought filled his mind, and that was to reach her side and protect her before it was too late. Jean began to move in Tori's direction and was halted by the one who had proven to be on the pirate's side after all.

"Jean, here, catch." Cisco had taken the soldier's sword and tossed it to the pirate who, with swift reflexes, caught it by the hilt. Now armed, he once again turned toward his lady, intending to step in and save her the horrible fate that was most definitely heading her way. "What the hell ever possessed you to act in such a reckless manner," the pirate mumbled under his breath as he began toward his wife? Jean knew better than to call out to Tori and distract her concentration at this critical time. Doing that would undoubtedly bring about her defeat and maybe her death. What she needed was his powerful blows, and she needed them right then if she were to live.

TORI had had no time to hesitate. She's pulled her sword from her belt and met the first blows from the soldier, who, with his own sword drawn, had rushed at her. Horror and terror hit home as Tori found herself in the midst of her first real fight. Unlike her spars with Dominique, she had no doubt that her opponent fully intended to wound or kill her. Whichever came first, he did not care, it seemed. He was only doing his duty, fighting to overcome her and win, thus preventing her escape. She, however, had no intention of allowing the man to gain the upper hand.

Laffite's wife was fighting to survive and terrified of making a fatal mistake because if she did, and he learned who she was, he'd use her to get Jean to surrender. She told herself that if she could just hang on, Jean or Cisco would come to her rescue. Both men were tops in the fighting department and would surely win their battles, thereby allowing them the freedom to come to her side. She'd heard Cisco call out to Jean and tell him not to kill the guard, and that had to mean he was about to win his fight, and that gave her hope.

Right then, however, her mind cleared of all else because to stray in her concentration would be fatal and something Dominique had told her she was never to do if she ever intended to win a match. As she battled, she could hear her teacher's words talking her through every action. It was like the old Frenchman was standing right next to her. "Thrust; now step back, that's the way — tip of the sword, up. Now swing, thrust," these were the instructions he was giving her, in her mind's eye. Several of her moves had caught the soldier off guard, and her confidence in her ability grew upon seeing that. She was doing so good that she found herself almost enjoying the fight and would have continued to do so if the soldier would just lay his sword down and tell her that she'd won. However, Tori knew this man was not about to do that, and this realization smothered her short-lived enjoyment.

Why was it taking Jean or Cisco so long, she wondered? Tori could hear them still fighting but dared not look. To take her eyes away from her opponent at this moment would be suicide. Every second counted now, and she realized this had indeed become her fight and hers alone. Tori knew there might not be enough time left for help to reach her. Therefore, she had no choice but to take a different approach to the situation or risk losing. Jean's wife had never dreamed that she might actually have to run her blade into anyone, and now that reality hit hard. Tori understood that it was run him through, or she might suffer a mortal blow herself. Her arms were getting heavy, and as she tired, her opponent sensed that he was gaining the upper hand. He swung his blade fast and hard, leaving her only a split second to react. She jumped out of the way of his thrust and spun completely around on her feet like she had seen Cisco do. It was this sudden movement that caused her hat to become dislodged and fall off. Without the support of the hat, her long chestnut curls came tumbling down.

The soldier faltered, shock registering on his face. This was no lad he was fighting; it was a woman. He screamed at her, "damn you, woman. You will die for this. No mere wench will ever get the better of me!"

Taking advantage of the moment, Tori swung hard with what she hoped would deal, such a wound, as to render the man useless. She aimed at his arm and slashed through his shirt, laying open a long gash that immediately turned his white sleeve blood red. To her horror, though, instead of dropping his sword in surrender, she saw how an added rage flooded him, instantly blocking any pain.

The blow had humiliated him and raised his anger, blinding him of all reason and sanity. To think that a mere woman was beating him was incomprehensible, humiliating, and unacceptable. Spitting at her through clenched teeth, he hissed, "You bitch, you'll pay for that." Then he came at her with a fury stronger than ever. He was using massive, hard swings, one after another, from one side to the other. They hit Tori's sword rapidly, with such intensity, that she only had enough time to block his next blow before preparing for the one that quickly followed.

For the first time during the fight, Tori's moves were pure defense, and not one opportunity arose for her to thrust or use any offensive actions. At this pace, she would not last long; no one could. So it was that Tori knew if she were to win, it would have to be right then while she still had the strength and wits to do so. The man was not thinking. Anger was clouding his judgment, and in that fact, she found hope.

Again, down came his sword connecting hard with hers. The clash vibrated up Tori's arm, hurting her shoulder. It was then that panic forced her to act. With no time left, her strength failing fast, she made her move. Instead of raising her sword to block his next blow, she raised it only halfway and moved forward instead of back. In a swift movement thrusting up and forward, she had the point of her blade at the man's throat before he realized what she was doing. He had not seen it coming, and by the time he realized what she was about to do, it was over.

"Drop your weapon, you bastard, or so help me, I will have to press the point home if you understand me? Do it now; drop it!" The tone of her voice, though shaking, was hard and cold.

The man could see that she meant what she said, but to give in to a woman, he would be the laughing stock of the whole garrison. How could he allow her the victory? His eyes narrowed in a dark frenzy as he began to calculate his next deadly move.

It was then that a male voice broke the silence that surrounded the area. "I believe the lady means what she says. You had best drop the weapon Monsieur because if you don't, then I shall have to help the lady in relieving you of it, and you don't want that, now do you?"

The man looked from Tori over to the person who had spoken up, and, seeing that it was Laffite himself, who stood there with a menacing look, he dropped his weapon and fell to his knees, begging for mercy. "Please, I had no idea he was a she, I mean, that she was a lady. You have to believe me. I would never have hurt her. I only needed to disarm her."

"Liar, you know you wanted to kill me." Tori pushed the point of her weapon into his skin, pricking the soft flesh and making him bleed.

Jean walked up to the man, and, looking at him, he saw nothing but a filthy lowlife that would have run his sword into Tori if he had had the chance. His temper was hot, and he had to vent it somehow. Hitting the man was one way to get even, and so hit him he did, over and over until the man's face was bloody and no sound came from him. When he stopped, Jean picked up the soldier's head and listened closely. Then, satisfied that he had not killed him, he let his head fall back. "Sleep well, you son of a bitch, and be glad I listened to my men; all need to live, they said."

Jean stood facing his wife, and their eyes locked on each other. Any anger he would have felt toward her at that point just evaporated. She was alive, and that was all that mattered. "You are the most stubborn, stupid, lovely creature, I know, but then that's why I love you." Looking at her standing there holding her sword in her hand, he found himself admiring the courage and talent she had displayed. The spirit with which she had fought and the skill with which she had done so truly amazed him. The fire that blazed in her eyes, the way her hair hung wild about her face, made her look every part, a lady pirate. She looked ravishing, and he was not sure at that moment in time which Tori he found more appealing, the lady or the pirate. He was so overcome by what he had just seen that if it had been under different circumstances, he might have very well taken her in his arms and shown her what emotions she had stirred in him right there. Instead, stepping forward, he wrapped his arm around her waist and turned to face their other companion.

Cisco laughed. "We have no time for romantic endeavors, no matter how hot you two are feeling. Come on, man, we have to run and hope they kept on waiting for us."

Jean grinned. "This man likes giving orders, does he not? Wise ones it seems, so come, my lady, we must follow him. Can you keep up? Your breathing is labored. If you wish, we can remain and hide; I still have many here in town who would take us in."

Cisco laughed but sounded very serious in his response to Laffite's statement. "You, Laffite, will do nothing of the sort. Tori can run and run she will, won't you?"

Tori laughed out loud. "Cisco, you know I will and can. So, let's run, okay?"

Tori and Jean ran then, following Cisco, who led the way. "Jean, old man, pick it up, let's move. If you would follow me, the rest of the escape awaits you, as your lovely lady has planned."

At the moment, his strange way of talking escaped Laffite, as his whole mind was intent on escaping safely. However, Tori had picked up on Cisco's modern English usage, and she told herself she needed to tell him to cool it once they were safely on the barge. The pirate's wife wanted to be the one to explain to Jean about her new friendship, not have him guess the truth, by Cisco's blunders.

In no time at all, the last of his crew were on the barge, being pushed further away from shore and safely headed home. They talked and laughed, each assuring the other that no one, not one soldier, had been killed. They had done it and had every right to be proud.

Tori sat, trying to catch her breath, while Jean looked at her and leaned closer. "It seems that I owe you my life, as well as my men. Did I hear right, your plan?"

Tori smiled and looked at him. "Well, not exactly all my plan. You will have to meet my new friend, and the rest will be explained to you. We will talk later." She turned her head and frowned at Cisco. "Loose lips sink ships," she whispered into his ear. "Get my point? I need to tell him about you, so watch what you say."

Jean just assumed Tori was thanking him for all his help, but when she looked back into the pirate's eyes, her expression had softened from one of excitement to love. "If you don't mind, there is something I have been missing, and I intend to collect." With that, she leaned over and kissed him. To Laffite's surprise, her kiss was not gentle but one that was full of passion. It was hungry and hot, not soft and romantic. She thrust her tongue deep inside his mouth and pulled him even closer. The message of the kiss burned into him. Then she pulled away slowly and, looking at him through half-closed eyes; she whispered, "You can count on more of where that came from, as soon as we reach Grand Terre, and you know what?" He shook his head as if to say no, I don't, and this made her laugh. "There will be plenty more for sure."

Tori snuggled into the safety of his arms and watched as the dark sky above her slipped by. The sounds of the men pushing and paddling with their long oars filled the night air. They were guiding the barge to safety across the Mississippi and into the bayous and toward home. Tori was physically and mentally exhausted, and as the sounds of the night faded into the background, she drifted off into a deep, exhausted sleep at last. While she slept, and they traveled closer to Grand Terre, Jean talked quietly with the man called Cisco.

Unable to contain himself, this new friend revealed some essential details of the night's affair. Jean learned almost all about what had happened since they had caught him. He heard how Tori, Cisco, and a friend of Cisco's, had come up with the plan, and as time passed, the more Cisco talked, the more Jean loved the lady who slept in his arms.

Over the course of the trip, a friendship between Jean and Cisco blossomed and grew deep roots that would last a lifetime. They had plenty of time to talk, and there was no stopping to camp. Instead, they continued through the night, guided by torches that marked the way. They were well into Barataria bay by dawn's light and moving swiftly on the outgoing tidal surge. Tori slept on as the sun rose higher in the sky, and Jean kept watch.

Cisco nodded off to sleep, and as his weary eyes closed, he smiled to himself. Loose lips, indeed. He knew he had, in the heat of the moment and excitement, maybe slipped up and used terms of speech that Tori understood but not so anyone else listening. Cisco promised himself he would not slip up again, and he knew why. He was not to be the person to explain who he was and where he came from. That, he was going to leave for Tori to do, as they had agreed. How was Jean Laffite going to react when he learned they were of the same time and that time was the future? He did not know, but he bet it was going to be one hell of a shock.

As they neared the home base, a voice rang out in the late

morning. It was the deep voice of Thiac, who had started to head back, after waiting so long, to see if everything was safe and well with the rest of the men. He pulled his little pirogue swiftly alongside the barge to see for himself that his main concern was indeed unharmed.

Jean motioned to him and, smiling down into the peaceful sleeping face of his lady, assured Thiac that she was unharmed, just sleeping.

"That's good, the little lady; she needs rest. Don't know how she been going about Boss. She hardly slept for days. Sure, is glad you back, Boss, now maybe she will rest and be a lady again, with you telling her what to do. This new Mizz Tori is awful hard on the heart and the mind."

"Thiac, this lady has never done what I told her to do, and you know what, I'm damn glad. Now, before we do or say anything else, there is something I want to do. I want to tell you that for what you have done, I am truly grateful."

Thiac grinned, his white teeth gleaming in the early morning light. He was happy; Tori and Boss were safe. Even his new friend Cisco was safe. "You don't need to thank me none. I just did what I was told and all. Seems to me we be even now too. That there be thanks enough. So, let's get us home cause that there, new friend of hers, and mine, he needs his rest too."

❧ Five ❧

John had handled his role expertly; even though he was worried most of the night about what was going on across town, no one suspected anything. It was late into the evening, when word reached the party at last. Two soldiers from the jails garrison arrived, with the news John had been waiting for, information that would tell him if all his efforts and plans had paid off.

ARRANGING the game and enticing the players had been hectic but straightforward enough. As luck would have it, one of the large plantation owners was in town, and John had informed him that he could arrange a private game of chance. It would be, he assured him, only players of his own standing and talent and all very discreet. Word of the upcoming game was then sent out via the coffee shop, where Edward was known to be that morning. Ensuring that the so-called private conversation was overheard, Edward soon learned that Mr. John Davis was looking for Mr. John Grymes.

An invitation to a private affair, to be held that evening, had to be delivered. Seizing the opportunity, Edward wasted no time. His appetite for gambling never ceased, and the chance to be in on a private game, one with high stakes, no doubt, was irresistible. He left at once for John Davis's hotel, confident that he would acquire an invitation one way or another.

From the moment Edward approached John at the hotel, with the excuse of finding out his credit standing, it became apparent to Davis that the man had overheard the conversation and taken the bait. John enjoyed listening to him and watched him squirm as Duval tried to ply information about the evening's events without looking too obvious. Finally, after letting him rattle on for a while, John spoke to him as if he had no idea that Edward was trying desperately to get himself invited.

Acting distracted, as if he were a man with a lot on his mind, John played his hand. Looking at his gold pocket watch, Davis made it seem as if he were not paying any attention to Edward at all. Then he allowed his expression to change as if an idea had just come to him. "Monsieur Duval, may I be so bold as to ask you for a large favor? I would normally use other discreet channels to gain such knowledge, but time has become an issue. I feel as if I can trust such a fine upstanding gentleman as yourself to ah… maybe assist me?"

"You may indeed, Monsieur, and please, I feel as if we have known each other long enough for you to call me Edward."

John just smiled and nodded his head slightly in agreement. The hotel owner thought this was rather like fishing. First, you hook him, and then you reel him in.

Thinking he was now on a first name basis and about to help Davis, Edward was feeling very sure of himself. After all, a favor done was a favor owed. He turned on the charm, and his words seemed to ooze from between his lips. "It would be my honor to assist you, and you have my word as a gentleman that whatever the matter pertains to, it shall be handled in the most honorable and discreet manner."

"Edward, my friend," John said, placing his arm around the dandy's shoulder and walking him over to a more private corner of the room. "It has come to my attention that you and our Governor are very close acquaintances. Indeed, I have heard it said that he holds you and your lovely lady in high regard. It is Monsieur Claiborne that I need to get this invitation to." He reached into his inside jacket pocket and took out the invitation. Twisting it around and around as if mulling over what to say, he slowly went on. "I was wondering if it would be possible for you to reach him for me? I have had no such luck in the matter. He is not to be found at home or at any other location that my contact tried. I'm afraid that I have no time personally to locate him at such a late hour, and he would be so disappointed if he missed this evening's affair."

Edward took the bait. "Oh, please do not think anything of it. It would be my pleasure to locate him for you, and I personally will pass on the invitation." Edward took the envelope from John's hand and, placing it in his jacket pocket; he continued, "I will take care of the matter right away." Again, he hesitated a second and then added what was really on his mind. "Although there is one small matter that…"

John cut him off mid-sentence. "That is very kind of you. These games don't happen often, and when they do, it seems that it's always spur of the moment. You know yourself when lady luck comes calling; she tells you that you feel lucky, you are lucky! One knows she will be at your side and my, how you want a chance to play. A man simply knows it's right to do so, does he not? That is how my client was this morning, insisting on a large, high-stakes game. Of course, I have to please my clientele, don't I? After all, that is what I have a reputation for doing," he said, laughing.

"Indeed, you do," Edward agreed. He momentarily waited before continuing, then not being able to contain himself any longer, he all but burst out his subsequent request. "May I be so bold as to inquire if this game would be open to a gentleman such as myself? Of course, I would understand if there is no room to accommodate me; it been such a late request."

It was almost laughable. Edward had played right into his hands, and ever the proficient actor, John looked genuinely horrified at having overlooked the obvious. "My dear Edward, please do forgive me. I should have known that you would want to join us. How very stupid of me. I said earlier that your credit is in excellent standing. I understand your plantation is doing very well this year." John started walking toward the hotel entrance, his arm still firmly around the younger man's shoulder. "It will be no problem at all to include you in on this evening's action. Consider yourself, my guest. We will meet in my private suite at around eight this evening."

Edward could not have been happier. Not only did he get himself an invitation to the night's activities, but he also seemed to have gained the owner of the fine establishment as a personal friend, something that up until then had looked highly unlikely. "Until this evening then. I will deliver your invitation to the Governor." He patted his coat pocket and curtly nodded his head. "Good day to you." With that, he swiftly departed, leaving behind him a delighted man.

So it was that Edward had been conned into thinking he had weaseled himself into the high-stakes game. John smiled; it had almost been too easy. Under normal circumstances, Davis knew Edward would have had his guard up. A dog like that always sniffed a con job out. But greed had blinded him and pushed his guard down, just like it had the commanding officers of the dragoons. A particular Revenue Officer, Walker Gilbert, and a Captain Andrew Holmes, both of whom hated Jean and were responsible for the tight security at the Calabozo, had also fallen victim to Davis's manipulation.

It had seemed justified and most prudent to include them in on the ruse. Greed had played its hand there also, just as he planned. With those two out of the way, John knew their men at the Calabozo would relax more, making Tori's job easier. Both officers were regulars at the tables but far from rich enough to join such a game, or so they would have thought. It had been merely a matter for John to explain that he would pay them a sizable amount of money upfront for their services. All they had to do was join the group for security reasons, of course.

A soldier's pay was not high, and an officer's not much better, so he knew they would jump at the chance to earn what he offered them. That was the bait. The hook came when John had explained that he did not want it evident to his guests that he had taken such security precautions to have them present.

"It would be most beneficial for all involved," John told them, "if you both joined in the game." He had explained that the Governor would be informed of their participation, so they did not need to worry. In fact, the Governor himself would look kindly on the arrangement; he was sure. Once he had settled their greedy little minds, John had reeled in his unsuspecting fish.

Only one guest had declined his invitation. While this did not disrupt the plan, John found himself baffled that such a man would pass up such a splendid opportunity. The attorney would always accept such an invite. Grymes had sent a note just before six that evening. It was brief and to the point. It merely stated that a particular young lady had required his services for the evening and that he and John would talk soon. John did not know who this mystery lady was, and he made a mental note to learn her identity because this female had to be very important for Grymes to miss out on the night's entertainment. The hotel owner smiled slightly. He knew that having personal information about his top clients was the best way to keep them returning to gamble. Knowing their likes and dislikes, weaknesses and strengths, were essential details. Catering to their needs was like chumming the waters; the fish kept coming back for more. Davis chuckled to himself; using fishing as an analogy was quite entertaining. He'd have to remember to fill Cisco in, as he was sure to get a kick out of it.

THE evening proceeded as planned. It had its ups and downs, but always the game continued. The house kept losing, just enough to feed everyone with winnings, some more than others, but always the results kept them playing.

The game was expertly executed; manipulated by his dealer, and with his discreet directions, it was perfection in play; so much so that John made himself a mental note to keep an eye on the man in the future. Cisco had taught him well, maybe a bit too much so. Knowing how to manipulate such a game could make the dealer a fortune, should he choose to use it for his own advantage during regular hours. Such an action would become detrimental to Davis's house profits. As for right then, though, the rigged game was proceeding as it should, and by the expressions of those involved, none were the wiser.

Edward hadn't had a streak of luck like he was having in a very long time. Sure, he had lost a few big hands, but all in all, he was ahead. Lady luck was on his side, and he loved it. The Governor and plantation owner sat looking very pleased with themselves too. Though not doing quite as well, the officers had more than they could have dreamed about, including money, wine, good food, and Davis's ladies hovering over them. Everyone was having, what they declared, to be a splendid game. That was until a knock came at the door, followed by the entrance of two very nervous-looking soldiers.

They quietly asked John Davis if they might have a word with their Commander, which of course, he quickly obliged. The whispering over in the corner of the room, amongst the small group, was like music to John's ears. The men looked too upset and nervous for it to be anything but bad news, and that meant things must have gone as planned. John understood only too well that he had to be very careful at this point. After all, he could never be connected in any way to the mishap that was about to be divulged.

"Governor." It was Captain Holmes who spoke. "Could I please have a word with you in private, Sir? It's about a very grave matter that has just come to my... ah... to our attention." He flashed Gilbert an outraged look. The bastard had pulled rank on him, making him the bearer of bad tidings. He knew Gilbert was trying to distance himself from the blame, not to mention from whatever adverse reactions the Governor would have.

Claiborne looked up angrily, laying the cards flat on the table. "You may not. Can't you see that I am in the middle of a damn good hand, and whatever you need... can surely wait?" With no response, he angrily snapped, "Well, can it or can it not wait?"

As he shifted from one foot to the other, the look of agitation on Holmes's face spoke for him. Seeing this, Claiborne impatiently snarled at him. "Oh, very well, if you must. You may continue. Quickly Sir!"

The Captain looked around the table. He was not sure, but maybe if he broke the news in the presence of witnesses, it would go easier for him. After all, it was not his fault, now was it? He had not been there at the jail. Some other fool's head would fall for this, not his. Holmes found himself silently thanking God for this small favor, and feeling a bit safer, he squared his shoulders and pulled himself to his full height. "Sir, if you beg my pardon, it is my duty to inform you that I have received rather disturbing news."

The Governor was at the point of exploding with exasperation. "I can see that, you fool. Now, get on with it."

"Yes, Sir. To the point then," he spluttered. "There has been an incident at the Calabozo. It seems… that Monsieur Jean Laffite has escaped."

Edward choked on his drink, spilling the wine down the front of his silk shirt, and John watched as the rich blood-red stain grew slowly across the dandy's chest. It was a stark difference from the pallor on his face.

As the color drained from Edward's face, the Governor's face did the opposite, his filled with color. It was then that Davis watched in horror as Claiborne's neck, which seemed to be bulging out of his collar, turned a deep purple. Then this plum color of rage rapidly crept upward, filling his entire face. Indeed, John thought, the man was close to having a stroke or heart attack. Why, at that very second, it looked to him as if Claiborne's head might explode.

With a burst of air and saliva, the Governor let go of his breath, roaring with rage. His fist slammed down so hard as to make the table shake. He rapidly pushed back his chair and stood to face the Captain. "What did you say?" He had screamed at the terrified man. Then trying hard to gain control of himself, he clenched his teeth. He was grinding them so hard that the sound was painfully audible in the silent room. His eyes narrowed to slits as the muscles in his neck contorted and flexed with each breath he took. Like a cobra, he hissed with the next question. Only his head moved toward the Captain, bringing his face within inches of touching the other. "How in God's name could you let something like that happen?" He then stepped forward, leaving no room between them, his chest pushing the Captain back as he cried out, "Just how did it happen? I want to know now! I demand some answers!"

Captain Holmes, genuinely shaken by the outburst and fearing for his own well-being, called on one of the guards, who had brought the news, to step forward and explain what he knew. The young lad, obeying his superior, stood at attention, looking straight ahead, as he repeated his tale. In a voice that trembled now and then, the man explained what he knew. "There had been not a sound or a warning, Sir," he told them. "It was as if Laffite had just walked out, Sir. In the men's defense, I might add that it is true that all the guards had been overpowered. Many still lay unconscious when I was dispatched with the news. None of them hurt beyond a thumping headache and a few broken bones. No one has yet been reported missing, and no one killed, Sir!"

Overpowered indeed, thought Claiborne. His temper seemed only to swell to new heights as he burst with indignation. "And just where in the hell were all the other men at this time, might I ask? We do have an entire garrison there, do we not? Are you standing there audaciously informing me that they were all knocked out?"

The young soldier's eyes moved to look directly at the Governor standing before him. He tried to clear his throat before answering, but his words still came out as a husky whisper. "Sleeping, Sir. They were all in their quarters for the night." Somehow, he found his voice then and spoke louder as if to confirm his following explanation. "Even if they had been aroused, they could not have helped. They were locked in Sir and the armory had also been barricaded. There was nothing they could do." He stepped back, fearing the Governor's next move.

Resigned to the fact that Jean Laffite had managed to escape, the Governor quietly and fearfully asked his next question. Claiborne's voice trembled as he spoke. "How many escaped?"

"Not one of the cells was left unopened. They all got out, Sir. Every last man is gone."

Claiborne once again lost control. He was beyond reason and stood yelling at the top of his voice. "Heads will roll for this." Then in a flash, he had his hands around the poor man's neck and was shaking him violently. Like a puppet on a string, he dangled the young soldier's body a few inches off the ground. The raving man's sheer strength easily hoisted the soldier and if he knew what he was doing or not, was anyone's guess. Holmes and Gilbert just stood there watching as the other young guard took cover behind two of the ladies. John and Edward moved quickly, fearing for the soldier's life. They pulled the Governor off the man, all the while trying to reason with him and bring him back to his senses.

It was Edward's voice of reason that finally brought calm back to the room. "Governor, please, it's not as if all is lost. Please, William, take a seat and let me explain." Claiborne slumped into his chair, physically and emotionally drained. He didn't even look toward his friend at this point.

Edward poured them both a drink and sat next to Claiborne as he spoke. "Monsieur Governor. It is not as bad as it seems." The opportunist always jumped at the chance to gain favor with the man while also aiding to what he hoped would be Jean's demise. "If I might add, it seems Jean and his men will be caught again, only with another charge to add to that of smuggling. This last folly of his will no doubt be of great help to you. Surely the masses will be swayed in your direction. Your conviction that he is no gentleman will be agreed upon. That he is nothing more than a hooligan pirate will be recognized once and for all. One can come to no other conclusions after his actions of tonight. After all, innocent men don't flee now, do they?" He slowly sipped his drink and let what he said sink in.

Seeing that the Governor was not entirely convinced, he went on smoothly and deliberately. "These new charges, and there will be many, won't there, Captain?" He looked toward the man, who simply nodded in agreement. "They will surely help in getting them all, each and every last one of them, convicted. The Laffite's are finished. After all," he smirked, "you still have all the proof you need in the warehouse. Jean Laffite and his men can be hunted down and brought in. Those who were not involved with the smuggling charge… all those down in their camp, at Grand Terre, along with Grand Isle." He took a deep breath before continuing. "Well, they can now be assured to be charged with aiding in his escape." Dramatically, he took a big swig of his drink, obviously reveling in the idea. "It will be quite enough to put the whole damn lot away, don't you agree?"

A smile slid across the Governor's face, and relief filled his voice. "You might have something there." Then with more conviction, he added, "Laffite might think he has won this round, but he has only hung himself and the rest of his crew; you are right there, my friend."

"Er… hmm…" Gilbert hesitated. Everyone turned to look toward the Revenue Officer. "Ah, to beg your pardon, Governor Sir, but there is more, I'm afraid." The small voice had squeaked from Gilbert in great difficulty.

He knew that the man would have to be told about the contraband sooner or later, and he being the Revenue Officer, would have that unholy duty. So better to get it over with, he reasoned, before the safety of those present. "You had best brace yourself because the news only gets worse, I fear."

"What else could possibly be worse? If you have more to tell, out with it. Blast it!"

"It's about the warehouse and the contraband inside. I have been informed that there has been a robbery. The merchandise is all gone. Sometime this evening, the place was raided, and well, the building is empty—not a sign of anything. Not even a break in the door or lock to show forced entry. It is as if nothing was ever in the buildings, to begin with."

This was more than Claiborne could stand. If what he had been told was the truth, he would be the laughingstock of the city. "No! I won't allow that bastard to get away with this." Jumping to his feet and once again slamming both his fists down on the table, he looked around the room at each and every person there. "Not a word of what has been said here tonight is to be repeated. Am I quite clear, gentlemen? John, I assume I can count on you for the silence of the ladies?"

"You may, and as always, you have my discretion and my confidence. I am sure, Governor, I speak not only for myself but also for each of us here tonight. You have our word, does he not?" John looked around the room at the heads, all nodding in agreement. "This is just a shocking situation. Shocking, indeed."

The Governor sat down in his chair, his hand shaking so violently that when he picked up his glass, the liquid inside threatened to spill. His head was swirling with turbulent thoughts, one after the other. One, however, surfaced above all others to become his primary concern. The events of this evening needed to be turned around somehow.

That bastard had to pay. "Edward, find me the State's Attorney. Grymes has to be reached. Tell him it is of the utmost importance that he meets me right away. I shall be waiting for him at my residence."

Edward was furious with Laffite. Not only had he once again slipped through their fingers, but he had also ruined the best card night he had had in a long time. Blast the man. He was like a cat with nine lives, but nine lives or not; even cats eventually die, he assured himself. "I shall leave at once, William. I will have Monsieur Grymes at your residence before the hour is out. Monsieur Davis, if you would be so kind as to take care of my winnings, I shall call for them tomorrow." With that, the dandy swiftly departed.

The evening had come to an abrupt end. Looking genuinely

shocked and very concerned, John escorted the Governor to the door. "If I can be of any assistance, please let me know."

"I will most certainly. Gentlemen, ladies, excuse me, please. I have important matters at hand to attend to." With that said, Claiborne was gone, accompanied by his officers and the guards from the jail.

The evening was at last over, and the room had been cleared, leaving John standing by himself in the now quiet surroundings. He closed the door and looked toward the table and the night's winnings. There was plenty of time to count up each gambler's total, and yes, he'd see that they all received a grand tabulation. However, for now, John just wanted to reflect and celebrate his great success in orchestrating and implementing the event. A happier man he could not have been. Slowly the hotel owner poured a glass of his finest champagne and toasted his friend's success. Ever the cautious one, the man reflected on all that he had heard and understood to have happened. It was then that he allowed himself to chuckle as he was confident that all those participating in the night's game suspected nothing.

There was one detail that needed his attention, though. It was a fact that both intrigued and baffled him. No one, including Claiborne, knew of Grymes's connection with the Laffite brothers, so the man could have safely joined the party. It was most unusual for the attorney to avoid him, let alone turn down such an enticing invitation. Sobering a little, John found himself hoping that Grymes knew what he was doing, and again he wondered just who the man had chosen to be with?

IT took Edward hours to locate the State's Attorney, doing so by accident in the end. He had tried the man's residence twice, each time to find it empty. However, on his last visit, he ran into the man as he was returning home. At first, Grymes had been in a splendid mood. His greeting was all smiles until he learned that the Governor required his presence immediately. After that,

Grymes became disgruntled when Edward would not divulge the reason as to why he had been summoned. His jubilant mood had soured, and the last thing he wanted was for Edward to accompany him. Whatever the Governor wanted to see him about was going to remain between them, especially if the reason he'd been called upon had anything to do with a particular secret, one that the attorney had gone to great lengths to keep concealed.

FOR most of the morning, Governor Claiborne and the State's Attorney were unavailable to anyone. Rumor had it that they had been in the Governor's study putting together a legal document concerning the Laffite's. By the time the day ended, the news was all over New Orleans that Jean and his men were free once more. It was announced that the Laffite's and twenty-five of their men were released on bond, awaiting trial. As far as William was concerned, Grymes had come up with a stroke of genius no matter what Edward had thought. The attorney had merely explained that they had nothing substantial to press forward without the contraband as proof of the smuggling. Therefore, delaying the court hearing was in the States' best interest. It was the only way they could buy time to gather other evidence and issue different charges. Besides, by doing this, the American could keep the truthful facts that the pirates had escaped custody and taken back all their merchandise. If this got out, he knew he'd be laughed at and maybe even replaced.

FOR hours after Grymes left him, Edward and a few others joined Claiborne and were all informed about the details that had transpired between the Governor and the States Attorney. Edward had been furious at first but then decided the situation could be turned to his own advantage. Every opportunity the dandy had during the casual gathering, he eluded, to the circumstances the Governor had been forced to take. In this way, the man's mood did not lighten. William continued to seethe, mainly when there was mention of the pirate and his ongoing activities and ever favorable reputation with a majority of the populace.

It was common knowledge that Laffite often sailed into the very heart of the cities port and was never confronted. The tax collector, it was said, always turned a blind eye when certain vessels docked. Claiborne even heard it was being said that Laffite held the key to the back door of New Orleans as well. Once rumors of the man's escape spread, and they would, if they hadn't already, there were going to be merchants in the city who were not going to be happy with him.

Duval would not ease up; he had to get the American to act against the Laffite's. "William, let me speak for all of us here." Edwards's tone was neutral at best, and if the American politician had paid attention, he would have seen the young Creole was placating him. "You were wise to listen to Grymes; he has at least salvaged this unfortunate situation. You will no doubt take the opportunity to gain the upper hand and gather evidence that will convict the swine once and for all." Those in the room audibly supported Edwards's remarks.

Claiborne rubbed his eyes. Many of the American merchants and quite a few Creoles in town were already telling him that if Jean kept his illegal business growing much longer, the pirate would monopolize the city's import trade. 'The pirate might as well own them all,' the voice inside his head shouted! William knew he had to do something soon about this horror of a situation but felt helpless to do anything more than he'd already accomplished. "Edward, if word leaks out that Laffite escaped, my job will be in serious jeopardy. Everyone must believe they are out on bail. Do I make myself clear?"

"You have our support, Sir."

"Do you think they will they accept what has been declared?"

Edward grinned slightly. "Most will, I am certain. We can but hope to avoid that anyone learns the actual truth. Should someone try to spread such lies and lies, I will call them; I will see to it that they are silenced. Any one of us gathered here will no doubt agree with me. Gentlemen, I am correct in this assessment, am I not?"

All agreed, and for a brief second, William's expression showed relief. It was then that Edward added another thought, a shot across the bow is how he thought of it. Keeping the stupid Governor stirred up was his intention. "Shame he is allowed to walk our streets without any risk of being accosted."

"Agreed, declared another. The man is guilty. Lock him up and put an end to it. The is no need for this sham or lack of justice."

William became more agitated just as Edward planned; he watched as Claiborne's face reddened with embarrassment and anger. "I should call Holmes in and demand they go and arrest the bastard. You are right, Sir."

One of the other merchants who had joined the small group spoke up. "I am afraid, Governor, that would do you no good. From our understanding of the details spoken here today, all evidence was absconded. Without the stolen goods, you have nothing to charge him with and even less time to retrieve what is necessary. It is my assumption that the merchandise will be sold at auction long before we can declare any of it as stolen goods. I, for one, will have to cut my losses."

The first gentleman who had spoken laughed at the merchant. "I'll be damned if I will pay twice for what is mine. We shall attend the auction ourselves and confiscate the lot of it; yes, that's what's needed. William, with your order, the garrison can accompany us, and even yourself..."

Edward did not like the way things were going. For a start, he much preferred any action taken, be recommended by himself. The dandy had to remain as one of the most trusted friends and advisors. "William, may I? It would be a most unfavorable, move I can assure you. Most of the respectable citizens of the state attend those sales. Would they not have to be arrested also? Besides, it's common knowledge that most of the homes in New Orleans, including your own, have merchandise purchased in this way. I am afraid, Sir, your hands are tied right now until the unfortunate events of his escape have been dealt with. Calmer actions are now, may I be so bold as to say, are needed to be calculated and enforced."

Claiborne had no choice but to take Edward's advice. After all, he made sense. Grymes's idea had allowed him a way to cover the embarrassing breakout and appease most of the merchants, thus saving his reputation. He'd simply assure them all that the States Attorney knew what he was doing. If it went wrong, let Grymes take the blame, not him. "You are correct as always, my friend. Let us have a drink and maybe start to calculate some of the actions that I will have Grymes draw up.

AFTER the States Attorney had left the Governor's residence and was riding back to his establishment, Grymes told himself he had bought Laffite some time, but it was now clear that things would have to change radically. The Laffite brothers could not keep going on the way they had. He had no choice but to talk with Jean as soon as possible. Also, he realized that he had better take care of his own affairs. Last night stood as a warning, one he would not ignore.

By the time Edward returned home to Simone, his sadistic temper was soaring. All day, he had stewed. Try as he might to get that fool, Claiborne, to go after that bastard Laffite, the meddling Grymes had stepped in.

Simone heard him storming up the stairs and braced herself. When he entered the bedroom, it was very evident that his mood was raging dangerously. To her, he seemed to be on the verge of losing any control he might possess. Edward slammed the door behind him and stood clenching his teeth, his features frozen in a thunderous expression. He spat his words out contemptuously. "It seems, my dear, that your lover, that bastard pirate, has once again slipped through our hands."

A sudden chill hung in the air as his words sunk in. Then, gasping, Simone whispered, "What in the hell are you talking about?"

"I will tell you, my dear. He escaped, got help, and walked out of the Calabozo with his men, too, as simple as that. While he walked, others stole back what they had been caught with, and now we have nothing. He is out and strolling the streets of this fine city, a free man yet again. Walking around as if nothing happened, I am sure of it."

"You have seen him?"

"No, I have not seen him. Can't you follow me here? It goes without saying that he will." Edward watched as Simone's mouth hung open in disbelief. "Oh, but wait, my dear, it gets worse. To conceal his humiliation at not being able to keep that rogue under lock and key, our esteemed friend, the Governor, had Grymes draw up a document saying that the Laffite's are out on bond. Can you believe it? Out on bond! What a laugh! Simply released! Not escaped and hunted as he should be." His face was a glowering mask of fury.

Simone's lips thinned with scorn, shock yielding quickly to anger, and the insolence was ill-concealed in her tone of voice. "And, you let William be smooth-talked into agreeing with this bond deal? You, stupid idiot, I can see I have given you far too much credit in the past—credit for your so-called control and manipulation over our dear American Governor. Seems without me right there, at your side, you are useless. I have to be with you to tell you what to do, don't I? You imbecile," she sputtered. Simone was so furious she could not go on.

The sudden silence that hung between them seemed somehow to shatter any remaining control Edward had. Transfixed, she coldly stared at the dandy, watching in horror as his whole demeanor grew in severity. His eyes narrowed, pulling the skin surrounding them tightly in opposite directions. This movement formed deep, angry furrows. Hatred and rage converted her lover's face into that of a demon. He was just standing there, slowly transforming as he clenched and unclenched his fists that hung rigidly by his side.

A growing alarm rapidly obliterated her anger. It rippled through her body, freezing her to the spot. As Edward started toward her, a wave of apprehension swept over her. Desperately she looked around for a way to escape; then, finally, Simone realized what she had done. Too late to take back her words, sheer terror took hold. Without warning, he flew at her, his hands quickly seizing her upper arms.

Her lover's face was so close; she could feel his hot breath escaping his mouth in rapid bursts; like a bull about to charge, he blew at her. She shut her eyes against the horrible image before her, knowing all too well what was to follow.

For one split second, he tried desperately to control his emotions. "You bitch," he said. Two small words were all it took to unleash the fragile control he had held. All his pent-up frustrations and rage finally found an outlet.

Simone's stomach lurched, and she stiffened under his grip, knowing what was coming. It was one thing to play rough, to suffer pain for pleasure but quite another to suffer his wrath when his anger took hold. When he was in such a rage, the last emotion on either mind was dealing or receiving pleasure.

Edward hit her then. Over and over, he slapped her. First, in her face, splitting her lip. Then came a full blow to the side of her head, knocking her flat on the bed. In vain, she tried to curl into a ball in an attempt to protect herself from his blind rage as he continued his onslaught. He ripped at her dress, tearing it away from her skin, exposing her bare flesh to his fists.

Simone gulped hard, hot tears rolling down her face, were mixing with her own warm, sticky blood. Her only hope was to reach him somehow with words because her strength was not enough to ward him off physically. Choking out screaming pleas, begging him to stop, fell on deaf ears, and to her horror, it seemed that Edward was enjoying himself because each blow that he dealt her was swiftly followed by another one far more violent.

In the end, Simone knew that she would have to change tactics if she was ever going to get him to halt his onslaught, and so from strength and cunning that she alone understood, the woman completely reversed her actions. Her tortured sob, her declaration of undying love for him, her begging for forgiveness over and over finally stopped the assault.

They stared at each other across the icy silence. The widow's lower lip trembled as she fought back her emotions of self-pity and struggled to keep from letting anger take hold.

Edward had used his fists on her before, but never to this extent, and never without warning. Simone found herself thinking it should have been he who deserved to be on the receiving end of such treatment, staying out all night, coming home when the day was over. Then like clouds parting, letting light sweep away the hell of only moments before, another thought entered Simone's mind. His clothes reeked of cheap perfume. Could it be possible, she wondered, that he had been unfaithful? Had guilt triggered his rage? Or could it be that he no longer found her attractive… that he no longer needed her at all? Suddenly, she was more frightened of losing him than she was angry at his cruelties.

Maybe he was tiring at times and brutal beyond belief, but she needed him. She could not let him slip away. Simone would not let that happen. The widow had to get him to marry her, to become Madame Duval. Oh, she had worked so hard for so long to gain respectability, something that she finally realized she would never have had with Jean. Sure, he would be good for the odd rendezvous like in the old days, but it was with Edward that she stood to gain everything with. Then she assured herself, as far as ever risking her standing with him, that would never happen. No amount of desire would drive her into Laffite's arms.

Duval saw the confusion on her face, a face that was swelling and turning a nasty shade of purple on one side. His voice was full of anguish, and with his trembling hands, he reached out gently, stroking at her bloodstained tears. "Forgive me. I was out of my mind." Finally, the realization of what had just occurred was sinking in. He had severely beaten the one person who was on his side. Simone was the one person in the world that truly understood him. How could he have done this? The corner of his mouth twisted with exasperation. She had asked for it, he told himself. He was not the guilty one here, was he? Simone had pushed him too far, and yet looking at her now, he was torn between hate and, God help him, lust. The dandy lowered his head, brushing her lips lightly with his. The bloody metallic taste mixed with the salt of her tears caused a strange reaction. To his surprise, it was exciting, and instead of being repulsed, the flavor acted as an aphrodisiac.

Simone recognized the change in him immediately. Her rigid body relaxed, her arms reaching for his jacket. Slowly she removed one article of clothing, then another, all the while kissing and caressing him. She would show him that she was the only woman who could give him what he needed, but one thing was sure, he would never know of the malice that she held for him at that moment. How was it, she wondered, that one could hate him and want him at the same time? Could it be that, on some level, she cared for him?

The passion in his eyes that raked her body stirred a far stronger emotion than hate, causing her to question further what feelings she was experiencing at that moment.

No sooner did she begin to wonder then another idea filled her mind. Simone convinced herself it was love. Yes! She told herself she hated and loved him at the same time. She knew beyond a doubt that she wanted him now and always. With this revelation came a renewed determination. One thing was sure, he was going to be hers, and no one would ever again take away what was rightfully hers.

Edward was no longer feeling any remorse for his actions. He did not even pity the woman in his arms. Simone had a sexual magnetism that made him feel like more of a man than any other woman ever had. Her very nearness kindled feelings of excitement and desire that made her irresistible, even now, battered and bruised; it did not matter. For him, he only saw what he wanted, and Edward wanted her. Duval entered her hard and fast, taking her, as he would have a common whore. The man didn't care that she dragged her nails across his skin. He didn't care that she was digging deep into his back, leaving angry, bloody lines. All he cared about was the pleasure he was feeling and nothing more.

Edward knew Simone had intentionally set out to inflict pain and hurt him as he had her. But, instead of causing him pain, she had aroused his animal instincts of pleasure. The man held no personal feelings or emotions when he was acting as he was then. Sex was a need for him, a hunger that had to be fed, regardless of with whom. To admit that he cared a lot for Simone was unthinkable. It would give her control. No, he would use her and continue to use her whatever way he wished, he assured himself.

He satisfied himself as his body gave a sudden shudder. Finished and exhausted, he rolled off her and lay on his back, breathing heavily. She lay still looking at him as he turned his head her way. Their eyes locked, and each recognized the inevitable. Words were not necessary; their feelings showed in their expressions and were felt in their souls. There was some tangible bond that drew them together. It did not matter if it was called love or hate. They were caught in its web and would always be so.

For right then, in total silence, they were content for the time being. The blood from their wounds was drying on their skin and the bedsheets. The bruises on their battered bodies were not half as bad as the wounds; each had inflicted upon the other's inner being. Neither would trust the other ever again, at least not in the way they had, and as Simone drifted off to sleep, she swore that one day very soon, she would be the dandy's wife. He owed her that much and more, for all she did for him and for all he did to her, all she suffered at his hands.

BACK on Grand Terre, Jean, Tori, and Cisco sat on Jean's verandah, watching the sun slowly sink on the horizon. The coastline's soft sounds were overshadowed by the resounding clamor of the wild and frenzied jubilation coming from where Laffite's men resided. It was evident to those listening that the men were all well into their victory celebration. And according to the pirate, it was a rambunctious party that could go on for an indefinite amount of time.

Jean had learned that nothing and no one would stop their drunken antics until they dropped from the sheer exhaustion of it all or until the rum and other liquors available ran out. So, upon arriving safely back, their Boss had declared that all the spirits from the warehouses was to be distributed amongst his well-deserving comrades. As for the safely stowed merchandise they had retrieved, he would hold a council meeting in the coming days to decide what was best for everyone. Grand Isle and Grand Terre exploded with joy, friendly banter, and mayhem upon hearing this.

Cisco was more than pleased with how things had turned out, but sitting there and not joining in the party was not his style. "Tori, before I leave you and Jean to join in the fun, is there any more of this vintage wine?"

"Vintage, you are a hoot. Don't worry; I will go and get one more bottle and not because you want more, but because I do." She was laughing as she left the veranda to go inside the house.

Jean chuckled. "You know Cisco; you earned it. You may have all the wine you wish. Call it my way of thanking you for everything. Most of all, for taking care of my wife."

Cisco smiled and nodded his head. "It was my pleasure for sure. Not always an easy job, taking care of her. Like I told you, in the tavern was the wildest; still, we got our men. Sorry, your men."

"I shall talk to Thiac tomorrow. His part played a stronger role than I had guessed. Important too. Intimidation, you needed that. To think that you and my wife planned this all, and it succeeded."

"Well, of course, it did. Besides, I had a friend get us the info we needed. I will thank him for you. I still can't believe I got to get the famous hero of New Orleans out of jail. Me, Cisco, friends with the pirate, who helped Andrew Jackson win the Battle of New Orleans."

Cisco had just slipped up without realizing it, and Jean, who was paying close attention, picked up on what he said immediately. "Battle? And which battle was that?

"You are a hero because, without you and your men, not to mention all the weapons you supplied, good old Jackson would have lost, and the British would..." Cisco stopped talking. He looked closely at Jean's expression, and then it hit him. "Oh shit. She hasn't told you about any of this, has she?"

"Told him what?" Tori was standing in the open doorway with a bottle in her hands. She saw they had been talking about something that had Cisco looking like he needed to run away and Jean as if he was ready to throttle someone. Laffite's wife handed him the bottle. "Here, pour me a glass and explain what you two are going on about? If it's the incident in the tavern, trust me, I was perfectly safe."

Jean turned in his chair and leaned his head to one side before pulling gently on his goatee. "We were talking about my role in a battle with a certain Andrew Jackson. Something that you have seen fit to keep from me, it seems."

Cisco interrupted. "Oh, man, I am sorry, Tori, really I am. I just assumed you had told him." He was genuinely sorry but more worried about catching hell from her. He stood up and looked from Jean back to Tori. One thing was clear to him, upset had arrived on the porch, and that meant he'd better disappear right then. "Well then, you two will have much to discuss, and I'm sure that you don't need the likes of me getting in the way. If you would be so kind as to excuse me, folks, the rollicking sounds that drift this way are calling me and my many talents. I think perhaps, I will join in and let you two enjoy the rest of the evening alone."

Cisco shook Jean's hand, and without thinking, he leaned over and kissed Tori on her cheek. He hugged her and held her close for a few seconds longer than seemed right to Jean. Then before the pirate could say anything to Tori's new acquaintance, the man winked at his wife, then saluted them both and departed.

Jean had been watching this display closely and found their familiarity just a little stronger than he would have liked. The two seemed to have formed a very close bond in such a short amount of time. Just how close, he dared not allow himself to imagine.

"You like him, don't you? I have seen the way you look at him." His words slipped out before he had a chance to think about what he was saying. "His actions confirm to me that he cares too."

"Yes, I do like him. He helped us when I didn't know what else to do or where else to go." She was puzzled by his sudden change in attitude. "You do like him, too; I know you do."

"It's not that I do or don't. I have not had the chance to get to know him and what he is up to. He is quite a character; you have to admit that." He wished he could stop, but he had to know what was happening here because his instincts told him something was definitely occurring. "It's how you two, look at each other. It's as if you are not telling me everything. I get the feeling that you both are hiding something."

Tori looked away from Jean. She knew that she had best tell him now, but how would he take it? On top of learning, she had kept specific historical facts from him; this all could be too much. He had a right, though, and for better or worse, she had to talk. "You are right. I am keeping something from you, besides certain historical facts, that is. So, hear me out, ok? We both are... this is hard... it's just that I don't know how you will take it. Cisco wanted to tell you himself, but he felt it would be easier coming from me. I have been waiting for the right time and now seems to be right."

Jean could feel his heart beating faster inside his chest. Had she fallen in love with the dashing young man? Impossible, he thought quickly. But, what other reason could there be for their closeness?

Could it be possible that they had been physically involved? Had Cisco taken advantage of her and her loneliness? Anger flashed through his body at the possibility. He told himself to remain calm, something easier said than done at that moment. His grip on the glass was turning his fingers white, and he dared not say a word for fear of the anger it would release. He had to let her talk first. He had to know, but God, if it were indeed what he feared, he would sail on the next tide. He could not bear to think of losing her to another man and damn it to hell; he owed that man his life! His hands would be tied; diplomacy would dictate so."

Tori turned to face him as she spoke; there was excitement in her voice as she hurried on. "This is sort of difficult for me to explain because I find it hard to think you will believe me. You will have to, that's all, and anyway, after you get to know him better and talk to us both, well, you will see it's the truth. Jean, Cisco, is like me. What I mean to say is… he is from my time. Jean, he's from the future!" There she'd done it. Now all she had to do was wait and see how the pirate took to the idea.

Jean did not know whether to jump for joy or to be jealous that this man had something in common with her that he did not. While acceptable, this news meant that Cisco would have a special relationship with his lady, which he could not partake in. Still, the pirate told himself this bond they shared was something he could learn to live with. Besides, it was not that he didn't already have an idea about the man; his actions and speech had subtly hinted at his origins. The way he spoke when his guard was down. He'd thought maybe the young Spaniard had picked up on some of Tori's ways; now he knew better.

The relief on his drawn face was evident, and Tori saw only too clearly that he had thought something far worse. To think that she might have been hiding something else was hilarious. "You fool!" she said, laughing. "You thought that I… you thought that we… slept together, didn't you? No, it's worse, you thought that Cisco and I had…"

"Call me the fool, but what else was I to think? I never would have guessed that what you were keeping from me was so innocent. From your time, you say? I have to admit that I had a feeling he was different. The way he expresses himself and the terms he uses now and then reminded me of you. I guess I assumed he was copying you. Your time, you say? Now I have two of you to contend with, and Madame, it will be my pleasure to do so, you can be assured." Jean opened the new bottle of wine and filled her glass. Then he filled his before placing the bottle on the table and picking up both glasses; he continued. "I think, my love, you will need this. You have a lot more explaining to do now we have cleared that small matter up. No more secrets, that was our deal, and it seems that you have broken that bargain."

He handed her the glass, and she gladly took it. There was no getting around it this time. Tori knew she had to tell Jean all she knew of his history. "I am sorry, but I didn't know when would be a good time to tell you about the battle and where he came from... Cisco that is... and as far as the battle goes, I wanted to, but if I were gone, you know, back to my time, history would go along, as it should. If I stay, I might mess it up by explaining things that happen before they do. It doesn't matter anymore anyway. I can see that now. So, what do you want me to tell you?" Tori was nervous, and it showed by the way she was racing on without stopping to think.

Jean reached across and stroked the side of her cheek. "Everything you know, and this time be honest."

"You are angry with me; I see that, but can't you understand my position?"

"I do not wish to understand; I wish to hear what you know. A battle sounds like a fact that I should know of. First, though, did you know about my arrest? That would be a part of your history, no?"

"God, no! If I had known, I would have told you. You have to believe me."

"But, explaining that fact to me, it would have changed history. This is something we both know you worry over. So maybe, you let me and my men get arrested and thrown into those cells because you also knew I would get out."

"I did not! I don't know every goddamned thing about you or what you did. I love you, love you more than history, and would never want you in that horrible place. If you don't know that by now, you don't know shit!" Tori drank the entire contents of her glass and handed him the empty. "I will have another if I may?"

Jean took her glass from her. Tori had made an excellent point. He did know how much she loved him. The problem was, he also knew how much she missed her child and her own time and how she feared greatly about changing things in this time, thereby changing things in hers. "I am sorry, my love. It is true, though; you do worry."

"I do. But I can see that you won't let this drop, so I will tell you all I know." She pulled the wicker chair closer to Jean. "My glass, please. Call it liquid courage."

"You have no need of courage, Tori. You have shown more courage in the past twenty-four hours than most women; no, all the other women I am acquainted with, and I have known many." A grin filled his face, and his tone of voice was lighter. It was as if he were trying his best to make light of the situation and alleviate any apprehension she might be feeling.

Tori sighed, "I suppose you are right there. I did fight my first sword fight and rather well. I will admit I would have had a bit of trouble poking my point home… I don't care to kill anyone."

A frown crossed his brow. "I blame Dominique for putting you in such danger."

"Oh, no, you don't. I made him teach me. He promised he would, and he did, and I did it so I could ask you for a match and show you all I learned. I never dreamed I would use my talent in the way I did. Besides, if Dominique had not taught me so well and I had not had the sword, the foil, or whatever you call it, made for me, well, I might be dead. By the way, I had no idea about the sword until Thiac gave it to me, right before we set out to get you and your

197

men. I had a short duel at the camp, but you can ask him about that. I can tell you; I proved myself enough to let him leave me be."

"Another good point, I suppose. I will still have a talk to my... to Dominique. Now, you need to explain to me more about how you came up with the plan to get my men and myself out of an impossible situation. Who else helped? Cisco mentioned another?"

Tori knew what he wanted, and she also remembered her promise. She had to change tactics fast so that Jean would drop his line of questioning. "I thought you wanted to know about the battle?"

"Ah, I see you are not ready to reveal your comrade..."

"Cisco's comrade, not mine, and you are correct. I gave my word."

"Well, you may keep your word." Jean hid his amusement by pulling on one side of his mustache. He had a good idea who this mystery man was. After all, he had heard how John Davis had paid a visit to Grand Terre. For the time being, though, he would keep that to himself. "So, tell, what is ahead for me, from this point forward? All you know and the truth. Every detail of historical facts you recall. No more holding back, agreed?"

"I will tell you all I know, and it's not that much, really. Like I told you, I am not from this area. In my time, I lived... oh; you know all that. Look, you are famous because you were, one, a pirate... two, you helped out Andrew Jackson, and we beat the British because of that. You were given a hero's celebration. Then, sometime after that, I think maybe a few years, I am not sure... you sail to a place, I know as Galveston. There you set up your headquarters and became very rich. There, that's it. Oh, and I think maybe, you were arrested more than once, but I don't know for sure."

"Hah! You told me you had no idea I was to be arrested, and now you tell me I am arrested twice."

"Hold up there. I was telling the truth. I had no idea, but Cisco knew, and I did not meet him until after you were locked up, so there."

"And, Cisco knows more? I shall have to talk to him."

"It won't do you any good. He knows about as much as I do—no good asking him for dates either. As I said, we are clueless when it comes to those. He will tell you that the cottage, the one Pierre keeps, the one in front of the blacksmith shop, is a bar, a tavern in our time. You know that already because I told you. As to the history you want, beyond what you now know, we can't help you."

"This battle with the British. Do you know when it is?"

"Sorry, I don't. What part of we don't know the dates, don't you get? Look, I can't tell you what I don't know. I have given you all I can." Tori looked at her glass and waited for his response. She was expecting more questions and prayed he did not push her for John Davis's identity.

Laffite sat, looking at her. Tori had spoken the truth; this he knew by her tone of voice and expressions. His love was upset, and he was making her more so by his continued bombardment of questions. They were questions she had no answers to; that was obvious. He'd confirm with Cisco that no dates were known because, without dates, the information was not so helpful. They would just be speculating about something, and often that did not aid anybody. One could imagine things to come, but there was little to be done without tangible information. Right then, however, he could do something to help matters, and that was to ease the tension between them.

Tori needed to change the subject. Get their minds off all the history that lay ahead and bring them back to what would be happening in the days to come. Better she did that quickly because she knew a tiny bit more about her pirate, facts that she intended to keep to herself right then. So far, he had believed her, but to keep on talking about his future role, could weaken her resolve. Tori did not want him to ask her for more details. It was not the time to tell him, and besides, it wasn't anything that he needed to know right that moment, nothing that could or would change his outlook.

Jean broke the silence between them. "It is best if I hold an auction soon, I think. It's something to do and something to look forward to. The men are going to need to keep themselves busy after this. Much of what is stored belongs to them anyway. What is paid for by the hotel owner, John Davis, well, some will remain his, and as for the rest, I shall give the man his money back and the chance to bid first on items he still desires. My men can't make use of the finery, but most will welcome the gold that it brings." Jean had observed her closely upon the mention of Davis; however, he saw no indication that she was about to mention the hotel owner's role in the escapade that had freed him.

Tori had listened to him and could not believe he had just dropped his interrogation as he had. Knowing Jean, though, she understood the matter was not over, just delayed a bit. No way was she about to interrupt him, though, for fear he'd jump right back into wanting explanations of things she could not or would not talk about. Instead of talking, Tori gazed into her glass and continued to hold her silence.

"This subject bores you?" Laffite had asked the question sounding genuine. "If you wish to talk of something else."

"No, please continue. I was simply thinking I have never been to a sale."

Laffite grinned at her. "January is always a good time to make certain merchandise available at the Temple. People are in town and will attend such an event." He slapped his leg. "Yes, there will be a short meeting of our council, where I will tell those attending of my intentions. It will be a meeting to keep that Italian on his best behavior. He feels as if I owe him for his part in the day's past. While I feel thankful for his role, I will in no way cut my men out of what should be shared by all, even by those who took no role."

Tori watched as he refilled his glass. She recalled that the area the Laffite's held their auctions was known as the Temple. Even the airboat Captains had spoken of the location, not that she could ever remember seeing the place. It was known that the pirate used the site because of its proximity to the city. What would it be like to witness such an event in person, she wondered? Then it hit her; she'd kept that piece of knowledge from him too. The fact that he was telling her something she already knew about reminded her to go slow because this what to tell, and when, was becoming more complex. For the moment, she was only interested in this sale he was planning because it could be fun to witness. Until now, Tori had not been allowed to attend such a sale but felt that she might be able to this time; she'd feel him out on the matter. "Jean, maybe I can go and see for myself how things are run?"

"No, this time is not safe. My men and I will have to be careful; I have no need to worry over you. My mind will have to remain, how do you say… ah yes, on point. Worrying about my wife is not on point. Making certain we do not get caught is."

"You are infuriating; you know that? Haven't I proved I can take care of myself? By the sounds of it, I am to assume we will not talk of this. Are there are other matters we can talk about?"

"There are. Come closer and let me hold you. I shall whisper my intentions into your ear."

How could she stay angry with him? He was so devilish in his ways. This man of hers was the most charming man she had ever met, and that added to the physical attraction between them. Laffite was like an overpowering magnet, pulling her to him. Still, for him to think that she would have fallen into the arms of another man? His suspicions earlier rubbed her the wrong way, and she wanted to teach him a lesson. "Hold me, you say? No way," Tori pushed him away from her. "If you want to hold me, it will cost you, and I'm very expensive."

"Name your price, my lady, and I'll gladly pay." His expression was what Tori would refer to as a rakish grin. "My world is at your feet. Just don't deprive me of what I so desperately need."

"Oh, really, Jean? You are quite something; you know that? One minute you accuse me of sleeping with another man, and the next, you want me to fall into your arms. Well, I have some news for you. If you want me, then you'll have to take me." She tried to sound hurt, angry, and tease him at the same time. It was only to teach the rouge a lesson, but she knew he'd seen through her little act, so she started to laugh, unable to control herself.

Jean could see the light in her eyes and the fun in her spirit. He knew she wanted him as much as he did her, and by God, he would have her. The pirate stood up, and in one move, was by her side. With the following smooth action, he swept her up into his arms and maneuvered her body over his shoulder, holding her captive, like a sack of grain slung over his back. With a swift turn, he marched into the house, and as he did so, he called out, "Carlotta, you and everyone else should go and join the party.

Enjoy yourselves." He audibly chuckled. "I know I will." By the time he had called out his orders, they had reached the stairs, and he'd begun climbing with his wriggling cargo firmly in his grip. Just as he stepped onto the landing above, the sound of a door slamming shut told him they were alone in the house. He was free now to continue with their little game without the worry of trying to keep things quiet.

Tori acted her part perfectly. She called for him to let her go, something she knew he would never do, and was glad of that. She beat playfully at his broad back with her fists, but instead of screaming to be put down, Tori found herself laughing so hard that she felt she would not be able to take her next breath. "Jean! I can't breathe, and this is no way to..." as she tried to catch her breath, the pain in her side made her call out in desperation. "Stop it!"

Jean paid no attention to her pleas or the pounding his back was taking. He merely carried his bundle down the hallway, determined to make it to their bedroom before putting her down, but upon reaching a closed door, he was faced momentarily with the challenge of opening it. Jean could not let her go to reach for the door handle, nor would he allow her to stand. Either of these actions would put a damper on the dramatics they both were enjoying.

Tori stilled herself and asked him in a mocking voice, "Now, what are you going to do, big boy?" The pain in her side had subsided, and again she found herself enjoying the pirate's antics.

He shrugged his shoulders and answered, "Only one thing to do." He faced the door and kicked it open with one, hard, determined blow of his foot. Once inside, with his foot reaching backward, he slammed it shut. Satisfied that it would stay closed, he marched toward the bed. Once there, grinning from ear to ear, he unceremoniously heaved Tori over his shoulder and dropped her in the middle of the bed, where she bounced twice, squealing with peals of laughter as she did so.

After a few more seconds of giggling, his wife fell silent and lay there looking up at him. Her face was so full of mischief, and yet she was, as always, so beautiful, he thought to himself. No matter the circumstance, he would forever find her most desirable, especially when they both had lovemaking on their minds.

Finally exhausted from her mock fight, Tori half closed her eyes and tried to relax her body and slow down her breathing. Her thick, soft lashes hid the slither of the opening; her eyes could peer through. The narrow gap was just enough to watch Laffite undress without him suspecting he was under such close scrutiny.

Jean watched her as he began to strip and could see only that her breathing was deep and heavy. It was as if she had just run a great distance, causing her chest to rise and fall, pushing her bust line precariously close to popping out of her gown. As so often before, he was mesmerized by the sight. He knew how her breasts felt beneath his hands. Of how her nipples would stand erect within seconds of his touch, and this drove him to act faster. He hurriedly ripped his shirt from his back and pulled free the buttons on his pants. At any moment, he fully anticipated her breasts escaping from the gown's confines and, if not by themselves, then by his hands.

His eyes were wide with expectations, and his lustful stares had not slipped by her undetected. Tori reached for the top of her gown, and, holding it up, she rolled over teasingly. For Jean, this action was like pulling down the blinds on what had been most amusing; his fun had been abruptly taken away.

"Why Madame, I had thought you were paying me no heed. My little vixen is sly, no? I should have remembered your skill of observing me while seeming to do otherwise." Jean had jumped onto the bed and forcibly rolled her back over, pinning her arms above her head. Bringing his head down on the pillow next to her cheek, he whispered close to her ear, "You shall have to pay the penalty for spying, a severe crime in this house. A crime, I might add, which dictates immediate action on my behalf."

Tori turned to face him as she answered his accusations. "I plead guilty to all charges, to both sly and spying, guilty as charged. Do with me as you will," she giggled.

His head inched closer until his lips were brushing against her own as he spoke. "I intend to, my love." Then without any hesitation, he released his hold on her arms. Gently but firmly, the pirate placed them at her sides. "Your punishment begins, but do not think that you are going to get away so easily. For your deceit, I will demand that you look at me." Placing his hands under her back, he raised her body off the bed a few inches as he spoke. "You will look into my eyes, and until I tell you otherwise, you will remain doing so, understand?"

Captivated, she answered him willingly, "Oui," while slipping her arms around his neck. Their eyes locked as he gently lowered her once again onto the soft bed and continued to remove the last article he had on. The sounds of his boots hitting the floor made Tori giggle again. "How do you always manage to leave your boots where I can trip over them? I know. It's because you are always in a hurry to join me in bed."

"I said, look at me. Your eyes have closed. They will not do so."

Tori could feel the heat of her blushing cheeks under such scrutiny. Jean was watching her every reaction, and would it seemed, continue to do so. She was embarrassed and growing even more so, as there was now an utterly vulnerable feeling sweeping over her. Her body knew what she wanted, but did her mind? 'Trust him,' a small voice echoed in the back of her head. And so, without taking her eyes away from his, she spoke the last words either would hear until their passion was spent, "Je t'aime."

Never in her life had she made love with her eyes open, let alone fixed on her lover's. Part of her wanted to look away, for it felt as if he was taking more of her than she had ever allowed. It was as if he were possessing her soul as well as her mind and body.

Jean's large, dark, fathomless eyes pierced her heart as he slowly and tenderly awakened her emotionally and physically. Each time her gaze would waver, or if she tried to close her eyes, his hand would hold her chin firmly and bring her gaze back to his. Not a word did he have to utter. He spoke through his expressions, and she obediently followed his commands; besides, Tori found it impossible to tear herself free of his hypnotic hold.

Held captive as she was, the lady realized that this gentleman pirate owned her wholly for the first time. Her body had always been Jean's to control and play like a beautiful instrument, but this time, the music that they made created a song that left nothing unsaid and merged their souls as if they were one.

Laffite observed the emotions emanating from behind his love's glazed eyes. He read their messages as clearly as if they were spoken out loud. Jean saw her pupils dilate, and the color deepen as he brought her closer and closer to ecstasy, and still, he waited, stroking and touching her body, with both his hands and his mouth. Then he finally entered her; he did so when her eyes pleaded with him and told him she was entirely his.

Tori drowned in Jean's love and in the depth of his gaze. She'd heard it said that the eyes were the gateway to the soul, and now she could see for herself that it was true.

What she witnessed as he gazed longingly at her told her he was diving deep into the depths of her being. She could see her reflection in the man's ebony eyes as clearly as if looking into a mirror, but that was where any similarity to a mirror ended. So large and dark were his pupils that she could not see where the deep brown's outer rim she knew existed, began, or ended. The colors readily joined and melted together, giving his eyes the illusion of being made up of one deep-colored orb, with sparks of emotions beyond the realm of her imagination.

His eyes may reflect like mirrors, she thought, but they were being used as weapons in a war that she had continued to fight on several levels. Up until this moment, she had had some control of her mind and her inner soul. Always, Jean had commanded her body, like a Captain did his ship, but now, what was happening was unique. Looking into his eyes, Tori knew she had lost herself completely. He had taken her to heights that were beyond anything she'd ever experienced or anything she could define, and with it came the realization that never again would she feel the same about him or herself. Her pirate now owned a part of her that she could never reclaim, just as sure, as she now held a part of him that she would never be able to evict. So, when he finally allowed her to close her eyes and silently drift towards sleep, Tori wondered to herself, did he realize just how high a toll his penalty had been for both of them?

As concerned as she was about going back into New Orleans, Tori knew she would not be able to change Laffite's mind. After all, Jean had explained, he was not a wanted man anymore, thanks to Grymes. He was a man out on bond, and this fact had amused him. To Laffite, the whole affair was now nothing more than a slight inconvenience and one to be ignored.

The trip they made back to the city was taken both by boat and horse, allowing long hours of isolation, in which Jean, Tori, and Cisco could talk freely. They were in one of the larger pirogues and escorted by two smaller boats, each with three men. The others were there only for Tori's safety, should they run into trouble, something Jean doubted but wanted to be prepared if the revenue men found them and decided to take their revenge for the humiliation they had suffered. Tori had not fought him on the subject but suggested that one boat stay well ahead of them and the other behind. Both she and Cisco had told him they needed to remain out of earshot so as not to be overheard. As Laffite never tired of hearing about the future, he readily agreed to this suggestion.

Cisco was only too happy to tell stories and enjoyed watching Jean's surprised expressions as they quietly discussed many subjects about the time from which he and Tori came from. Tori's new friend was always careful about what he divulged, though, because, like Tori, a deep-rooted fear about changing the future clung to him. He felt this way, only because he knew Tori would one day try to go forward, and if she succeeded, then history had to be as close, if not identical, to how they had left it. To do that, Cisco had agreed with Jean's wife that the history they needed to keep on track was where the pirate was supposed to help Andrew Jackson win the battle. But, suppose he talked too much about the wrong subject? In that case, he might inevitably change the man's mind on that action, so Cisco remained careful while trying not to look like he was keeping something from the ever-inquisitive privateer.

Laffite was not the type of character to give up on anything, and so he always brought the conversation back to the subject that bothered him the most. Try as he might, he found that Cisco either knew no more about the immediate future than his lady or was unwilling to depart any such facts. "Are you two sure that this so-called Battle of New Orleans is fought with my help," he said, frowning? "It seems to me that before I go offering my services to defend this America, I should have more, much more information. That is prudent, don't you think?"

Tori knew he was trying to pry deeper. She also knew that deep down he understood the implications of all they had told him and what it could mean to New Orleans and all of America. Tori also understood the knowledge he now possessed continued to be difficult for him to believe or accept as a definite fact. It was something she expected, as he was ever the practical man. Jean could not accept the knowledge without proof or dates.

Tori had observed the man closely hour after hour. She saw he had his doubts, as it often showed on his face, but what could she do? One fact was clear; they had to reach Jean somehow, no matter how stubborn he insisted on being. So, while the men talked of inventions and a time that brought both problems and solutions, Tori sat deep in thought. As they made their way through the bayous, it became apparent to her that it was time to get Cisco to talk to John, to get him to open up and reveal himself to Jean. Between the three of them, perhaps then they could come up with some hard facts that would persuade Jean to accept his future role.

As darkness approached, Tori leaned over to whisper in Cisco's ear while Jean was distracted, giving instructions to the men guiding the boats to shore. "Look, I know I gave my word and you too, not to expose John's secret, but trust me here, we need to get him to talk to Jean."

"Reading my mind, are you?" Cisco grinned, and then just as quickly, a far more severe expression filled his face. "Look, I agree with you on this. Just leave old stuck in the mud up to me. I will send word as soon as I can. That, or you will see us turning up at your doorstep. I can't give John time to change his mind once I convince him to join us. You just try and keep that man of yours out of trouble, and most of all, out of jail. Remember what John said. Laffite's destined to be arrested again, and I, for one doubt, they will be so stupid as to let the pirate escape so easily next time. That is if it happens at all. Oh, shit, you understand, right?"

"I do, and trust me; I get it. Now, you talk to John, and I will try my damnedest to keep Jean under control if that's possible."

Cisco saw Jean looking their way, and even though his expression seemed calm and not upset or suspicious, he did not need the pirate thinking they were planning anything.

"Jean, my man, you take it easy and try listening to your wife, ok?"

"I assume you mean well, with such a jest. Your man, indeed."

The men from the other boats were laughing among themselves.

Two looked Cisco's way and shook their heads. The Spaniard was crazy because he sure sounded it.

Jean frowned; Cisco needed to understand where he stood, and quickly before such an odd statement was spread among his men. He spoke up loud enough for all to hear him. "Such a suggestion is artfully wrong I can assure you. I am now and always will remain my own man. There again, just what am I supposed to take easily? Don't answer; it will only confuse the situation I am quite certain. As for listening to my wife… I fear after the past few weeks' events, it will be almost impossible not to do so. Your horse awaits you. I suggest you leave this mode of transportation unless you plan to return to Grand Terre.

Cisco laughed and shook his head. "Only when the two of you are there shall I dare return. Thanks for the ride."

Laffite chuckled and pulled Tori close to his side. "Take care, my friend. I hope to see you soon. You are always welcome at our home."

Cisco let out a whoop. He was so happy and proud of himself that he did not mind what he said or did right then. "Damn, he called me a friend, the most famous pirate I know, called me friend, and invited me over." With that, he ran to his horse, mounted, and rode off, still hooting and hollering, "you're the man!"

Jean looked at Tori with a puzzled expression. "Don't mind. You can explain that idiom as we ride the last of the way." He helped her mount her horse and was pleased to see her sit the animal sidesaddle. It had been a point of contention, and after many hours of heated arguments, he had made his opinion known. Tori had thought her way out of doing so was to claim she could not ride in such a manner. Jean, however, was one step ahead of her. While they spent their time in Grand Terre relaxing and planning, Tori took riding lessons from one of the men. A sidesaddle was acquired, and against her better judgment, after a few days, the woman from the future found herself enjoying this new seating arrangement as she called it.

209

"You are comfortable, are you not? It is the proper way for a lady of your standing to ride and be seen ridding such."

"I am quite comfortable, thank you." She was polite but still angry at having to ride the animal his way, even if it did make sense. So, without looking at him and with a sly grin, she turned the mare toward home. Tori had plans to show him that she was not one to control.

Jean had witnessed her expression and decided it was best not to ask what she was up to. He thought it more prudent to pretend he suspected nothing. "Then, come Tori, we will take it slow, but we do need to arrive as soon as we can. I am certain Bessy is worrying, and if I know Grymes, he too will worry and want to see me as soon as possible. While my days away have been entertaining and enlightening, that time is over."

"On the contrary, Jean, I rather think it is all just beginning." She kicked the side of her horse and galloped ahead of him, not ready yet to face the onslaught of numerous questions she knew her statement would invoke. Besides, it was fun to show him that going slow was not on her agenda and that she could handle her mount at full gallop just as good as anyone, sidesaddle or not.

WITHIN hours of Jean being back in town, they had visitors. Word had spread rapidly, and once again, they were receiving invites to dinner. They were no longer shunned but instead were in considerably greater demand in Tori's estimation. This assumption was reached by judging the flow of written inventions stacking up on Jean's desk. This kind of two-faced falsehood and hypocrisy upset Tori and made her rage inside. She recalled only too vividly how many of their so-called friends had turned their backs on her, and Tori had no intention of forgetting or forgiving them anytime soon, and she let Jean know just how she felt. "I don't care; what you say, they are all horrible. You should have seen the way they distanced themselves from me at the dinner. Some even turned their backs on me. If Cisco had not rescued me, I don't know what I would have done."

"They are what they are, and does it matter in the grand scheme of things? We have so much more to think about at this point. If you and Cisco are correct, days around here are about to become far more interesting than people turning their backs on us or not." Jean raised one eyebrow and inquisitively looked at her. "How about a drink before dinner?"

"That goes without asking, and make it a double if you please." She was about to continue with her rant about New Orleans's citizens when the sound of Bessy's voice echoed their way.

"I know you understand that waiting until I announce your arrival is expected, so why you following me like you is expected?"

"Because I am expected, and I know my way."

The door to the living room pushed all the way open and revealed a frustrated housekeeper. "Lord helps me, Miss Tori, but this here Massa Grymes, he says he is expected and won't wait in the hall like most decent folks does."

"Oh, Bessy, don't worry, your head any, Mr. Grymes can come on in, and maybe you can set another place at the dinner table?"

"I rightly can and will do so." Bessy stepped aside and let Grymes walk past her before she turned and left, mumbling away as was her norm. "Never saw, no decent folk, acting like they can just walk in as if they, owns the place..."

Laffite chuckled and walked toward his attorney to greet him, and Tori frowned. It was unlike the man not to follow protocol and barge in as he had, and for her, his actions could only mean that something was up.

"Sorry to push in like I did, but I wanted to talk about a most pressing situation." He shook Jean's hand and then hugged Tori. "Dinner sounds like a wonderful idea, but I have other matters to deal with this evening. I, however, have heard through the grapevine..."

"Grapes talk?" Jean was grinning as he handed Tori her drink. "I take it you have picked up a term or two from my lady, but talking grapes?"

"Actually, I learned this term an hour ago from an acquaintance of yours at Davis's establishment."

"That would have to be Cisco, right?" Tori was fishing but didn't want to seem so. She desperately wanted to know who taught Grymes the saying and why he was so intent on using it? Was he trying to learn more about their friend? Could it be Cisco slipped up or had John Davis confided in Grymes about his origins? If he had done so, then surely, he would have divulged Cisco's identity too.

"You would be correct. The young man Francisco, the dealer, has some strange colloquial phrases. If I did not know better, I would think he had more in common with you, Tori."

Now, it was Grymes's turn to fish, but Tori would not take the bait. She looked right at the attorney as if she had not even heard his statement. Change the subject, she told herself. "You are here because you learned what, may I ask?"

Grymes frowned briefly and then looked at Jean. "You are still intent on having your sale at the Temple?"

"I am."

"Jean, this is not a good idea, considering your predicament. You are, after all, out on bond."

"Thanks to you." Jean handed his attorney a drink and smiled. "I think maybe there is more you wish to say on the matter?"

"You damn right, there is!" He turned back to face Tori. "Can't you make him see to reason? I can tell you this idea of his is not going over too well at the Governor's office."

Laffite laughed. "Ah! So, our American friend has word of the sale. Magnificent! He always purchases the finer quality items at top price."

"Jean, this is no game. Do I have to remind you that if caught, you and your men will find yourselves right back in those filthy cells, and this time there will be no slipping out." He shot Tori another look that implied, 'I know more than you think I do, and you were behind his escape, of that I am certain.'

She wanted to laugh but chose to frown instead. "John, what's that look for? You can't blame me for what Jean does or doesn't do."

"Madam, I, in no uncertain terms, place any blame for his actions your way, I assure you. If I implied so with my manners, excuse me. But, surely, you see the situation here. If found, your husband, his brother Pierre, the whole lot of them, will be caught and arrested."

Again, Laffite laughed out loud. "I think you underestimate me, John. Besides, I have given my word that Tori can do a bit of shopping herself. She can talk me into anything, it seems, only takes her longer on some subjects." Jean winked at his wife before turning his attention back to their anxious visitor. "Sorry, but this sale will happen, and the Governor cannot stop me, and you, my friend, will not change my mind. That is not your job; your job is to represent me when needed. Now, dinner is waiting, and I am hungry. You do wish to join us?"

John was frustrated and angry, though he kept in check the second emotion. There would be no changing the pirate's mind, and knowing that, he decided to leave. "No, thank you, I have a prior engagement, as I said. I shall take my leave." He finished his drink and handed Jean the empty glass. "You had best watch your back, my friend. You have made a few more enemies, and the Governor is at the top of that list. If you have the sale, it might be prudent to keep Tori out of harm's reach." He did not wait a second longer but turned and walked to the door. Once opened, he looked back at Tori. "See if you can't talk some sense into your husband. He is one stubborn man, but maybe he will listen to you." With that, he left, leaving the door behind him open.

"Jean, I think I will take another double if you don't mind. The man has reason to worry, and now I am more worried than before. Is it wise to hold the sale? I mean, isn't there another way to sell all the booty?"

"You talk like it is nothing but trinkets, a pirate's horde." He was chuckling again. "It is all, top quality merchandise, not just simple

213

booty, acquired by 'privateers' no less. He had emphasized the word privateers. "As to why I choose to sell now, it is my decision. Besides, there is no better way to disperse it all. Grymes did have one good point, though."

"And that is? Or should I dare ask?"

"You can ask, and I will explain. You will not be joining me this time; next time, I assure you, you will shop till your little heart is so tired, you beg to leave."

"Jean, you can't... you said I could go."

"I did, now I say you can't, and that is that. I am hungry. Let's not talk about this anymore. I fear it will spoil our dinner. We will talk after if you wish, but know this, my mind is made up."

"Grymes is right."

"You agree? That is good."

"Not about me not attending, you idiot. I agree with him about the fact that you are one stubborn man. Bessy!" Tori went to the door and called out to their housekeeper in a tone that did not sound too happy.

THEY had picked at their dinner, which Tori had Bessy serve in the living room. Somehow sitting in the dining room didn't feel right. Besides, it was a more intimate setting, and she needed that atmosphere to calm down and prepare Jean for what was to come later that night. Cisco had sent her word that he intended to visit and bring John Davis, even if he had to drag him along. Tori could only pray that John would come of his own free will and want to help them. Picturing him been dragged along against his better judgment was not something she wished to do, let alone see. The image was pushed out of her mind, and having accomplished that, Tori's mind was free, to confirm all facts that were floating around in her head. With John's added knowledge of New Orleans's history and Jean finally having the proof he needed, they would not be so helpless. They would not have to sit and wait blindly for everything to unfold around them.

Tori continued to sit in front of the fire with her back to Jean so he would not see her concern. It was impossible not to worry over Cisco, saying he would drag the man to meet them, knowing full well how clear Davis had made his position known. They had given their word he would remain plain old John Davis, with no time travel connection at all. Now, she and Cisco were going back on their word to appease Laffite and his endless number of questions. Were they right in doing so, or would the move prove to be disastrous?

It had been over an hour since they put their plates down, and still, Tori had not brought up the subject of the sale. She understood the pirate better than he knew. He was itching for a discussion on the matter, so he could demand that the issue be closed. Besides, if he thought she was sulking about not going to the sale, it was good because it helped her hide that her worry had nothing to do with the subject. Jean was being kept clueless as to why she was acting as she was, and for Tori, that was important.

They were sitting in front of the fire, each waiting for the other to raise a topic of conversation. During this awkward silence, Bessy burst into the room for the second time that night. "Massa Jean, there be that young man, who was here before, when you be in jail." She looked at Tori with a worried expression, and then upon seeing that her Mistress didn't seem upset by her slip up, she continued. "He said dat he got to see you and dat you would be happy to meet his friend. I ain't got his name, but he, look like a fine gentleman's to me. It's dat young pup; I ain't too sure about. You want me to tell him to leave, 'cause I will be real glad to if you want…" she rolled her eyes. There was nothing else to say on the matter. Bessy still thought it best to keep the dandy far away from Jean. After all, he was the same fool who had been with the Mistress behind the Master's back. And now he had returned. It smelled like trouble to her. Yes, Sir, big trouble. She realized that her speech pattern had exposed her worried state of mind, but Lord, how was she supposed not to be so worked up?

Tori could tell the housekeeper was upset and all for no reason. She had to make that point clear, or the poor woman would have a fit. "Bessy, by the way, you are talking; one would think you are worried. There is nothing to worry about, I can assure you. Calm yourself, and you may show them in." Laffite's wife knew who Cisco's friend was. It could only be John, and if that was true, Tori knew that Cisco had reached him, and he was ready to reveal his identity to Jean.

Bessy was still standing in the doorway, looking even more perplexed, so Tori quickly spoke more, hoping to calm her and get the woman to leave and tend to her duties. "I completely forgot, Bessy," she added in a hurry to smooth things over. "It's my fault. I asked the gentlemen to call. There is a matter we have to discuss. Please go ahead and bring them back, and Bessy, don't you worry any," she said, smiling at the woman before continuing. "The young man in question is a friend of ours, and Jean knows the other fine gentleman well. Now, you go along, hurry. We must not keep our guests waiting." She turned to Jean, who had a puzzled look on his face.

"I don't know about you," said Jean, "but I was rather looking forward to enjoying an evening together. It is always delightful to smooth the rough waters between us." He looked toward the doorway and cocked his head to one side. "Who do you suppose Cisco has brought with him? Someone who wishes to meet the famous pirate, maybe?"

The man was teasing her again, and she knew it. "Can you be serious for once? And don't you worry, I'm sure that you will find this evening far more interesting if our guests are who I think they are. However, something tells me that you will want a good, stiff drink first." No sooner had the words left her mouth than they were joined in the room by their company.

Cisco entered, followed closely by a somber John Davis, who looked anything but glad to be there. Jean looked at him and then at Tori. His face remained a blank mask to hide his surprise at learning that the friend, John Davis, was the mystery guest. "I think, my lady, you are right. A good stiff drink, as you put it, is in order. Bessy, you may leave. We will take care of ourselves for the rest of the evening. In fact, make sure the house is empty. I don't want anyone here to disturb us. Gentlemen, you will join me in a drink, I am sure."

As Bessy left, she was relieved to know that her Mistress had been right. There would be no trouble. Sure, was strange, though, him asking for her to leave and for the house to be empty. Ah, huh, it was strange, but then white folks be that way.

Jean handed out the drinks, including one for Tori, who stood frowning at John. Cisco was the only one who seemed unperturbed as he helped himself to the leftover cold meats and delicacies on the table. "Lucky for me, you two like to eat in here and not the dining room. This is too good to waste, and my boss has not fed me much today." He shoved a large piece of chicken into his mouth, followed by a bite out of one of Bessy's slices of cake. "You know, I just started my first shift when I decided that more important matters were nagging me."

Tori shook her head while giggling. "Help yourself, by all means, don't worry about us, isn't that right, Jean?"

Jean looked from Cisco to John and then to Tori. His face was still a blank mask concealing his emotions. "You had best join us, Cisco, and eat later. I have a strange feeling that somehow you are a part of all this. Whatever this is?"

"That I am, and you are right; I do need to pay attention because it should be good." He walked to the chair next to Tori and sat down, looking from John to Jean and back again.

Laffite ignored his antics and turned his attention toward the less than happy John Davis. "John, I think somehow that you are about to become far more than just a business acquaintance, am I correct?"

"I think you are. Cisco has spent the whole afternoon convincing me that I am needed here and that you and Tori are to be trusted. Before I go on, however, I must have your word as a friend and a gentleman, that our friendship along with what I am about to disclose, all of it, remains a secret among us. Your discretion in this, your guarantee, is the only way that I will remain here this evening. Unlike these two who gave their word to me and broke it..."

Cisco sprang to his feet, exclaiming in what sounded like a wounded tone how he felt. "We did not, did we, Tori? I mean, you are here telling Jean, not us. So, how'd we break our word? That pisses me off."

Jean cocked his head and looked puzzled. Cisco had used modern terms, and it had not shocked Davis. Things were rapidly turning far more interesting and a lot more complicated than him giving his word. Sensing the gravity of what John was about to say, Laffite hesitated only momentarily before speaking. "You have it," he said, walking up to John and offering his hand. "My word is my honor, as you know."

Tori stood up then, rocking slightly, side to side; she could not remain seated at a time like this, nor could she standstill. Now, she understood why Cisco was always jumping around. The tension and excitement at that very moment kept her on edge.

Using the excuse to fill a glass with wine, she tried hard to contain her bent-up emotions and concern. She had kept her word. Both of them had. Now, however, they had placed Davis in a situation where he was about to break his own rule and include yet another person with his secret. In a soft tone of voice, she spoke to Davis. "You know how I feel about this, John. I will always respect your wishes." Laughing softly, she whispered, "Have no fear; you will always remain the invisible partner in crime, of that I can promise."

John drank all of his wine and, placing the glass down carefully, he raised his head and looked at Jean. "I will be upfront and to the point then. It is as simple as this. I have known Cisco here for a very long time. One could say for centuries. You might say we came to New Orleans from the same place as your Tori. I am one of them, you see, and between us, we hope to be able to put our heads together and keep history, as we know it, as it should be. On track… so to speak." He coughed and looked at both Cisco and Tori before continuing. "I am here to offer my support and my help in any way it counts, so long as you need it."

All eyes in the room were now on Jean's face, watching to see what his reaction to this new piece of news was going to be. Cisco thought of the saying, 'you could hear a pin drop,' and Tori worried that Jean would be upset, that she had kept this vital piece of information from him. However, what they observed was an outwardly calm man whose only giveaway, that he was inwardly excited, was the twitch of his lower lip.

"I am no longer shocked by anything that pertains to my wife. Surprised maybe, but shocked… no! Things are beginning to make more sense now. I guess you helped in a far more significant way with the escapade that acquired my freedom? I am correct, am I not? You are, until now, the unnamed individual that supplied Cisco with the pertinent information required?"

"You are indeed correct in that department, but only a few of us know of my involvement, and I intend for it to remain that way."

Jean's eyebrows dropped in a slight frown as he considered what John had just said. Did the man not realize that most of Grand Terre knew of his role in the escape plan? Maybe it was something he chose to ignore or not worry over. If that were the case, Jean decided unless John brought the subject up, it was closed for discussion. He looked at Cisco and noticed that he sat beaming like he had just won the best poker hand of his life. His beloved Tori's expression was one of a different kind. To him, she looked a bit worried, and he could guess why. They had promised each other no more secrets, and here she had kept yet another. Still, it seemed she'd no choice in the matter, as he now had no choice but to agree to Davis's terms, whatever they were. He owed the man his heartfelt thanks and more. "For my freedom, I am indebted to you, and it is a debt that I will pay. Name your price. You shall have anything you want."

Davis nodded his head. "You can do only one thing for me, Jean, and that is to listen and learn from us." He pointed toward his cohorts. "It is my hope to keep the outcome of history as it should be and only that. I think maybe your wife had it right when she said that it is perhaps destiny that has brought the three of us here together and not a coincidence."

Tori interrupted. "Jean, are you ready to listen? Can we try and sort it all out?"

"My love, it looks as though I have no choice in the matter. We have all night, and we have plenty of fine wine and more than enough food leftover." Laffite looked toward Cisco and added, "Bessy had expected one more for dinner; he did not stay. So, let us begin."

"To drink or eat? Or both, maybe?" Cisco was already heading toward the food.

"Cisco, you are impossible," snapped John.

"No, just nervous and maybe a bit excited, but never impossible."

THE small, unlikely group of conspirators had moved toward the table, and Cisco ate while the other three sat and drank. During the hours that followed, the three time travelers began to share theories on time travel and ideas about destiny. First, though, the talk was about how and where John had fit into the grand-scape of things and what he had done to aid Jean's escape.

Jean had laughed when John described the looks on both Claiborne's and Edward's faces. He had been very impressed with how the whole plan had come together. One fact that stood above all others; and had surprised him the most was that after dealing with John for a few years, not once had he guessed the man to be anything other than what he portrayed.

From that discussion, they found themselves embroiled in a long night of drinking and explaining to Jean all that they could about New Orleans's history and what was to come. He was like a sponge, soaking up all the pertinent details, interrupting only to ask questions, and always wanting more explanations and descriptions. For hours they talked, covering the one subject most present on their minds. What were they to do about the upcoming battle?

Try as they might, neither John, Cisco or Tori could agree on the exact date of when the Battle for New Orleans began. Davis knew it was fought in the month of January but not the exact date or the year. He had not yet studied the events surrounding that fight in great detail and was just as frustrated as Jean over his lack of such grave information. "I apologize for my ignorance on the matter. I only wish I could impart more."

Tori reached across the table and patted his hand. "You know more than Cisco and I, and what you have shared will help us. It's not our fault we were raised in other parts of the country and that the details of this battle were not taught to us. You would think that schools would want to teach about the last battle fought against a foreign enemy on American soil. It was a defining moment in history. I mean, if we lost, our country would have turned out far, differently; that or many more lives would have been lost before we won our complete independence."

Cisco sounded glum when he spoke. "You know, I didn't look at it like that, but you are right. I bet you can go all over our country and ask about the battle, and only a few will know about it. I mean, I knew that the British burned down the White House and then lost against us and signed a treaty, but this battle, nope, didn't have a clue. Look, John, my man, stop beating yourself up about it."

Tori nodded her head in agreement. "John, you can't blame yourself. Maybe, more will come to mind as the days pass; you don't know it won't. Cisco or I could jog your memory, or ours, who's to guess?"

Cisco made a disagreeable sound as he added his thought about this. "Him, guess… well, that will be the day. Old stuck in the mud won't stick his head out if we can't come up with cold hard facts to back up the next move. I need another drink before I explode."

Jean had sat silently listening to them as they all discussed the reasons behind what they knew or not. It seemed that it was what they didn't know that was most important to him. He no longer doubted that a battle would be fought or that he would somehow be instrumental in the outcome, but the where, when, and how still eluded them all.

After more hours of discussions, it was evident to John that all they had as a certainty was the battle's outcome, as it was written in their time, and that Jean played a strategic role. Just how they would ensure that the outcome remained the same way was–in his mind–going to be a monumental task. Worse still, his concerned expression and attitude were evident to all there, and Cisco worried that the man would choose not to be involved. After all, he only ever took risks on deals he felt were in his favor.

Cisco was getting frustrated at John and his ever-pessimistic mood. He was about to let his friend have it when Tori broke into the heated conversation. She spoke with an edge to her voice, forcing even Cisco to listen. "Look, you two. I've been thinking about this a lot, and well, it just does not make sense one way or another. Seems to me we have two choices. One is to sit back and do nothing and see if it turns out the way it should. The other is to get involved. We could organize ourselves with what we know is going to happen and use it to see that the outcome is what history wrote. The thing is, which one? If we sit still and the outcome is different because we did not help, we are in trouble. If we help and screw it up, we could be changing history. The fact is, we are damned if we do and damned if we don't."

Davis mumbled under his breath, "doesn't matter what we do or not; we will be making history, written or not."

Cisco fell silent; a scowl hid his usual smile. John, exasperated and fed up with going around in circles, spoke up. "Trouble is, we don't seem to know too damn much if you ask me. Therefore, how can we get involved at any point, especially if we don't know what we are doing? I vote to leave it alone. Besides, why do we care what happens? None of us will know the repercussions of what happens here because we won't be in the future to see the outcome one way or the other. Screw history up is one thing; screwing up our life here is quite another. Let's not be stupid. I vote to leave well enough alone for now."

Cisco was not about to stand for that plan of action and immediately reiterated his point of view. "Always the cautious one, John. As Tori here said earlier, had it occurred to you that we three might have come back in time for just this purpose? To help, so to speak, and if we don't, well, we could very well change the outcome of so much, including our own existence, for one. I mean, if things go differently, then maybe you and I, even Tori, won't get born, and all this will be changed because we won't come back to help or not help. Shit, it's confusing the hell out of me now."

Angrily, John snapped quickly back at him. "And did it occur to you that the opposite could be true? You are talking gibberish and drunken talk at that. I can't make heads or tails of what you are going on about."

Tori spoke up then, fearing a fight brewing between her two friends. "Guys, guys, please. Let's not fight amongst ourselves. Squabbling is not going to help Jean or us. What we have to do is approach this systematically and then decide what to do."

Still somewhat agitated, John could not let the subject drop. "And just how do you go about that, may I ask?"

"Indeed, you may, John. The way I see it, we make a list of all we know about this time and what will happen. Writing things down sometimes helps. But sitting around waiting for the outcome, one way or the other, won't prove shit. Look, we all agree that Jean had the supplies that Andrew Jackson needed, along with men. That's a start! Thanks to you, John, we also learned that Jean would meet

223

with the British, who would offer him a ton. That should signal that the battle is close, right?" She looked toward Jean, who had been quiet for some time. Tori was hoping to get his opinion.

Jean could see clearly, what they failed to acknowledge. "My friends, this discussion is going nowhere except around in circles. It is rather like a dog chasing its tail; in the end, he succeeds in catching it. We will no doubt become clearer on this subject as events leading up to it occur. From what we know, and that seems to be far more than we thought, we will be very aware when the time is close at hand. Until such a time, I agree with John. Let's just keep a vigil and act accordingly." Jean looked at a very frustrated Tori, and placing his arm around her waist, he drew her closer. "My lady, do not look so depressed. I have no doubt that we will have enough signs to alert us and guide us in the time ahead. Don't you agree, gentlemen?"

"I do, most heartedly," said John sounding much relieved.

Laffite bowed slightly toward him. It was like an unspoken agreement had been reached between them, but Jean did not end there. "I do have one more question we have not discussed, John. Tori mentioned I would be arrested again. Is this so?"

"I had thought so. It was a story I overheard, but I am now not so certain. It could be that this last experience you had, thrown into jail, was the first and last. We can but hope and keep up our guard, just in case."

"Ah, so like much of what we know, our history is not set in stone. We beat the British; if I step in, that is the only fact we can be sure of. I need to read the signs as they present themselves and decide upon my actions as I see fit. John, like you, I take no risks, not unless those risks are in my favor. I have a little to go on and must trust to you three and your memories."

"That's about it, I am afraid."

"Well then, here is to keeping our destinies on... how do you say, on track?" Jean raised his glass and toasted the moment.

Feeling much calmer now that he had the levelheaded Jean taking his view on the matter, John went over to sit at the piano and began to tinker with the keys. Cisco may not have liked what Jean had just said, but he smiled and nodded his head in complete agreement. Like always, he wanted action, not this sit around and wait option. Though nothing had really been solved, he was pleased with the way things had gone and looked forward to many more evenings such as this. "I may not agree, Jean, but majority rules. Besides, until such events start to guide us, we can meet and have get-togethers like this. Isn't that right, John?"

The hotel owner looked up and frowned. "No, I totally disagree there. We can't afford to be known as friends now or ever. Too many questions and unwanted inquiries would arise."

Cisco scoffed. "For who? For you, I think. You and your, wanting to keep everything secret," Cisco slurred. His drinking of the evening was finally catching up to him, clouding his judgment and making him careless.

Tori could see another confrontation building and acted quickly to diffuse it. "I agree with John. Things need to appear the same. Or nearly the same, as they have always been.

We can explain your friendship, Cisco. But, to have such a high-profile friend as John all of a sudden, is dangerous. Don't you agree, Jean?"

"Most certainly, and I did give my word, at the beginning of the evening, that John's identity and his connection to the future would be kept amongst us. My word is my word, Cisco," he added sternly. "I suggest you take heed and do likewise or run the risk of upsetting me." He shot the younger man one of his inscrutable grins.

Suddenly, John played a piece of music that drew Cisco and Tori's attention away from the subject at hand and brought instant relief to the strained atmosphere. The soft notes floated across the room, and the familiar tune was recognized immediately by everyone but Jean.

Cisco laughed out loud, "Now that's what I call appropriate. If ever there was a song for you two," he declared, as he looked at Jean and Tori, "it's that one. Don't you agree, Tori?"

She did indeed and laughed with him. "I had never thought of it, but yes, you are right. It could be our song."

Jean suddenly felt left out of a joke. "We have a song? Please explain, this should be interesting having my own song…"

"Not you, us." Tori was laughing. "You will understand once you hear the words, I am sure of it."

John could see the perplexed look upon the pirate's face, and as he slowly played the beginning of the tune, he said, "I have not known you and your lady long. Oh sure, I have known of you, but until this evening, I could only assume what I have now seen for myself… experienced witnessing, what is whispered around town… Tori is truly the love of your life, your lady. Please allow me to play a song for you, from our time, that I know you will approve of." With that, he started to play in earnest, and softly the words escaped his lips as he effortlessly sang the melody.

Tori pulled Jean to his feet and, putting her arms around him, started to slowly sway to the music, with her head resting on her pirate's shoulder as they listened closely to the words. She knew the famous Kenny Rogers song all right. She had heard it many times before, but listening to it now, brought tears to her eyes.

John continued to sing as Jean and Tori held each other in a loving embrace while listening to him, and as they did so, it was as if no one else was in the room. The pirate would squeeze her closer to him whenever the words seemed to express exactly how he felt, and she did the same to him.

Cisco sat mesmerized by the pair of lovers and the dance that played out before him. But, most of all, he was deeply moved by the love that radiated between his two friends. He sipped on the last of his wine and found himself wondering if he would ever find such a love as the Laffite's had.

John, carried away by singing one of his favorite country songs, found that it now had a meaning to him also. Because of this, the man put his whole heart and soul behind the lyrics. He did not look at the couple dancing to the melody until the last words of the song left his lips. It was the sight of Jean's tear-filled eyes, followed by Tori's look of wonder, that caused him to act on impulse. Putting his finger to his lips to silence Cisco, who was about to clap, John stood up and walked toward the door, motioning Cisco to join him, and together they slipped from the quiet candle-lit room unnoticed.

Jean and Tori stood in each other's arms for what seemed to both of them an eternity. Each was caught up in the haunting melody and its meaning. Jean bent his head down close to her ear and whispered. "That, my lady, is exactly how I feel." He turned to thank John and ask him about the lyrics, only to find both he and Cisco gone. Smiling, he looked into his lady's face. "I think we have very wise friends, my love. Now, let us not waste these precious moments alone. Let us take full advantage of how I… we feel. Come with me." He kissed her lips lightly before guiding her upstairs.

Tori did not talk. She walked with him, the song playing again and again in her mind. It was their song and would be from now until she died. Kenny Rogers's song 'Lady' was perfect, and Laffite's wife smiled to herself, content for the moment. Then suddenly, a sad feeling swept over her. She thought of another era and another song, 'Tommy's song,' but that melody was not so clear now and belonged in another time far away. At least, for now, she could push it from her memory and concentrate on the man who filled her whole life. Jean gave her life meaning, and he did so with abundant love.

ᴥᖱ Six ᖯᴥ

In the coming months, life went on as it had before Jean's arrest. Nothing much changed as far as the pirate was concerned, except that the business grew day by day. Laffite and his men had held one of their infamous auctions in the bayous, its total success spurring him on. Both he and Pierre openly walked the streets of New Orleans with confidence and an air about them that demanded respect. To many of the merchants who were demanding justice, it seemed that the Laffite brothers thought themselves above the law.

Grymes had tried to persuade Jean to lay low but failed in his attempts. He worried day and night about his client's blatant flagrancy as his continued warnings fell on deaf ears, rendering him powerless to do much more than worry. However, the attorney's frustration dimmed because there was hope in knowing that Claiborne seemed helpless and had his hands tied, yet, for how much longer, he wondered? The Governor would be pushed too far one day, and then Jean and his whole operation would find themselves in dire straits.

Edward and Simone had temporarily put aside their goal of contributing to Jean's demise. Edward had proposed to Simone, and she willingly accepted. Not wanting to wait and afraid he would change his mind, Simone immediately started planning the wedding day. The Spanish beauty had specific guidelines given to her by Edward, but she had free reign other than those few suggestions. He had stipulated that he wanted a small but well-attended wedding, one befitting his standing in society.

Simone would have married him in a back alley if she had to. True, she loved him in a sort of sick way, but she was far more in love with becoming Madame Duval than spending the rest of her life as Edward's kept woman. She told herself that her wedding was to be the month's social event, and the woman was eagerly counting the days.

As a wedding gift for his bride-to-be, Edward had purchased a new home for them and arranged to reside at John Davis's hotel until Simone had furnished their elegant abode, as she wanted. Leone's townhouse, their current place of residence, was to be sold, along with Simone's smaller establishment, the one she had been driven to live in, upon the loss of her former husband and his money. They would keep most of the elegant pieces of furniture from Leone's, but Simone insisted that her tiny establishment's contents were to be sold. She wanted as little as possible to remind her of her disastrous former life.

The idea of making John Davis's establishment a temporary home didn't bother her. After all, it was the best New Orleans had to offer, and Edward had acquired a suite of rooms, sparing no expense. It was expected that Simone was to have her own room and be attended by her female slave. To do otherwise would not have been acceptable as decorum dictated that separate living arrangements had to be held until they were wed. What the public accepted and what they did when prying eyes were no place to be found was another matter. One door connected Simone's room from Edward's suite, which meant that nights were not lonely, and his lady kept her respectable standing. If anyone questioned or wondered about their living quarters, Davis had given his word it would be handled delicately and in such a manner as to clear the young couple of any wrong proprieties. Knowing this, Edward was confident no one would ever be the wiser, and as long as his future wife could continue to live in the style that she was accustomed to, he remained content. Had either the dandy or Simone realized how convenient this arrangement was to their sworn enemies, the conniving pair would have been far from pleased.

GRYMES was smiling, so Jean assured himself that the news had to be agreeable. At least whatever the man had to share was sure to be a change for his attorney, who was always trying to convince him to live a quieter lifestyle. "Well, then you had best tell us, for I fear if you do not, you will tease my wife to the point of exasperation."

Grymes chuckled. "I most certainly will not drive your wife to such a condition. I came here to inform you both about a small bit of interesting information. Imparted to me, I tell you, by Davis himself. Edward and his soon-to-be bride will be living at the hotel until Simone has decorated and furnished their new home, given by Edward as a wedding gift to his bride. It's all the talk in the hotel's dining area. The ladies are all over themselves, trying to become the first to gain an invite…"

Tori could hardly stand it. "Oh, please, stop it; you are making me ill with the thought of those two becoming the talk of the town." She was serious about her statement, and Grymes knew it.

"I beg your pardon Tori, but that is not my intent. I came to share the news because it is good for us, for both of you, don't you see? We can quite easily keep a closer eye on those two while they are there. After talking to Davis about the activities of the night you escaped, it is my opinion that Edward holds sway over our esteemed Governor's continued vendetta toward you and yours. The man has acquired a close friendship, as you know, and this allows him to not only be privy to all that is going on but to manipulate, ah, shall we say, certain objectives, to his desire. For these reasons, I deem it most prudent to spy on the couple while we can. Davis assures me their every word will be reported to him directly. All of their plans and actions will be at our fingertips."

Jean grinned. "That is good news for us and not so for them. Not that I fear them, and they have left us alone for some time now. I doubt we are…"

Tori hastily butted in. "Jean, you can't mean that? They have not left us alone, and they never will, I can tell you that. Don't you agree, John?"

"I do, and Jean, you would do best to listen to your wife."

"I do listen; I just don't always agree."

If Jean had been serious, Tori would have argued with him right there and then, but she saw what Grymes did not; her husband was goading her and did not mean what he implied at all.

"Jean, you should listen and agree more. Tori has a level head about her. Davis wanted me to inform you that his new employee, Francisco, would also keep watch. Seems Edward is back to his old gambling habits whenever he gets the opportunity, and that is quite often. If the man is not by Claiborne's side, he is seated at the card table. The Spanish gentleman in question has assured Davis that he intends to report any pertinent information. However, Francisco will not be seen visiting here if he should be invited, which he often has been of late. You do, after all, seem to have a bit in common;" he glanced toward Tori, "it seems... no matter, I digress. He will arrive discreetly and leave the same way. Can't tip our hand, don't you agree? Your continued friendship with Davis must remain cloaked. Francisco's friendship, you can explain away simply enough, but let's hope that is not necessary. Of course, you will be able to talk with both at the hotel, nothing unusual about that. I recommend that your conversations be of topics that can be overheard and nothing that will raise suspicion about your relationship with either the owner or his employee."

Tori had begun to laugh and could not stop. It took her several minutes to gain her composure and talk without bursting into laughter again. "I am sorry, really, I am. It's just the name, Francisco. You see, we both know him by the name Cisco and to hear you standing there calling him Francisco, well, it just cracks me up."

"Ah, Tori, one does not crack up," Jean was amused and twisting his mustache, a dead giveaway, that he too was finding the moment comical but did not wish for Grymes to realize it. "John, you will have to forgive my wife; she often finds things amusing that we would not. Again, I thank you for your visit and your continued guidance and due diligence in regard to our wellbeing."

Grymes nodded his head. "Right then, I shall take my leave." He turned and walked toward Jean's wife. "Tori, I would rather make you laugh than see you angry or sad. Both of which you may find yourself experiencing if you can't keep your husband under..."

"Enough," snapped Jean, "or you may find yourself none too happy."

The sharpness of Jean's tone warned his attorney not to push matters further. Grymes knew it was best; he departed before someone said something they should not, mainly himself. "Then good day to you both. Tori, you take care. Jean, we will talk soon, when you are more agreeable, I hope."

Tori smiled, the pair may argue, but both knew their bond of friendship would last a lifetime. As for their enemies, those two seemed as if they would last just as long. She agreed with Grymes and his continued worry over Edward and Simone. "Before you go, John, do you have word on the wedding date?"

"It is to be two weeks to the day and held at the Governor's home. Such is the high-standing Claiborne holds of Duval. I myself have an invite, one I can't turn down without raising suspicion as to my feelings toward either Claiborne or the soon-to-be wed couple. May I ask why you inquire? You're not expecting an invitation, are you?"

"Oh, heavens, no. That's one invitation I would turn down if we did get one. No, I was asking because with Simone and Edward so busy with wedding plans, we can safely assume things for us will remain quiet. It's just nice to know."

"Indeed, it is. I am off then. Till next time." He bowed his head and then did the same in Jean's direction. Without further words, he then departed.

Tori was frowning and sat down, still looking toward the door where Grymes had just stood. His lady looked deep in thought, and whatever she was thinking had her looking very solemn. Jean quickly realized he had to alleviate her anxious mood. "Tori, something troubles you? I would not overly worry about Duval..."

"I am not thinking about them. It's Grymes, his implying that I seemed to have more in common with Cisco. You did catch that, right? You don't think he has put two and two together, do you? I mean, he has never spoken a word about me to us. Not one question about where I came from. Not even when we confided in him and Leone about, well, you know. Leone had many questions but accepted the fact of time travel; Grymes acts as if he never heard a word of what we confided; why is that do you think?"

"That is just John. He is a man that deals in facts... in substance. You can't prove to him your story is true. He knows about you, and that is enough for now. Let us not worry."

"How can you say that? If he suspects Cisco, how long before he connects Davis too? I, no, we all gave our word that his identity would remain intact. I will have to speak to Cisco and tell him to cool it and to be extra careful around people. It's not like him to slip up, and he most certainly can't afford to slip up now."

"Agreed, we will both have to mention it to him. This term, cool it? You like to use the weather or one's own temperature to describe many situations. When you are hot, hot in the cot, that I understand but cool it? One can only surmise its meaning, and I have long since learned it is best not to do so with you."

Tori burst out laughing. "I do forget myself, sometimes, don't I? You have only to ask, and I will explain. If you cool it, I will try to make myself clear and use terms you will understand."

"My understanding is growing. My American vocabulary is slow; I admit that. I do catch things, though, words here and there. Odd terms that have strange meanings; however, I do like it when you explain yourself, now; if you cool it and come here, let me explain myself." He held out his hand and waited, knowing that his love could never resist him.

ALL who attended the wedding declared Simone was a radiant bride. Edward was a handsome, proud groom, and both he and his wife beamed with happiness. The bride had looked as if nothing in the world could be wrong. She smiled and laughed with the guests, all of whom had no idea that the beautiful female was far from happy on this, her wedding day. The new Madame Duval was furious at Edward's lack of progress with the Governor regarding placing Jean back in jail. It had been her utmost desire to forget about the Laffite's on this her most spectacular accomplishment. Her wedding was to have been nothing but a victory celebration in her mind, but it had not quite happened the way she had imagined.

The day had started as a dream wedding and ended up as a nightmare as far as she was concerned. All the bride had overheard repeatedly, at their reception, had been talk of Jean Laffite. Laffite, how dashingly handsome, how successful... and on and on went the praises until Simone was sick of it. Her new husband had to be told that such conversations had ruined her day. Edward had to do something about the situation, and that was that.

Duval knew his wife very well, and seeing that something had greatly disturbed her, he set out to learn the cause. Taking her aside, he asked in a concerned voice, "Are you sad that you married me? Or could it be that your wedding was not as grand as you would have wished? Perhaps you wish we had married in the church with a larger guest list? Or dare I assume my sweet Simone..." he hesitated, then taking her hand in his, he continued in a husky tone of voice. "Is it that you can't wait for this gathering to be over? That you have far more critical affairs to attend to in that beautiful mind of yours?" Edward ran his hand down around her waistline, and once it rested on her rear-end, he'd squeezed a hand full of flesh, kneading it suggestively in his palm as he spoke.

She shot him a smug smile, then let it quickly slip away. "Oh, Edward, my dear. Besides this night's upcoming duties, as your bride," she whispered, turning her salutary smoldering eyes up to meet his, "I want you to know that I was thinking about our life together, as man and wife," she lied. "It was wonderful; the wedding... you were right to keep it small and elegant. I am the envy of many, I am sure. Being married in the Governor's home and attended by only the highest in society. No bride could have asked for more. As for changing my mind, you, silly man, I am the happiest woman in the world. I am Madame Duval and very proud of it. I am your wife and, as such, will see to it that the Duval name is one to be reckoned with." She turned away from him and looked around the room. A sigh escaped her as she turned back to face her husband, thinking how she felt and why. 'Now that you are besotted, it is the time to tell you what's really on my mind, you fool.' Having Edward's full attention, she spoke with a touch of sadness in her voice. "There is, however, a dark cloud that has descended upon our day. It is the one reason behind some of my gloom. Have you not noticed the talk? Always it is about Laffite. It sickens me."

Edward had indeed been fully aware of the discussions that floated amongst his guests, and his mind filled with hate. 'Damn that pirate and his ability to overshadow what should have been the happiest of days, both for myself and my bride,' he thought.

"Edward," Simone said, using her sexiest voice, the one that pleaded and could not be easily ignored. "You know how grateful I am to you for such a wonderful wedding gift. The house is going to be the talk of the town when it is finished. But, my dear, if you want to make me... us... truly happy, then you have to find a way to put Jean back where he belongs, in chains. If ever you could give me a wedding present that I would love, beyond all others, it would be that. How can we be happy with that man walking the streets? The bastard mocks us, I tell you. Worse, the pirate, he mocks me. He knows he used me and would do so again, I am certain, regardless of you being my husband."

She was lying, but Edward did not know that. His jealousy of the pirate, having bedded his wife and now hearing that he'd do so again, was like oil to the flame. He would destroy the Laffite's, all of them before he would ever allow the man near what was his. "I agree with you, my love. I have delayed long enough. It is time to get back to work and destroy all of them. By that, I mean his men, his brother, as well as his whore of a woman. I intend to begin this very second. William is departing our gathering here to retire to his library, as is custom after a meal. You ladies may talk about today's events, our new home, and whatever else you desire. I do so hope, my dear, that you will find the opportunity to darken their glowing enthusiasm about that loathsome pirate. I shall do the same, but discreetly so. William is about to hear from me how the shadow of Laffite almost destroyed your day. So worried are you about how the citizens of this city are laughing behind his back." Edward had a wicked grin, and as he cocked his head to one side, he knew Simone had understood his intentions. "Now, if you will excuse me, my love, I shall begin." He left his bride's side and joined the men as they made their way toward the library.

The ladies left alone could concentrate on the bride and make small talk until their husbands returned. Knowing that Edward was plotting and planning, Simone relaxed and began to enjoy all the attention that now came her way. It was the consensus that the day had been excellent, and many told Simone how fortunate she was to have found Edward. Then, the subject changed to the new home, and how long did Simone expect it would be before they took up residence there? Simone was in her element at last. As Madame Duval, she was respected and her future secure.

THE day after the wedding, Edward insisted on paying Claiborne a visit and join in the meeting the man had called for unexpectedly. Upon his arrival and before the Governor called the session to order, the dandy took William aside and spoke in earnest to him. "I assure you, William, I am here with my wife's blessings. We are to take a trip to our plantation soon, and it will be there, we will celebrate our life together. Today, my visit is at my wife's request; she feels that you need to understand your current situation. Simone is in full agreement with me that I share with you; all that is being talked about behind your back."

"Talked about? What do you mean by that? May I ask who is talking?"

"Many are, and as always, I am your friend and confidant. I assure you I am here, only to inform you of your standing at this point in time. I thought it prudent to do so. If the Laffite situation continues, and the man is allowed to continue to walk the streets, as if he owns them, there will be trouble. As you are well aware, the Creoles are romantics, and they support the pirate and his illicit dealings, while the Americans do not. Those people are whispering about electing someone who will rid them of the brothers. Both Pierre and Jean have to go, and by that, I mean caught and put in irons or, better hung. Only then will the people of this city see what I know to be true. You, Sir, are the right man for the job."

By the time Edward had finished explaining things to Claiborne and done so in such a way as to fan the flames of hatred, he felt most confident that his mission had gone exceptionally well. The Governor had been increasingly agitated by the fact that Jean was able to carry on as he pleased. It further infuriated him that his friend Edward had just confirmed that a large portion of the local population and most of the Creole merchants seemed to be on the outlaw's side. As if that was not bad enough, this was occurring while the new and growing American side of town was screaming for something to be done. He had been unaware that many of them were threatening his re-election if something wasn't accomplished soon. William was genuinely upset because up until this moment, he had allowed himself to think of the talk as mere rumors.

Grasping his opportunity to continue, Edward added his final and most pertinent blow. "It would not surprise me, William, if you were to learn that Jean had the State Legislature in his hip pocket. My estimation is they are likely profiting from the pirate's activities themselves. Why else do they turn a blind eye, I ask you? Once again, I must reiterate, something must be done soon about this intolerable situation, or else we will all become the laughing stock of this fair city, and you, my dear Governor, will be without a job."

Claiborne shook his head in denial. "I can assure you that that will not be the case. All morning, even before your arrival, Edward, I was plagued by this very dilemma that you have brought to my attention, to our attention." He looked around the room at those gathered for this meeting. "Gentlemen, let us begin. I brought you here to discuss a certain matter pertaining as to what I should do about a certain problem pertaining to that hooligan pirate?" He looked at the young Duval. "This is your worry Edward, as it is mine, and indeed all of us here this morning. You see, gentlemen," he said, now addressing the whole room, "Laffite's bond has been forfeited, and as such, I was forced into taking action. I had the State's Attorney draw up a proclamation before you arrived, which by now has been posted." A rumble of voices, each expressing their own view on this piece of news, echoed about the room. "This day will go down in history. Not only is March 15, 1813, the beginning of your married life, Edward, but it is also the beginning of the fall of Laffite and his Banditti."

"But may I ask what was said in this proclamation, Sir?" a voice asked from across the room.

"Indeed, you may. Keeping to the point," the Governor continued, turning to face the gentleman who asked the question, "it has made my standing on this Laffite matter very clear. He is an outlaw engaged in unlawful activities. Activities that neither I nor this fine state will stand for any longer. I have also made it clear that this fine city's citizens had best desist in any such subversive practices with him. I had surmised, Laffite had a following within the Creole community, not all mind you." The Governor smiled and nodded his head in Edward's direction. "There are decent upstanding gentlemen, of Creole heritage, like yourself." He then looked around the room and ended up staring at two of the most prominent merchants. "Certain Creole merchants had best stop purchasing items from the Laffite's or suffer the severest punishment."

William looked back at Edward, whose stunned expression was

mistaken for one of concern. "So, you see, my dear fellow, I have taken it upon myself and my duty as Governor of this here fine state to see to the end of the unlawful trafficking on Barataria Bay and thereby put an end to the whole illegal activities. Jean Laffite's cruising of the high seas, plundering for his own gain, is about to be... how do you say... fini!"

Edward had had no idea that any such proclamation had been handed out, but now that he knew, he would, of course, let his Simone believe it to be one of his ideas, a small wedding surprise for his bride. Oh, this was going to be an excellent beginning to his marriage and an exciting start to Laffite's end.

TORI came downstairs to find Grymes and Jean deep in conversation. They didn't even stop talking to greet her when she entered the room, which was a reliable indicator that whatever they were discussing was serious. Laffite's wife did not interrupt but stood to listen to the lawyer.

"I tell you now, I have drawn up the papers, and he is moving ahead. I had no choice in the matter. You, Sir, are a wanted man. You have read them, they are a copy true, but they are what Claiborne now holds in his office, I assure you. I told you to stop your activities, to slow down. You have brought this on your own head Jean. My advice to you both," he looked toward Tori when saying the word 'both' and hesitated before continuing. "I can't see any other way forward; you need to leave town as soon as you can." John turned back to face Jean and finished his statement in an even more somber tone. "Remain gone for a while. At least until I can sort through all the legalities of your predicament."

Jean turned his back on Grymes as if not wanting to listen or even consider what he was talking about. He was treating the news as if it were nothing more than a mere inconvenience, and this action caused alarm. Grymes had to reach him, or Laffite would suffer the consequences, which were dire in his estimation. "If you don't wish to find yourself back in jail, you need to return to Grand Terre. I will get word to you as fast as possible, but this will take time, my friend. Jean, this is no trifling matter; these charges are cause to take note. Please, I insist you take precautions, if not for yourself, then for your wife." Grymes looked very worried as Jean handed him back the papers.

"I don't like it, what you are asking of me, but fear not, I will take your counsel and do as you ask. We were due to pay Grand Terre a visit anyway. I tell you now, I am not backing down, rather, taking the advice of my attorney and friend. Tori, I take it you have gathered enough, standing there, to know we are leaving as soon as you are ready. I will explain on our way. John, if you will excuse us, we have a lot to do. I thank you for allowing me to read those and for your wise words."

"You are most welcome. I had hoped it would not come to this." He folded the papers and put them inside his jacket. "Unfortunately, it has, and I will deal with it, but I need you to listen to me and follow my instructions to the letter. Do I have your word?"

"I can guarantee you I am abiding by your wish John. You have my word, Sir. We depart today."

"Your word is good, and I am most grateful for your change of heart. For a second there, one would have thought you had no manner of notion to take my advice. I must be on my way and you two on yours. Until we meet again." Grymes shook Laffite's hand, then briefly hugged Tori. "Do try to keep your husband out of trouble and remain safe, my dear." Then without further word, he hastily departed.

JEAN and Tori wasted no time. Within the hour of John Grymes's meeting, they were headed toward Grand Terre and the safety therein. The only thing utmost in Jean's mind was that he had been publicly declared an outlaw. America had turned on him while he did all he could to make it his ally. Spain and England were his enemies, and now it looked as though the very country he was supposed to help save had declared him, Jean Laffite, a foe.

This latest development was something that even Tori and her friends had not known about. Could it be possible, he wondered, that they were wrong about other such facts? One thing was certain; to stay in town would be suicidal. He had been declared no better than a Banditti! On top of this slur, he and his brother were now wanted. His so-called bond had been forfeited, and it was said the merchandise was missing and presumed back in pirate hands. He could be arrested at any time, and if that were so, his brother was also in danger!

While preparing to depart, they sent word of their new predicament to Pierre and hoped he too would leave town, thus remaining out of the law's reach and Claiborne's clutches.

Pierre, however, had a mind of his own. The man sat at a small desk in his Mistress's cottage and began to write. He was not about to turn tail and run, let alone run from the upstart American Governor. "My brother may run and hide, my dear," he told Marie, "I shall not. To leave your side would cause me great distress, and so I choose to remain. This idle threat toward myself and Jean is nothing to worry over. I would dare say it will all blow over before anything comes of it." With the note finished, he folded it and sealed it with a wax stamp. "See to it that Jean's boy returns with haste and hands my response to his Master as soon as he is able. Then you and I shall take a stroll and enjoy the day."

The note was delivered just in time, and though it was short and to the point, it did nothing to relieve the Laffite's concerns. Tori read it after Laffite and looked up into his worried face. "Jean, Pierre claims it is not he that Claiborne wants; it's you. He says right here that he has no intention of leaving the city. Is he crazy?"

"No, my love, not crazy, just stubborn. I think after we are gone, he will return to his senses and depart for Donaldsonville and the safety of the home he has there. Once he sees it is a serious matter, he can, if he chooses, depart for Grand Terre and make it to us without detection. As you know, the routes are well patrolled, and my men will keep an eye on my brother, fear not. We must depart and concentrate on slipping past Claiborne's soldiers. Time is of the essence. All we can do at this moment is pray Pierre understands what he is risking."

ONCE he got word of the proclamation, Cisco dropped by, only to find Jean and Tori already gone. Bessy handed him two letters that Tori had left for him. One was addressed to him, and the other he was asked to deliver to his friend. With no name on it, the housekeeper assumed he would understand just which friend it was. He read Tori's short message, explaining the predicament they now found themselves in. Then it went on to say that once they were settled in Grand Terre, she would contact him. Cisco smiled as he read the last line. It said he would always be welcome.

ACROSS town, in a hotel room, Simone was laughing and hugging Edward. "You did it. Why did you not share your plans with me, though?"

He kissed her on the cheek and grinned. "In case they did not come to fruition. I wanted to tell you only when his fate was sealed, as it was today."

Simone spun around laughing. "Oh, you have made me the luckiest woman around. I have married a brilliant man and one who has kept his promise. I feel as if I want to shout to the world. I want them all to know how happy I am."

Edward reached out and caught her by her arm. "You can't do any such thing. I am not to be seen taking credit for the pirate's fall. Remember, as always, it is William who takes the credit. Now, that Laffite's life is, how can I say, ah yes, in the hands of the law, we shall take a short trip to the plantation. It is time you visited the house;

after all, you are the home's Mistress, are you not?"

"I am, and to that end, I very much look forward to the visit, but I also wish to remain here and see Laffite arrested."

"I doubt that will happen anytime soon. My man has informed me that both Jean and the bitch have left town. How they got word of what William was doing is a good question but worry not, I am certain things will work out our way. Come, let us depart as soon as possible and not worry over the pirate and his demise."

"Worry? I will not do such a thing. I will celebrate. But, Edward, should we take the trip now? I mean, I have so much to do. There is so much to take care of. Maybe, we can delay it for a few days. After all, I shall have to pack, and you will have to gamble a bit, as lady luck seems to be smiling on you."

Edward was in agreement on that subject. She was right about waiting a few days, as there were indeed affairs to be taken care of. First, he would have to send out word that he and his wife would be at the plantation and more than delighted to entertain all. The man also knew he'd add; they hoped to be visited by all of their friends during their stay at the grand old home. Then he'd sit back and see who was willing to venture forth and declare themselves friends of the Duval's. It would be interesting to see if any of his brother's acquaintances would align with him now that he was in his rightful position. Those that didn't would be duly noted and ostracized by his family ever after.

THAT night they celebrated, and Simone was in her glory. So, sure of herself and her standing, the very next day, the scheming female had hired two dock workers to sell the contents of her townhouse. Simone knew Edward had planned and agreed on such action; she just hastened the move. She had even instructed them to remove all other articles she left behind and make sure the larger pieces went curbside display to obtain the best bids. The men were to bring her the funds the sale would create and do so discretely. But, by the end of the day, the beautiful bride was bedridden and seeing no one. Fatigue was her excuse; vanity and greed were her crimes.

DOWN by the French market, a free woman of color rearranged three pieces of furniture in a room above a small shop. She had acquired the expensive dresser at a sale the day before and, so far, had not regretted her extravagant purchase. It had been sheer luck that the piece had become available to her, and from the moment it was hers, the woman told herself God had blessed her and helped her to find a way to acquire it.

All her life, she had dreamed of owning a small, nicely furnished home, and after long hours of backbreaking work, her dream was, at long last, realized. For two years, she had been buying one piece at a time, mainly from the sales that the Laffite's held, but since hearing of the Governor's proclamation, she had thought it best to look elsewhere for what she required. That was when she had stumbled upon the purchase of her life.

It had not been easy to locate what she desired because very few people sold their furniture. The few odds and ends that she had seen over the past year were well out of her price range and not always just what she had in mind. Then, while delivering two gowns that she had created for her prominent customer, she overheard them talk about the sale of a particular home and all the contents therein. It was to be held at a modest townhouse, not far from where she was right then. Thus, it would allow her the opportunity to stop there without going too far out of her way. That's when her luck began, and God guided her.

The Mistress of the home, where she delivered her work, was going to see for herself if there would be any item she might like to purchase. They seemed to talk about such an event as if it were amusing to do so. It was during the fittings; the dressmaker also overheard the older woman say that it would be a surprise if she actually would acquire anything; she just wanted to see the kind

245

of furniture the establishment held. It seemed that the woman and her daughter were only going to satisfy their curiosity. It was not her place to listen or comprehend their conversation, but she continued to eavesdrop. The seamstress understood she was to be seen and not heard and never impart her opinion no matter what. So, she did what was expected and kept her head down and all musings to herself. Instead of listening to the women's continued gossiping, she paid close attention to how excited she was at the prospect of seeing what was available and kept her emotions to herself.

Her mind was on her job and dreaming about finding an affordable piece of furniture to add to her growing collection when, to her utter surprise, the client had inquired if she would care to walk with them? Of course, the excited mulatto had agreed, never expecting the outcome would reward her so richly.

THE three women had arrived at the location, just in time to find two large men carrying out a heavy piece of furniture, which anyone could see, was of top quality. The men were grumbling amongst themselves and not too quietly either. "I tell you she was a real bitch, talking to you like you was dirt and all. I, seen her likes before, moved up in the world fast like and then thinks they are better than us. Get as much as you can, says her, and be quick about it. Telling us, she'd know if we kept anything on the side. What the hell does she know, I, asks you? Then making us carry it down here and outside, just to show off what she was selling and not needing. Never had to do the likes of that, ever."

"Me neither," puffed the other man carrying the heavy load. "I tell you, I be in full agreement; she wants to show folks that she has no use of this and all the rest we have to bloody well drag down here. Advertising she got better, now, she is. If it weren't that my missus needs the rent, I'd a told her where she could shove this here dresser."

They put the massive chest of draws down and stepped back. "I got an idea; let's sell it quickly like, for far less a sum than we could get if we waited. First-person, to make an offer, gets the bloody thing, what says you?"

"Justice, I say, that's what it is. First come, first served; it is then."

That had been the very moment the seamstress had stepped up, never thinking it was indeed possible to strike a deal but willing to try. Her first offer was too low, even for them, but then the most surprising thing had happened, just as the church bells rang, God, it seemed, stepped in to help.

Her client, Miss Elizabeth, stepped in front of her and made a slightly higher bid, and the item sold. However, before she could feel sad that the most desired piece of furniture was out of reach, the woman turned to her and pulled her aside to talk. That's when they had made a deal, and what a deal it was. It would be hard work; during hours, she'd usually rest, but that was not going to be a problem to keep what she wanted. "Yes, praise the Lord," she murmured. "For five gowns of top quality and the promise of a quick delivery on all five, I got myself some fine-looking furniture. Miss Elizabeth nice too, 'cause she only wants the five gowns and nothin' more. Yes, I get to keep my coins, which means I get to shop again, anytime I want to. Find me something nice to go with you; I will." She stroked the large ornate piece lovingly. Then, taking a rag with a small amount of beeswax on it, she began to polish the wood to a high shine. "That Miss Elizabeth, she is real, good to me, buying you for me and letting me work off my debt.

Now you be mine, and I be so proud." She hugged herself briefly and then went back to work, cleaning, while she continued thinking. 'Lord, them, white folks, they don't know what they has most the time. I ain't never goin' to sell such a fine piece, no sir. Never could make me enough to buy the likes of you again.'

The seamstress happily hummed a tune as she carefully and lovingly cleaned and worked at erasing any touch of white folks, fingerprints, on her prized possession. Each drawer she removed was wiped both inside and out. This was followed by a closer inspection and waxing of the inside area before sliding the draws back in place. Not one space was left untouched, and that was how she discovered the document.

During the dresser's interior examination, much to her surprise, a parchment was found. If she had not been so thorough in her cleaning, the paper would have gone undiscovered and wedged for eternity inside the back of the dresser, she told herself. Fascinated, she took the large sheet in her hands and unfolded it carefully. It was torn in one place, where the drawer, at one point or another, had caught it, but other than that, it seemed to be intact. Just what it was, she could not tell, nor would she dare speculate. Nevertheless, something told her this was trouble, and the nervous woman had no idea what to do about it.

Thoughts, such as taking it to Miss Elizabeth or the church, raced in her mind. Sitting down, she spoke aloud. "No, that would not do." The female looked back at the place she had found the article. "I could just put it back and forget it, but that be like lying, and that be a sin," she whispered to the heavens. 'Oh Lord, what's I goin' to do about this here paper?' She raised it and studied it closely. She would have learned how to read and write if she had had her way, just like the white folk did. Oh, she was smart enough; she knew that, but it was not that easy, was it? She shook her head sadly. There was no one willing to teach her that she knew of, and she didn't want to spend her hard-earned money on paying someone either. Then a sly smile crossed her young face as her mind tackled the problem. 'For years, she had been learning herself, hadn't she? Not easy to do, but not impossible either.'

"Maybe, I could, like see if I know'd any of these here words? If'n I knows some of them written down, that could help me some. Yes, that's it. I'll just take me a look and see." She held the document in her trembling hands and carefully looked at the words placed neatly in dark ink. Whoever had written those words sure did a purty job, she thought. Then an idea fleetingly crossed the woman's ever-curious mind. 'Maybe, I can, git me some paper and try to do me some purty lettering?" Sadly, she shook her head. 'Nope, can't do that. It's not right to do so, white folks not liking that, and I know'd it. Still, can't help to try and read a bit. All I has to do is look closer and see for myself if there be a word or two I gits.'

She recognized a few small, easy words, scrawled in penmanship that was as foreign to her as the language it was written in. She knew a few English words, but most of her self-taught reading dealt with French. So, there was her first clue, she told herself. It belonged to someone who spoke English. What else did she know? The house, where the drawers and document had come from, was not in the new district, no way. It had come from a small townhouse in the French region. So why was it written in English? Better still, why had it been lost or hidden at the back of her drawers? She looked up at the piece of furniture once more and then down at the paper. It was a puzzle, and puzzles could be solved if you worked hard. 'Maybe it fell out of the drawer and got pushed back there. Maybe it just got lost like, not hidden.' The woman examined the article still closer. It looked very impressive, and elegant too, a love letter maybe? Whatever it was, she just knew in her heart that it was important to someone.

The woman stood up and looked inside the empty space to make sure there was nothing else. Upon finding nothing, she picked up the document and looked again closely as if expecting to learn the mystery behind its appearance. If it had been lost, she told herself, someone would have looked for it and most likely found it. This conclusion frightened her. "No, you was hidden, and you be trouble just like I told myself." She put the paper down quickly, acting as if it were going to bite her hand or worse. Then her eyes registered a name that she recognized. Looking closely, she found the title at the very top of the paper and then again on the bottom. It was one English name that she knew, but to make sure, she would go out right that second and walk over to where it could be compared with the sign. If it matched, she'd see it, and if not, only then would she have to think about things more.

"I know'd it already in my heart Lord, it be the same name. Yes, I do. How else I know that there, name if it weren't the same? Lord, you done showed me the way, and I done know what to do. I just return it to this here person, whose name I see. Yes, that be the right thing for me to do." Quickly she put on her cape and stuffed the paper in a large pocket, out of sight.

The woman had to hurry; the day was already growing late, and she did not want to spend one more night with this document in her house. It was going to take her some time walking to the building, where she had seen the name. Because of that, the woman prayed there was enough time before the white folk left for home.

Stepping outside her small shop, she found herself thinking how white folk were lucky to have their names on their shops. With trembling fingers, caused by her anxious mood, a brass key turned and locked the door. It would not do her any good to carry on so, she told herself. 'I has to calm myself some, or folks a going to see I ain't acting right. Then some might think I be up to no good.' While taking in a deep breath, her eyes looked upward. What would her name look like written above her door, she wondered? Gazing at her sign, she grinned.

The seamstress had made it herself and been very proud of it. It was not her name, but it was what she did. She had painted a needle and thread and surrounded it with a design like lace. No, it was not her name, but it had worked just fine.

Calmer now, the woman turned away and started walking briskly toward the American section of the city. How was it, she wondered for the first time, white folks knew what kind of shop somebody had when all it had was a name? Suddenly, and for the first time, she figured it out. "That's what the other letters be about. They are telling the peoples what they, needs, to know." Then with pride at having solved another one of life's many mysteries, she concluded that her sign was better by far. 'Cause, if'n you can't read, you still know'd what I be sellin'. Her spirits soared. 'Yes, I be smarter than most folks think I am.' Determined that she was doing the right thing, she hurried on her way, passing the grand hotel and unknowingly the document's former owner.

EDWARD had thought that Simone had destroyed Leone's will the same day he had stolen it. Instead, she had hidden it away at the back of her chest of drawers. Ever scheming, his wife had done so as sort of an insurance policy of her own.

Should Edward ever choose to leave her, she'd use it against him and bind him to her. That had been the plan. Simone had told herself that she would burn the document; once she was Edward's wife; that part of the plan, however, was never put into action.

Simone remembered the will she had stashed away, but by the time she returned to the townhouse to see what remained, all within had been sold. Not wanting to raise Edwards's suspicion, the desperate woman set out on her own to locate the men she had hired. It was a task that cost her quite a bit of money; in fact, the desperate female used all the funds that came from the sale, an amount that her husband was unaware of. But, loathed as she was to part with such a sum, Simone understood she had no choice.

Using her wits and money, she was able once again to talk with one of the men who had done her bidding. He had co-operated as best he could and seemed genuine in his answers. Simone had no reason to doubt the man and dismissed him once she was satisfied. After he left the small dockside inn, Simone went over and over each word he had spoken.

"Ma'am, you told us to sell it all and be quick. You did not tell us, to keep no record, of who bought what. We just did as you told us. I wish I could help you, but I can't. I don't even remember who came by or who took what. Just they all paid, and we gave you the total." He had sounded so sincere in his explanation that Simone believed him. Had she known the man was lying to her and doing so in such a blatant manner, she would have pressed harder to reach the truth and then seen to it that the individual was punished one way or another.

Simone had walked back to the hotel in a desperate state of mind. With no way to locate the furniture and retrieve the will, what was she to do? The guilty female made herself sick with worry and was a complete wreck by the time she reached their rooms. In fear, Edward's wife took to her bed, sick with a headache, and asked that she not be disturbed. Due to her sudden illness, the trip to the plantation had to be delayed, and the doctor was called. The physician told Edward bed rest was the best he could offer. The strain of the wedding and being a new bride were to blame for her melancholy mood and painful headache; however, he assured the newlywed that his wife would soon return too normal, and her pains would be no more.

Edward was disappointed that his new bride was indisposed but not enough to keep him away from the card tables, particularly where the man called Francisco dealt. He always had a certain amount of luck when with him, and the man was easy to talk to.

Simone continued to hide her fear and worry as the days slipped by. She even took to sleeping alone, fearing she may talk in her sleep and reveal her secret. Her nights were filled with vivid dreams of Edward holding the will and demanding that his wife accept the fact that their marriage was over. She could not help her dreams, but during the daylight hours, Simone would sit and go over all the possibilities she could conjure up, driving herself, still crazier with concern.

If the document were discovered and fell into the wrong hands, all would be lost. Those that found it would either turn it over to her husband or, worse, to that bastard Grymes. Then she told herself that would not be the worst; she could find herself blackmailed if the person realized the importance of the document. Life, it seemed, had once again dealt her a hard hand. How could she have been so stupid as to forget about the blasted will, she'd ask herself repeatedly? And this one question haunted her day and night with no solution in sight.

In the end, Simone surmised that all she could do was wait and see if the new owner of the chest of drawers discovered its hidden secret. No doubt, if it were found, it would be so immediately. As it had not turned up and each hour passed with no news, Simone began to allow herself to believe she had gotten away with her deceitful act. Feeling safer and not wanting to give herself away, Edward's bride emerged from seclusion.

As the days slipped by and still the will did not surface, she convinced herself that it was indeed safely and securely hidden and would never be found. If and when it was, she would most likely be dead and buried after a long and joyful life. Her headaches vanished, and life progressed happily once again. For Simone, the matter of Leone's will was once more conveniently dismissed.

UPON arriving at the building, where the seamstress was sure she had seen the same name written on the paper, she hesitated. Her hands now trembled as she took out the document to compare the letters. The woman knew that she had to be very careful at this point and not let anyone see her. Looking around, she found that she might have a chance to act unseen if she acted quickly, as not too many people were walking by. The few that did pass her paid her no attention like most days, which gave her confidence. Feeling better about chancing a glance, the nervous female looked at the name written on the paper, then at the one on the sign. Sure enough, they were the same; of this, there was no doubt. However, the rest of the writing before her was far too difficult for her to make out. Sure, she knew the word, 'at,' that was simple, but the rest remained a jumble of indistinguishable words. They were far too difficult for her to make out, and she'd not stand there attempting to do the impossible. Knowing she had the right place and the correct name was enough for her. In her mind, there was nothing left to do but knock on the door.

JOHN Grymes had been working late and was about to leave when a knock came upon his door. Typically, one of the junior lawyers would take care of answering the call, but he had let everyone go early, something he always did when he was working on Jean's behalf.

He answered the door while putting on his coat, thinking it would be nothing more than someone delivering a message.

A woman of mixed heritage and not at all unattractive, but not what he would have considered pretty either, was standing before him. She was dressed in an outfit that, while denoting her class, was clean and well made. Her face, young in years, was somehow older in expression. Her posture was upright, and her gaze was somewhat uncomfortably forthright.

"May I be of some assistance?" His voice came out sounding somewhat surprised and unsteady, even to his ears. However, she didn't seem to notice as she nodded her head in the affirmative.

"I'm sorry to be here so late and seeing you about to leave and all. I won't be a keepin' you long. I have to see the man, whose name is written right there," she pointed to his name printed on the small plaque. "Will he still be here?" The lady had spoken in English with a heavy French accent, and though her grammar was poor, her overall demeanor was open and honest.

Grymes did not recognize this woman, and the fact that she asked for him caught him off guard. "May I ask why you wish to see him?"

"That's between him and me. You may tell him that I think I have something he has lost, and I would very much like to return it to him, personal like. It being the right and proper thing to do."

John looked closely at her, quickly trying to size her up. She was apparently determined to reach him and seemed to be telling the truth. But just what was it that she had of his, he wondered? He'd not misplaced or lost anything that he could recall. John looked at her more closely. The female certainly had courage, standing there, demanding only to see him. She also looked frightened half to death, as if not wanting to be seen standing there. He took a step forward without thinking; he looked up and down the street before turning his attention back to the stranger. One thing was clear; the Creole had come unescorted and was standing her ground, which he found intriguing.

The woman was a proud individual, and despite her apparent fear, her eyes never left his. Grymes smiled kindly toward her, trying to ease her discomfort as he continued to scrutinize her. She was fascinating to him, a real enigma if ever there was one. The woman seemed self-assured and yet uncomfortable at the same time. The manner in which she was dressed and her thick accent told him something, though. The astute Grymes determined that she was from the other side of town. His guess was that she was a free woman of color and an intelligent one.

But why point to his name and not just ask for him outright? Just what was her connection to him? What on earth could it possibly be? No matter how much he tried, the attorney could not imagine under any circumstance why this woman was insisting she meet him. One thing was evident: his curiosity peaked, and he knew that he would have to find out what was going on. "Please come in," he said, standing back to let her pass through the entrance before closing the door. "I think maybe, I had best introduce myself to you. I am the gentleman in question. The one whose name is on the wall outside; Mr. John Grymes at your service."

Her mouth dropped open, then just as quickly, she recovered her emotions and openly stared at him. John saw her disbelief, so he nodded as if to confirm she had heard him correctly. He took her by the arm and escorted her from the entrance hall and into his office. "How can I be of assistance? You say you have something I lost? That seems highly unlikely, as I am not currently aware of any article missing, and may I add; I do not think we have ever met. So, indeed, what makes you think, this article you have belongs to me?"

The woman looked at him, suspicion on her face. "Yes, that's right enough. I don't know you. Know who John Grymes is, though. Just 'cause I'm me, and uneducated don't mean I'm stupid. I've been around this here town some and in many fine homes. Peoples talk, and I listen. Just never met you before or seen you. How'd I know you be this here, Monsieur Grymes, the State's Attorney?"

The mention of his position caused him to pause briefly. This person standing before him was not stupid, and those she came in contact with were fools if they thought so. Grymes knew he had to get her to believe him so they could proceed, and he had to do so in a forthright and straightforward manner that she would understand. Also, he determined it would have to be handled so as not to insult her or diminish her quest. "In answer to your question, you can't know for certain, but you seem to be an intelligent woman. Look around you; this is a private office. This is my office, and here on the desk is my name." He pointed to the small brass nameplate. "I can assure you I am, who I say," he said, smiling at her. "You have my word on that." John softened his tone and talked to her in what he liked to call his parent tone. "This being my office and us standing in it, well, I could not be anyone else now, could I?" Giving her some time to think about that, he walked around his desk and pulled out his chair, seating himself comfortably. He then reached and opened a drawer, taking out a pen and ink, along with some paper on which to write.

She had watched him, and seeing he knew where things were kept; the female made up her mind; he was telling her the truth. Besides, she wanted to get rid of the document and be on her way home as soon as possible, so delaying further asking more questions was pointless in her estimation. "I found this in my chest of drawers," she held up the paper, "stuck way in the back. I was cleaning, you see, and I think maybe you owned the drawers before I bought them."

He raised his eyebrow at this. He had sold no furniture now or since moving here. The woman was obviously confused. Easy to do, if you can't read, he figured.

She saw the look on his face. Clearly, he did not believe her. "I did buy them. Miss Elizabeth, she got them for me, and I paid her for them." She pushed the paper across the desk toward him, quickly withdrawing her hand.

It was on the tip of his tongue to tell her that he had not sold any chest of drawers and just what made her think the papers belonged to him when his mouth slammed shut. He recognized his handwriting immediately, and still further to his astonishment and sheer delight, he saw the document for what it was. "You found this at the back of your drawers?"

"Yes, Sir. Like I done told you, it must have got stuck there, and I got it, and I see'd your name right there on the top and the bottom. Then I told myself that I had best bring it to you and all. I hope I did, right? It is yours, isn't it?"

"My dear lady, you did far more than right. Yes, it's mine, and yes, I did misplace it quite a while ago. So long ago that I completely forgot about it." He looked again at the folded paper to be sure he was not dreaming and then back at the woman. "Madame, I did not get your name. You are...?"

"Why'd you need my name now? I'm in trouble, aren't I? You think I took it? I didn't! I swear it! Oh Lord, I know'd that it be trouble when I first laid my eyes on the thing." She was backing up toward the door as if getting ready to run. Her hands were twisting on themselves, and she was all but crying.

Grymes knew he had to calm her down, so he stood as he quickly spoke. "No, no! You are not in any trouble, I promise you. I just wanted to thank you by name, that's all. It was very good of you to return this to me and, might I add, very clever of you to figure out it belonged to me. If you wish to keep your name to yourself, then that is up to you." He was using that parent tone again as if he were reassuring a child. "If it makes you feel any better, then by all means, please do so. I do think that you should be rewarded for your honesty and integrity, though."

"I know 'bout honesty, but that other, I ain't knowin' 'bout. I don't need nothin'. Just want to go home and forget about it; that's all."

John reached into his jacket and took out some coins. "Look, I would not feel right if you didn't take something for your trouble, and then we can say goodbye and forget about it, yes?"

Seeing him counting out the money and knowing it was a comfortable sum, she rapidly reasoned with herself that it was only fair to take his reward. "I will be thankin' you then," she said, holding out her hand.

John dropped the coins into her palm and would have gladly paid her much more for the document but felt it more prudent to make light of the matter. He told himself 'it's better if she forgets about it and goes on her way.' Grymes wanted no one to know, especially Edward and Simone, that he had the will back, safely, where it belonged. He'd been careless once before, but never again.

Smiling at the amount of silver and happy to be finished with the ordeal, she turned to leave. Then, thinking that she really could trust this man and maybe someday might need a favor from him, she turned and spoke up. "Je suis, Mademoiselle Musette DuPree." She was smiling now. "I own a small dress shop at the end of Toulouse, close by the corner of Dauphine. It is a shop outside of which hangs my sign. It ain't got fancy words like you have. Just drew me a picture, showin' what I, does. I sew, make gowns for the fine ladies."

"That, Mademoiselle DuPree, is very clever of you. I can truly say it is my honor and pleasure to make your acquaintance." John was beaming and meant each and every word.

He was thrilled; he had let this woman come inside instead of turning her away. Thank God for small favors and kind acts, he told himself, as he walked back around his desk toward the seamstress. "And now, if you would please excuse me, I do have an urgent matter at hand. I was on my way out if you remember? However, let me assure you that your meeting with me will always be remembered. I seldom forget those whose character is upstanding and as forthright as yours. Should you ever need my assistance... well, it goes without saying, does it not? I am now and will always be at your service. Now, however, I must insist that our meeting come to an end."

"Merci Monsieur Grymes, and please don't bother yourself. I have kept you too long, for that I am sorry. I am glad to have been of some help to you. I will let myself out. I'm in a hurry also, wanting to get back and all. Maybe we will meet again someday, oui? Maybe, your wife, she would like a gown? I would be honored to make her one. Until then, au revoir." It was obvious to Musette that she was no longer wanted. She also knew that she had done nothing wrong to warrant his eager dismissal of her but was wise enough to know when to take the hint and depart.

Before any further conversation could take place, or before she got herself into some kind of trouble with this important man, Musette knew to get, while the getting was good.

John watched as she turned and hastily departed. The sound of the outer door closing let him know that he was once again alone in his office. Standing there holding the will, the attorney felt a tinge of guilt for the way he had hurried her out, but his excitement over what he now had in his possession had warranted her quick dismissal. Grymes had not wanted her to see how very glad he was to receive what she had given him, a task that had been very difficult because he had wanted to shout out in joy. "Leone, my friend," he spoke softly, "God smiles on you this night. I would have bet my last coin that never would I have seen your will again. I hold in my hands, once again, the proof necessary to oust that bastard and his wife.

Jean and Tori's son, Christopher, was to have been your heir, to have your estate, once he came of age. It states here; also, that should he not inherit, then his parents would. Sadly, we both know that the child died, and I see the wisdom in all you requested. I hope the lad is with you, and both of you are now at peace. By God," his hand hit the desk, "I will see to it that Jean and Tori inherit, what is rightfully theirs, and I can, at last, keep my word to you! Do you hear me, Leone?" he shouted. "I can keep my word!"

Instantly John set to work writing an urgent message to Jean, explaining that he had some important news for him, and urged Jean to contact him at his earliest convenience. He did not even hint at the urgent information, just in case the message was to fall into the wrong hands. From here on, he told himself, he would be very cautious. The attorney dipped his pen into the ink and added, 'You will not be disappointed. Your humble servant John Grymes.' Smiling, he finished the letter and headed for the blacksmith shop, taking the will with him. Once there, he would pass the note to Thiac, who, in return, would see it delivered safely to Laffite. Then he intended to place the will with a colleague he trusted. His law partner, Edward Livingston, would ask no questions and keep the document hidden until needed. The man would also act on his behalf, should anything befall the States Attorney; this was a certainty and comfort to Grymes. Retribution was within his grasp, and nothing and no one was going to stand in his way.

WITHIN a few days, Jean received Grymes's message and read it out loud to Tori. "What do you make of it?"

"I'm not sure. It seems to me that the information he alludes to could be nothing but good news, though. Jean, do you intend to go into the city anytime soon?" Concern filled her voice. "It is still dangerous for you. I'm afraid you will be taken into custody."

"No, my love. I intend to stay right here for the time being. You may relieve yourself of any worry in that direction. I am not so stupid as to place myself into the Governor's hands so easily. Maybe we will go later in the summer when things have calmed down."

"And, how do you think they will do that, may I ask? You are causing far more trouble these days for yourself. Why, only yesterday, I saw another of the ships sail in loaded down with the contents taken from... Jean, are you listening to me?"

"It is of no concern to you," he snapped. "I have given you my word that no American ships will be taken, have I not? That is, what you're asking, isn't it? Well, my love, for your information, it was a British ship that was taken." His temper was rising as he continued sarcastically. "The Americans will soon forgive and forget, or I will earn back my dignity by taking still more English vessels. That is how it is done. I fight this war for them, and all is forgiven. I take the British ships, as we are at war with them still. The war of 1812 is far from over if I listen to you. According to Cisco, even after they sign the treaty, it is a ruse. America will forgive me soon, right? Why else would I join them against the crown? Better they come around soon, I tell you. They care not right now, but they will, according to you, John and Cisco. I, however, tell you now that I continue to pray you are correct in that account. Much more of this waiting will give me far more cause to raid on the high seas and tempt me into such action that I may give the American's something to cause a greater worry than they can imagine."

He had spoken with such a sarcastic tone that Tori found herself irritated and angry. How dare he doubt her and their friends and what they knew! "You are impossible!"

"And you are unreachable. I shall take my leave before we disagree further."

"Jean, you come back here," she called to his back. "I'm not finished."

"Well, I am! I have to attend to the day's work. We will talk more over dinner, oui?"

Tori knew they would not. They talked less and less these days about his work at Grand Terre. Jean had put a wall up between them, and he was securely hidden behind it for better or worse. She knew he was having trouble with Gambi; there was nothing unusual about that. There was also another pirate, who she had not met. His name was Humbert, and Dominique claimed he respected the man. As for Jean, Tori could not judge if he felt the same. Either way, this new pirate brought in boatload after boat-

261

load of goods, and some of the men were becoming increasingly upset by his success and their lack of luck.

The pirates were angry that their Boss would not allow any American vessels to be taken, which caused much strife. Then there was the increase of the Governor's men, patrolling the waterways and confiscating all they could. It had been hinted to Laffite that maybe one or more of his own men had been paid off and informed the authorities of their routes and times of shipments. This situation had forced Laffite to move some of his operations to an island further West along the coast. Cat Island quickly grew, and new routes North toward the Mississippi were developed. On the far side of the Mississippi, the town of Donaldsonville was now a major hub for smuggled goods going to the city.

Jean faced all the changes and difficulties and dealt with each as they arose. Meetings at all hours were held and, more often than not, behind closed doors. To Tori, it seemed that Laffite was consumed in proving his worth to the Americans while keeping control over his empire. The task was taking its toll, both on them as individuals and their relationship.

Over the last few months, Tori had seen how Jean had changed and how he acted more like a pirate than a privateer. He was often gruff and guarded, leaving Tori to wonder why? If he blamed her for his troubles, why didn't he just come out with it instead of lashing out at her with these small but upsetting blow-ups? And if that's not what was bothering him, then what was? If only he would talk to her or Dominique about what was upsetting him, she might be able to help, she thought.

Tori had noticed a sad, lonely look replace his angry scowl as he walked toward the beach. Laffite's wife couldn't help him, and she couldn't reach him, but she could be patient. In time, he would come around; he always did. Still, the waiting was difficult, and she was lonely. Because of this, thoughts of the lake and going home began to cross her mind more often, and dreams of Linni filled her nights.

❦

JUNE was upon them, and with it, the heat of the summer once again blanketed the bayous. For hours, in the hottest part of the afternoon, Tori would lay in the hammock strung under the front verandah. She would lie there, trying to catch the sea breeze and fan herself, desperately trying to cool off.

The afternoons were the quietest and calmest part of the day, mainly because it was too damn uncomfortable to do much else. She knew that Grand Terre was far cooler than up in the city, but it sure did not feel that way to her.

The bay waters sparkled and danced as the small waves rolled into shore. The deep green and blue hues of the Gulf shimmered through the heat waves. Those rippling waves rose off the land, making the Gulf look more like a mirage than an actual body of water. Even the birds that generally danced about the water's edge were gone at this time of day. Nothing, it seemed, had enough energy to disturb the tranquil picture that lay before her.

Tori dozed on and off, debating whether or not to go for a swim. The humid air was so thick and heavy that it was an effort, even to breathe. The heat was so oppressive and worse still; it caused her to sweat like a pig, she angrily thought. Her mind continued to wander. 'Deodorant and maybe air-conditioning, now that would be worth moving for. Only neither are available, are they?' Tori could see no use in wasting what little energy she had, just to get up and change into her breeches and top, to walk down to the beach to swim? She was drenched anyway, and swimming clothed, as she'd have to, was just ridiculous.

Rivulets of sweat trickled down the sides of her face. Her entire body was covered in a light film of moisture. Tori's damp blouse, along with the rest of her garments, literally clung to her flesh. Frustrated, the short-tempered woman lifted the wet blouse off her skin. When she did this, a waft of even hotter air escaped from within the confines of the garment. Angrily, she hiked her skirt up over her knees, telling herself that maybe, the idea of a swim was not so bad after all? However, all thoughts of swimming left her at this precise moment, as the tranquility surrounding the village was utterly shattered.

A loud clanging of a bell echoed across the whole area, something Tori had never heard before, and it unnerved her. Birds took flight, and men and women, from all directions, ran toward the Gulf beaches. Something was wrong, and even though Tori could see no threat, she knew this was no drill; whatever was happening was very real. Never had she seen the village react in such a frantic manner, and again, her nerves fluttered.

Like everyone else, Laffite's lady knew not a ship could come or go that Jean was not informed about. His network of spies covered many square miles of territory, and each could signal another, relaying the identity of any given craft sighted. All along the shoreline, the men kept watch for many miles in both directions. So how any vessels could have slipped by unseen seemed unlikely to be the culprit for the village's arousing.

Tori placed her hand on her brow to block out the bright sunlight to see better, and still, she saw nothing that could have raised the alarm. If they were under attack, where was it coming from, and who was attacking? These were questions she wanted answered, and so without hesitation, she ran toward the beach, along with many others.

Once standing at the shoreline, Tori witnessed several rowboats already reaching the sides of two larger ships anchored not far away. Looking back along the beach, she saw other fully-loaded small boats pushing off. The men were shouting orders to each other and seemed to be in quite a hurry to depart. Tori looked back toward their destination and frowned. One of the large vessels anchored offshore was Jean's, and the other belonged to one of the Italian pirates, but which one she was not sure. She could not spot Jean on deck, but there was no doubt that they were readying to make sail.

So many new ships came and went each day, it seemed, and there were many new Captains, and sometimes, merchant ships from France or the islands docked at Grand Terre rather than go up the river. But no strange ships were currently anchored, and as far as she could tell, none were approaching to do so. It all seemed so confusing; why were they boarding and making ready to sail in such haste?

Observing both ships' decks, she saw they were a hive of activity. Then, as more boats pulled up alongside the Italian vessel, she witnessed the pirates hastily climb the ropes that hung over the side of the hull. Tori stood transfixed as the sails of this boat dropped, even before the last of the men had boarded. It was as if the ships were in a race to see who could up anchor and sail free before the other.

Looking around for answers as to what was happening and why Tori saw a face she knew. It was one of the pirates who had helped her get Jean and his men out of jail, so she felt she could trust him. "Hey, you, please, can you tell me what's going on?"

"Aye, I can. Seems our men spotted two bloody, begging your pardon, English ships trying to sneak up on us. Coming from that way, they be." He pointed off to her left.

"But, aren't the British camped out that way," she pointed East, knowing the British were camped at what would be known as Pensacola, Florida.

"Well, these buggers ain't coming for us all easy like, hell no. They be sailing up from the other way. I guess they think the sun will be blinding us to their arrival. They don't know the Boss, though; he'll be blinding them soon enough. I heard tell, the English were not far from Last Island, them be barrier reef islands, Ma'am. So, don't you worry any. Our man said those ships been sitting there for a bit, waiting they are, for the tide to turn, Ma'am."

"The tide?"

"Aye, but don't look so upset. Boss has most of his crew, and Gambi has his. Between them, they will make short work of the Red Coats. You see. I am, right. Besides, they got Dominique on

Boss's ship, and he has him a fine eye when it comes to his cannons."

"So, I have been told."

"Miss, I was there when Boss got the word, and I heard it all. It was said the English were moving slowly along the outer banks. Bidding their time seems like. Boss thinks someone told them about us here, about Grand Terre and all. Told them that this time of the month is when most of our fleet is out, what with the moon going dark. Anyway, Boss thinks they are waiting for the tide to turn. That be when it's low, real low like, and our ships at anchor run the risk of running aground, trying to leave. Well, that's when they will strike. See, no one's looking that way for them, the English that is, and the tide will be low when the sun is just high enough off the water to blind anyone bothering to look. Cunning, if you think about it. Boss said it was a good plan but not good enough. That's why they are leaving in a hurry. The tide will begin its turn soon, and Boss plans to use it to his advantage. So, them, bloody English, will never see him coming. Then he will blow them out of the water."

"You mean to tell me they are going to fight? A battle at sea?" She looked back at Jean's ship, which was now at full sail and moving out into the Gulf, followed closely by Gambi's vessel.

"Miss Tori, Ma'am, you ain't got to worry much, Boss ain't lost a battle yet, and now he knows them, English bastards, begging your pardon, be trying to sneak upon us. The surprise will be theirs I assure you."

"Why is he turning? Is something wrong? Gambi's following, look."

"Yes, Ma'am, that's what he has planned. He's going to hug the shoreline."

"Oh my God, that's crazy; what if he runs aground?"

"He got him a good crew, and the tide is high right now."

Tori looked at the man. "Not for long, though, right? Is there enough time for them to reach the British ships before the waters begin to recede? How far is this Last Island?" She looked back at Jean's ship, chewing on her lower lip with worry.

"Not far. It is close to Cat Island, and we have many men working there, and ships come and go, as you know. Good thing we do, or those Red Coats might have sailed right to us, destroying us. I reckon you will hear them cannons rightly enough. Boss, he will use all his force to be sure, and if I was among those English sailors, I would be a fearing what I see heading toward me. You need to excuse me now, I have to prepare, in case them bastards, pardon my language, do arrive here. You best be heading back to your house now. It is safer, rightly enough. An', Miss Tori, I'd find me that little weapon you had with you last time we were together. Just in case, not meaning to scare you or anything, just help, is all." With that said, he touched his forehead with his two fingers in a quick salute and was off.

Tori was left alone, standing on the beach along with a few women and children, all of whom were watching the Gulf. Jean's ship was getting smaller as each second passed, with Gambi's following close behind. She tried looking ahead of them to the horizon, but try as she might, she could not see a sign of the British anywhere. Then she began to worry about another fact besides the battle that the ships were sailing toward.

Could this be how the British arrived to talk to Jean like Davis had told them happened in history, and if so, and the pirates fired on the English, would he be changing things? Tori prayed this would not be so. "Oh, come on. They take British ships all the time; this could just be that" she whispered under her breath. Laffite's wife took one last look at the two ships, which were now so tiny on the horizon that they blended into one tiny dark shape. There was nothing left for her to do but depart the beach. She turned and walked back to the house quickly, with all intentions of changing into her breeches and retrieving her weapon.

AFTER months of attacks and significant losses, the British had been pushed too far. So, it was deemed necessary that the Barataria port be destroyed to protect the English interests. Too many of their supply ships from home had fallen into pirate hands, something they could not afford. It was also deemed that holding Grand Terre, plus Grand Isle, and having them as a British base would prove most beneficial. They could easily man a blockade of the Mississippi River from that advantage point. With New Orleans cut off, the invasion of the American city would be guaranteed. Once the British had a foothold, they would control the whole of the river, and by doing so, the American's were most assuredly to lose the war that they thought was over.

JEAN and Gambi set sail, each taking the best men they could get for their ships on such short notice. Laffite had shouted across to Gambi as their vessel's anchors were hoisted. It was crucial that the Italian follow him and stay close behind until they needed to strike if they were to succeed. "I trust you will know what to do when the time comes," he had called out. "Let us go and show these English a welcome they won't soon forget." There arose loud cheers from the decks of both ship's decks, and even those onshore joined them. They watched Boss take his place at the helm of his ship, and Gambi took his. Simultaneously, they began to spin their ship's wheels as their sails filled with the wind.

Jean paid little attention to Dominique and what he was doing; all he cared about was guiding his ship toward the contact point while not running aground. What they required for his plan to work were surprise and speed, and as the vessel's sails billowed, it became evident that speed would not be a problem. Lady luck, it seemed, was on their side because the offshore wind had picked up.

Only once did Laffite look behind him to gauge the Italians distance from his own, and a grin filled his face when he saw the other ship closing the distance between them. Knowing this, Jean estimated it would be only a matter of moments before Gambi was sailing in Laffite's wake. Once that was accomplished, the Italian pirate would have his hands full, maintaining such proximity. Once he entered and crossed over the swells, Jean was leaving in his wake; the Italian's ship would have smooth water to glide along, thereby gaining a faster speed than his Boss was traveling. The pirate was a skilled seaman, though, and would not get too close. Seeing they were catching up and obeying his orders, Laffite looked forward and spun the ship's wheel once more.

GAMBI was known to be headstrong, but he was no fool, and he knew that Jean had a keen sense and was sly like a fox. He would follow Laffite anywhere, knowing this. Sailing out into the Gulf would have been the Italian's move; had he been giving orders, then he would have turned and come up behind the enemy. The Boss, however, was doing the opposite. He had turned his ship until he was hugging the coastline; Jean was sailing right toward the enemy and directly into the sun. As close as he tailed Jean's vessel, Gambi knew he'd only have seconds to turn into deeper waters should Boss's ship run aground. 'Mere seconds to avoid the same fate,' he thought, with a frown crossing his brow. Maintaining a safe distance and leaving enough time to maneuver fast enough was, in his judgment, critical. Still, he pushed his vessel a bit closer because he trusted such a fate the Boss would avoid at all cost. Upon seeing Jean's ship turn again toward the shoreline, Gambi followed and spun his ship's wheel as Laffite had just done.

As Captain, Jean was relying on the skill of the young pirate up in the rigging. This lad would call down directions to him, so he could steer the ship clear of water too shallow for their hull to pass over. From up high, the young pirate could see the coming depths in the pristine waters that the crewman, standing lookout on the bow, could not determine until they were almost on top of the shallows.

Jean had no intention of running aground as his ship picked up speed and raced across the water, tempting fate. His plan would work as long as the lad above kept his eyes on his task, and Dominique kept the crew working on their preparations while remaining as quiet as they could.

Laffite's ship was La Diligent, and it was formidable. She usually sailed with a crew of eighty or more, and right then, they had just over half that number. On her decks were a dozen fourteen-pounder cannons, and should they need, all the men were well armed with both cutlasses, knives, and guns. He had everything he required to do what he intended.

As Tori began to change her outfit, her mind raced with questions and known facts. Jean's ship, the one he now sailed aboard like a mad man, was unlike the one Tori had traveled on. It was far larger to start with and was constructed for battles at sea. The ship that had taken her to the islands and back had been faster. It also maneuvered easily because of its size. He was not on that ship, though, and she worried. It was true, the La Diligent was quick, but she wondered, could it respond to the Captain's directions just as swiftly? Pulling on her breeches and reaching for her top, Tori hesitated for a second while her mind continued to race.

Both ships were sailing under Cartagena's flags, and she knew the vessel that Gambi was manning, the Dorada was just as deadly as Jean's. Maybe more so, because unlike Jean, Gambi delighted in being cruel, and cutthroat fit his description the best. Frowning at this thought, she pulled her shirt over her head and then sat down to pull her boots on. Tori had feared Chez Nez until she got to know him and win his respect, but Gambi was the killer and was a man she had good reason to fear always. Still, he was one of Jean's men and trusted to a certain extent. She stood up and looked in the chest for Dominique's gift. Her sword lay waiting, along with a handmade leather belt designed to hold the weapon in place at her side. Tori hoped Jean knew what he was doing by having Gambi tag along. That pirate was out for blood, and because of him, all his crew would be worked up long before they met their foe. Dominique would maintain Jean's crew and have them ready, but Gambi would not care how bloodthirsty his men were as long as he won.

With her outfit complete, Tori headed downstairs to wait. Only time would tell if she would have to fight or not, and as horrible as that thought was, the very idea of her gentleman pirate on board, a ship with cannon fire aimed at him, was even more terrible.

THE tide was turning, and it was Laffite's estimation; he had less than half an hour left, where he could continue to safely maneuver his ship, as close to the shoreline as he had been doing so far.

Gambi continued to follow his Boss close behind, and it did not take him long to realize Laffite's wisdom. He knew if they remained on course, they would meet up with the British ships within a very short amount of time. This would keep the enemy well away from Grand Terre and Grand Isle. By doing that, they most likely would save Cat Island as well. If the Boss's plan worked, the British Captains were about to get one hell of a welcome party. "You up there, keep your eyes sharp; if I have to come about rather than ram up the Boss's ass, you best let me know." There was laughter all around. "And you, you swine, keep your eyes out for the first sign of the enemy. I'll not have Boss say we didn't do our best. Rum for all when we return victorious and with luck a new ship to crew." Again, there was a burst of cheering, but it did not last long because the men had jobs to perform. Besides, each knew that what they were about to do would most likely cost lives. Any one of them could be injured or killed, and this sent a wave of silence momentarily across the deck. Each man's mood went from jubilant to somber as, one by one, they either decided the odds were good for them, or they were encouraged to think so by the man standing next to them. It was the idea of taking a prize ship and beating the British at their own game that speared them on, and as it did, excitement filled their hearts, not fear.

THE British were under orders to wait until the tide was low and the sun still high enough to blind those onshore who may be looking their way. It was a brilliant plan. When they left their home base, they had taken a path across the Gulf that took them well out to sea. Then after several days, they had turned toward the coast. Once they were close to shore and reached the outer barrier islands, they had dropped sails and waited. As the English suspected, the area where they first sailed along the shoreline was free of pirates. They knew about the activity at Cat Island, but it was Grand Terre they had to destroy. If the weather and tides held, the way was clear to attack the pirates from the West. It certainly looked as if it would all be over before they knew what had happened.

What they had not spotted was the small group of men crouching in the dunes spying on them. From this group, word was sent to Cat Island, and from there, it reached Grand Terre, having been transported via a small, swift two sailed sloop. It had taken just over two hours for the report to reach Laffite, and in Jean's estimation, that was time lost that none of them could afford. It was Laffite who calmed the men, explaining what he thought the British Captains were up to. Then he'd given the command to man the two ships he thought best equipped to annihilate their foe. The other vessels could sail out into the Gulf if they wished, but they were not to follow La Diligent.

AT last, the tide was retreating, and so the British Captains gave the command to proceed. With their sails up, pushing the ships steadily toward Grand Terre, the British prepared for their victory. It was the last time on their voyage that they would feel so confident.

Jean and Gambi met the intruders just past the tip of Last Island. Cat Island had a few smaller vessels anchored, but most of the activity was inland. After hearing the British were close, they had acted quickly and moved the merchandise off the beach area and toward the inland waterways. Not all goods would be transferred this way, just those which were more valuable. As the two ships from Grand Terre sailed swiftly by, those onshore waved, but none called out. The sound could carry, and if the British were still anchored, they might hear the cheering on the wind and be tipped off.

Laffite saw the men on shore; he could have called out to them and been easily heard as they were sailing that close to the beach. Instead, he gave his crew orders that it was time to maneuver slowly into deeper waters and make ready to attack. What the lad up in the rigging saw, that those below or onshore could not, was the two British ships under sail, heading right for them, and he'd alerted Laffite. "Boss, they are dead ahead and under sail; silly sods don't see us because they are not looking, I reckon."

Jean chuckled to himself. He had guessed right, and now his plan to attack would begin. "Dominique, get your men ready to fire. You there, go to the stern and signal Gambi, just in case he does not see them."

"Will do, Boss, but if them, British are close, you can bet Gambi smells 'um."

A few crewmembers laughed, but not for long. They were preparing to fight and had no time for fun and games. Jean turned the ship's wheel hard to his left, and immediately his vessel responded and began to turn away from shore. Then just as quickly, Jean straightened his vessel's course and called out his orders. "There they are, stand ready to shoot on Dominique's orders. Dominique, you know the drill; wait for it. I don't want them sunk. I have no intention of taking either. Give them something to think twice about, and I shall attempt to remain out of range of their cannon."

Dominique called back in a stern-sounding voice. "You got it, Boss. You get them bastards in my sights and leave the rest to me. I'll give them a tickle or two.

"I repeat, just wound them; we don't want them sunk."

"Wound it is, Boss. Shame 'cause I would like nothing better than to sink the buggers. Soon as they fire, count on me to know what firepower they have onboard; we won't take a hit if I can help it. You heard the Boss men make ready all cannon; on my command only, will you fire."

They came into view of the unsuspecting British, taking them by total surprise. Until that moment in time, the two enemy ships had thought the going was clear. The British were so cocksure of themselves that for a brief moment, they had relaxed their watch. The shock of seeing two pirate ships boring down on them forced the British Captains to maneuver to an attacking position as best they could. These were veteran sailors of His Majesty's Navy, and as such, they were able to ready themselves for battle rapidly. Had they been anyone else, Laffite would have expected them to falter, but he knew the British Navy and all they were capable of. As their ships turned broadside, so did Laffite and Gambi. Now, the men on shore stopped what they were doing. They watched the events off in the distance unfold as four ships sailed horizontally to each other and out into the Gulf waters beyond to battle.

TORI listened to the sound of cannon fire echo through the heavens for what seemed like years to her. She could only imagine the carnage that was taking place on the decks of all the ships involved. The hardest part for her was waiting and not knowing who was winning. She worried about Jean, about all the men from Grand Terre. Then looking down, at the sword, in her hand, her eyes filled with tears. She loved the older pirate in charge of the cannons, and for a second, she allowed her fear to grip her mind. "What would I do if I lost you now, you, old fool? Dominique, you damn well better not die on me, not now. Not this time." She had spoken these words while looking at the gift he had given her. If she had to fight, there was no doubt in her mind that she'd do just that. 'Keep Jean safe, Dominique, keep them all safe.'

THE British fired first, and their shot fell just short of hitting Laffite's ship. The second shot landed much closer but in the space between Gambi's ship and Jeans. Gauging the distance and using his knowledge, Dominique called for the forward cannon to fire. This first shot hit the aft bow of the closest British vessel. It hit above the water line and scattered debris over the deck. Not waiting for a second longer, the older pirate called out loud. "Boss, give me one more shot, then move us slightly East, remain broadside to them. Men, fire second and third volley now!"

In rapid sequence, two booms sounded, one on each side of where Dominique was standing. This was followed by the sound of four more cannons firing from Gambi's ship, and all watched as one hit its mark and others went beyond their target. Dominique's voice bellowed loudly. "Boss, turn her now. Ready all cannon men. Wait for it... wait, on my command only."

Laffite did not hesitate; he slowly turned his ship's wheel, guiding the boat gradually Eastward but maintained a broadside position to the English. As Jean attempted to remain out of range of the cannon fire, Gambi had stayed on course. It was then that the Italian took a hit to the bow of his beloved ship. Luckily the cannonball skipped high and just struck the top of the railing before splashing in the water on the opposite side of the intended target. The splintered wood scattered at a high rate of speed, and several of the pirate's crew found themselves impaled. Cursing the enemy, Gambi turned his ship slightly East as Jean had done. He despised doing so, and had he not given his word to follow Jean's orders, the Italian Captain knew he'd have turned West and, with guns blazing, taken at least one ship and sunk the other.

After much firing from both sides, and just as the sun was setting, the battle ended. Silence, at last, invaded the heavens. The booming sound, which had echoed across the water, and filled the heavens for miles, ceased. The British could see that the fight was a losing battle, and after suffering substantial damage and many casualties, they hoisted full sail, taking advantage of the stiff evening breeze, and quickly departed. Their attempt to dislodge the Baratarians had failed. It would be impossible to dislodge them; they would later tell their superiors, who immediately began considering alternative neutralizing methods.

THAT night in bed, Jean and Tori talked for hours. Outside they could hear the celebrations going on. Laffite and Gambi's men were given their rum as promised, and now they bragged how they had beaten their enemies. Tori knew they had lost men and wondered how their friends could be celebrating instead of mourning? She guessed it was their way and, having done so she decided that asking Jean to explain it to her was far from easy and best forgotten. There was one thing on her mind, and knowing she'd not sleep until answered, she looked at Jean and asked in a soft but serious tone. "Jean, the British have made a move, one that we did not know about. You don't think they were trying to meet with you, do you?"

He looked at her and grinned. "It is my experience that sneaking up on someone like they tried to do today is not the way to engage in polite conversation. Their intentions were clear. Make no doubt about it; they were on their way to bombard our home. I fear that they have spies in New Orleans and possibly even here."

"Why would you say that?"

His expression had turned to a far more worried look as he answered her. "You saw the bay today. Only two ships, worthy of the fight with any hope of winning, were at anchor. All the other ships that could have sailed with me today are at sea. Someone had to have talked. Luck had nothing to do with the British knowing when to attack us. We were the ones who got lucky today. Sadly, a few had no luck today. The lady, called death, visited the enemy along with us. Both Gambi and I lost some good men, and for what? To watch the British sail off, to let them go so they could report back to their commanding officers, and all because of a tale of how I am to meet with them one day."

"It's not a tale, it is history, and you know it."

"I may know what you told me, you and the other two, but I don't have to like it. I made Gambi an angry man today by stopping him from going after the British. He is out for blood now."

"Not yours, I hope."

"With that man, one can only guess. He is not one to play cat and mouse like I am forced to do at this point. Jean placed his finger on her lips to keep her from talking. "We shall go to town tomorrow. I need to talk to Grymes, and maybe we could both talk to Cisco and Davis again. This waiting for something to happen is driving me crazy. I need to be doing more."

Tori pulled his finger away, "I agree with you, and who knows, maybe it will improve your mood to be with friends and away from here for a while. There is so much going on each day. You have lost merchandise and even changed your routes to stop the taxmen from taking shipments. Boats come in here and now at Cat Island also. People from all up and down the river come to buy what you have to sell. They will continue to come as long as they can get a bargain. You do all this in the open… you and Pierre. He is as bad as you, now that he is healing. The stroke no longer keeps him home. I have heard he even goes to sea. I thought he was the brains behind all this, and now I see he is…"

Jean interrupted her. "He is much improved. True, my brother sails out, and who is to blame the man? He is, after all, taking a more active role in our enterprise.

"Is that what you call your pirating now?"

"Privateering Madame. We sail under papers from…"

"Oh, don't give me that, she snapped back. "The only real privateer here is Beluche. At least, he got his papers from America. He's legit. Then there is Humbert, who I have heard from Dominique, served under Napoleon in the Imperial Guard, whatever that is. I would assume this gives the man some credit toward being called a privateer instead of a pirate. If he has papers or not, I don't know, and maybe I don't care. As for all the others that come and go, well, if you ask me, as I said, Beluche is the only one who is legally operating in the Gulf."

"He is in their eyes, but he still works for us." Jean chuckled, trying to lighten the mood. "It is because of him you can take Cisco and Marie a gift for her potions. I have in my warehouse a bulk of cochineal."

Tori couldn't help but giggle. "What the hell is that?"

"Ah, finally, something else you don't know." He stroked some hair away from her face and let his fingers trail down her neck. "It is a purple dye that is used for many things and can be used in food without harm. I think maybe your friends will like a thoughtful gift."

"They are our friends, and yes, I bet they will, but do you think it's safe to go to the city?"

"I am no fool, my love. We will remain safe; we will leave before we are taken into custody. You have my word on it. Besides, I have much to talk about with Grymes and with my other attorneys and friends. It is imperative that I go, especially after today."

She tried to smile at him, to let him know he could open up. Instead, he turned from her and softly spoke. "I told you, I do not wish to talk about today, and that will be your next inquiry, yes? You had best rest, my lady. Tomorrow will be long and hot."

Within moments, his breathing had become regular and deep. Tori assumed he had fallen asleep, exhausted from the fight with the British, and who could blame him? They would have plenty of time to talk about what happened in the days to come. He needed to sleep, and so did she. With Jean at her side and knowing Dominique was safe, too, Tori slipped into a fitful sleep. Her dreams were of battles at sea, a sea that was red as blood. The blood flowed from the ship's decks, and the nightmare was endless. Soon the horrors were of battlegrounds and men marching to their deaths as she frantically screamed, trying to warn them.

Jean, unaware of Tori's nightmares, lay awake beside her. He had only pretended to fall asleep, so his lady would rest. What he had told her was the truth. The trip back to New Orleans would be long and hot. That, though, was the least of his concerns. He was wondering if today had been the first sign they had been waiting for, and if so, then from now on, things would never be the same. His privateering days were numbered, and for who knew, how long?

Lying there besides the women he loved, he found himself wondering why he listened to her? He wanted to leave and keep his life as it was. Maybe take Pierre's advice and some of what Tori had mentioned and move to this Galveston place. Instead, he was supposed to become a hero and maybe settle down. It was true he dreamed of becoming an American citizen and a respected man, dealing in a legal enterprise, but was it to be so, or was it only a fabrication of Tori's desires? Davis's and Cisco's, too; they had aspirations along with the need to remain anonymous, as far as their history went? Could he trust in all they had told him? They knew so little, really, and he was a man who needed to know far more before he made a move that could cost him everything he had built.

"I received your message and came as soon as I could. You know, of course, that Claiborne and his wife have joined Edward and Simone at their plantation. With them out of town, you are relatively safe. However, I would highly suggest you don't go parading yourself up and down the streets as your brother does in Donaldsonville."

Jean chuckled. "I have no control over my brother's actions, as you well know, and I am not so inclined to tempt fate, so you may relax, my friend. Thiac told me about Edward; that is why Tori and I are here at our house and not hiding in the blacksmith shop or the cottage. So, now, tell us before we go any further. Just what is this news that is so important that you mentioned in your letter? I know," he laughed, slapping his knee, "the Governor has forgiven all, and I am no longer wanted." He was making a joke and yet hoping at the same time.

"No such luck, I'm afraid. So, don't go getting all worked up." He could see Jean's mouth tighten and knew only too well how his moods had been swinging back and forth because Tori had kept him up-to-date, bless her. She had sent him regular letters, which Thiac himself had delivered. "Look, you two. I will come right to the point. You most certainly are not going to believe it, so here, look at this for yourselves, as I explain how it came into my possession." He handed Leone's will over to Jean, who shared it with Tori. As recognition crossed his friend's faces, he told the tale of just how it had all come about.

"And, that is how she left me, sitting in my office with that document in my hands. I tell you, I got good and drunk that night, but not before securing the will in a very safe location, where it has been until this evening. You do realize that we can go to court as soon as you want and take back what is rightfully yours. You should be able to take possession of the plantation and the townhouse, well not that residence, Edward has sold it, but the rest is yours. Just as soon as the judge verifies the document, you will own it all. Then, my friend, the gentleman pirate, can settle down and become an honest citizen and a fine plantation owner!"

Jean laughed, and Tori could hardly believe what she was hearing. She could never picture Jean Laffite as a plantation owner, no matter what Grymes said. In all the stories in her own time, not once had Tori heard anything close to Laffite becoming a plantation owner. There again, she did not know that much, and it could be possible, unlikely, but possible.

It was Jean who responded to Grymes. "John, you know you make it all sound so easy, so simple in fact, that it tempts me, my friend. But, how am I to go to court and fight for this," he held the paper up, "when I am a wanted man? And how, may I add, would it look if the State's Attorney were to suddenly be standing by my side, as my attorney? No, I'm afraid that this matter will have to wait for the time being. You shall have to place this back safely wherever it is you kept it. We will handle one problem at a time. Leone's plantation will have to wait."

Grymes looked shocked and then dismayed. Of course, he had known that it was almost impossible to act right away, but anything could be worked out, and he had his word to keep to his deceased friend. "Jean, are you certain? I can leave the State's Attorney's office; just give me the word. I would be free to represent you. We can fight this and win. I can take on a friend of mine, another attorney. Edward Livingston is a fine upstanding gentleman and talented, I assure you. My associate and I would become your official representatives. He's very clever and far more gifted than me in many areas. With his talents and mine, we could get all charges dropped. There are ways, you know."

Jean reached out and placed his hand on Grymes's shoulder. "I thank you for your offer. I might need to take you up on it one day, but I have my reasons to ask you to remain in your position for now. In so doing, you will better serve this city and myself. You'll have to trust me on this." Jean walked toward Tori, who also did not look too pleased.

Grymes begrudgingly nodded his head. "I still would have loved serving Edward and Simone the eviction papers. Do you know that they would be out on the streets, with no damn place to go and no money except the small allowance left to Edward? Simone forfeited her income when she remarried and sold the townhome, as you know. It would have been such sweet justice to see that pair get what's coming to them."

Tori frowned. "I thought they had purchased a new house. Larger than Leone's was. That would remain theirs, right?"

The attorney nodded. "That is true, but from what I hear, Simone still has to furnish the place, and as they will be in need of money, I don't see them keeping the house for long. I will see they get what is coming to them, I assure you."

"And, you will," Tori said. "I, for one, want to be there when you tell them. But Jean is right. We have to wait a while on this. We have our hands tied, and to tip them off about the will might spoil any chance of winning in the future." She frowned at John and then turned her attention toward Jean. "I agree with Jean. We have no choice but to wait. Too many battles, at one time, tend to weaken one, right?"

Grymes stood up and went to where the bottle of wine sat on the table, and he filled a glass. "Do forgive me, but a drink is in order. Just knowing that you will act one day shall have to be enough for me, even though I may not understand your strategy. I will see to it that the will is placed safely away and will be returned to you, should something happen to me." He drank the contents of the glass. "And now, if you will excuse me, I do have other matters to take care of. I hope to see you both soon. Maybe dinner one night?"

Jean walked John to the door as Tori sat thinking. The plantation was theirs, and with it, the lake had once again become within reach. Was that the real reason Jean did not want to fight for their rightful place as the owners of the Duval plantation?

Unbeknownst to her, that thought hadn't yet occurred to Jean, for he had far more pressing problems to deal with. The evening was now clear and safe for Cisco and John Davis to join them as planned. He needed to talk to both of them and once again see if he could extract any further details that could enlighten him on the events that lay ahead. There was also the challenge of getting his brother Pierre to come back to Grand Terre with them.

NOTHING was solved in the short visit, one that would have been extended by many more days, had it not been for the return of Edward and his party. They had come back to town early and, once again, unknowingly caused Jean to head back to his home base. Once there, Laffite's frustration built, and his need for work grew. Like his brother, who had refused to join him at Grand Terre, Jean

282

became ever more aggressive and daring. It seemed to Tori that he was pushing his luck too far, and one day, in early October, his luck, it seemed, ran out.

JEAN had felt the need to be useful and ventured into the bayous. Tori, not relishing the idea, had elected to remain at the house no matter how badly she wanted to spend time with him.

It was to be a single shipment of goods taken up the waterways toward New Orleans. Everything had progressed like always, and Jean relaxed in the cool of the bright sunny autumn day. The first part of the trip was uneventful, and now after transferring the contraband to a smaller boat, they slowly pushed their way through the marshes and toward their flat barge, waiting for them on the Mississippi. From there, the goods would cross the river and dock just outside of the city. Thiac and others would see to it that the merchandise was distributed among some of their trusted shop-keepers to be sold, and the few goods that top clients had already purchased would be delivered directly to their destination.

Without warning, a shot rang out, and before anything could be done, Jean found himself fighting a small platoon of dragoons, headed by the Revenue Officer, Walker Gilbert himself. The surprise attack had caught him and his men off guard, and quickly they lost control of the boat and its contents. For a brief period, the goods were in Gilbert's hands. Then, as the soldiers began their way toward the city, Jean and his men followed closely until the opportune moment. Laffite was not about to allow any skirmish to be lost, especially where there was merchandise involved. He and his men fought back this time, ready and more than able to take on the platoon. The fight was short and bloody, and when Jean had his boat back in their possession, one of Gilbert's men lay severely wounded on the shore. Laffite ordered them to push off, fearing that his men, who were thoroughly worked up and bloodthirsty, would do more. He left Walker Gilbert and his men in the swamps empty-handed to fend for themselves and never looked back.

WHEN word reached the Governor of the skirmish, he was furious at his military and revenue agent's inadequacy. Once again, he voiced his frustration out loud to his friend Duval. "Edward, this Laffite and his cutthroat mob of pirates have to be stopped at all cost. It is high time they are brought to justice and made to face the charges against them in a court of law. No matter how many men I send into the blasted swamps and bayous, the area is so vast that they succeed where we fail. Goods arrive in Donaldsonville every day." He saw the look of shock register on Edward's face. "Fear not, I have kept my men busy and know many of their routes, but the bastard always evades me." He hit his desk hard with his fist. "I am stretched to my limit and demand better of my legislators. They sit and smirk and cough and delay, all while buying from Laffite and others associated with them. Do they think I do not know how they conceal their amusement at my continued failures? Now, to hear that blood has been spilled… that the pirates are so brazen, as to attack without regard to life or limb… it is too much! I will have justice."

"I agree with you, William. To be made the laughing stock of the city, yet again, is so unjust. The man has not stopped his movement of plunder and slaves into our city; it is true, and to do so, using such a vicious act as to attack your Revenue Officer and his men, well, it's outrageous." Edward was adding fuel to Claiborne's temper, and he intended to continue.

The Governor spun around and faced the Creole. "I have had it! Enough of this. I will not be made a fool of any longer. I shall petition the State Legislature for help in destroying the pirate stronghold. This time they will listen, and they will act by God."

Edward smirked behind the man's back but kept his tone of voice sounding stern and supportive. "That seems to be your only option and a fine move if I might say. One that is by the law and makes you appear strong to all who consider you weak."

"Edward, I am going to be seen no other way, other than a strong Governor. The legislature will rule in my favor, for how could they not? I shall send word today, and then we will await a reply."

Edward wanted to make a move sooner, as the Governor's way would take time and support, something he doubted would happen. Not willing to give in so quickly, the dandy came up with another idea to help further the cause of Laffite's demise. "Until then, William, may I suggest you have the military guard the river-front both here and upriver."

"Fine suggestion. I will send for Gilbert immediately. Who knows, lady luck may play into our hands, and we might catch the bastard."

OCTOBER turned into November, and still, no answer came from the legislators. For Claiborne, it became apparent it was time to enlist the Mayor's help and anyone else he could think of asking.

"Edward, Simone, and you, my darling wife," he smiled at the young woman. "I have been thinking and have concluded that we shall have a dinner, to be held here, a dinner that will to all invited seem harmless enough. However, it will, in fact, be held so I might engage those who attend to join me in my cause and bring about action from the States Legislature, who so far has done not a damn thing! My apologies, ladies."

"None needed William," spoke Edward looking toward his wife. "I agree, we all know how frustrated you are, and I think it a wonderful idea, don't you, Cayetana?"

Everyone looked her way, but it was her husband who spoke. "I have no need to confirm with Cayetana; her look of approval tells all. Let us drink to the coming together of like minds, intent on the destruction of the Laffite's and all they stand for."

Edward raised his glass in a toast, and William, looking very pleased and confident with his new plan, joined in the toast. He, however, failed to understand the strange expression upon his young wife's face.

So it was, on the 23rd, of November 1813, that Edward, Mayor Girod, and a few significant merchants, along with their wives, gathered for dinner. As always, the subject of Laffite surfaced, and Claiborne talked to all those present about his number one nemesis. "Ah, but Girod, my friend. As Mayor, you do not have the problem on your shoulders as I do. You can always pass the problems, no matter what they are, onto the Governor's office," he laughed.

Everyone watched as the translator interpreted for the Mayor. When he finished, the Creole spluttered at the Governor's remark and was not above taking offense. He was, however, an intelligent man. One who understood that if he was to be re-elected in the fall of the following year, he was going to need this American Governor on his side. He ignored Claiborne's remark but did not forget it.

Edward had seen the flash of anger cross Girod's face and rightly guessed he had taken offense at what William had implied, so quickly he moved to smooth the man's hurt feelings. He addressed him, speaking in French so the Governor could not understand a word spoken. "Mayor Girod, my friend, the Governor is so upset by the news that comes his way. I assure you he meant no ill toward you and the difficult job you so masterfully control. He is but a simple American, who has no idea of our ways, is he not?" Edward felt sorry for the Mayor. Besides, he and Girod were the only Creoles present, and as such, Edward felt obligated to stand by the man; at the very least, to look as if he was. Duval would do anything and say anything to see his ultimate goal met. "Excuse me, William, for speaking French, but I find it easier to converse with the man on a level he understands. I just told him what a fine job you are doing, and we are lucky to have an American such as yourself fighting for us and against our common enemies."

"I try my best. Please continue to speak with him in French, do all you can to sway him to our cause."

"I shall then, with your permission." Edward turned back to the Mayor and again in French continued on. "Each day, it seems news of Laffite's activities flows into this fool's office."

The pair quickly got caught up in a serious conversation, and as the Governor could not understand a word of it, he turned to Simone, who gladly took advantage of the opportunity to play her part. "I myself do not know how you cope, William. Really, I don't," Simone spoke coyly, setting him up for her husband's continued manipulations. "Pray... tell me, whatever became of your request to the State Legislature for money and men to destroy the settlement at Grand Terre?"

"They did nothing, my dear. Nothing! But don't you fear. Unlike others," he said, flashing a look towards the Mayor, "I shall not sit idle while that damned man makes a fool of me. Did you know, my dear, that he is actually in town at this very moment?"

Simone let out a small gasp. "So, it is true. I was surprised myself to hear such dreadful information, and no one is lifting a hand to help apprehend him or that brother of his. Why, William, we often see many other acquaintances of the Laffite's too, and they hail him as a hero. Did you know the pirates openly sell their goods on Sundays while we sit in church? Knowing you are not Catholic and do not attend our services, you may not be fully aware of this. I declare, they shout so loud as to drown out the choir. I fear that they are not men of God; the devil helps them. By the time your men arrive to arrest them, they have departed, and with their merchandise, I might add. It would seem that they have help among the citizens. I don't know what can be done to stop them... really I don't."

Simone's husband interrupted the conversation. "Maybe I can be of some assistance there. It seems to me that you can now, with witnesses to this last skirmish, name the man outright. You could even offer a reward for his capture. That would, I'm sure, entice someone to take action. Maybe, one of his men will be greedy enough to take the bait. None of them have any scruples, you know," he said, dabbing his lips with his napkin. Then, looking around the table at the other guests, he remarked, "delicious food this evening, but I, for one, have lost my appetite. Laffite has soured my stomach, and I do agree with the Governor; something has to be done. A reward is the next best step; it seems to me. What say you?" The group talked about this idea and, in the end, were convinced that it was the only thing to do.

Claiborne liked the idea and heartedly agreed. "I will have the posters made up tomorrow and spread around town as soon as they are printed. With luck, Edward, we may finally snare that sly fox."

Edward's wife dropped her knife onto her plate on purpose to gain full attention. The noise of the silver hitting the china did the trick. Everyone at the table turned to look her way. Without so much as an apology for her clumsy manner, she spoke lightheartedly. "Why, Governor, I think you give the man too much credit. The very thought causes me pain. You are the sly fox; outwitting that horrible snake in the grass is what you will do."

Everyone laughed, including the Mayor. He thought that if Laffite were caught, he could use the occasion to help his re-election. If anything went amiss, well, it would be the fool of a Governor's blunder, not his. Oh, he liked that better, and he laughed even more at the very thought.

William was in such good spirits that he missed the hint that Mayor Girod had understood English far better than he let on. The Creole may not speak it, but he did grasp a lot of what was spoken; hence, his full belly laugh, at the Governor's last grand statement.

JEAN had been staying at the blacksmith shop since arriving in town. He'd made plans to leave the next day and head back to Grand Terre as all of his business had been accomplished. He had only one regret but understood it could not be helped. The man had missed visiting with Pierre's Mistress and her children. They had moved into another cottage that his brother had purchased for her, on Dumaine Street. It was safer for them, Pierre explained to

Jean. Meetings at all hours with their Captains and buyers placed his love in danger, and he was not willing to do that. Jean had seen sense in his move but still regretted not being able to visit with them as often as he was once accustomed. As for Pierre, he found it far easier to slip into town and visit Marie and the children undetected. Unlike the cottage in front of the blacksmith shop, which was always busy, the new location was more remote and less visited by outsiders.

CISCO had been on his way home when he spied a crowd around a coffeehouse. It was after all too late in the day for such a gathering, and being nosy, he made his way to see what the fuss was. At first, he caught only snatches of conversation. Something about Laffite being wanted, whatever that meant. Jean had been wanted for months; that was nothing new. Anxious to learn more, he pushed his way to the front of the crowd to find out what it was they were all so worked up about. In seconds he learned the truth behind the excitement. Posted on the wall of the popular restaurant was a notice from the Governor. It was dated November 24th, which meant it had just been put up. He read it and then quickly turned and set out to find Thiac because Cisco knew only too well that he had to get word to Jean and Pierre immediately.

JEAN and the smithy were starting their second bottle of wine together when the sound of someone banging on the front door filled their ears. The blacksmith shop had been closed for two days now, so no one was expected. Thiac had put out the word that he was putting in a large balcony iron grill over in the American side of town. As it was not uncommon for the shop to be closed at odd times, due to his line of work, so none had cause to doubt the explanation. "I'll be seeing who it is. You best stay out of sight,

Boss," he murmured.

Jean sipped his wine and smiled. "Bet, it's my brother. Have him join me in the side garden."

"Yes, Boss. If it's him, I sure will."

Cisco was about to give up when the wooden door gave a groan and creaked as it opened. Upon seeing Thiac's friendly face, he pushed on in and sputtered, "Shut the door. I need to talk to you. I need to get a message to Jean and fast. Can you do it?"

"Well, now, pends on how fast you be wanting it to reach the Boss. If you like and it be, real important like, well, you could take it to him yourself." Thiac was grinning and obviously enjoying the moment.

Frustrated, Cisco snapped back at him with a slight tone of anger in his voice. "Don't be stupid, man. I can't just take off and head down to Grand Terre. But this is important, very..."

"Well then, you had best do as old Thiac said and deliver it yourself," Jean interrupted. He was standing in the back doorway, leaning against the frame, smoking one of his thin cigars. He was relaxed, tanned, and smiling as if nothing in the world could bother him.

Cisco, who was happy to see his friend, walked quickly over to him, and the two briefly embraced. "What are you doing in town? I could have sworn you told me that you and Tori would not be back until it was safe? Nothing has changed in that department, you know. That's why I'm here. Look, I think we are both going to need a drink on this one. May I join you?"

"Go right ahead," Jean said, pointing to a couple of chairs sitting in front of the fire. On the table was a bottle, and as they walked toward the seats, Jean looked back at Thiac. "One more glass is needed. Our party grows." His humor was in such high spirits that Cisco almost hated to dash it so soon.

Jean took a seat and picked up his glass. "So, do tell me. What is so damned important for me to know? If it's about the skirmish my men had with Gilbert a while back, I already know. I was there," he laughed. "Had a bit of fun. Hard time getting the men to leave, though, I'll tell you that. We have lost some shipments and let the word out that I have moved my base of operation, which slowed down the revenue men a bit. They seem to not like going into our territory. Give them an excuse not to, and they don't. From the look on your face, I take it that your news is not about that. So... what is it?"

"You have a price on your head. The Governor has named you and put a reward out to anyone turning you in. The posters are all over town, and more are going up each hour. It said you grievously wounded one of Walker's men." Cisco took a long drink of his wine, and Jean slowly refilled his own glass, listening closely as Cisco continued. "It went on to say that anyone helping you is just as guilty. And then, it said, get this, five hundred dollars would be given, to anyone delivering you, to the Sheriff of the Parish of New Orleans.

Jean frowned and spoke in a severe tone. "Thiac, go out and retrieve one of these posters Cisco is talking about. I want to read this for myself." He was no longer laughing. A thunderous look had clouded his eyes, which seemed to darken as the storm inside grew. "Cisco, my friend, I think the time has come for us to pay a social call on John Davis and his fine establishment. Thiac forget going out. I will read this so-called reward poster for myself. If Claiborne thinks for one minute that I'm going to run and hide any longer, he is gravely mistaken." Jean was past reasoning, and even though Cisco worried about what he would do if someone tried to make good on the Governor's offer, he could think of no way to prevent Jean from marching out the door.

Once outside and walking toward Davis's Hotel, the two instantly became aware of the looks and stares from many of the citizens. They would tell others that Jean Laffite, it appeared, was not impressed with or afraid of the Governor's reward. He was openly strolling the streets of New Orleans, and many would tell of how he even stopped to read the reward proclamation himself.

Cisco was worried and kept a close eye on those standing close to them. "Jean, my man. I don't think this is very wise of you. Standing here as if nothing is wrong, reading your own warrant for capture is crazy." Cisco reached up and took down the paper. He folded it up neatly before handing it to him. "May I suggest that you read it when we arrive at John's. Besides, I have just had an idea that you will no doubt find amusing." He pointed at the reward sheet, now held in Jean's hand. "Put that in a safe place. We will need it before the night is through." Cisco was all but dancing with joy. "I tell you, Jean. I would love to say that what I'm about to suggest was my idea, but then I'm not sure. It's just so damned confusing. I keep saying that, don't I? No worries, come on. Don't just stand there. We have work to do, and boy, are you going to enjoy yourself." He slapped Jean on the back and smiled.

Cisco's face was lit up with one of his infectious grins. Jean had seen his enthusiasm before but never accompanied by such uncontrollable excitement. Watching his friend, he found his foul mood replaced by a heightening curiosity.

They continued their stroll to John's, and many more fine citizens of the city crossed paths with the pair. It became only too clear to them both that many were admiring his indifference to danger. They openly laughed and talked among themselves about his nonchalance, and a few even called his way, smiling and offering their support. One very evident fact to all was that no one tried to take the Governor up on his offer. The reward might as well have not been posted for all the good it was doing.

John Davis was told right away that Jean and Cisco had arrived, and rather than greet them himself, he sent word to Cisco that they join him in his suite. He had read the proclamation earlier, and he too had an idea as to what should be done about it.

"JOHN, can you believe it? Have you heard?" said Cisco as they entered the private rooms. "Jean, give him the copy. Come on, man, let him see it." Cisco could hardly contain himself.

"Steady on there," laughed Davis. "I take it you are referring to the Governor's latest and greatest? There is no need to show it to me. I have already read it. The point is, Jean, what are you going to do about it?"

"You can't be serious?" Cisco laughed. "We know just what in the hell he is going to do about it. It's the same thing that he did do about it. You do know what I mean, don't you, John? Hell, don't tell me; I finally know something about our Jean here that you don't."

John smiled at Cisco. "Oh, I doubt that very much. I see from your face that you know about the counteroffer?" Both Davis and Cisco were laughing now, and Jean found the whole situation just a little more than irritating.

"If you two would find the time to let me in on your little secret, I would be ever so happy to sit and listen." He tried to sound stern, but seeing the two friends all but celebrating the poster; he found himself caught up in their enthusiasm.

"You might well indeed sit and listen," Cisco said, pushing him down in a chair. "Jean, my friend. You will not believe this one, but it seems we know exactly what you are about to do. Old Davis here has had his memory jogged like mine. You are going to have this reward rewritten. You are going to post them all over town." He was laughing so hard that he found it hard to go on.

Davis broke in. "What Cisco here is trying to tell you, Jean is this. "In our time, the story is told, of how you, yourself, posted a reward, this time with William Claiborne being the one wanted. You offered fifteen hundred dollars for his delivery to you at Grand Terre, or was it Cat Island?"

Holding his sides, Cisco added, "You signed your name to each one of the posters, and it drove the man up the wall."

"Up the... wall?" replied a puzzled Jean.

"Crazy. It drove him crazy!" laughed Cisco.

Jean loved it. He found the humor in the situation to be just what he wanted. He could see the Governor's face in his mind, all red and bloated, as he was informed that he was a wanted man. Yes, let him feel for a while; what it was like.

"You say that I did this?" asked Jean.

"Indeed, you did," answered Cisco. "And, the people of this city enjoyed the joke as much as you. If I remember correctly, it diffused the whole situation, and soon the reward for you was forgotten." Cisco looked toward John for confirmation on this.

"I can't tell you much other than that," Davis added. "I do know that no one was able to collect either reward because, as far as I understand, nothing was ever done. I can tell you this," he said a bit more seriously. "I think this is one of the signs we have been waiting for, telling us that we must start to think seriously about what is ahead of us. It seems history is playing its hand, just as it should. The cards have been dealt, and we are all playing the game now."

Cisco stood dead still for the first time in an hour and looked gravely at both his friends. "I did think of that. I mean, is it our idea to put the other reward out, or was it just because of history and such? It does get fucking confusing at times."

Davis frowned. "I don't think it much matters. The point is this: if you follow our suggestion, Jean, then history marches on as it was written. If you choose not to, then it is rewritten. What you do from now on is going to affect far more than just this," he said, holding up the poster.

Jean understood the gravity of the situation. He also knew that what they had suggested was something that he very well might have come up with on his own. It was too damn good to resist either way. If history said he did this, then let it be so. After all, who was he to rewrite what was to be? He smiled broadly at them both. "You two are far too serious for such a prank. I, for one, think that it is too good to resist. Now, how do you propose we go about getting this done?"

"Payback's a bitch," laughed Cisco.

"You should know,," added Davis. "Well, it will be a long night and much to do. Let's not sit around doing nothing. Let's get rolling."

Two days later, the City of New Orleans rocked with laughter just like John and Cisco had predicted. The people had treated the two posters as nothing more than a joke. Besides, what else could they do? Each day, they would hear about the Laffite brothers walking the streets openly, with no one attempting to stop them. The Governor, on the other hand, was not to be seen. He had become the laughing stock of the whole affair. Jean had a sense of humor and open defiance that the Creoles could admire, and their so-called Governor and his proclamation meant nothing!

Claiborne was far from amused when he got the news of Jean's counter-offer, but before he could let the incident vex him, other pressing matters came to his attention. The dispatches from Washington were not good. It was becoming clear that the British would attack New Orleans and that the Federal Government had its hands full. They would not be sending help to far-off, Louisiana, any time soon, if ever. William Claiborne was left to deal with the worry of how to protect his city and state, along with dealing with Laffite and his men. The pirates were one problem. The British and their possible invasion were another. They were separate enemies for now, but what if Jean and his men were to join forces with the British, he wondered? What then?

⊰ Seven ⊱

Jean and Tori had decided to spend Christmas 1813 with friends and family instead of by themselves at Grand Terre. Tori had insisted on remaining cautious, and the pirate had given his word that at the first sign of being in danger, they would leave the city. Once they had arrived, though, it became evident that as long as they remained among friends, their safety was all but guaranteed. On Christmas eve, the pair made their way through the French Quarter toward the gathering that had been arranged. It had been easy to move around in town, under the cloak of darkness, avoiding their usual haunts. Those that did recognize Jean did nothing more than make the appropriate greeting. So, the pair hurried on with little difficulty, to the new cottage, on the edge of town.

The small gathering included Pierre and his quadroon love, Marie Louise Villars. Also joining them were Dominique You, Cisco, Marie Laveau, and a small assortment of young children, all of whom called Pierre, papa.

Tori and Jean enjoyed the laughter, and excited squeals of joy, as each of the children was given a small gift and sweets. Dominique doted on them all in turn, showing a softer side that not many people knew he had. Always a favorite of the children, he was often nearly smothered by the tiny giggling admirers. However, one young man always stood above them all in his affection, and tonight was no different.

Young Pierre Junior, who was the spitting image of his papa, sat with the older Dominique for most of the evening, listening to his tall tales. His face was filled with admiration, and the boy's eyes expressed the trust he felt toward his uncle. The child was handsome, with features so much like his father that no trace of his interracial background showed. It seemed a shame, Tori thought, that such an adorable child was doomed to live under the shadow of his black heritage and his circumstance of birth. He was a bastard in the eyes of the church. And as if that was not enough, Pierre's son would have to live with the fact that his papa had chosen to leave his mother and take another woman and have another family. Last but not least, he was one of the Laffite's, a name both loved and hated at the same time. For Tori, it all seemed too cruel.

Cheering cries from across the room drew her attention away. Pierre and his Mistress sat on the floor playing with the youngest child, a chubby, happy rollicking toddler. The two of them were helping the baby walk and laughed as she seemed to do better each time. It was evident to anyone watching them that they were very much in love, and witnessing this display of affection herself; Tori finally understood how Pierre could have made the choices that he did. Love was a powerful emotion; it could destroy as well as dictate one's future. She shuddered at this thought. Her love for Jean kept her by his side for now but would it always?

Unlike Jean, Pierre's life was far more complicated than she could have ever dealt with. He had a wife and children he very seldom visited but took care of. He had left them with his father-in-law, in a fine home with a lifestyle that he supported. To him, it had seemed the only workable solution. He'd left his wife for his first mistress, who was responsible for the two young children that sat with Dominique. Tori frowned. Pierre tried to see the children as much as possible, at least that's what she'd been told. However, more and more, they were being pushed aside to make way for his new life. If not for Dominique insisting the children be included in the gathering, Tori sadly had to admit Pierre would not have missed them. It was just a shame that so many lives had to be disrupted and hurt for him to find his happiness. This thought made her ask the question, wasn't she doing the same by staying with the man she loved? How many lives was she hurting, and how many more would she hurt by the decisions she made?

Looking at the man she loved, Tori recalled that Jean only laughed about his brother and his lifestyle, saying that it was Pierre's business. Dominique never commented one way or the other. After all, this sort of thing was commonplace, so why should he say anything? Tori looked away. 'Some people never learn,' she told herself. Maybe though, Pierre had finally settled down. Only time would tell, and as far as history went, not one of the time travelers knew what the years ahead held for Jean's brother.

Young Pierre and his baby sister Marie, who was nearly four, were the first to leave. Adelaide, his first mistress, arrived at the door but refused to enter, choosing to wait outside for her children. Tori wondered if her decision was out of pride or hurt and thought it probably a bit of both. Pierre had been sensitive to her choice and not pushed the issue. Instead, he sent a Christmas package, along with the children. To Tori, it was clear that the gift was his way of easing his guilt over the situation and nothing more. When they had gone, Pierre turned his attention again to the love of his life without a second thought.

Once the older children had left, the evening started to wind down quickly, and within the hour, the cottage was left to six very grateful adults. Not one would admit that the children and their antics had bothered them, but the silence that surrounded them, at last, was received gladly.

Dominique and Cisco swore to each other that children were only enjoyable when you knew they could be given back to their parents. Jean had laughed at this remark and reminded Dominique how he had tried so hard to convince the young Pierre to remain longer only a short time ago.

A sly smile left the older man's eyes, and a grin slipped across his face. "So, it seems that you have caught an old fool in his true feelings toward one, and I might add, only one child. Not that he is a child anymore. The boy is almost a man after all." His tone had changed mid-sentence, taking on a more defensive air. Cisco's Marie wondered if she was the only one to see beyond the older man's facade. He always tried to laugh off the lonely shard of ice that held his heart. He seemed nothing more than a happy rogue on the outside, while on the inside hid a man who sometimes longed to have more.

Dominique knew only too well that he himself would never know the joy of being a father. His heart would always have that agonizing void. It was a space that somehow felt smaller by the company of Pierre's son. He looked toward the fire and tried to pull himself together and conceal his secret ache. He would have to hide his emotions more carefully, he thought. After all, they needed him and his strength, not his weakness or self-pity.

Marie's eyes filled with tears as she closed her mind to Dominique's. His thoughts would remain his. The knowledge of his pain had been shared briefly, but his anguish, that would never again be touched by her. Marie sat down by the fire and sipped her wine sadly, wondering what else the night would bring forth. As she sat watching the flames and thinking, the occasional echo of children's laughter grew fainter, and the living room gained an air of expectancy about it.

Cisco and Tori had been talking quietly when Dominique realized that they were both looking toward the door every few minutes as if expecting company. Even Jean seemed somewhat on edge, and now, come to think of it, Dominique was sure that they were up to something. The familiar twinkle of amusement slowly crept back into the old sea dog's eyes. Dominique's longing for a life he would never know was safely put away, for the time being, in anticipation of what would soon be far more interesting than moping he was certain. He felt sure something was about to occur, but what?

The fire had new logs to burn, and the wine had just been restocked when a loud knock at the front door sounded throughout the house. Cisco looked up at Tori and, cheerfully squeezing her hand, said, "This is it then. Here goes nothing."

Dominique's eyebrows rose involuntarily, and he dared not speak, as he knew it would be a waste of his breath. No one was about to let him in on what was happening, that was for sure.

Jean stood with his back to the fire, facing the open doorway as two more guests entered. At last, he had both of his friends together for the first time. They were all here now, and Jean winked at Tori, who knowingly nodded her head slightly and smiled. Jean did not hesitate; he greeted the new guests before anyone else could utter a word. "Gentlemen, please come in and join our little gathering. It is about time that we all got to know one another as the friends we are. John, for the sake of sanity," he said to Grymes, as he handed John Davis a glass of wine, "I think we shall have to call you Grymes. My friend here," he said, looking toward the hotel owner, "would be appalled, if I tried to call him Davis. Tori, hand Grymes a glass while I explain this gathering." Jean filled his own glass and turned to face everyone before he continued. "Now, as to why Tori and I have gathered you all here, I shall start at the beginning and explain. Dominique, for what you are about to hear and become a part of, I know you will hold it in your care, as you would my life. I chose both you and Pierre to join us for reasons that I shall keep to myself." He held up his hand to silence him. "You have the wisdom and the courage, my friend, to hear and become a part of what is in store for you."

Dominique chuckled. "And here I thought we were celebrating the season! A lie if ever there was one. Should have known you were up to something. Ah, but Tori, you wound me, keeping secrets from me." He had placed his hand over his heart and looked very sad, then just as fast, he raised his glass and spoke with a hint of laughter. "To whatever the pup is up to now."

Jean chose to ignore this last statement and faced the worried hotel owner. "John, I gave you my word on a certain matter, and it will remain so. You know you are as much a part of this by your involvement and knowledge as you are for any other reason. That is why you are here." Then, smiling, he added, "And we love your music." His voice, light but sincere, had eased the worried frown from John's forehead.

"Grymes, my friend, you, of course, have no idea what is going on. At least, if we have been careful enough, you don't. I see by the expression on your face that this is true? Well, you are about to be changed for life, and believe me, the role we are going to ask you to take on will cost you." Jean's face had taken on a more distressing look. "We have all talked about you and your upcoming role and decided that you had to be told everything and brought into our confidence." Jean stared at his friend, who had a very perplexed look about him.

Jean and Tori had told Grymes once about her time travel in a meeting with Leone years ago but had not mentioned it since. They would now try again. "I am sounding like a fool here, aren't I? And you and Dominique, along with my brother, need to be, as Tori would say, filled in before we can progress. Gentlemen, may I suggest you sit and listen till all is said, and try to keep an open mind."

Pierre frowned as he stood up and reached for his lover's hand. "I think maybe you can hold this meeting without us, and I prefer it so. Any pertinent information that should be shared, I trust one of you will take me aside later. It is not that I do not believe, nor that I do not wish to take part, just that for us, it is best, we go upstairs."

Jean nodded in agreement. "If that is your wish. I think it best. We will talk, my brother, when you are ready." He hugged Pierre and then gave Marie a kiss on each cheek. She could be trusted; he knew that, but Jean saw the wisdom in his bother's request. The less that she knew of what they would talk about this night, the better.

AFTER Jean finished explaining the time travel, along with what history they knew, to Grymes, it became quiet in the room for the first time in nearly two hours. The attorney looked around at the people he called friends and saw that they genuinely believed in what they had told him. Even the solid of mind, and true skeptic, Dominique seemed to accept it.

Having heard this tale before, Dominique knew there was more to come, so he remained silent. Things were getting interesting, and he hated to spoil all the fun. The look on Grymes's face alone made him chuckle. The expression on John Davis's face told him that more excitement was about to happen. For right then, however, his full attention fell on the attorney.

Grymes was scowling; he did not find anything amusing as he looked around the room. All of them were educated and intelligent, but time travel and history? The attorney was torn. "Look," Grymes said, his voice sounding strange even to himself, "I wish that I could believe all you have told me. Jean... Tori... how can I put this? As incredible as it seems to me, it's not that I don't want to believe, understand me? It's just..."

Tori, worried. She had thought that Grymes would have accepted their tale and been ready to join forces with them without any reservation. He was, however, on the verge of total denial. If they lost his support because he thought them all crazy, it would be far more challenging to continue. She looked toward Jean for help and found he was staring at John Davis and not paying any heed to Grymes or what he was saying.

They had not revealed Davis's time travel identity until now, enabling Jean to keep his word to the man. All Laffite said was that not only did Davis believe in Tori and Cisco, he'd also played a significant role in getting Jean and his men out of jail. With so much information presented to them, Grymes, and Dominique, who had suspected the truth behind Davis's part in that escapade, now had confirmation.

Although Davis's story was secure, Jean desperately needed his help in gaining Grymes as a significant player. To do that, he would have to step forward and reveal himself but would he? It was that question in Jean's eyes that Davis could see. Was he going to risk his identity or hold back and risk history? Grudgingly the man knew he had no choice. A small voice whispered in his head, 'I told you so.' He looked away from Jean's probing eyes and gazed at the floor. "Tell one person, and soon there is another and another," he mumbled to himself. It was evident to him that exposing his darkest secret: his existence, as one of the damn time travelers, was about to come to light.

"Grymes!" Davis snapped. "I think maybe you had better listen to them." He looked up and into the eyes of the State Attorney. "I know what they are telling you is the truth." He stood and walked toward the attorney, standing inches away from him, as he continued. "I know because I'm one of them. Not just a good friend. I'm a traveler in time. I'm not crazy or am I a fool, but what I do have, besides the truth, is knowledge about you. I think maybe you and I had better take a walk and sort all this out."

Grymes shook his head. "A walk won't be necessary. If you have to say anything, I think it best you say it here and now." He looked around the room as a grim expression filled his face. He forced the next words out of his mouth. "We are among friends, after all, are we not? So long as you are not about to tell me my death date or some such disturbing fact, please continue; you, Sir, have my full attention."

Within the next hour, they had won him over. Then, at last, after his numerous questions had been answered, the room fell silent once again.

It was Tori who stepped forward and raised her glass. "Friends, may I suggest that we get to the real reason why we are all here. It is nearly 1814, and due to certain events that have occurred and the knowledge we three have," she looked toward Cisco and John, "we can all be assured that 1814 is the year we must start to prepare for the British and the Battle of New Orleans."

John Davis raised his hand in protest. "I think maybe we should still tread slowly. I agree that we all can start to prepare, but none of us are sure this is the year, are we? We have to go slow."

Cisco jumped up. "But the reward and the counter reward prove that history is going as it should. That is to say, with our help. If I had not suggested the reward for the Governor, well… it could have all been changed, right then, history I mean. I say we move ahead. Start to get things in place."

Jean raised his hand and looked around the room as he spoke. "I am not about to go in circles again. We have gone over all of this before, and we agreed that we would take events one at a time. First things, first. Grymes, you have been added to the group because not only are you one of my trusted friends, but it seems that you have a large part to play in the upcoming events." Grymes looked puzzled yet was willing to listen to what Jean had to say.

"You have told me this, Jean. What I would like to know is just what is it that I am supposed to be doing? Or, more importantly, what is it that you think I am going to do?"

Jean grinned. He had been waiting all night to drop his bombshell, and now seemed the appropriate moment. "You, yourself suggested, just what that is, John. Cisco and Tori already guessed what you would do. Let me explain before you say anything, and you will understand. Not long ago, you came to my house and offered to become my attorney. You were willing to resign from the state's position and represent us in the fight to clear my name and gain back a certain piece of property. If you remember, I asked you to wait… that you would be of more help where you were. Nothing has changed yet in that department. However, you will be glad to know that you will become my attorney in history, that's according to the three individuals standing in this room. It was Davis who knew this interesting information, how or why he came across this, he has not divulged, but Tori and Cisco support him, and it seems highly plausible. However, that is all we know at this time. Just what it is you did for me… for us… is still a mystery."

Grymes's expression showed he was stunned. He looked toward John Davis, who merely nodded in agreement, and at Cisco, who was smiling, like the devil himself. Tori was the only one who seemed to mask whatever feelings she might have on the matter, and something told him that she was not revealing everything. He would talk with her himself, at a later date, and in far greater detail, that was certain. "So, what is it you want me to do?"

305

"Keep your eyes and ears open and stay close to Claiborne and his cohorts," replied Jean. "It's nothing that you haven't always done, oui? Also, see if we can't get at least one more gentleman from the legislature on our payroll. The longer they stall the Governor and his requests to arrest me, the better. We need time right now." He turned toward Dominique, who had sat listening with no comment. "Dominique, my friend, now for your role. I need you to start to move flints and powder. You have to place as much as you can in secure places in the backwaters. Make sure that each stash is hidden and known only to you, myself, and maybe one or two others of your choice."

Dominique smiled. "Like the old days in France, oui? It will be my pleasure to play your game. I can add more to the stash, no? More than just flints and powder, maybe? But, Boss, to hide as much as I think you would want me to, well, I will need some distraction for the men. Something to keep them busy and their minds off what it is crazy Dominique is up to."

"I have thought of that. I shall have a large sale… the largest that we have ever dared to hold before. The posters are being printed as we speak. I have set a date, January 20. That should give you some time to ready yourself. All of the slaves we have, and any that come our way, are to be sold. No more from Grand Terre, under any circumstance shall we sell." At this statement, he caught his wife's eye and saw the pleased smile play upon her lips. He knew only too well how she felt about the selling and moving of slaves. That she should think, he was doing this to please her, suited him, and he would say nothing to change her opinion.

The absolute truth behind his decision was simple. If Grand Terre was in danger of the British or the Americans, then he wanted only his able-bodied men at the ready. He did not want to worry about the blacks' welfare or the chance of having escaped slaves running about causing havoc. He would see to it that any human cargo taken would be moved through Cat Island. The monetary value to be gained by selling slaves was lucrative and necessary. That money, he told himself, was needed to aid in the lean days ahead. What his lady did not know would not hurt her, and it would keep certain Captains happy too. The slave trade was alive and well, and there was nothing he or Tori could do to change it. "So, it is agreed that we proceed carefully, and all keep our eyes open… and I might add," he said, looking at Dominique, "our mouths shut."

Dominique shot him a dramatic hurt look as he moaned and placed his hand again over his heart. "Ah, Boss, you insult me. I would never reveal what has been said here tonight, not even to my lover on the pillow. May, the Saints hear my oath. Not even under the drink will I talk." He rolled his eyes toward the heavens as if the angels themselves were listening to him. Then looking toward Jean, he spoke in a tone so soft as to hardly be heard. "I can carry a secret, as well, you know." Standing, he walked toward the fire and bent to light his cigar from the embers. "Besides," he said, inhaling deeply, blowing the blue smoke out into the room toward Cisco and John, "who would believe the ravings of an old fool if I were to tell such a wild tale? I ask you all, who in the hell would even listen?"

Marie broke the room's laughter as she walked up to Dominique, and looking into his eyes, hissed, "The devil himself would listen if he thought to gain by the information. I suggest if you don't wish him to come a calling, that the cat holds your tongue."

Dominique blanched at her mention of the devil, and like a child scolded by his mother, obediently nodded; he understood what she was implying. No devil was going to show his face, any place close to him, or what he knew.

Tori smiled at the loveable old pirate, as she called him. He was a good friend and could be trusted even if Jean didn't think so. "Dominique, you will be fine, just do what you have to and make sure you stash as much as you can because it takes a lot to fight a battle and win."

"Tori, my sweet woman, you do not know this, but I am only too well aware of how much powder and firepower it takes to fight a battle. I shall not let you or Boss down. I will take leave right now and begin my task by morning. There is, after all, a warehouse full of what we need, and I assume Boss, it is no longer for sale."

"It is not. Take who you trust from the docks but be careful because once they know the location of such a prosperous horde, they might be tempted."

"That you can leave up to me. I have no intention of leaving it in one place for long, and those who move it to the last place I have in mind, well, those I would trust with my life."

Dominique walked to the door and turned as he opened it. "I will see you soon, Boss. There is much to do, and sitting here with friends is nice, but that is not how one wins." The door closed on his laughter.

Cisco laughed. "Just like him to listen to the plan and laugh at us. Well, I, for one, say there is nothing more we can do tonight other than drink and party." Cisco was filling another glass of wine and, as always, had found the lighter side of the situation. "Plenty of time to begin working tomorrow, if you ask me."

"I did not," chuckled John Davis as he stood up. "I think the tables require your talent, and you still work for me. So, I suggest you leave the drink and come along."

"Spoilsport."

"Just practical, that's all. Jean, Tori," he nodded his head. "I will be in touch soon. Keep me posted. Grymes, will you be joining us this night, or do you have other plans?"

"Nothing to keep me from a little gambling. I will join you. Besides, I think we still need to chat. Something we can do while we return to the hotel."

Cisco laughed again. "Hell, it's going to take much longer than a short walk to fill you in, old man. I bet you have a ton of questions."

John Davis shot Cisco a stern look. "Might I add, you need to step back into this era and sound as if you belong before your mouth has you flagged as a crazy man?"

Everyone laughed, and Cisco nodded his head, seeing the error of his way. "You have me there—time to be me. You sure you want me to work tonight? I could slip up, you know?"

"He has a point there, John," added Tori. "Maybe, best to give him one night off. It can't hurt, right?"

"I suppose you have a good point, but work, he will. Jean, the posters announcing the sale will need to be put up. I suggest that our friend here organizes that task. Keep him busy and out of trouble." Both Davis and Grymes laughed at the perplexed expression on Cisco's face.

"EDWARD, have you seen these posters? They're all over the town, and everyone is talking about it and planning to attend. Edward, where are you? Do you hear me?" Simone was screaming from room to empty room, looking for her husband. He had said he would be here to meet her and discuss the furniture she wanted to buy for the house. So, where was he, she wondered?

Edward sat in what would be the front parlor. He had heard her call for him and knew only too well what she was yelling about. It was that damned Laffite again and his sale. The brazen bastard was going to have the largest sale of exotic goods, and everyone he knew was planning to attend and purchase what they could. All of them thought of the illegal sale in only one way, to gain cheaply, what they wanted, and to hell with how Laffite had acquired the merchandise. Not that any of that mattered right then. He had to deal with his wife and what he knew she was going to suggest.

Simone burst into the room. "There you are. Didn't you hear me calling? Here, look at this," she said, holding out a sheet of paper toward him.

He raised the announcement off his lap and showed it to her. "So, I see you have one also," he answered sarcastically. "It is kind of difficult not to pick one up, isn't it? They are the talk of the town. The city seems to think it fair game." He didn't look at her when he continued. Instead, he was reading the list she had given him a few

309

days ago. "You have here," he said, pointing his finger to the list, "quite a number of items that will, if ordered regularly and rightfully, take months to obtain."

Simone's eyes narrowed as she looked at him. Just what was he getting at, she wondered? "Are you implying something?"

"Simply, that Laffite will have some, if not all, of the items that you require to furnish this place, and in the style you want. It could be outfitted in a matter of days, not months, that's all." He looked at her knowingly.

"You mean to tell me that you're willing to line that man's pockets with gold just because you can't wait to have the place furnished? I thought you wanted him destroyed as much as I do? You actually want to tell me you wish to support him and this sale?" She was waving the paper in the air angrily. "How could you?"

Edward stood up and glared at her. "Now, don't go getting yourself all upset until you hear me out. And don't go acting the upright citizen with me either. I know you better than you know yourself." He walked to her side and stroked the side of her face lightly. "You can't stand there and tell me that you had not planned to suggest we go to purchase a few things, now can you?" He looked her straight in the eyes and watched as the guilty color rose on her cheeks. She spluttered, trying to say something, but knowing that he had seen through her, she decided to remain quiet.

"I thought not. Now, if you don't mind, I will tell you what I have come up with. I think you will find it mutually beneficial to our needs. We will end up with merchandise, and Laffite will end up hanging himself." His sadistic look of joy was spilling forth as he hatched yet another of his evil plans.

THE day of the auction started early. The weather was mild for the middle of January, and the dawn's light found many camped close by. These hardy people had decided to brave the night under the stars to be among the first to purchase items or place bids on particular objects and more lucrative merchandise before they were snatched up. As the sun rose over the horizon, many were waiting for the bidding to begin. Still, many others continued to turn up. They came on foot, on horseback, some in wagons, and others in carriages. Tori was amazed to see such a mix of people. Plantation owners from Mobile and still further away had come to purchase slaves, the last of the pirate's human cargo, Jean had assured her.

In contrast, many of the more exceptional citizens of New Orleans came to buy luxury items like silks and furniture. Many free blacks sought spices and cloth or things they could sell at their stalls in the French Market and make themselves a nice profit. They understood that there was money to be made because not everyone would make the trek into the bayous, and those who didn't would be searching the market for items that they hoped to buy at a lower price than in the shops.

Jean's wife stood looking around the area, which was quite an expanse. Every place she viewed, deals were being made, and cash was changing hands. Never had Tori dreamed that Laffite had so much and such a variety. It amazed her even more as she strolled among the aisles, how easily the goods were sold. Jean's men were everywhere, and even though it seemed to her that items could be picked up and stolen, she took comfort in the knowledge that Dominique assured her; it never happened that way. Who, after all, would have the courage to steal from Jean Laffite, he'd asked, laughing?

Food was being sold, and drink was readily available. Children ran and played among the most prominent pieces of furniture while their parents inspected the items. Others played at games, while some of the adults, who dared, tried their luck at the odd game of chance. The atmosphere surrounding her was rather like one would find at a carnival, and everyplace she looked, people were enjoying themselves.

Dressed as a male and with her hat pulled down low, she was able to walk among the crowd unnoticed and unbothered. It amused her to listen to the ladies in particular, many of whom openly spoke of the handsome Laffite and how charming he was.

After overhearing just such a comment, Tori was smiling to herself when she recognized the voice coming from directly behind her. She stood still, pretending to look at an item, and listened even more carefully to what Simone was saying.

"Are you sure all the items we want are safely on the way home? After all, we don't want them to be confiscated as evidence, now do we? Edward, are you listening to me or not, and where are the Governor's men anyway? I thought they would be here by now."

That was all Tori needed to hear. Quickly, she made her way over to where she had last seen Jean and Dominique. He had to be warned, and the sale stopped before it was too late. Damn Edward and Simone. Would they ever leave them alone, she wondered?

Jean saw his lady pushing her way frantically toward him. The look on her face told him something was very wrong, and he excused himself from a small group of ladies that had been overjoyed at having a chance to barter with the pirate. They had been haggling over the price of an English silver tea service and continued to do so, even after he left them with one of his men.

"Jean, I need to talk to you," she said, panicking as she grabbed his sleeve and pulled him away from the crowd. "Simone and Edward are here, and I heard them talking, and…" she had to stop to gain her breath. "You have to call off the sale and get out of here now. Save some of this quick," she'd whispered into his ear while pointing at the merchandise all around them. "Edward's purchase is safe on its way. He will get to keep his stuff, but you will lose yours. The Governor's men are on the way." Suddenly she stopped talking. Was he smiling at her? He was, damn him. Did he not understand what she was trying to tell him?

Jean slipped his arm around her waist and pulled her closer. "My, my, you are panicking over nothing, I assure you. Come over here and let me explain something to you." He guided her from the area to a secluded spot by the water's edge. "You do look ravishing when you are all worked up, even dressed as you are."

Tori stomped her foot and hit him on the chest hard. She was about to repeat this action when he caught her hand in mid-flight and pulled her close to him, laughing as he did so. "I think you had better calm yourself down, or you are going to give away your disguise, and such a nice disguise it is, I might add." He had patted her rear with his hand and looked around her shoulder, admiring the view of her behind in breeches.

"Jean, there is no time for foolishness," she said, slapping at his hand. "You have to get out of here before you're caught."

"And what makes you think that I will be caught, huh? You think that I would hold such a sale without having precautions?"

"Well, no. I thought you would have some, but Simone and Edward made mention that the..."

He kissed her hard on the lips quickly and pulled back, smiling. "Do you know that I love you more when you have that angry flare about you? It makes my blood run hot and my mind crazy with wanting you." He saw her flush a deeper red before tears of frustration pricked her eyes. Upon seeing this, he knew he would have to tell her. It was cruel to keep her worrying unnecessarily. "My love, you do not need to worry your head or your large heart about my safekeeping. I will not stop the auction, as there is no need. However, I will send some of my men to take back the shipment that those two pompous, so called elite citizens think is safely on its way. Call it a lesson for all the trouble they caused me this morning."

Her eyes narrowed. "What trouble is that?" she asked, not too sure she wanted to know.

"I had a run-in with a few of the Governor's men early in the morning. My men knew of their whereabouts long before they were within reach of this site. I personally met them to persuade them to give up on their mission." His face went grim as he continued. "One of the fools did not want to listen, and one of my men acted too hastily. He shot and killed the man." The look of horror on her face as his words sunk in scared him. He was no cold-blooded murderer and would have done anything to change the event. For him, right at that moment, it was imperative that Tori understand that.

"If I could have stopped it, believe me, I would have." His hand took hold of her chin, and he held her face so she could not look away as he went on. "Two other men were shot but not killed. That was before I got everyone under control."

"Jean, this is not good. Let go of me," she pulled his hand away. "You know this will mean that you are wanted for murder. He will stop at nothing now to get you. Damn you, Jean. You might have given Claiborne and Edward the ammunition they need to come after you full force!"

Quick-relief filled his soul as he saw that she was more worried about his safety than angry at what had happened. "You need not worry about that either. Without proof of what happened, they can do nothing. None of his men there, this morning, will talk against my men or me. It was just an accident, and that is what will be reported." He smiled so gently that she was not sure if she had seen his lips curl up in a grin or not. Then she looked at his eyes that appeared so serious. Tori could see the lines that extended each side and watched those lines deepen as he frowned. "Neither will they be coming here."

Now she did look horrified. Had Jean killed them all to silence them? If so, how would she ever forgive him for cold-blooded murder?

Confused at first by the look upon her face, he laughed out loud as he realized what she was thinking. "I simply sent them back home to New Orleans with their pockets filled with trinkets for their loved ones. They are thrilled and contented men, believe me." He hugged her to him and could feel her body shaking as he held her close. "Nothing is going to happen to me. After all, I have a battle to win, oui? You seem to keep forgetting that, and I have to keep reminding you." He held her for a few more seconds and then pushed her away. "I have a sale to finish, and you have some shopping to do. Now, smile. Think about Edward's and Simone's faces when they realize they have been outwitted once again."

Tori laughed and cried at the same time. "I think I've had enough excitement for one day. Thinking about those two right now, well, it's too much. I do admit, though, I think they got exactly what they deserved. Simone is going to have a fit, you know? Poor, poor woman!" she giggled while looking for her in the crowd. "That picture in my mind is better than any shopping. I'll enjoy the image and wait for you down by our boat." She looked into his eyes and, in her soft sexy voice, added, "I take it we are still going back to Grand Terre tonight?"

"That we are, my lady. Maybe sooner than you know." His dark eyes gazing into hers spoke volumes about how much he wanted her at that moment. It had been months since he had put his emotional needs before business, and he was tired of it. His men could just as easily finish up the sale for him because Jean Laffite realized he had more important things to attend to.

EDWARD sat sipping his strong coffee, listening to the conversations that were going on around him. He was in no mood for company and especially that of his wife. More than once that morning, he had thanked God silently for the brief stay in giving her the news about their shipment. When she realized that all the merchandise they had bought would not be delivered and was instead back with that filthy swine, the lady would be impossible to calm down. He shook his head at the thought and gave a slight shudder at the next. Simone would sleep for a few more hours yet, and by the time she was up and about, Edward hoped to be well out of her reach. He had taken the easy way out; he knew that. Writing her a message just seemed the simplest solution to a difficult situation. It was not that he was a coward, he told himself, but damn it to hell, he was just in no mood to hear again how much she wanted that pirate's head!

EDWARD drank more of his coffee au lait and sneered as he listened to the conversations around the tables in the restaurant. They spoke of Laffite in almost endearing terms. Even now, after killing one and wounding several others of the Governor's men, Laffite was considered a fair and caring individual. It made him sick to his stomach to listen to the fools talking about how generous the pirate had been. They went on and on about how he had loaded the soldiers with gifts instead of killing them and had sent them home safely. No one spoke of the injured or the one that was killed. Murdered was more like it, he told himself. Edward wanted to scream at the top of his lungs, to shout out that Laffite was not a hero. He wanted to make them see the truth, that the man was nothing more than a cutthroat pirate, one who had bought the soldiers off. That was all the bastard had done! And, he had gotten away with it. The dandy stood up and left disgusted. Better, he spent his time more productively. He decided to stop in for a much-needed visit to his so-called friend, the Governor.

Claiborne had once again failed to stop Laffite. And Edward was growing very tired of the man and his office. What kind of Governor was he anyway? He would have to apply more pressure and get him to act now. Indeed, in the wake of what had just occurred, while it was still fresh on everyone's minds, the man should petition the State's Legislature again, asking for the funds to form a militia. They needed a military to oust the thieves and murderers from their stronghold. The statesmen would have to agree to that. After all, how many more letters from the Governor could they ignore, he wondered? And why was it that all requests made involving the Laffite's, fell on deaf ears? Was it their way of getting back at the American? Would it have been different if he were one of them? No, he doubted that. Well, they would have to listen now. This time, they had no choice but to act. As for himself, he would never ease up on the Governor. Angry and determined, he began making his way toward Claiborne's home, his walking stick hitting the cobblestones hard with each step he took.

Duval had come very close to the reason why the American Governor got nowhere with his petitions. Claiborne's continued pleas fell on an uncooperative group. Again and again, they promised to listen and to come up with a solution, only to turn around and do the opposite. The American Governor was treated as if he were a man, to be tolerated and no more. He had no power and little or no control of what was going on around him. Without their support, his hands were tied, and they liked it that way. He was their puppet, and they pulled the strings of running the city any way they thought would benefit them. It felt good to control the Americans and their stupid interference, where it was not wanted. Most of all, they admired Jean, who was one of them, who kept the Americans in their place. He was, to them, a valid symbol of defiance, with actions that were always carried out in an honorable manner, of course. Knowing they were driving the Americans and the Governor wild only added to their self-satisfaction.

The Laffite's had continued to ship their goods into the city, most of the time under armed guard and at night. Many knew that he and his men could just as easily move anything they wanted, day or night, and not be stopped. The waterways and the purse strings of the city belonged to Jean, and everyone knew it. Besides the Laffite's, many profited from the enterprising deals. But many more, primarily the Americans, were not, and Claiborne was caught in the crossfire. The State Senate was openly hostile toward him. The city's citizens called Claiborne a tyrant and a fool, and the American merchants were demanding something be done.

On top of all this, Edward was always around, adding fuel to the fire. He continued telling William how he was being played for a fool. The dandy was determined to keep the whole situation explosive in hopes that something would be done.

IN the spring of 1814, Congress repealed the embargo and non-importation laws, but New Orleans had her financial hands tied behind her back. The city banks under strain suspended payment, and about this time, word came that the French Emperor had fallen from power. England was now free to turn all its forces toward the United States, and it wanted Louisiana back as an ally. The Creoles, who held no loyalty to the Americans, had begun to talk about becoming independent. The whole city was openly laughing at the Governor and his continued failings at apprehending Laffite or his men. By the time summer arrived, the Governor was pushed to his limits. He understood that something substantial had to be arranged, both to gain respect and to put an end to the thorn in his side, the Laffite's. So it was that Claiborne set out to organize a friendly grand jury chosen from American merchants and bankers. Held in secret, they called witness after witness, who all swore to acts of piracy by Jean Laffite, Pierre his brother, and their men. By the end of the lengthy hearing, Claiborne finally got what he wanted. Satisfied, he sat back and watched as indictments were drawn up against both the brothers and two of his lieutenants. "These pieces of paper," he said, shaking them toward Edward, "will be the end of that damned man and my humiliation. Now we will see who will dare laugh at me!"

Duval was concerned. After all, Laffite had always found a way to avoid any form of punishment for his crimes. "William, before you do anything, may I add a small suggestion. One that might be prudent." Edward wanted to make sure they had the edge on things. "Before we, excuse me, you, send out word of what is written there," he said, pointing to the papers in William's grasp, "why not act first and then tell the citizens of this city what the Laffite's have been charged with after. We don't want those two to slip out of town and into hiding, now do we? Believe me that is exactly what they will do if they get one sniff of this. You have been most prudent until now; why not continue?"

William looked at his friend with appreciation filling his voice and expression. "Point well taken, and I'm in full agreement with you. I will have a platoon of my finest leave immediately to apprehend those bastards once and for all. And this time, they will be held and not given any chance at bond or escape. We finally have them, I tell you. Tonight, they will be caged up, and we will celebrate!"

JEAN and Tori were home relaxing when the news of Pierre's arrest reached them. Dropping everything, they both fled into hiding, slipping from one safe house to another until they arrived in the attic at the blacksmith shop. Thiac had closed shop after a platoon of dragoons had searched it from top to bottom but worried that they would return any time. It was not safe for the pair to hide in the cottage or his shop, but where else could they go?

"Boss, Mizz Tori. It ain't safe here now for you two. I ain't one to tell you what to do, but I think it best, if'n you's head out of town as soon as I can get me two horses ready." He did not wait for an affirmative answer but turned and left to get the animals.

Tori touched Jean's arm lightly. "He's right, Jean. You know he is. This is one of the places that they will keep searching until they catch you. Look, there is nothing we can do for your brother at this point, but we can prevent you from getting yourself thrown into that hellhole with him."

Jean placed his hand on top of hers. "I agree with you, but neither can we ride out of here in broad daylight. Claiborne is no fool. He would not have arrested Pierre if he were not confident about catching us both. The roads will be heavenly patrolled, as well as the river. We have to wait until dark at the earliest. I agree waiting here is no better." He removed his hand and began pacing up and down, already feeling confined. The cottage was a trap, and he knew it.

Tori tried to soothe his agitation and asked him softly the one

319

question on both their minds. "We have to find a new place to hide then, but where they won't look?"

No sooner was the question off her lips than realization flooded Jean's face. "We will go at once to Marie Villars's. My brother's mistress will take us in and be only too glad to do so." He grabbed Tori's hand and pulled her to the stairs. "Thiac, leave the horses," he called out, "we are walking."

"How you be doing that?" A very puzzled male voice called back.

"On two feet just like anyone else, you fool," laughed Jean.

Thiac met them at the bottom of the stairs, looking very anxious.

"I knows, how you walk, Boss. What I mean is, how you going to escape to the camp when you on foot?"

"We will take the horses later. I'll send word soon. Now, my lady, are you ready? We best move and move fast and pray to God that we are not seen."

MARIE had received word about her beloved Pierre and was beside herself. Her younger sister had tried to tell her to stay calm and that she was sure Jean would have his brother out of jail very quickly. But Marie, pregnant again and due any time, was not so sure. She could do nothing but sit and stare out the window or pace frantically back and forth.

Pierre's lover saw Jean and Tori long before they got to the house and rushed to the door to let them in. "Jean, do you know anything about what they have done with my Pierre? I'm so worried. But, thank God you and Mizz Tori are safe."

Laffite's wife reached out and hugged the frightened woman. "Marie, I want to thank you for letting us in. Jean thought that it would be the best place for us to hide for a while. We will leave out the back if he sees anyone coming for us." She turned her head to look back at Jean, who was watching out the window.

Marie knew Tori well and had spent many hours with her but never before had she seen such a look of fear and worry cross her face. Tori had deep lines that filled her forehead, lines of concern that she had no idea would stay with the woman for many months to come. "Don't you fret yourself none, Mizz Tori. Jean is a fine and good man. He wouldn't do nothing to hurt me or the children." She smiled at the little one playing quietly and stroked her large round abdomen as she talked. "Pierre would want to know I took care of you both, and I know that Jean will take care of him too. He won't be in that jail long. I know he won't."

THAT night, when Jean felt safe enough, he sent for Grymes. "I tell you, John, if I thought I could make it out of town, I would not be here. I agree with you, though; to leave now would be foolish. It is doubtful that anyone will search here for us. Besides, my brother, God love him, has a hidden space between the walls upstairs. It is large enough for Tori and I to hide in if anyone comes looking."

Grymes didn't like the idea of them hiding, even if they were concealed by a wall, in a hidden compartment. Somehow, he had to make Laffite see that he needed to get out of town as soon as possible. "Jean, that may be so, but you will have to leave as soon as you can. You can't just hide here, not now. I stopped by Davis's hotel and had a chat with him. He believes that this arrest is yet another sign that things are fast approaching the time of which you will be needed. He said that he told you, that Tori and Cisco both told you, that the Laffite's got arrested again, and even though it's only Pierre in the cell, he thinks this is that time."

Laffite nodded in agreement. "I guess so. He did say that if it happened again, we've kept things on track, as you say. I didn't think much about it. You know how all this knowing and not knowing goes."

Grymes nodded in agreement. "Trust me; I am beginning to grasp the situation. I knew about the grand jury meeting, and it was Davis who convinced me to let things play out. Forgive me, Jean, but I listened to him as he made a valid point. I could not tip my hand. Still, if I had done something, your brother would not be sitting in that jail."

"Nothing to forgive, John. You will try to see what you can arrange as far as my brother's release, though?"

"I will begin right away. I have my contacts and can remain your friend, still unknown friend that is, for a bit longer."

Jean slipped his arm around Tori's waist, and he pulled her close. "That the so-called grand jury has found me guilty of crimes of piracy is the least of my concerns right now. Obtaining my brother's freedom and getting us safely out of here is paramount."

Gryme's nodded his head, and with a stern expression, he spoke. "I shall depart then. I will not return here, just in case I am followed. You will get word from me as soon as I have news. Tori, take care of yourself and keep him out of trouble. One Laffite in jail is enough, and Davis is still unclear as to who ends up in jail, one or both of them."

Tori tried to smile but found it challenging. In the end, she gave up trying to hide her worry and spoke with a tremble in her voice. "I will be okay, thanks. Now you better head out. Give my love to John and Cisco and tell them I'm ok. We will leave as soon as Jean gets word it's safe to do so."

Two days later, news came by way of Cisco's visit. "It is no good, I say. You run the risk of getting caught; staying here while we try to find a way to get your brother out is better. Bond has been denied, and they are holding Pierre in a secluded cell, chained, I might add, and with full guard. So, there is no chance of breaking him out either. I couldn't run the risk of talking to Grymes, so I learned all this from a very full of himself, Edward. Man does he like to brag while playing cards, only when he's winning, more's the shame. Also, I have a bit of news you might like. This is from Davis, who wants it passed on to you. Jean, Grymes is going to resign his position this time and take you on as his client. Is it agreed? Grymes said Davis told him it's written in history. The man seems to know more than he is letting on. Anyway, just hope it's the right time and all."

"Jean," Tori whispered. "It is history, and I think this time he is right. You have no choice if we are to get your brother out, and you know that. John knew about this secret grand jury, but only because someone told him, which can mean only one thing. They told him to test him. He must be suspected of a connection to you already. His spying days are over for you."

Jean only nodded his head. "I understand what you are saying, but no, I do not agree that this is the time. That he is to become my ally at such a difficult time does not bode well. It will not be easy and might be foolish, but I prefer to keep Claiborne and his cohorts guessing. They maybe think Grymes is the spy among them; let them continue. His partner Edward Livingston can represent us as he has in the past. Let's keep John in his position for as long as we can. Cisco, you find him and tell him my decision is final on this."

Cisco grinned. "You have it. As for Livingston, he is with us full force on this, and he can be trusted to work hard. A better partner Grymes could not have asked for. He is experienced, and his knowledge of the law is outstanding. He is highly regarded, as you know, and his reputation speaks for itself. I have had the chance to not only meet the dude but talk in length too. We have talked long and hard about you and your circumstances, and he feels as I do. You are no pirate, and the charges should be dropped. He will fight this case and win you wait and see. I know one thing, John will be disappointed that he can't be the one to handle the case, but spying does occupy his time in a way he enjoys. I know he will listen to you and what you suggest. Just hope you are right on this. I can also tell you that he intends to keep our time travel and knowledge out of Livingstons' way. He will not be told now or ever, so you can rest your mind on that little detail. Thus, he will get your brother off and do so, not knowing the full story."

"That is good to know. You understand I gave my word to Davis, and I intend to keep it." Jean had a worried expression that he tried to hide from Cisco's prying eyes.

Seeing that the conversation was making Jean uncomfortable,

Cisco simply nodded his head in agreement and hastily spoke. "I shall depart then. I will not return here, just in case I am followed. You will get word from me as soon as I have news. Tori, take care of yourself and, like always, try to keep your man out of trouble. One Laffite in jail is enough, and like I said, Davis is still unclear as to who ends up in jail, one or both of them. Either way, Pierre will be freed."

He sounded so sure that for a second, Tori felt as if it would be so. But then she had an uneasy feeling that anything could happen and not necessarily the way she thought it would. She looked at Cisco, and for the first time, saw him clearly. Gone was the happy-go-lucky personality. He was taking everything very seriously, and at last, she glimpsed the educated man that he was, not the airhead playboy he portrayed.

Cisco saw Tori looking at him and guessed she was appraising him. "As for my spying days, well, let's just say I still have an ace up my sleeve, as does Grymes. He wanted me to tell you that he has ways and certain contacts that will continue to keep a close eye on the Governor and others. Oh, hell. He guessed you would ask him to remain where he is. I Should have known it. Had to give it a go, dangling the thought of his quitting, that is. I Just hopped he could do it representing you, is all. Like I mentioned, the man says he has others spying for him and not to worry. Love to know who these others are?" Cisco smiled and then walked toward Tori. "It is time you took this man of yours out of here to safekeeping. Jean can't stay here, and you both know it. Look, I'm sure the roads will be patrolled, but you only have to ride a short way until you reach the river and freedom." He kissed her on the cheek. "Keep safe, and I will get word to you as soon as I can." He continued in a very gentle tone. "Don't worry; this too will pass."

NEWS of John Grymes's law partner representing the Laffite brothers spread as fast as a wildfire. Duval only laughed at the foolish American. He could do nothing this time. The pirate's days were numbered, and with one Laffite out of the way, the other would soon follow, he was sure. Claiborne had gained back his former high standing among the American merchants and a few of the Creole society but still had a long way to go among the general population. As for John Grymes, he'd keep an eye on him too. Someone on the inside was telling the Laffite's what was going on, and if not Grymes, then who? Until he or Claiborne knew, they would tread carefully around the so-called District Attorney.

THE courtroom was packed. Pierre, on one side, was standing between guards. On the opposite side, Edward Livingston was looking very sure of himself. He briefly looked at the crowd behind him and nodded when his eyes locked with his partner Grymes, who was seated not far behind Pierre. Livingston looked back toward Pierre and was pleased to see that the man was following the instructions he had given to him the day before. He'd entered the court doing just what he should, and the response had been just as he'd predicted. Whispering sounds had filled the air when Laffite had dramatically entered the crowded courtroom. The cause for this uncommon display of anger was evident.

All the people had seen for themselves what up until then had only been rumored. Laffite was indeed shackled. The leg irons had jangled as he'd shuffled to his chair; the crafty pirate had made certain of that. He needed the sympathy of both the judge and the people who could influence the court's findings in his favor. Jean's brother had been held for six weeks now, and it was clear that prison life was beginning to take its toll.

Pierre's attorney began the hearing by demanding a bond be set for his client due to his failing health. It was a very unorthodox beginning but direct and to the point. "It is evident, your honor, that the man is suffering beyond what any prisoner should. Due to his failing health, that you yourself can witness," Livingston pointed to Pierre, " I implore the court to set bond so that Pierre Laffite can be properly taken care of while waiting to face the unwarranted charges against him."

Mr. John Dick, the prosecuting attorney, had a long disregard for John Grymes and his law partner. This fact was well known in town. His loathing of Livingston was evident in his voice as he responded to Livingston's request sarcastically. "Well, well, such a beginning of what I had hoped would be a great deal more professional. At least my standing as a law-abiding citizen and true representative of this court will prove Mr. Livingston's assumption incorrect. To say that his client's condition is a concern and reason for bond is utter nonsense and totally fabricated. I stand firm in regard to this request. The prisoner should not be granted bond. I base this on the sheer facts known to this court. The first fact is Pierre Laffite and his brother slipped bond a year ago. This alone makes the man a high-risk prisoner and…"

Livingston hit back quickly. He stood abruptly and faced the judge. "I object. My client is neither a risk nor is he healthy. If not allowed bond, in his weakened condition, as is plain to see, he is in great danger of becoming gravely ill. My client suffered in the past from a stroke. I fear his continued imprisonment will be the cause of another."

The prosecuting attorney was not about to allow Livingston to succeed in obtaining a bond, and he interrupted his opponent. "I can assure the court that is pure fabrication. I myself took liberties to have Mr. Laffite examined by more than one qualified physician, as you yourself can see in the documents I supplied you. Those very documents that you have there before you. Each physician concluded that he might be slightly weakened but is in no way in danger of becoming, as Mr. Livingston would have us believe, gravely ill."

"I object…"

"Denied," the judge's mallet sounded as he hit the desk to silence the room. "Continue Mr. Dick."

"Your honor, you will see that it is advised, in order to counter any malaise, Mr. Laffite may be suffering; that he be allowed to have the restraints removed once a day and, for a short time, walk outside in the air. If the court will allow such, then the prisoner is more than capable of awaiting his trial in jail as the law requires for such a man with his reputation and disregard of the law."

The crowded room erupted, with many calling out in favor of Laffite. Before Livingston could respond, the judge's mallet fell several times; hitting his desk hard, he called loudly for silence in the courtroom. Once control of the outburst was obtained, all listened carefully to the ruling. "I will not have any disruption of the proceedings. Should anyone dare disobey this fundamental directive, they can be assured to pay for doing so, both by a sizeable fine and a stay in jail. This ladies and gentlemen, is a court of law and will be conducted with full dignity and standing. Outbursts on either side will not, I repeat, will not be forthcoming."

No one uttered a word, and satisfied he had gained complete and utter control, the judge turned his attention back to the prosecutor. He looked directly at Mr. Dick without any sign of emotion. "I have before me your report Mr. Dick and agree with the findings. Accordingly, the prisoner shall remain in jail, with the conditions of his incarceration followed as suggested."

For the second time since his arrest, a bond had been denied. Also, this time, the judge set a trial date. Gryme's listened as the orders were given and shot his partner a knowing glance. He was angry and felt helpless right then because all he could do was watch and listen.

"The prisoner will be escorted immediately back to his cell, where he will remain until his day in court." The judge's gavel sounded, putting an end to the day's proceedings.

John wasted no time in joining his partner to see what else could be accomplished at this point. "Did you have any idea that such documents were handed over, stating that doctors agree Pierre is healthy enough to stand trial and remain in chains? I know even with my contacts and position I had no idea." He looked at the empty judge's chair and mumbled to himself. "It seems very likely I was correct; they do not trust me."

Livingston continued folding up his papers and responded to his partner. "I was not told, and had I been; I would have had our own doctors examine Laffite. Their findings would never have matched what was said here today. You can be most assured of that."

Grymes spoke louder, "I tell you, Livingston, Pierre Laffite is ill, and if I were his attorney, justice would have been served here today. He would never languish in jail in his condition. This is preposterous!"

The court, filled with a buzz of utter disbelief and anger; imagine a Laffite, especially a gentleman like Pierre, having to endure such harsh conditions, they whispered among themselves. All watched as the prisoner was escorted away, and most concurred with what John Grymes had said loud enough for everyone to hear. The man was in ill health and deserved better no matter his crimes.

The court's general mood was turning against the prosecutor, and it deeply angered the man. He had won his case and would have thought that the public would be more than pleased, but none it seemed were. Looking over toward Grymes and Livingston, Mr. Dick's face flushed with rage as someone called from the back of the room, "American pigs!" The room fell quiet as the caller explained that treating Laffite with such disdain was nothing short of abuse. Finally, he pointed at Mr. Dick and continued. "It is a perversion of justice, I tell you, handled by a stupid, ignorant baboon!" Some laughed while others angrily supported this last statement.

Mr. John Dick had had enough. He turned his anger and full attention toward Grymes. Playing to a packed crowd, he openly charged Grymes of having been bought off with pirate's gold. "You, Sir, by allowing your law partner to represent known pirates, is as good as doing so yourself. Grymes, you have lost all honor in so doing. Why I suggest you have indeed fallen below the standard your office deserves. By accepting large sums of their gold for representing scum, you are showing everyone that you feel as if you can take the law and use it to set free those guilty of smuggling, and dare I say... worse!" A smug, satisfied look covered his face. "I suggest that you have not one ounce of integrity left in you. Upholding the law is something those of us, with our oaths intact, will see accomplished. Unlike you, I can't be bought off!" Again, the surrounding area was filled with whispers; but the prosecutor was satisfied he'd made a valid point. 'Let them take that and think about it,' he smugly told himself, confident he'd won the moment.

Grymes was visibly shaken as he slowly turned to face Mr. Dick. Someone called out from the back of the room, but those around him silenced the man. All could see that things were getting interesting, and not one detail did they want to miss out on witnessing. All held their breath and waited to hear the response Grymes would give to having been charged with such damaging accusations. It was clear to anyone looking toward the confrontation that both men were at the point of no return.

A continued hush fell over the people as they waited to see what would happen next. John's integrity was something that he held dear, along with his reputation as an honest lawyer. Money had never been the issue, nor would it ever play into his practice of the law. To stand accused of such an outrage was unthinkable. With cold, calculating eyes and a voice that was laced with contempt, he faced his accuser. "You, Mr. Dick, have gone too far in your opinions of my character. To imply that my partner or I would use the law to line our pockets with illicit earnings is preposterous. To do so in private would have cost you a blow to your foul mouth. To stand there and accuse me in front of these fine and upstanding citizens, many of whom are not only clients but friends, will cause you profound consequences. You will have to pay for this outrage. I will not stand for such a slanderous attack on my integrity; as an attorney or as an upstanding man of my position."

He walked toward Mr. Dick with long slow strides, his footsteps echoing as they crossed the polished wooden floors. "I demand satisfaction, Sir. He slapped his open hand across the prosecutor's cheek. "You will have until this afternoon to think upon what you have done." His eyes were cold and calculating as he stared at his opponent. "We will duel in the style of true gentlemen. Gentlemen like my client, who will, I am sure, be only too happy to make me a loan of his dueling pistols." He could see the attorney's face drain of color and thought for sure that he was about to offer him his apology for his outburst, so he continued before the man had the chance. "I will expect you at sunset.

My man will deliver the directions as to where we will meet." With that, he turned and walked through the people who parted in silence as he left.

Grymes may be an American, but he had become one of them in that one act. The Creole population now supported him, and that would be so for the rest of his life. For the next few hours, the whole Cajun and Creole population, along with many American citizens, would hold its breath and await the outcome of the duel.

Cisco quickly followed John outside the courtroom. He made sure not to leave his friend's side from that moment on and remained with him through the hours leading up to the event. Never having seen a duel before, he found the whole procedure intoxicating. Later he would explain to Tori how the entire day had a surrealistic feel to it as if he was watching a movie. He would tell her he couldn't quite believe it was all actually happening.

As the sun slowly set over the field and the enormous moss-covered trees cast long dark shadows across the ground, Cisco called out the paces for the duel. His excitement far outweighed his concern for his friend at that moment, and it was not until the absolute horror of the pistols firing at each other rang out in the open air that rationalization took hold of him. He held his breath, as in slow motion, he saw John lower his hand and drop the gun to the ground. Grymes just stood staring at his opponent. Cisco followed his gaze and saw two men standing over the fallen man. He was moving and crying out in what could have been a mixture of pain and anger, but at least he was alive.

The duel was over in seconds, and satisfied that his honor and reputation were restored, Grymes joined Cisco. He was limping as he walked, and it was then that Cisco saw the bloodstain. "Is it bad? You know you have been hit, right?"

"I do, and we won't know how bad until we get it looked at but not here. I won't give that bastard the pleasure of knowing his aim was good enough to cause me harm. Come, let's go to Davis's establishment, and if we need, we shall send for a doctor."

Word of the duel and its outcome reached Pierre in his cell. He smiled weakly as he was told that Grymes had wounded his opponent, who would most likely carry the bullet and the pain for the rest of his days. Grymes's wound to his calf was but a graze. Justice, he thought, was maybe not so blind after all.

A small glimmer of hope accompanied this thought. With Mr. Dick severely injured, he would not be able to meet the trial date. That could be good for him, for it would allow more time for his defense and maybe even his release from the hellhole where he was held under close guard. Yes, he held out hope, but unfortunately, he knew his health was suffering, regardless of what those doctors had said, and with it, his mental state. No matter how he tried, depression was taking hold, as sure as the chains around his ankles.

The long hot summer months were intolerable to many unlucky enough to be held in any one of the cells. But to Pierre, who was ill and embittered, it was like a death sentence. He did not know how much longer he could hold on under such conditions. He prayed for what he often dreamed about—standing as Captain on the deck of a ship, sailing with a cool breeze on his face.

GRYMES and Cisco decided that they had to meet with Jean. Livingston was working day and night on their case to no avail,

331

leaving Grymes no alternative but to turn to Jean and his connections. It had become evident to all involved that Claiborne was not going to be reasonable in this case. Pierre had weakened over the summer months, and now came news of the British.

More intense fighting had broken out up North, and as the days slipped by, it became apparent to Cisco and John Davis that they now knew the date of the Battle of New Orleans. Grymes looked at Cisco and spoke with a stubborn tone. "It is settled then. We ride for Grand Terre and decide with Jean and Tori what to do. One thing is clear. We have to get Pierre out of that place and soon." He was looking very concerned and a little lost.

"You worry too much," said Cisco. "I'm not too worried about Pierre. I'm sure he will be fine. If Jean wants him out, then he'll go and get him, mark my words. More legal work for you," he chuckled, slapping his leg and laughing even louder at the glare that Grymes shot his way. Worried for a second, Cisco decided it best to change the subject. "Look, we need to meet with Jean and Tori to discuss many things. So, let's do it. Besides, I love it down there. Anything is better than this place right now; you have to admit that."

JEAN and Tori had kept to themselves, safe in the confines of Grand Terre. It was a waiting game that they played these days. Wait and see what would happen with Pierre. Wait and see what that idiot Claiborne would do. They had to wait and see when the British would make their move, and through all this, keep a close eye on the business.

Dominique had succeeded in his mission. Only a chosen few knew where he had hidden a substantial amount of powder and flints. With that job finally finished, the pirate found himself with time on his hands and nothing left to do. His answer to his idle hours was to sail off on a voyage that he swore would be profitable. Other Captains came and went. All left merchandise at Cat Island

and sometimes even dropped off their goods with Laffite at Grand Terre. Nothing had changed to them, and as long as the money was excellent and the ships were easily taken, the corsairs continued to plunder. Some talked about moving the center of operation along the coast to another port, though, and these rumblings reached Jean's ear. Tori told Jean that she thought that the new position would be the place she knew as Galveston; she did not tell him that Jean himself would set up his operation there after the battle. From there on, though, she did not know what happened and dared not even think about it.

WITH Dominique gone and the days long and hot, Tori found herself growing even more restless. She knew about the news delivered to the State Legislative, telling of the Capitol's House in Washington and how it had been burned. Grymes had sent a copy of the report as soon as he had read it himself. It stated the capital had been burned on August 24; that many buildings, including the one in which the president resided, had fallen to flames. It was the year 1814, and even though the war of 1812 was almost finished, the British action was a huge indicator for Tori and her comrades. The crucial historical event could only mean it was a matter of time now before the British would come to make their offer to Jean, and this was what worried her day in and day out. The constant battle Laffite fought to remain free and hold his dignity was one battle that the Boss was growing tired of. Frustrations grew, and his anger smoldered.

Jean had become very hostile toward Claiborne due to his brother's treatment at the American's hands. Not to mention the disbelief of how he himself was looked upon by many of the citizens. Accused of being a bloodthirsty pirate and forced into hiding was humiliating, and it infuriated him. He was an educated privateer, successful in all aspects, and soon to be in higher demand if Tori was correct. If it had not been for his lady and her so-called history lessons, he was not so sure that he would side with those who did nothing but scorn him.

Jean lay in bed many nights, thinking how easy it would be to take his brother and leave the area. There were other locations from which he could continue his business, and with so many now following his command, he did not doubt that he and all who joined him would become very wealthy. Then the pirate would look at his sleeping wife and reflect on all she had told him. According to her and her friends, he would never become the hero he was destined to be if he left now. Part of him wanted that, but more, he wanted his love to be happy, and if waiting a while longer made her so, then he would continue to remain. He would, however, unknown to Tori, begin to make secondary plans. Plans that involved leaving the American shoreline and sailing off for unknown parts.

GRYMES and Cisco's stay with Jean and Tori was full of long discussions about both the British and Pierre and his predicament. Jean had decided long before the end of the first meeting just how to handle the problem with his brother. As to the British and their arrival, it was back to the waiting game.

Laffite received reports on the enemy's activity and where they were at all times. This news he kept to himself, and as the days slipped by and the reports remained consistent, Jean began to wonder if the British were actually planning on moving their fleet toward the Mississippi. He knew if he had such an armada to command, that is exactly what he would do, but Jean was not their commander, and as long as he continued to receive updates on what the fleet was doing, he decided to concentrate on another situation that needed his immediate attention.

For three days, the friends enjoyed Grand Terre and all that it had to offer. Each night's meal was elaborately set before them and always served with excellent wines. The china, crystal, and silver shone in the soft candlelight. Never had Grymes expected or imagined the wealth of his client. The so-called pirate's hideout was so luxurious that it rivaled many of the finer plantations along the river, outdoing most of them by far in its furnishings alone. He would remember and talk about his visit with Jean for the rest of his life, constantly reiterating that the man was a true gentleman who knew how to appreciate the best life had to offer.

In the hallway, Tori and Grymes spotted Jean discussing something with Cisco in earnest, which Laffite referred to as a 'small problem.' "It is nothing to worry your head over," he said to Tori, "and I assure you, my love, that you and Grymes have no need to concern yourselves."

The worried look on both Tori and Grymes's faces caused Jean to weaken in his resolve to maintain his secret. He hugged Tori closer to him. "Look, I will tell you this. It is just a small surprise for Pierre's Marie. With the new baby's arrival and her love kept in chains, she needs some cheering up. I will explain it better as soon as I'm sure it can be obtained." He smiled at Cisco, who had the same look of mischief that Tori had come to be wary of.

She couldn't help it; the words spilled out. "Cisco, you look like the cat who ate the canary; come on out with it. What were you two talking about?"

"Sorry Tori, mum's the word. You have to ask your husband for the details."

Laffite laughed at both the foreign expressions his wife and Cisco were using, but it was the look on Grymes's face that had him entertained. "Mr. Grymes Sir," he chuckled, "they do talk a strange form of your American language. I wouldn't let it worry you. Now, I suggest you come to my library; I have something to discuss. You too, Tori, not that I could keep you from joining us, could I?'

Cisco took Tori by the arm and whispered in her ear. "Wait until you see this. I went weak in the knees when he had me help bring the boxes into…"

335

Jean did not look back, but his voice sounded as if he knew exactly what Cisco was up to, and he spoke in a stern tone. "I suggest Cisco that you hold that tongue of yours, or you may find yourself on my bad side. Come on, don't saunter like you are out for a stroll."

Before Cisco uttered another word, he was hurried along into Jean's library. Cisco smiled at Tori as they entered and placed his index finger to his lips, indicating that she, say nothing. Upon seeing she was going to cooperate, he gently guided Jean's wife to a chair that sat directly across from her husband.

Once Jean was behind his desk, he looked at each of them while stroking his goatee. Whatever he was up to was entertaining him immensely. His free hand rested on top of one wooden box, and his fingers were tapping ever so slowly as if he was contemplating what to do next. Tori studied the man's expression, but it was to the desktop that her eyes looked. There were two identical boxes, and she wondered more than ever what the pirate was up to? Never had she seen the objects, and looking toward Cisco got her no answers, as his eyes were staring at the desktop in anticipation of what was about to be revealed.

"And now Grymes, to the matter at hand. You will no doubt be wanting some of the money that I owe you. Fees due and a small amount to aid you in all your upcoming hours of assistance." Jean lifted both lids simultaneously, revealing the contents therein.

Both Grymes and Tori inhaled audibly as the gold and silver coins within the box's caught the light. Stunned, John sat down and then laughed out loud, demanding a drink. "A view like that can put a man into shock, so I feel the need of a tonic, the fine wine kind of tonic."

Cisco whistled. "Holy shit, it would seem I'm in the wrong profession. It's a pirate's life I need!" He immediately shut up when he saw the look of thunder on Jean's face. "Begging your pardon, Captain, but it's the truth. Just stating the obvious here."

"Privateer is the occupation, and you don't have it in you. You may also consider the use of such vulgar terms while my wife is present. She is a lady, and language such as calling a certain nasty substance holy, you know, it's not to be repeated."

Tori laughed. "Jean, I can assure you two things; first off is I agree shit is not holy, and second I am not offended by the use of the word."

Jean frowned and then turned his attention to the objects on his desk. "I have no need to hear such strange comments; there is work to be handled. So please, my darling wife, let us change the subject to why we are here." He pushed both chests toward John, and he spoke as he did so. "I think that should cover things for a while. It amounts to around twenty thousand apiece for you and Livingston." He shot another meaningful look, Cisco's way. "You and Cisco can leave in the morning for home. I will make arrangements for you both to travel up the river by boat. It will be safer. A long way around, I know, but I don't think you are in any big hurry to return, are you?"

John submerged his hand in one box and lifted some of the gold coins. "No, not at all. No hurry here. I had hoped to stop along the way back. Have to check in on a few clients, you understand?"

"Yes, I know exactly what you mean, and I can't agree more," said Cisco, reaching over to try and touch the coins in the other box, only to have the lid slammed shut by Jean.

"I bet you do," said Jean. "Don't you go getting any ideas."

"Who me?" questioned Cisco, while trying to look shocked and a bit hurt.

There it was again, Tori thought, the look that spelled trouble. Her counterpart had something planned. What it could be, one could only guess, and her mind wandered back to the small chests loaded with pirate treasure.

Grymes laughed. "Oh, don't you two worry. He's with me, you know, and I'll see to it that he keeps out of harm's way and out of my cash." The lawyer dropped the lid on his box, winking at Cisco as he did so. "I think we all could use a drink."

Jean wholeheartedly agreed. He seemed pleased with himself about something, and it had nothing to do with drinking or smoking.

The man was in a good mood, and nothing was about to spoil it. "I agree, John, and I think some fine brandy and a good cigar will meet the needs of all." He looked toward Tori and grinned. "Well, maybe meet the gentlemen's needs. My wife will have to settle for just a brandy, won't you my love?"

"I guess so. I have no delight in those," she pointed to the larger specimens of cigars. "Jean knows I prefer the thinner, lighter ones."

Cisco chuckled. "No cigarettes here, but hey, bet there is no brandy like this in our time and if there is, it has got to be damn expensive. Settle for one glass and join us?"

"How can a girl say no. Besides, I don't want to miss anything, and I have a strange feeling that you two," she looked at Jean, "are keeping something from me."

"Us, never. You keeping anything, Jean?"

"Just this glass of brandy." He handed Tori the drink and lightly kissed her on the cheek.

LATER that night in bed, as she was drifting off to sleep, Tori spoke to Jean. "I tell you, those two are up to something, and you put them up to it. I swear, are all the men in my life keeping something from me? I ask you… are they?"

"Seems that way," he teased. "If, however, you come closer here, I have something I would never keep from you."

"Honestly, Jean. I don't know if you're the horniest man I have ever known or if you're just trying to change the subject once again."

"A little bit of both, I think, my lady. You have nothing to worry your head about. Now come here."

JOHN Davis was pacing back and forth in his office while Cisco and Grymes sat watching him. "You mean to sit there and tell me that the two of you left Grand Terre just over a week ago? That you had yourselves a gambling spree all along the Mississippi until you lost how much?" John Davis's face was a cross between frustration and pure amusement, but the look he now shot Cisco's way expressed another emotion, anger.

The younger man sprang to his feet to say his piece. "Actually, it was the entire sum Jean paid him, all twenty thousand of his and twenty of Livingston's. You have to admit when you come to think about it, it's totally outrageous. Ah, but what a time we had. I'm telling you if I died right now, I would be happy." He sat back down and rubbed his forehead as if a headache was annoying him.

There was no doubt; both had been on the binge of a lifetime, and neither showed remorse. Davis was at a loss what to say, and it showed in his actions. He paced back and forth, looking from the attorney to his card-playing friend. Cisco he could understand, but John Grymes? Never! He had thought that man quite levelheaded. That was until now. Both of them looked guilty as hell, and he, for one, was glad they felt so. Then, seeing the younger of the pair begin to try and talk his way out of the deplorable situation, he reacted. "Oh, for God's sake, shut up, Cisco. If you don't, I might very well kill you, and believe me, right now; it would not take much to oblige."

Cisco shut his mouth and looked at his friend. At least Davis could find the story amusing; maybe once he knew the whole plan, he would.

The hotel owner ran his fingers through his hair and inhaled deeply. When he felt he was back in control of his emotions, he spoke. "Look, you two, while you were both having the time of your life, the rest of us have been trying to hold down the fort, so to speak. All hell is about to let loose around these parts. If that's not bad enough, I got to see Pierre last week, and I fear if we don't find a way to get him out of that place soon, we might as well kiss his ass goodbye."

"Just what do you mean by that?" asked a concerned Grymes, straightening up in his chair as he did so.

"I mean that the man is going to die," answered Davis. "If you can't get him out right now, at least find a way to get the chains off him. I'm telling you that we have to find a way to deal with this and other matters that are just as serious, maybe even more so. It has come to my attention that the Governor is not giving up on Jean, and he is gaining support in that quarter."

Grymes's face filled with annoyance. "I bet he is, and let me guess who is behind the drive to capture Jean. Sure bet, Edward Duval for one..." He spat out the name.

"As always, you are correct, but more than just Edward. There are others. I have not had any means to find out what it is they plan to do next. I have needed the two of you here, and now you sit and laugh at the wonderful time you had at Grand Terre and the trip home." He marched across the room before spinning around to face the two men again. He had no need for words. His situation, their situation, had become only too clear to everyone.

Grymes shook his head and stood up, looking at Davis and Cisco. "Gentlemen, I think we all know what we have done and not done. That is irrelevant now." He started to chuckle as he continued. "I must say that I, for one, will never forget the days past. I hope that one day soon, I will get to tell you the whole tale," he looked at the flustered Davis. "All in all," he paused to clear his throat, "there is work to be done, and the time to play is over. I will leave at once to see Livingston and see what else I can learn from a few trusted friends in Claiborne's camp. I'll come back this evening, at which time we can all put our heads together." He walked to Davis and reached out his hand.

"Until later then." Davis took his hand and firmly shook it.

"Glad to have you back regardless of your idiotic actions."

Cisco was relieved to see the two of them make amends. He knew it would take him a little longer to get Davis to forgive his involvement in the so-called grand escapade, but he had no fear that the man would come around in the end.

TWO weeks had passed, and Grymes had worked relentlessly on Pierre's case. Both he and Edward Livingston had built what they thought to be a strong case in their favor. It should have been clear-cut. The chains should have been removed, but they were not. The date was now August 10, 1814, and after much discussion, it had become evident that if they were to ever get Pierre out of jail, it would have to be done other than through the law.

All of them knew that it was perilous for Jean to even think about coming to town, and to add to their problems, they also realized that they could not run the risk of meeting with him themselves. The dire issues were quite plain, and worse still, not a single problem would be solved quickly. So it was that Grymes found himself revealing his long-kept secret.

GRYMES took a deep breath, and looking very serious as he spoke, he began. "I do have a solution to just how we may get all that we need. First, we have to get word safely to Jean and he to us, right? The idea of having him come into town is crazy. To damn risky, but we do need a meeting. Look, what I mean is this. What I'm about to reveal to you three must remain with you." Grymes looked at two men who sat with bated breath and then at Marie Laveau. She was another story; he had the strangest feeling that she already knew what he was about to say. He watched her face as he continued. "You all know that for some time, I have had my source within the Governor's compound, that I have always had my ear to the door, so to speak. It is more than just knowing someone, and it is that someone I will now reveal to you. She has agreed to this, so I am not breaking any confidence at all."

Marie's face was still not showing any emotion, but she did seem to nod her head ever so slightly. He continued. "I have been involved with a certain lady. She has been in my life and is my life. There is no easy way to put this, and you may be shocked, but please do not judge her too harshly. She loves me and is willing to aid us in our cause." He held up his hand toward Davis. "She does not know everything. To put it simply, I have told her only that we are trying to help America and need Jean for that. Look, the lady is married, and that is why I have kept our affair secret."

"Oh shit! It can't be!" Cisco began to understand. "Damn. That's who has kept you busy all these years. How many has it been, two?"

Davis was grinning. He didn't speak, just nodded his head to affirm his understanding of what Cisco was implying.

Grymes chuckled. "Now, wait for a second, both of you. I have not told you her name."

"There is no need to, is there?" laughed Marie. "It seems quite clear to us all that the lady in question is none other than William Claiborne's wife herself, is it not?"

The look on Grymes's face confirmed it. The lovely Cayetana was the woman he was involved with. It was true, and he beamed, as he could share this fact with his dear friends at last.

"My God, man. You are either very stupid or very brave," Cisco said, slapping him on the back. "You, sly old fox you, and right under the bastard's nose too. I thought I was good, but this takes the cake."

Grymes made a strange expression. "Takes the cake? A saying from your time, no doubt? Look, the fact is she is going to be our go-between.

I have arranged for her to visit an old friend South of town, far enough out to be safe for Jean. The family are also good friends of Jean's but will not be told of their guests' connection. I have to protect my love and my client. It will be up to them, or I should say, up to Cayetana to make contact and relay all. I know she is capable. After all, look at what we have accomplished all this time, under everyone's noses," he laughed.

Cisco joined him laughing. "Brilliant. It's so fucking brilliant. Are you sure I didn't think of this myself?" Cisco was excited, and it showed in the way he almost skipped across the room. "You have outdone yourself, and I can't wait to meet this lady and tell her a word or two myself."

"You shall have a long wait, my friend, on that I can assure you," giggled Marie.

Grymes chuckled and then straightened up and spoke. "By this time, three days from now, if all has gone as planned, we should have news on how to proceed. Jean will be informed as to what is going on with us and be updated with Claiborne's actions and his scheming."

They all raised their glasses and toasted the new couple. "To John and his lady," Cisco announced joyfully.

"Here, here. To the happy couple, and may they one day truly be together," added Davis.

No one heard Marie whisper in Grymes' ear, "They will."

Grymes nodded his head slightly to let the woman know he had heard her. He gave no other indication that anything was amiss, let alone that the voodoo girl had just confirmed what he desired the most in life. He turned and looked at the small gathering. "So, now all we have to do is wait until the meeting has taken place, and my Cayetana tells me what Jean has to say. I can only pray that time is on our side and that Jean is as brilliant as he claims."

Davis was quiet and looked as if something was upsetting him. He knew he had to speak but hated the idea of ruining any plans. "I have one question that we have not considered. The British are supposed to meet Jean. Historical fact. What happens if they arrive when Jean is gone?"

It was Grymes who answered. "They won't be missed. Jean's men know their every move, I can assure you. Before Jean leaves, he will have reports of their activities and whereabouts. I know he will not attempt such a trip should any British ship be in the area. It is one of the conditions, a caveat of sorts to the agreement for the meeting. As for now, please excuse me. I have only a matter of hours before the Governor's wife departs for a short visit with friends. Till next, we meet." With that, he was gone, and those left behind prayed silently that all would go as they planned.

TIME slipped by, and before the week was up, Cisco and Davis sat once again listening to Grymes. They had been called to his office, supposedly on hotel matters, but now they sat waiting to hear details of the event concerning Jean and Cayetana. Grymes held nothing back as he began to tell them the news.

"The meeting went as planned. My love performed beautifully, and no one was the wiser."

It was anxious Cisco who could not contain himself. "You mean to tell me it worked? It did, right, or you wouldn't be here? Oh, do give, I'm dying to hear." Cisco loved it; excitement was bubbling within him, and he wanted the details. "Come on, spill it."

Grymes paid him no attention; instead, he looked at Davis and continued. "She said that it was late afternoon when Jean arrived and shocked her hosts with his unexpected visit."

Cisco immediately jumped in with a question he was dying to have answered. "What happened? Did they try to get him to leave?"

"If you will remain silent, I will tell you. Now, where was I? Oh yes, Cayetana said she almost burst into laughter as she watched them quickly cover their guest's identity. Jean, thank God, was traveling in disguise, and Cayetana pretended not to recognize him.

They were left alone after dinner, and it was then she was able to tell him why she was there. Not just as the Governor's wife, you understand? My beautiful, brave woman was able to convince Jean that she was telling the truth and that we had arranged for the meeting. Please don't ask me how she did that. I'm still not clear on that detail myself. Anyway, the point here is we got our message to Jean, and he got his to us. They parted ways the next morning, much to the relief of their hostess, I'm sure."

Davis smiled slightly. "My congratulations to your lady. Indeed, she has pulled this off admirably, and her actions truly humble me.

344

The Governor's wife risked a lot."

Grymes nodded his head in agreement. "No one even suspected them, and to be sure, no one ever would, she devised a scheme, a cover story of sorts. Cayetana told a few of her close friends, in strictest confidence, that she is, after much thought, convinced that she met the Pirate, Jean Laffite. Oh my, how she tells them in great detail, what a fine gentleman he is and how handsome!" They were all laughing and more than pleased with themselves, however, the time had arrived to end the meeting and move on.

"Cisco, we have some business to attend to," continued Grymes. "I suggest that we all pay close attention from here on out. According to Jean's letter, and Davis agrees with it whole heartily, things are about to begin in earnest. We already know Claiborne has been receiving letters from the President, as well as writing them. They are letters pertaining to Jean and his situation and letters about the British, and so forth. We all agree that the time is very close at hand… no, change that, Gentlemen, it is upon us." He looked gravely toward each of them. "We must keep our wits about us. It is imperative that any communications between the British and Jean, between Claiborne, and whoever, are seen by those; all need to know what's going on. Be they enemies or allies; all communications must be intercepted and placed in the right hands. From here on out, gentlemen, we are at war! What each one of us does in the next few months will affect the outcome of not only Jean's pardon and Pierre's release but… our countries future history."

No one uttered a word. The three men sat staring into space, each deep in their own thoughts. It was no longer a game, for it was now a matter of grave consequences, of which there could be no mistakes. One slip-up on their part would be devastating, not only for each of them but for everyone involved.

❧ Eight ❧

September 1814 had been unusually warm and quiet. The summer storms had ended in the first few weeks of August, and with them, the humidity. Days felt more like spring, followed by cooler evenings and gentle sea breezes washing in off the tranquil gulf.

Ever since Jean's trip upriver and his meeting with Cayetana, he had stayed close to home. Any further news from the city came by way of Jean's elaborate network of men, which he had doubled, all up and down the bayous and coastline. Daily reports came in from all sources, most were trivial enough to be ignored, but some were significant enough to be questioned.

Jean and Tori were well aware that many British ships had been spotted days ago off Pensacola's coast and that rumors ran rampant among the populace that the British planned to invade. Day and night, the horizon was kept under close scrutiny until they received the news, they knew was inevitable.

Both had been awake for hours, enjoying the splendor of the magnificent dawn. The first warm rays of the sun had begun to chase away the crisp morning air, and the cooler weather kept them beneath the bed covers. Like new, young lovers, Jean and Tori had renewed their lovemaking with such a passion that it often left them drained and contentedly basking in the afterglow. This was the case when word finally came. Standing by the open bedroom door, Tori had listened to the message given to Jean and to his calm response.

"Dominique, I take it the news is such that you have found your way up here and now disturb my morning tryst?" Jean chuckled

347

and tried to sound serious but failed to do so. "Brave soul you are, I must say." This statement was followed by all-out laughter.

"Boss, this is no laughing matter. I am here to tell you that two British ships anchored offshore and raised the flag of truce. Many of the men were unsure as to how to handle the matter. And as you were indisposed, and I capable of tending to the matter..."

All signs of Laffite's playful banter vanished. "You mean you wished to see for yourself what they were about, and I take it you have?"

"Aye, that I did. Rowed out to the ship and had a quick chat with one of the Officers and learned what they wanted, that being a meeting with you. I told them you would be more than willing to talk, but here and not on board one of his Majesty's ships. I was very convincing always had a way of dealing with the enemy. Straight to the point I was and set a time, told them Beluce would meet them on the beach and escort them here. I reckon that should happen within the hour."

"Well done. I would never have thought to allow you to go. It worked to our advantage it seems. You, meeting the British, and not myself, that is. It was smart that I did not go out to their ship, or they maybe would never have agreed to meet me here. They maybe would have found a reason to keep me hostage... such is their way. Next time though, don't go off on your own; remember, I am the Boss, and you need to clear all actions from now on with me and only me. So much rests on what and how we make our next move."

"Awe, Boss, I agree; it needs to be so."

"I suggest that you return to the beach and escort them yourself and see to it that Beluche keeps the men under control. Let us see what we can do to help history and America."

"Aye, Boss, I will be on my way then. You had best hurry; it would be nice to have them meet you in a dressed condition, and not as you are, naked as the day you were born." He turned and was chuckling as he hurried off downstairs. He called out playfully as he descended the stairs. "Sorry for the interruption, Tori, but duty calls. His, not yours." He was enjoying himself and continued to chuckle as he left the house.

Laffite stood there for a second, thinking about what Dominique had told him. The British had two ships, just like Davis had said they would. They were going to come ashore to meet with him. It was happening as was written; this had to be the big meeting they all had been waiting for. The game was afoot, and his role was about to take center stage.

Before he returned bedside with the news, Tori was already preparing herself for the meeting with the British. It hadn't taken her long at all to realize that the historical event between her love and the British was indeed about to happen.

"I see my lady has been listening at the door again. A nasty habit that is my dear." His face was anything but worried, unlike hers.

How he could simply stand there and joke at a time like this was beyond her. "Jean, this is it, I know it, and you have to take today seriously. Not act like it means nothing?"

He looked at her with a puzzled expression. "And just what are you doing, may I dare ask?"

"I have had a change of mind. I think it's best if I attend this meeting with you, considering your flippant response so far." She saw his eyes darken and his lips tighten, forming that stubborn glare he always had when things were not going to plan.

"Don't look at me like I am nuts. I need to dress, and as your wife, I should be..." she looked at him and saw his continued dark expression, "now, before you say anything, hear me out. I know we thought that I should stay out of the way, but Jean, can't you see I'm needed? Besides, if you plan to entertain these so-called officers of His Majesty's Service, men who are expecting to meet with nothing more than a heathen pirate, well, wouldn't it be to our advantage to upset the apple cart? Think about it for a second. We know you entertain them lavishly and shock them by how refined a gentleman you are, but what if you add a hostess. A hostess, which is far more than merely a hostess. One that is your wife!"

349

"No!" he snapped sharply, silencing her speech and halting her actions. "I know that you mean well and that your idea has some merit." The sharp edge to his tone had softened as he took her in his arms, continuing with his explanation. "We discussed this meeting at length, did we not? All of us went over what little you know about what is to occur. The point that this meeting is about to take place only strengthens your case and shows me that we have to play it out, as close to how you and the others remember it was written. Look, my love." He lifted her chin and gazed directly into her eyes. "Was there any reference to a beautiful lady at this meeting, let alone my wife?" He continued staring at her as he tilted his head slightly. "You have been most adamant that we do nothing to change history. If you attend, you will not only be changing it; you will be making it. Do you understand?"

"I suppose so. I still think that..."

"Tori, it is true; we can't afford to change history, to add or subtract in any one place. It is like you have so often explained... what we do; it could drastically change the outcome. If you join me today, it will do just so. If I allow that to happen, everything could change. Time and history could sweep you from my arms." He held her close and could feel the slight shiver of her body as his implications hit home.

Tori buried her face into his shoulder and spoke softly. "But, Jean, how do we know for sure I was not with you? Just because history did not mention me, or should I say, just because we could not recollect me being there..."

He squeezed her arms tightly in his grip as he pushed her away from him. Jean had intended it to make a point, but his grip had caused her to wince, something he never desired. Laffite released some of the pressure but not all. Tori had to be made to understand, and time was running out. His viewpoint had to be made, and his love had to understand and agree. "I'm not going to change my mind on this, and deep down, you know it's right. In everything I have ever done in life, I have always found it best to go with my first instinct, and my lady, my instincts in this matter are quite clear." He finally released his grip and walked over to his wardrobe. "I have very little time to dress for my guests. Will you assist me or not?"

Tori was beaten, and she knew it.

To try and sway him once his mind was made up was like trying to change the current in the sea. Nevertheless, his reasons had held some merit, and she knew that they had all agreed on how things should play out.

"Tori, my love," he said softly as he pulled on one of his best shirts. "I love you more than life itself, but you have to trust me in this. I will need a clear head to play the game that is about to begin, and having you there would only distract me." A grin filled his face. "You are always a distraction to me..."

"Oh, stop it. Your point is well taken, and I give you my word that I will stay hidden if you give me yours." She placed her hands on her hips. This was a clear indication to all who knew her that she was determined to have her say and her way. "You are to come up here immediately. I mean the moment they leave. You give me your word!"

"You have it and more. Should I feel at any time that I need your advice or counsel, I will seek it." He had finished dressing and stood before her. "Well, Madame, do I look like the rogue you think I am, or do I present the image I require, one of the Gentleman Pirate?" He was laughing and obviously did not need a verbal answer, for it was written clearly on her face.

The sound of approaching voices below halted any further conversation. Jean raised his eyebrow in acknowledgment of his guest's arrival and quickly drew Tori into his arms for one last kiss. His lips pressed firmly against hers, which were trembling. He needed to assure her, so Jean's arms wrapped briefly around her shoulders—and then he was gone.

The privateer was on his way to keep history, or make it, or both. It was so confusing, like Cisco was always saying. Tori sat down on the bed, resigned to the fact that she was going to have to try and entertain herself or go crazy for the next few hours, wondering what was happening downstairs. "So, we now have one date confirmed. September 3 in the year 1814 is the day that Laffite met the British. God help us all but most of all, help my husband."

JEAN received his four guests in his study, walking toward them from behind his desk as they were shown in.

Clearly, he had them at a disadvantage.

Not one of them could contain the surprise of their surroundings or of the image of their host. He chuckled inwardly but reviled nothing to the men as he surmised what they must have expected, compared to what they now encountered.

"Gentlemen. I am Monsieur Jean Laffite at your service." His face was calm, his voice friendly, but his dark eyes, black as onyx, said something very different that only the most discerning individuals could have understood.

The first two British officers looked directly at him, while two who accompanied them stood toward the back of the room. They were looking at their surroundings with stunned expressions. No doubt they all saw standing before them a man who was to be reckoned with, and judging by the surroundings, they'd say he was no uneducated buccaneer like they had been led to believe.

The officer in command stepped forward, extending his hand. "Captain Lockyer, of his Majesty's Navy. And may I present to you, Captain McWilliams of the Army." This man quickly stepped forward and shook Jean's hand, curtly nodding his head.

Jean greeted the two warmly. "My pleasure." His grip was firm, and his gaze was direct. At least he now knew who the two senior officers were in this game he played. The two other lieutenants were introduced and greeted just as warmly. But to Jean, they no longer held any importance. These men would be tolerated yet of no consequence to what was obviously about to take place.

Jean offered each a chair and returned behind his desk, seating himself comfortably before looking toward Captain Lockyer. The officer was carrying a pouch that obviously contained the letters the man had been instructed to deliver, along with the British offer. How would they feel, he wondered, if they realized that Jean was well aware of the reason behind their visit? Or was he about to learn something other than what his time traveling friends had knowledge about. He was so deep in these musings that it was the sound of Lockyer clearing his throat that brought his full attention back to the meeting at hand.

"As I was saying, Mr. Laffite, we are here to deliver to you an offer, one that I am certain you will find to your advantage, Sir." He patted the pouch on his lap and then placed it on top of Jean's desk.

Jean found that he was in no hurry to dispense with the business of discussing the letters or the British terms about to be offered to him. After all, he knew what he intended to do about both. Instead, he wanted to learn as much as possible about what was happening with the English fleet.

For Laffite and for all those involved, such as Davis, Grymes, and Tori, it seemed prudent for him to glean any other information his guests might unwittingly pass on. No doubt, he could, over drinks and a meal, coerce his present unsuspecting company into divulging further information. Details that would be useful to know.

"Gentlemen, I do not know what the customs are, where you are from," he lied, "but here on Grand Terre, it is the custom to dine first and do business second. Therefore, you would honor me if you joined me in my midday meal. Early as it is, I think a good meal and drink will be most welcome. Let me show you some true Southern hospitality." He carefully watched the reactions of the two senior officers. It was evident that they were not opposed to the idea, nor were they tempted. Duty, it seemed, was to be their first priority. What they needed at this point was a slight push in the right direction. "I will not take no for an answer," Jean said, laughing lightheartedly. Then with a far more threatening glare, he added, "to do so would truly offend me."

"On no uncertain terms do my comrades or I have any intention of causing such offense. Sir, we gladly accept your invitation to dine. I am sure many an alliance has been achieved over just such occasions and a bottle or two." The British Captain smiled, then added a slight chuckle and was joined by his fellow officers.

"Very well put." Jean's supposedly good humor had replaced his glare.

To look at the pirate, one would have thought him to be thoroughly enjoying the conversation and company. At least his guests thought so. Not one of them had any inclinations otherwise. Laffite opened the office door and called out his instructions. "Carlotta, please see to it that my initial plans are canceled. We have more important guests to entertain." After this, he turned back to face the British. "The best part about being me is that I can do as I please. My initial guests for lunch can wait. They will miss a good meal, but you have piqued my interest. Let us proceed, shall we?"

Jean led them to the dining room, which had been set and ready for days. An oversite, which could have raised a red flag. It was his quick wit and cunning mind that avoided what would have been hard to explain away. In all her planning to impress, his love had not thought how Jean could explain the already waiting setup. It would have looked like he was expecting them all along, which was not what Laffite wanted them to think. Lucky for him, he had devised his ruse, and none seemed the wiser.

Tori had added the elegant touches to the room and table, herself, wanting to achieve the desired effect of opulence without being ostentatious. Had she been there to see the British reactions, she would have known that she had succeeded. To say they were stunned would have put it mildly, Jean would later tell her.

Every detail from the table settings to the food itself had been thought out carefully. The wines and brandies to be served were only the finest. Over the next three hours, the service and meal would have rivaled the best homes and restaurants in the world. Jean proved in conversation to be a gentleman of high standing and one that was world-traveled and educated. It became evident to the Captains and their Lieutenants that they had significantly been misled in the reports about the leader of this stronghold. They had found themselves a charming host instead of the blood-thirsty pirate they had expected. Talk varied from the discussion of the artwork on the walls to the food and wine at the table. For at least half an hour, Jean had guided the conversation, learning about each of the men and their service to the crown. The men were proud of their service and were only too willing to expand on their personal careers and lives. When the politics of the day had been reached, Jean wisely guided the men from the dining room to the sitting room.

No matter which room they entered, they were greeted with still further signs that they were dealing with a man, nothing short of an aristocrat. The British no longer talked at him or down to him. Instead, they found themselves addressing him as they would a superior or a man of a well-to-do family with connections. In short, Jean had earned their respect and was held in the highest esteem.

THE hours slowly ticked by for Tori upstairs. She had given up trying to stay busy by sorting her closet or tidying their room. It was a useless task and unnecessary. In the end, she had decided to dress and sit and wait for Jean's return.

Laffite's wife sat in a chair on the verandah and waited while sipping a glass of wine. The afternoon was peaceful enough, and the day's end would soon be at hand. Her favorite part of the day, sunset, was only hours away at most. She found herself daydreaming about what was going on downstairs when one of the many songbirds sitting in the large tree by the house took off for what seemed at first no apparent reason. Then she heard the angry voices and the screams of protest.

A robust English accent was demanding to be released when still another louder voice, with a Creole accent, was calling for the spy to be hung or turned over to the Americans.

Not understanding what was happening, Tori jumped to her feet. What had gone wrong? She did not know but was damn well going to find out. Turning to head downstairs, she bumped right into Jean and his grinning face. Without uttering a sound, he took her in his arms and kissed her long and hard.

Her mind was swirling with questions, and her impatience was multiplying. Then just as suddenly as he had taken her into his arms, Jean released her from his grasp. "I would like to join you in a glass of wine, that is, if any is left." He was looking around the room for the bottle.

"Wine, you said? Jean, have you gone mad? From what I just heard going on out there, you had better explain to me fast what went wrong."

"Nothing went wrong. It all happened just as you said it would. I have in my possession four letters, all asking me to join the British against the Americans. For the last hour and a half, I have been badgered, bribed, and in the end, threatened. It was all as you said and more. But one thing we did not count on was the need to buy time with these bastards and to get them to leave without suspecting they had been; how do you put it… ah yes, snookered?" He laughed at the word. "I must say, I rather like the sound of that one. Well, anyway, my lady, I decided that if I were to excuse myself for a short time and arrange for my men to drag them off and lock them up, that would get them out of my house, don't you see?"

"No, I don't see. How in the hell is that going to make them think you are considering their offer, may I ask?"

"You may," he smirked. "God, you're beautiful when you're angry."

"Just shut up," she stomped her foot, "and explain to me, or so help me, God, I will show you just what angry looks like!"

"In that case, I guess I have no choice. It will be like this. In about half an hour, long enough to scare the hell out of those four, I shall arrive and demand they be turned free. You see, they came expecting to find pirates and did not. Now, however, I believe they have! I think they needed to see I was Boss here. But they also need to think that I have to convince my men to join me on the side of the British. If I had just agreed, well, they are not stupid. Tricky bastards if you ask me. Anyway, I will explain to them; I need two weeks to round up all my men, as my territory is vast." He twisted his mustache and grinned while doing so. Then, I will send word back to them. They will think they got out of here with their lives by the grace of God, luck, and my help. I tell you now, not one of them will suspect anything other than that, which I intended. We will have our time to get the letters to Claiborne, and he, in turn, will have time to do whatever is necessary to protect New Orleans."

"You amaze me; you know that? You came up with all that just off the top of your head?" she said, throwing her arms around his neck. "Have I told you lately how much I love you?"

"Not lately, no. You may, however, be ready to show me when I return from saving four trembling British officers," he said, slapping her lightly on her rear end before finishing off her glass of wine in one gulp. "Oh, and when I return, remind me to tell you how I avoided a disaster we had not thought of. The dining room already set up ahead of the surprise British visit." He watched as her expression went from shock to a look of curiosity. Then, before she had time to begin with her questions, he left, knowing that she'd be waiting for his return and all the details he could supply.

TORI decided it was best to wait for Jean's return in the sitting room rather than upstairs. She wanted to read the letters with him for herself and discuss their next move. Her wait was not long, and judging by the look on his face, all had gone as planned.

"I take it that your little charade has worked?"

"That is an understatement. I never saw four more grateful men row out in their gig, nor so fast, I might add. I tell you, the size of the wake they left behind them could have rocked my own ship."

"Oh, Jean, stop," she laughed. "You're making my sides split."

"Now, why in the Lord's name would I wish to do that? Some of your sayings are beyond me, and they still keep coming after all these years." He looked so perplexed that it sent another wave of laughter over her. Jean, not grasping what she found so damned funny, turned and left for his study. 'Women! He would never understand them,' he thought.

Tori pulled herself together, and taking two glasses of wine, she followed Jean to explain what had her laughing so much. When she entered the study, she found him reading one of the British letters while the others lay open on top of his desk. Picking one up, she asked, "May I?"

Without even looking up, Jean nodded his head. Tori sat down and looked over the first document. It was nothing short of an appeal to the Louisianans to join the English against the Americans. She had difficulty understanding and following the rambling letter but could see how it would not help Claiborne listen to Jean. It had been handwritten by Edward Nicholls and signed on August 29th. Nicholls also wrote the second letter; it was dated August 31st. This document called on Jean, and his brave men, to enter into the service of Great Britain. It also asked that they stop all hostilities against any allies of Great Britain. That meant the Spanish would be off-limits. Tori looked at Jean when she realized this, but he was busy reading the following letter, and so she went back to reading hers. Jean was offered the rank of Captain and the promise of lands, equal to his status once his service was no longer required. This was followed, by the notice, that all his ships and vessels would be placed under the orders of the commanding officer of Pensacola headquarters. It explained how Captain McWilliams would answer any and all questions Jean might have and that Captain Lockyer, of the Sophia, would also be of any assistance he could to aid Laffite's transition from civilian to a member of the Royal Navy.

Tori looked at Jean, who was still going over one of the letters with a complete lack of emotions that astounded her. To think he had read these letters in front of the British and maintained his composure only gave her a more profound admiration for him. Stop hostilities against Spain, his sworn enemy? That must have made him want to laugh out loud. Or maybe it was thinking of all the British ships that Jean and his men had taken over the past few years and how upset the British had to be on that front. It amazed her even more so that now they believed just because they asked, he would stop! She took a sip of her wine and picked up the third letter. It was written by the honorable William Henry Percy, Captain of his Majesty's ship Hermes. He was, by the looks of things, the senior officer in the Gulf. The letter was to Lockyer and, in short, was an order for him to go to Grand Terre in an effort to persuade a one, Jean Laffite, to join their ranks.

Jean had finished reading the fourth letter and handed it to Tori, who took it without uttering a word. This letter had been written on September 1st by Captain Percy and was the one that upset her the most. Percy made it very clear that Jean's ships, Barataria and Grand Terre, should be destroyed if Jean and his men decided not to join forces with the British. The letter explained that should they choose to say yes, the already mentioned land and rank, payments, and full pardons awaited him and his men. Briefly, she looked into Jean's eyes and saw he was watching her closely. The problem became apparent to Tori that Jean was caught between a rock and a hard place. She looked back at the letter in her hands and folded it up slowly. If they could not get Claiborne to listen and believe that the threats were real, that Jean's offer to help was genuine, then they would be left alone to face the British, or worse yet, join them. Tori looked again at Jean's face; his eyes so dark that she had no need to ask how he felt. It was the question of what he was thinking or planning to do next that plagued her, but she remained silent.

"You know, my lady, the fools, believe that my men would follow me if I choose to join them. Now, that is something which they are gravely mistaken about. More than half my men hate the British, and no matter what they are promised, they would take great delight in fighting them. The problem is that I am not sure as to just how many British they would be taking on. I know, you, John, and Cisco say a couple of thousand, but nothing other than a slight hint that a sizable force is on its way could I get out of any of them or these letters. I sat and politely drank and ate and fished for information and learned not much more than you yourself now know."

"You have done everything you could and more." Tori reached across the desk and stroked the back of Jean's hand.

"I have bought us time for now, and I am sure Captain McWilliams left here certain I would consider joining them. Time... time is something I need more of and don't have." He sat back in his chair, rubbing his chin. "We have to move on this," he said, waving one of the letters. "I need to write my own letters and, along with these four, have them hand-delivered to the right people. I'll start with one to Jean Blanque, my trusted friend, who also happens to sit on the State's Legislature. The other, of course, will be to William Claiborne himself, and the last will be to our new friends." He chuckled as he spoke. "The British; I have to make sure I can delay them, as long as possible. These documents will leave tonight... and then my love, we wait. Wait and pray that history repeats itself and our Governor listens."

EDWARD sat quietly, watching and listening to the ongoing discussion. It had become only too evident to him, in the past half-hour, that he and Simone had been right all along. Laffite had paid off certain members of the State's Legislature, and Edward felt confident that he now knew the identity of at least one.

Jean had received the correspondence early that morning and immediately taken it to the Governor's office. In the pouch had been four letters, supposedly from the British, along with two from Laffite himself. Edward had no doubt that the documents that

William now held in his hand were genuine and that Laffite was sincere in his offer to aid in defense of the city. This, however, was not going to happen if he had anything to do with it, and he was determined that he would have a great deal to do with it.

The committee that sat around William's office was one that Edward knew he could manipulate. It consisted of military advisers from both the Navy, Army, and a few of the States Legislators, along with Girod, the mayor. To sway the Governor against Laffite proposed no significant problem. Doing it in a manner that did not arouse suspicion was quite another.

"Gentlemen," the Governor said, silencing the room. "As you all have now had a chance to read the letters and look them over carefully, I have a couple of questions before I make any decisions. First and foremost, are these letters before us genuine, and if they are, is it proper that the head of this here fine state corresponds with Laffite or any of his associates?" He shot Jean Blanque a dark look as he asked this question. "Your input and opinion would, at this time, be gratefully received."

The room exploded with each man trying to make his thoughts on the matter heard. To Edward, who remained silent, it seemed that only two of the committee members were siding with Laffite: the mayor, who in Edward's opinion was a fool and sorely afraid of the so-called invasion, and the Major General Jacques Villere. Monsieur Villere was adamant in his belief that the letters and Laffite were exactly what they seemed to be and that, yes, the Governor should, at this time, consider corresponding with Laffite. He had William listening to his advice while the other fools sat quietly.

Duval could not afford to remain silent any longer. "William, Governor. If I may be so bold as to suggest a solution to this dilemma we have here," Edward drew everyone's attention by calmly walking to the center of the room. "You have here a fine and upstanding committee. Representatives of the highest and most moral standing." He smiled toward each, including, I see,

Monsieur Jean Blanque, it is good to have you.

Blanque shifted uneasily in his chair. "No one here wants anything but the very best for our fine city and its citizens, just as you yourself do. It would seem that a majority vote could not be ignored or wrong in its advice. I, therefore, propose that a vote on the matter would put to rest any doubts, one way or the other."

Villere was immediate in his response to Edward. He could see only too clearly the direction this meeting was taking. "It is my belief, Governor, as I stated before, that the letters are genuine and that Laffite and his men are very much needed. Should the British choose to invade us at this time, we have little or no defenses available."

"That Monsieur is just my point," Edward spoke softly but firmly. "We have no real proof that the British do intend to invade now, do we? All that we have is the word of a mere pirate and a few letters, all of which could have been drawn up by the man himself. We even have a reason why he would concoct just such a ruse, do we not? His beloved brother sits in chains as we speak, awaiting trial for crimes that could cost him his life. It is my opinion that this is his true intention behind this move. He intends to free his brother by any means necessary. Using the threat of the British and gaining friendship with you, Governor, that would help him, would it not?"

Claiborne nodded in agreement. "So true, Edward, but surely we have to consider the fact that the man is telling us the truth. We have had warnings about the British, and we are at war, or has that small fact slipped your mind?" William looked genuinely concerned, and his emotions had sounded in his question.

Edward remained calm, but his voice betrayed the anger he held carefully in check. "I have not let anything slip my mind, Monsieur. But, if you would hear me out, I shall offer another thought on the matter. If these so-called letters are actual correspondence, then they can only show us that Laffite is a spy. I suggest to you, Governor, that the man is playing you for a fool while he aids our enemies. His stronghold, if in the wrong hands, would be of great military use. He is strategically placed and well situated. As you yourself know, his camp is all but impenetrable. So no, I say Laffite is not to be trusted, and furthermore, I think that he and his men need to be neutralized."

Villere was outvoted in a matter of seconds as the seed of doubt grew against Laffite rapidly. In everyone's mind, it was not inconceivable that the pirate was capable of double-dealing and in league with the enemy.

Patterson and Ross, both of whom were anxious to attack Laffite's stronghold at Barataria, insisted the Army was more than ready to do so at once. Was the Navy behind them, they questioned?

Outvoted, Villere had no choice but to nod his head in agreement. Jean Blanque and the mayor could only look at each other in despair, while Edward smiled to himself. Things were finally going his way, and he was sure they would continue to do so.

No one noticed the door to the Governor's office slowly close. Nor was it unusual for anyone on the outside to see Cayetana depart the building. Had they followed her, however, they would have been quite surprised at her destination.

UNDER the pretense of a business matter to do with her husband, Cayetana was shown into Grymes's office. Once alone, she was able to divulge all she knew.

"You are sure of this? There can be no mistake?" Grymes's face was filled with concern about what she had just told him. If true, it meant that he and Livingston had just run out of time.

"John, my dear, I would never have risked coming here like this if I was not certain of what I had overheard. It is just so lucky that I decided to visit my dear husband and that the door to his office had been left ajar, is it not?"

"That, my dear, is an understatement. What you have just told me is going to change many people's lives. There is something that I now have to set in motion. You, my love, must leave here right now before someone questions the validity of your visit. I suggest that in case any questions do arise, just let us say your meeting here today was for a friend of yours. After all, you would never break a friend's confidence, and I am obliged to remain quiet." He smiled into her face and saw only loving eyes looking back at him.

Grymes could see how she trusted him and cared for him, and it tore at his heart. He continued to speak in a loving tone, filled with concern. "You would not exactly be lying in the matter. Therefore, I feel it the best explanation. I would never ask you to lie for me or do anything that would be detrimental to yourself."

"My darling, you should not ever worry about such things. What I choose or not will be up to me, and because of my deep and abiding love for you," she said, touching his cheek softly with her hand. She stroked the side of his face, "I will always hold you and your happiness close to my heart. Please take care in whatever it is you are about to do and know that I will continue to aid you however I can." She stood up on tiptoe, placed a kiss on his fore-head, and then lowered herself down gently and kissed him on his lips. "I had best depart while I have my wits about me. I declare you do such things to my mind and soul as to drive me wild in my thoughts."

"Cayetana, my love," Grymes said, kissing her quickly on her mouth before pushing her away, so he could look into her eyes, "what you do to me is beyond words."

"Not beyond physical, though," she laughed, her eyes dropping down to his erection.

"Why Madame, I declare I have no control where my body and you are concerned. Now before we completely lose our heads, you must depart." He walked behind his desk and sat down. "I love you and always will." His eyes spoke of this love as he called his assistant in the outer office to come and escort Mrs. Claiborne out. Then he set to work on the next order of the day, one he had hoped to avoid and now found impossible not to.

CISCO had been with John Davis when the message arrived that Mr. Grymes required an urgent meeting. Within an hour of Cayetana's visit, the two men had placed Jean's wishes regarding his brother into action at long last. It was a plan that had been hatched months ago and set into motion on an evening long ago at Grand Terre.

"Cisco, are you listening to me? We have to get this payoff into the right hands and from there, used as planned," Grymes ordered.

Cisco looked worried as he reached for one of the pouches. He saw Davis was frowning, but he made no comment his way. "Are we damn sure that this gold will be enough to sway all those involved to do what we want? I mean, they could always turn on us, on me. I am the delivery boy, after all."

"I assure you we already have them in our pockets and have done so for a while. Hell, even I don't know who they all are. I do know I have been talking to a one, Mr. John Holland. He is the guard that watches Pierre's cell. He is an honorable man with high ethics, or so says Claiborne himself. Let us hope the guard will aid us in our actions."

"Well, he better be what you say because he does not get any of this to sway him, that much I do know. Just seems such a shame to have to turn this all over to the other greedy sons of bitches; when you and I could have had so much fun with it all."

"Ah, but we did. Don't you remember all the gambling on the trip home?" he laughed. "Such a tale we told, and I for one shall tell it till my dying day. To have gambled away, forty thousand dollars, on such a spree. Ah... that my man, is what dreams are made of." Grymes had a far-away look in his eyes. He seemed to be relishing the tale that he had told to so many.

Cisco found himself looking at his friend and realized that Grymes had told the fabricated story so often that a part of him had actually come to believe his own lie.

Jean's idea and plan was brilliant and totally untraceable. The people involved were well covered and would never be found out. So, all that was left for Cisco to do now was meet with the two politicians and then wait.

He took the leather pouches in hand. There were three pouches in all. Two were to go to Jacques Villere and the other to Blanque. Then it would be their task to make the connections within the confines of the jail and deliver the hefty bribes.

The pouches were placed out of sight in pockets that were on the inside of the coat Marie had made him, saying it would be far better to conceal the gold in such a manner. "Just in case you should be stopped or even robbed," she had laughed. Cisco had to admit it was a great way to transport the wealth of gold and silver coins discreetly. His Marie always surprised him, and this was one such time. He would be sure to tell her all the sewing and concealing of pockets was top-notch. "I shall leave now before I get tempted," he said, tossing one last pouch in the air before dropping it into the secret pocket. "I tell you, it's not easy giving this to those bastards, and the only reason I'm doing it is for Jean. You will have the carriage waiting for us, as planned?"

Grymes smiled. "That I will. If all goes as it should, we will meet two hours after midnight." The attorney reached out his hand and took Cisco's, shaking it firmly. "Good luck and be careful. Remember, two of those are for Villere and the other…"

"I know who gets what. You must be sure to have our getaway waiting for us, and I will do the rest. Once the money has crossed hands and the doors opened, I will escort Pierre to you, safely under the cloak of darkness. God, this is right out of a Bond movie, I tell you."

Grymes looked at Davis, who had remained silent during this exchange. "I have no earthly idea what he is babbling about."

"I do, and it's just his fantasy and one that might serve him well. If he acts like Bond, we will succeed. History is about to be made, safely securing the events that must unfold as they should."

The attorney looked back at the younger Spanish gentleman. "I do see you are confident in achieving our goal. May God be with you John, and Cisco, don't get caught, or all this would have been for nothing. The plan is only now going into action because it has taken time to win over those inside, don't lose sight of that. We are out of time and can't afford to begin again. Be careful, that's all."

"You be careful. You have to be seen in public for the next two hours. Make sure Davis is too. Just cover all our bases."

Grymes held out his hand, "I will be seen, don't worry. Now go. Time is running short."

THE evening was damp and chilly as Cisco walked toward the church. The man-made his way cautiously and tried his best to act normally. He found himself watching his surroundings closely as he walked to the rendezvous place. Most people did not even look his way and those that did moved on without so much as a greeting. The walk from Davis's hotel to the area behind the church was not far, and he had no idea how long he would have to wait, but wait, he would. "Just hope you two are prompt, 'cause I doubt even I can stand around for long without drawing attention," he mumbled to himself, pulling his coat collar up. "September 5th, another date we will have knowledge of if we pull this off. By tomorrow, Pierre should be safe, and we will be one step closer to victory. So, all I have to do now is wait and pray we pull this off."

The area behind the church was where his two contacts had designated a meeting point. It was, after all, very close to where they held Pierre. The small street between the church and the jail was all but empty at this time of night. Those who had been there only a few hours before to sell their goods, their pirate booty, were long gone. Villere had let the word spread that the army was going to make a raid in hopes of catching some of Laffite's men. That had caused quite a bit of hasty action, as many departed quickly, believing the rumor.

THE hour was getting late, and Cisco wondered how long he should hang around before calling it a bust? He scanned the area, and still, he did not see either one of his contacts. Then, just as he was about to give up and return to Davis's hotel, he saw a familiar figure walking his way.

Jacques Villere had waited until Edward Duval and William Claiborne had left the building before making his way to the rendezvous point. He had seen how the dandy looked at him, summing him up. Villere had spotted Cisco long before he had looked his way, and it amazed him that the man was not paying better attention to his surroundings. The young fop, who Laffite trusted, did not even attempt to meet him halfway when he did spot him. He was trying his best it seemed to be inconspicuous, and then without warning, he called out. "Jacques, my friend, how are you? It has been a while." The young dandy approached him and offered his hand in greeting, only to quickly change his mind and curtly nodded his head instead.

Jacques Villere answered with a slight smile. "It has been a while."

"It has indeed. What brings you out at this time may I enquire?"

"Just needed some air before heading home or maybe to Davis's for a chance at lady luck. And you?"

"Taking some air, myself," Cisco lied.

The pair looked around, and seeing no one was paying any attention; they lowered their voices. "I trust you have what I came for?" The older statesman had a puzzled look about him, almost as if he could not imagine why Grymes or Laffite had given him this delicate task.

"I do indeed. Two pouches that I might add are none too light in weight." Cisco looked around once more as he reached into his pockets and pulled out the two pouches. "I suggest you conceal these fast."

"I have myself two deep pockets, such as yours, had this transaction in mind when I chose to put this on." He nodded his head. "Nice to see we think alike." He took the pouches and placed them into his coat pockets. "I see what you mean, a good sum and heavy like you said. Still, I won't be burdened long. Now, if you will be so kind as to excuse me, I seem to have forgotten some papers back inside. Ah, just in time, I see your next visitor is approaching; good day, Sir."

"Good day then, and may lady luck grace you too," Cisco replied to the man's back as he walked away.

Villere did not respond to him; he just turned and walked away with a far quicker pace than the one he had used when walking toward Laffite's friend. No sooner had he departed than Cisco felt a firm slap on his back. "What are you doing here, Cisco, my friend." Blanque was standing just behind him and smiling. Cisco faced him and nervously replied to the man's friendly greeting. "You are lucky; I mean, Villere indicated to me you were here, or I think I may have… never mind, you are here. I have a small heavy pouch, and you need to keep it out of sight. Here, take it and for God's sake, make this work because this waiting is driving me… well, I don't like it." He handed Blanque the pouch and watched as the man placed it out of sight in the pocket of his coat.

"You have done well; now it's up to us. If you will excuse me, I have someone I need to meet before changing the guards. May I suggest you wait in one of the taverns until you are needed."

Cisco exhaled and spoke quickly. "You can suggest all you want, but I have my instructions, and like you, I intend to follow them."

"Then good luck my friend and until we meet again, which I hope will be under easier circumstances. Good day." Blanque turned and walked away, making sure not to look back in case they had been seen. It was then that Cisco decided that he would wait in the safety of the blacksmith shop for the next few hours.

PIERRE was weak but hopeful that, at long last, he was going to be free. One of the many guards he had good dealings with, by the name of Holland, had told him earlier that he should be ready to exercise when his escort came. Anyone overhearing this exchange would not have thought twice about it, as Pierre was now allowed to walk outside his cell more than once a day. The guards had been instructed to do this, but his excursions were never at the same time. His leg irons had to be placed back on once he returned from his walk, and that was the worst, and he swore never again to find himself in chains.

The hour was late, and each one had crawled by it seemed. The darkness was the worst for Pierre. He would lay there and wonder about so much and worry about his Marie and the children. At least during the day, he could occupy his mind with other thoughts.

This night, however, was different as he waited and wondered which guard it would be that Jean had found to bribe? It was evident that he had succeeded because no guard had ever taken the time to speak to him, let alone tell him to be ready for anything. It could be the guard who had spoken was the one, but Pierre knew better than blindly trusting anyone, especially a man who could be bribed.

While Laffite's brother was musing about this, he heard the footsteps approaching and then the sound of a key turning in the door of his cell. He stood to face the man and his dimly lit lantern, knowing his time in jail was over at last. The irons, which usually held him chained, had been removed hours ago, so there was no worry about any delay. Holland, who had said be ready, had dropped the key to the leg irons inside his cell. This action had spoken volumes to Pierre, so no other words had been necessary.

Pierre was cold, weak, and hungry, but he was also free at last. He took the heavy coat offered to him and wrapped it around his shoulders as he made his way forward, following John Holland closely. He assumed that he had been chosen because of his commitment to the Laffite's. Only later would he learn that the man was just a guard who believed in justice. He had not taken any bribe but instead had taken it upon himself to aid in Laffite's escape. He walked him to another guard and left him in this man's care with no questions asked. This was the guard who had taken a large amount of gold right before he played his role in the escape plan. He also learned that the man sailed out on the early morning tide, wealthy and happy to be free of his military life.

CISCO had left the blacksmith's and was now waiting on the steps of the church. It was late, and no one was about. Even the moon had disappeared from sight, and the river beyond was just a dark and boat-free silent waterway. Maybe it was good that the rain had decided to show up when it did. That had to be a huge reason why people were hunkered down in their warm and dry homes.

The impatient man pulled his collar up and pressed his back up against the church wall. At least standing where he was, it kept the brief showers off him for the most part and also helped conceal his whereabouts. Looking up at the sky, he could see that the inclement weather was dissipating, giving him hope. The carriage ride North would not be so challenging if the roads remained somewhat dry. As exciting as the prospect was of accompanying Pierre Laffite to safety, he did not relish the idea of doing so on flooded land.

Cisco had been standing there for about half an hour when he heard the sound of footsteps making their way toward him. Off to his left, he listened to another noise and knew it was the sound of a carriage approaching. "Perfect timing and a good omen, if I might say so," he whispered to himself. This was it, the moment had arrived, and with no time to waste, he stepped out of the shadows and made his way quickly toward Villere and the man he was helping to walk.

"Villere, the carriage is here; let me take over. Pierre, Mr. Laffite, I am Francisco and your friend. I am to take you to Donaldsonville, and from there, you will be taken to Grand Terre and your brother."

Pierre nodded and spoke weakly. "As I have been told. What is

371

next?" He looked behind him looking worried. "Villere said something about a carriage."

"It is here as promised. If you look this way, it approaches, see?"

A carriage traveled rapidly toward them and pulled to a stop a few feet away from Villere. The statesman quickly reached for the door pulling it open. "Come now; we need to hasten. I should hate for us to delay and be found out. Villere turned to face Pierre, who was attempting to straighten his posture and stand on his own. Once he felt steady, he looked toward the younger man.

"I thank you for your part in this adventure. You can be assured I will never forget this and should you ever require my assistance."

"Please, I am a friend; you can call me Cisco; Francisco sounds too formal, and we are about to spend quite a bit of time together."

"We are? Well, I am honored to do so."

For once in his life, Cisco found himself wishing that Pierre would shut up and stop trying to be the gentleman. All this proper do this and say that, could get them caught if they did not depart right then. "Please, allow me to help you." He reached for Laffite's arm, but the man was not interested; he just ignored the gesture and addressed Villere.

"And, you, Jacques, I am in your debt. I have one request, though." He coughed and swayed slightly as he did so. Cisco took the man's arm and firmly held on. Pierre did not seem to notice or care; he kept on talking to the statesman. "Please, I ask a favor, and after all, you have risked seeing me freed; I admit it maybe is not my right to do so. But if you could find your way to let my Marie know that...."

Cisco waited no longer; he began to guide the sick man toward the carriage without giving him a chance to listen to a reply to his request. Once by the carriage step, he forcibly helped Pierre up and then settled him inside as he spoke. "That has been taken care of. I assure you. All the details I will explain once we are on our way and out of town. Villere, you are needed at Davis's where you have been playing cards all night, beating Blanque and Grymes, I hear." Cisco climbed into the carriage, not waiting for a response.

Villere laughed. "A second bright spot in the evening then." He looked inside and directly at Laffite. "Pierre, take care, my friend, and we will see each other soon. My best regards to Jean and his wife. You are in trusted hands and none better, I dare say, to see you safely to Donaldsonville. I must be off, as must you. Driver, you may depart and hurry, please. Stop for no one." He closed the door and stood back.

The carriage pulled off seconds after the door closed, and Villere watched it until they turned out of sight. Then with his part in the plot completed, he turned and made his way to Davis's. All had gone to plan so far. With luck, the rest of the escape would be as easy as the first part.

CISCO looked at the gaunt man, who was Jean's brother. He had only seen him from a distance, and even then, he had not seemed in the best of health. Now, he looked even worse, if that was possible. His cheeks were sunken in, and his eyes seemed slightly crossed. Could be he had suffered another small stroke; at least that was Cisco's diagnosis.

Someone had placed a woolen blanket on the seat across from them, and there was a small basket, which he assumed had some food for them. The ride was going to be long and cold, and even though he had been assured that it was easy going after leaving town, no one had mentioned the weather or temperature. 'Easy indeed, but then what did anyone in this time know of easy going. Potholes and flooded dirt roads were far from easy,' he thought. 'Give me a modern highway and a mustang, and he'd have the man safe and sound in no time. Warm too, nice heater turned up high, instead of a single blanket to keep the chill off.'

The sick man was grateful for the blanket but shook his head no when the basket was put on the seat between them. His hands were trembling, and try as he might to put on a good front, he could not fool his traveling companion. Cisco had seen to all Pierre needed in those first few moments, and so rather than risk being noticed or recognized, while traveling the city roads, he lowered the wick on the oil lamp that hung opposite them. Once he had taken care of that, he settled back confident that they had just pulled off yet another jailbreak. This was sure to piss off many and none more so than the Governor and his cohorts.

Pierre coughed, struggling to catch his breath. The man's chest sounded congested and was most likely the beginnings of pneumonia.

The months in jail had been harder on this Laffite than any of them had guessed, and it worried the modern doctor. He couldn't do much, but he could offer something that would ease his discomfort. "Here, I think this should warm you up and give you a boost. The younger man handed Pierre a flask and watched as the grateful man began to consume the contents. "Better ease up there, don't need to deliver you drunk, do I? I mean, Jean and Tori will have my head if I do."

"Tori will not mind, and as for my brother, he will not dare speak of such, and you have my word on that. If I, his older brother, can't drink as much as I wish, then I have given him full reign over me, and that will never happen. Just a shame we only have this," he held up the small silver flask, "to drink while we make our way. It's a longer trip than you know until we reach where I need to be." He lifted the flask to his lips again.

Cisco laughed, "I see you are very much like your brother; stubborn to the end. Besides, who said that's the only drink I have?" He reached into his coat and pulled out a slightly larger flask, and then from inside the basket and buried under the food, he pulled out a bottle.

Now it was Pierre's time to laugh. "You, Sir, are to be commended, and I am lucky my brother has chosen such a brilliant strategist. So, let us talk about all I have missed. First, though, tell me how this all came about and what took Jean so damn long to get me out of that hell hole? Then maybe you can explain to me what the British are up to?"

SIMONE had enjoyed a deep and peaceful sleep and had awakened with a smile on her face. It was a smile that had remained on her lips from the moment Edward had returned home the day before.

He had been brilliant in his handling of the committee. Soon, very soon, Jean Laffite would be joining his brother in chains. His fate would be worse than his brothers, though, for he was now considered a spy. Trials were not needed if such was the charge. He would be shot or hung without delay upon being caught.

'My how the grand fall,' she thought. Edward was still sleeping next to her, his breathing deep and rhythmic. Half of her wanted to wake him; the other just wanted to enjoy the feelings she was having all to herself.

Slipping out from the bed, she decided to get their cook to make them an exceptional breakfast, and then she intended to dress and do some shopping. Her home could have been fully furnished by now if it had not been for that damn pirate, taking back what she had bought. Her temper started to rise at the thought. But then, if he had not, she would not have had the delight in all the shopping she had been doing as of late, and she did so enjoy shopping. So, what, if it was slow going, it only extended the fun and joy out of locating each and every extravagant article of furnishing.

The drawing-room was already furnished. Simone had seen to it that some of the pieces had been transported from Leone's plantation in order to do so. 'Her plantation house,' she reminded herself. Looking around her, Edward's wife delighted in all she saw. It was the kind of room she had always dreamed of having, and she enjoyed sitting in it for hours on end.

This morning would be no exception. She would have the cook set up breakfast in there also. While Edward slept in, Simone would begin to make her new list of friends to invite over. A small celebration would be in order once Jean was in chains. Edward's wife entered the room and found her coffee was already waiting for her, and after she explained what she wanted for breakfast, she sent the small kitchen maid out for the daily paper. Her husband did so like to read it while he had his coffee, and she intended to spoil him today, a reward of sorts. After all, he had kept his promise, and in a short time, they would read all about it in the paper themselves.

The new Madame Duval started making notes in her daily planner as to whom she would see and whom she would invite to dinner that coming weekend. Her mind kept slipping from her task at hand to that of what was sure to be the day's headlines. Laffite declared a spy! Her daydream grew and grew in its splendor as she sipped her coffee and grinned a wicked sort of smirk.

When the young girl returned with the paper in hand, Simone could hardly contain herself from snatching it up. She could hear Edward making his way down to join her. He was whistling a tune and commenting to someone that breakfast smelled wonderful.

Simone took the paper and dismissed the child, who left as fast as she could. Even though the girl could not read, word was around the town of the headlines it held, and she did not want to be anywhere close when her Mistress read what she already knew. The last time bad news had been delivered, the slave doing so had been sold as if it was her fault and that was after a beating.

The paper was folded in half, with the front page clearly visible, exposing the giant headline in bold print. ONE THOUSAND DOLLARS REWARD. Her hand shook as she continued to read, unable to tear her eyes away from the page.

Edward saw his wife standing in the drawing-room reading the paper she held. She stood so still and was so intent that he was sure she didn't even notice that he'd entered. Watching the way, she glared, however, the way she looked down at the newspaper, indicated clearly to him that something was wrong.

Simone looked up slowly toward her husband and just handed him the paper. Words could not escape her; it was as if she would choke to death on what she just read, and nothing was going to help. Edward's wife could not even catch her breath, and God help her; the room had started to spin.

Fearing Simone was about to faint, Edward took her by the arm and led her to the couch. Once there, he physically forced her to sit. Then he read what it was that had so obviously upset her. Within seconds he was sitting next to her, his mouth hanging open, his head shaking no.

Simone looked at him. "You can sit there and deny it all you want, but you had better believe it," she said in a hoarse whisper.

Edward shouted his response. "If I believe this to be true, I tell you, I will personally kill whoever is responsible for letting him out."

"Edward, I wish I could believe that. However, you know as well as I do, once again, the Laffite's have gotten away. Their money and power have to be destroyed if they are ever to be brought down. Don't you see that? You won't find out who he bribed, but mark my words, that's how the bastard got his brother out. And you won't find him so easy to put back either. If we are ever to see Jean fall, and I mean fall, he has to be rendered defenseless first. As much as I wanted to see his brother stand trial, I want to see Jean pay for his actions. Take away his men, his money, his power, and then his woman. I hate him. Do you hear me? I hate that he always seems to get what he wants. Well, no more!" she screamed, her voice getting louder. "Not again. Not now, not ever!"

Edward's wife then threw herself into her husband's arms. He could feel her shake as she cried the tears of hate and frustration. Soothing her and making her happy was second to what he most wanted, and that was just what she needed, Jean's destruction. "Simone, listen to me. I will dress and leave at once and see what is going on. Simone! Please, my love... listen to me." The sobbing started to slow down as she struggled to listen to his words. "He is nearly ours. It is so close, I tell you. I will work day and night from now on. Jean is already suspected to be in league with the enemy. Time is running out for him, and soon your tears and my anger shall have revenge. I swear to you it will happen."

In the coming days, Edward kept his word and stayed close to the Governor and his advisors. So it was that two days after Pierre's escape, the dandy was there when Jean Blanque delivered still more letters. Pierre had intercepted a letter that his brother had sent when they reached the small cottage in Donaldsonville. It was another British correspondence, and knowing that he was up to date on all goings-on, the older Laffite took it upon himself and wrote a letter to be delivered along with the other document. In the letter, he offered, like his brother had, all his services and support. Then again, three days later, another letter dated September 10th was received from Pierre, who was now thought to be residing at Grand Terre. This one asked for a reply as to whether or not the Governor would accept the Laffite's offer. Little did those who read these correspondences guess that the escaped fugitive was no place near Grand Terre; he was instead safely hidden in a home on the banks of the Mississippi.

The letters fell right into Edward's plans. He continued to claim the brothers were nothing more than spies. To Colonel Ross and Commodore Patterson, Edward's warnings about Barataria and the treasure it held hastened their desire to attack the stronghold.

Slowly and methodically, Edward worked on the committee, who finally decided to listen to him. No further correspondence was to be made with Jean Laffite or his associates. He convinced the Governor and his men that communicating with spies was not to be endorsed in any form. Most now concurred that they needed to eliminate the pirates before allowing the British fleet to anchor off their stronghold. Edward and a few other statesmen made sense to the Governor, who was listening intently. He had a decision to make; therefore, a meeting was called, and those who attended spoke up. William turned to Commodore Patterson, and together they set out a plan to disarm the Laffite's and take possession of their famous Grand Terre. Edward, as always, was in the thick of things. He encouraged those who were hesitant to go up against the pirates with the promise of recovering Laffite's stolen treasures. His most vital point of view was that those they caught would be hung as traitors, swayed those few holding out.

On September 11th, before the light of day, three loaded barges filled with soldiers and ammunition left New Orleans and sailed down the Mississippi to join with six gunboats and the Navy. The destination was Grand Terre. The mission: capture Jean Laffite and take possession of the stronghold before it fell into enemy hands. If they put up a fight rather than surrender, then they were to be hunted down and shot. Dead or alive, the end was finally near for the brothers and their men.

JEAN was up and getting dressed before Tori fully realized why. Panic hit her as he shouted at her to do the same. "Tori, do you hear me? Get dressed fast, and I might add, make it faster than you have ever done so." The air was filled with noises that made no sense at first. She could hear screaming and yelling but could not distinguish what was being said. Tori looked toward Jean, who had fully dressed in just a matter of minutes and was now frantically pulling on his long leather boots.

"Jean, what is it? What's going on?" Her voice betrayed her emotions. Her eyes were filled with dread. "Look, I am trying here." She was putting on a blouse and reached for a pair of breeches in the chest at the foot of the bed. Once she had a hold of the pants, she turned to face Jean as she pulled them on. "What in the hell is going on? Damn, my boots, where are my boots? Jean, answer me; what's happening?"

"An alarm has been raised. It would seem that we have unwelcome visitors. In short, my love, we are about to be attacked if we are not already." As his last boot slipped on his foot, he walked quickly toward the far side of the room, where he kept his weapons. Fastening his sword belt, he looked anxiously toward her. "How long before you are ready?"

"Ready for what?" Tori had found her boots and was pulling them on.

"To get the hell out of here if need be," he snapped. Then seeing the flash of terror cross her face, he softened his tone and added, "sorry. It's just that until we get down there, we don't know who or what is happening. Something tells me our British friends have grown weary of waiting for my answer and have decided to take matters into their own hands. If that is the case, then I have to get you to safety and try to keep this place from falling into the wrong hands. Now, come on and bring your sword just in case." He tossed her weapon toward her as he spoke. She caught it easily and headed toward the door, following Jean.

Before they got halfway to the shore, it had become clear that it was not the British that now threatened his home but the Americans. 'How could this be,' a stunned Jean questioned himself?

For the first time in his life, Jean was at a loss as to what to do. He turned to Tori, who, like himself, stood looking at the force headed their way.

Dominique appeared from nowhere, his emotions written clearly in his demeanor. He was furious at the pigs that now threatened him and his home. It hurt his dignity to think that they were insulting him in such a manner. Gentlemen did not fight with such a lack of honor. There were rules to how one fought a battle. And the Americans were nowhere close to abiding by any such rules.

Jean cared not how his first in command was looking at the situation. What he wanted from his lady was an explanation; maybe she understood what was happening. "You did not know of this?" he asked angrily.

"Do you think that I would have kept it from you if I had? Jean, you know me better than that," she replied just as angrily.

Dominique looked from one to the other and then stepped between them. "It does not matter now who knew what. The point here is being made very clear. The American pigs are about to take from us all that we have. Are we not going to fight to protect our homes and our men? Are you going to stand and gape like a young fool? They have betrayed us, no? Look for yourself. Look."

He physically turned Jean's body so he could look back at the small span of water and the flotilla that grew closer and closer. Six gunboats sat offshore; all guns pointed at them. Safely behind them sat a schooner Jean recognized as the Carolina. It was an American vessel, and there was no doubt in that fact.

"Look closely at the words on the white flag she flies," added Dominique. "Do my eyes deceive me, or does it say, Pardon to Deserters?" He spit to the side. "I tell you now; we must fight. The men await only your command. Already we have ships armed and moving out, but most are not manned and sit ripe for the picking." At that moment, gunfire came from one of the small boatloads of soldiers headed for shore, quickly followed by a loud boom of cannon fire.

Behind them, the front porch of Laffite's house exploded into bits and pieces.

Jean drew his sword, raising it in defiance. His face filled with rage, his voice exploding his order of "fight!"

With the boom of yet another cannon, it was clear to him that the Americans were not there to talk but to destroy. He watched as two of the pirate ships were fired upon and taking direct hits; they burst into flames.

Grabbing his arm, Tori desperately dragged him back a few paces, screaming all the while above the mayhem for him to listen to her. "Jean, please, you have to leave! Look, I don't know what is going on here." He shot her a dark look that seemed to question her sanity. "Oh, stop that. Of course, I know what's happening. I just don't know why. I do know that you can't run the risk of being captured or, worse yet, killed. Jean, are you listening to me? Do you understand what I'm telling you? This was not in our plans. Something has either gone very wrong or just was not known to us. One thing is certain; you have to leave!"

A bullet whizzed by their heads, making Jean pull her down lower to the ground and out of the line of fire. Anger and pure rage filled his mind at seeing how helpless the situation was.

He did not want to listen to her anymore about history and what he was supposed to do. Hell, it was his home that was under attack, and his men who stood a good chance of being killed or captured.

Another part of his house exploded as it took a direct hit. The explosion threw Tori into his arms shaking and crying. She realized that her life was also in jeopardy. To see something happen to her or to see her in chains if they were caught would destroy him and Tori knew it. "Jean, there is not much time," she begged.

Dominique, who had listened to her plea, marched up to them both. "I will stay and fight. I must. You have to listen to her. She is right, Boss. You have to leave. You have no choice. If we win, then you will be back. If not, then you will be safe. Listen to me. I know it is hard to run, but sometimes you have to do that."

Another bullet whizzed by, followed by a cannon blast that landed not far from where they stood, spraying sand and dirt all over them. Laffite's decision had been made for him. Without a word to either of them, Jean took hold of Tori's hand and pulled her back in the direction of the house.

Seeing that Boss and his lady were listening to reason, Dominique turned to face the invasion, putting the safety of his two dearest family members out of his mind. They would be long gone should they lose the fight, and something in his gut told him that was exactly what was about to happen.

Tori and Jean ran to the area behind his house, and there they found a pirogue pulled up on the small sandy beach. In seconds Jean pushed the vessel into the water, and once floating, he helped his wife into the small craft.

The noise of the ongoing battle behind them was frightening, and neither wanted to leave but understood they had no choice. Rapidly they made their move, and soon the pair were sitting in the small craft, which Jean paddled toward the first bayou he knew would have them hidden quickly.

Tori only looked back toward the house once. Judging by the billowing black smoke, it was burning. Like thunder, the sounds of gunfire and cannon continued to fill the heavens, and once or twice she caught a glimpse of people running toward the inland waterways. This was a grim sight and meant those left fighting, were most likely losing the battle. Fear for Dominique gripped her as it often did when he was in danger. Tori knew then without a doubt the man would stand and fight as long as he could to give her and Jean ample time to escape.

HOURS had passed, and the sounds and sights of Grand Terre had fallen away. Either the dense foliage blocked the echoing volleys across the swamps, or the battle was finished. Either way, until they reached a safe location and got word back from the area, they would not know the full extent of the carnage.

Tori kept looking toward Jean, who had not uttered a single word. The expression on his face told her he needed time to think things through. Not once did Jean slow his pace, and neither did he look at her. She understood that the pirate had one mission right then, and that was to save her from the very people she claimed he was to support and fight alongside. Knowing it was wise to remain silent for a while longer, Tori looked out over the swamps and fought the tears that wanted to flow.

IT was impossible to put up with his mood any longer, and so she broke the silence. "Jean, can you talk to me? I have kept to myself, but I can't go on like this. Jean, I did not know about this; please, you have to believe me on this."

He looked at her then and stopped his paddling. "We shall have to keep going; I intend to make it into the city before those bastards return. I am certain that all is lost back there; the point is why? If I had guessed they would turn on me as they have done, I could have prepared and to hell with history and keeping it, as you say, on track. I was a fool, only keeping watch for the British when I should have kept watch on the Americans too."

"But you do, believe me, right?"

"I have no idea what I think or believe right now. One thing is clear, my love, I have many allies and far more enemies. Some have made themselves known, like Edward and his wife, Claiborne, and the British. Those are against me; now the Americans, they have declared war as far as I am concerned."

"I don't know that you can say that. Let's wait until we have a chance to talk to Grymes and others. There has to be a reason for all this."

"Reason or not, they have taken away all I have built. Killed many, I am sure, and my home, our home, is gone. Claiborne has shown me he has no intention of listening to me, of letting me help, and why should I?"

"You will do it; I know you will. Andrew Jackson will be your ally and your friend."

"I am not convinced of that anymore. Tori, please let me alone to my thoughts, and if it helps you any, I know you did not keep such a tragic event from me. It was clear to see by the look of horror on your face as we approached the beach and more so when we saw the American ship. The attack did show me that we don't know anything for certain. I have just got one brother out of jail and now fear that another will lay dead on the beach or taken to be hung."

He looked away from her, not even realizing what he had exposed. Tori said nothing, it was not the time to do so, and she understood there might never be a time that was right. One thing was clear to her, Dominique was Jean and Pierre's brother as she had suspected; he had just declared such. "Jean, please try to understand…"

"Oh, I understand, all right. I have a choice to make, and right now, that choice is easy. To hell with the Americans and what they have done. No more talking; let me guide us to the place we need to reach. From there, we will make our way into the city, and then and only then will I consider all my options." He turned away from her and began to paddle again. His mood was somber, and reaching him, trying to explain more was impossible. She's let him alone and let him paddle through the bayous while she prayed that he'd come around.

THE afternoon was hot, and she was thirsty. Looking out over the bayou and the water beyond, Tori licked her dry lips. She pulled her hair up off her neck and wished she had something to tie it up, to keep it off her back and thereby help rid some of the heat she was experiencing. 'Surrounded by water and not a drop to drink,' she thought. Her throat was dry, sweat dripped off her face and ran down her back. Jean's shirt was soaked from sweat, yet he never complained or slowed down, so, how could she? How long the journey would take, Tori had no idea, just like she had no idea if this pirate would stand alongside Jackson and the men from New Orleans against the British. His resolve to help had been shaken and maybe destroyed to the point where history would be changed. Chances were, if that was true, everything would be changed for the worse. She continued to pray that once they reached the city, Cisco, Davis, and others could help convince him he had to aid those who had just turned against him, but how? With thoughts and questions filling her mind, Tori remained silent and could only hope that the news would not be so devastating in the days ahead.

Her hand gripped the small sword that lay against her leg, a gift from the one person besides Jean, who she loved. She wanted Dominique to be safe for both her and her husband; because if he were not, they would be devastated, and Jean would never agree to fight for those who hurt or killed the man. How could she make Laffite change his mind and stay on course to be at the battle and help save America? When could she take the opportunity to express her concerns? God help her, she should not begin to cry? If Jean saw her cry, it would only worsen the situation, but thinking of everything she knew to be accurate, how could she stop?

The beautiful house and all it contained were gone. Carlotta, was she safe? The children, did they manage to escape the bombardment? So many questions were left unanswered. Tears filled her eyes, and try as she might, Tori could no longer stop the emotions flooding over her. As Jean continued to paddle, lost in his own ponderings, his wife quietly looked at the passing country through clouded tear-filled eyes. In the end, she gave in and allowed her tears to fall—as the shock of what had happened enveloped her.

THE past two days had become a blur. They had been lucky to escape capture unharmed and still luckier to have made it to the blacksmith shop undetected. Word had been leaked that Jean and Tori had escaped to Cat island, and from there, they had taken a boat and left for destinations unknown. This had been an idea given to the pirate by his wife, who told him if everyone thought them gone, they would not come looking for them.

It seemed to have worked; because Claiborne and the city had accepted the plausible idea. With one urgent problem under control, the pair could face the numerous others that they faced. At least for the time being, they found themselves hiding and hoping for news about the fate of their friends and home. However, with each passing hour, the agony grew.

Jean had sent word, via a hand-carried letter, to his brother Pierre and told him he was to hide with his Mistress, who he was sure was with him. He was also to see that the rumor of where he and Tori were was to continue; everyone had to think he was sailing someplace in the gulf, maybe even with Pierre safely onboard with them. Lies could be planted and allowed to take root if whispered into the right ears.

With many friends telling such news up and down the river and in town, they had a chance of remaining undetected. Once the letter was on its way, Jean was able to relax safe in the knowledge that for a short time, his brother would also be secure from capture. Once night fell, he would find a way to send Tori to Donaldsonville, too, in case the soldiers came looking for them. What he had not counted on was her stubborn streak.

"I tell you right now; I am not going anyplace without you." Tori was walking back and forth while fuming at the very idea that she would listen to Jean and run. You will have to realize that you need me, and I am sure Cisco and the others will agree."

"What am I to do with you? I could tie you up and ship you like a bundle of cotton, all wrapped up nice and warm and…"

"You will do no such thing. So, get that idea out of your thick skull. We are a team, and we need to keep focused on what is going on. If you are worried about me and not doing what you have to, well, we all lose, don't we?"

He walked over to her and took her in a loving embrace. As loathed as he was that she was correct, he had to admit it. "You can stay for now, but heed me, if things don't go as you and your friends think that they are supposed to, well, I will ship you out, and you won't stop me."

"Deal. You won't have to, though, I am sure of it. All we need to do is keep our heads, and everything will go to plan."

"I assure you I fully intend to keep my head right where it is, thank you. Now, come, sit with me. I want to go over everything one more time."

TORI and Jean kept themselves hidden in the small secret room above the shop, while Thiac kept up his work as usual. If they were found out, the chance of escape would be slim. However, after discussing their options, both agreed the cottage was the safest location and the last place anyone would look.

The news was slow in coming. For days they sat waiting and wondering.

As days passed, Jean knew it could not have gone well for his men. He only prayed that those he cared about and loved, like Dominique, had not been lost to him forever. Just about the time, he could stand the waiting no longer, Thiac came up to bring them the news that Cisco and friends would arrive that night to talk. They had told the smithy only that Grand Terre was no more. All was lost and or taken by the American's. Jean's only reaction was to take Tori in his arms and hold her close. Thiac knew the pain the man now carried, but he also realized that as long as Jean had breath in his body, he had a fighting spirit in his soul.

LATE that night, in the dimly lit room, the small group met. The first order of business, as Grymes referred to it, was to tell Laffite what news they had of the British. "Our man, who as you know is one of yours, the one you sent to Mobil to keep watch, he returned. We got the news before Claiborne, and no, we did not tip our hand and run to him as I wanted."

Jean tensed up but remained silent. He wanted this information whether it was good or bad, and judging by the expression on Grymes's face, it could be either/or. "So, sending him to spy paid off? I am glad of that."

"It was smart, and it is important news. We learned that on September 15, the British sailed to Point Mobil and attempted to take Fort Bowyer. According to our man, sorry your man, the Red Coats marched from Pensacola, the land assault failed. Fort Bowyer repulsed the British warships, which were sent to give support. The batteries there crippled the Hermes; many men died, sad to say, theirs more than ours if that helps. The British set that ship, ablaze, so we couldn't use it. For three hours, they bombarded the area but could not dislodge our troops. The three other ships sailed off with their tails between their legs," he laughed. "You might say they got a taste of what is in store for them. Our spy did learn that the main force has sailed from Jamaica and is heading for us. Gentlemen, they mean to conquer New Orleans; there is no further doubt on that subject. Little more was shared our way, and the man refused to return, claiming he wants to fight alongside Boss."

Jean lit a cigar and sat back in his seat before talking. "I will have to thank him and pay him for his troubles when I have payment myself. He did well, and for that, I am grateful. Is there news of Jackson?"

"Only that he will be coming our way, but word of his movements and the number of men he has, is hard to track. We know only that he intends to come here. For now, there is nothing further to report."

Jean leaned forward. "I will see to it that more men are placed in areas of weakness. What we lack in numbers, we will strengthen with information. Now, I feel the need to have something more than wine. Thiac, see to it that we have the other bottles brought up."

The smithy didn't utter a sound; he just turned and left the room to retrieve the bottles Jean had requested. After he left, Laffite spoke, adding, "tonight will be long, I fear."

They would talk for hours, and Jean would finally learn the truth about his home base. All had been confiscated or destroyed. The Misere and General Bolivar, his prized ships, were among the vessels taken and now sailed under the American flag. There had been twenty-seven ships at anchor when they were fired upon. Some were burned by the pirates, and others sunk by the invading force. No vessels remained under the control of Laffite's men.

"It is sad news that Grand Terre has been completely ruined; not a building was left standing. And, as Patterson had not enough men to sail the vessels, they captured, he destroyed... but then you would have guessed as much." Grymes stood up and continued to talk but without looking at Jean. "They plundered, burned and killed, all in the name of duty! The warehouses were emptied as even the pockets of those fallen were emptied. I know this is hard to hear, yet you have need to know and won't rest until you do."

Jean sat at the small table and reached for Tori's hand. He held in words he wanted to say because if he spoke, Jean was sure Tori would worry about his commitment to the American cause.

"Gambi's ship Petit Milan is no longer his to command, and I hear he is like an angry hornet in jail. Anger drives him, but it has not swayed him from us just yet. As to your home, it is a pile of rubble with nothing of value left in its charred remains. Ross took what he wanted, not the man following orders for the right reason. Patterson has begun to make a list of all cargo and ships taken, and I will have a full list of what was stolen and of each vessel floating or not; also, the count of dead and…" Grymes stopped talking when Jean abruptly stood up.

"I learned that many of my men had been taken prisoner, but still more escaped, fleeing into the sanctuary of the swamps and backwaters, that they know like no others. For now, those men and women are safe. For that, I can be grateful, I suppose." He looked at Tori and retook his seat. "I shall try to remain an optimist for you, my love. Right now, at this moment, I am more determined to seek justice."

Davis spoke up, sounding very determined. "And you will have it, Jean. Tell him Cisco; he will, won't he? Grymes, you know he did nothing to deserve all this."

Jean sat still and deep in thought while the others sat and spoke in lowered voices. He had only asked to be told the truth about what had happened after they left the beach, and now that he knew, the shock of it hit him hard.

All he had worked for, was gone, taken by those he was supposed to help. How was he going to be able to help without his men and ships? How was he to gain his men's support? How would he get them to join him after they learned what he just had? One thing was sure, even if he could get back his ships and weapons, it did not guarantee any of his men would fight beside him against those who had burned them out.

Grymes looked at his friend and hated to add to his burden but knew that to delay the rest of his news would not make it any easier. "Jean, there is one other piece of news that you should know." Jean looked up, dreading what else he would learn.

Grymes wanted to give him some hope, even if he felt at that moment the possibility was bleak. "It's about Dominique. He is, I'm afraid, one of those captured and brought to jail. There are eighty at last count that sit with him, and every one of them is ready to join you if they don't hang before..." he stopped talking because Laffite had begun to laugh.

For the first time since everything happened, the pirate chuckled and then broke into an all-out laugh; he could not help himself. He had been so sure that Grymes was about to tell him that Dominique had been killed. To hear he was instead sitting in jail seemed like a blessing. "Is that all? That, my friend, I can fix. Those walls have not done a good job of holding me, or my men, in the past."

Grymes shook his head. "That might be. In the past... it is just that don't you see, the past? This time your men and Dominique will either swing on a rope or rot in a stinking hole; of that, you may be assured. You have been lucky and had the financial backing to obtain freedom, to buy what you needed. That has changed. I hate to remind you of one fact. You have at this time, nothing. You are broke!" he quickly added. "Don't go giving up. No Sir! We have some plans, Edward Livingston and me. I assure you, we believe that we can fight all this in the courts and, in due process, get back most of what you have lost, along with a full pardon, as you are guilty of nothing. At least, nothing that they have charged you with will obtain you the rope. The same goes for Dominique. A privateer and a pirate are two different entities completely. If they do not agree with that, you will have enough money to bribe..."

"Grymes," Jean held up his hand to stop the man from talking. "I

391

am sure you and Livingston have every good intention of helping me here, but the problem is, as I see it, that all of what you intend takes time, and time my friend, is something we don't have." Jean looked at the other two friends as he spoke. "Cisco, John, I need you two to put your heads together along with my lady here and try to figure this mess out. Just what are we supposed to do now? I know what I want to do, but what must be done is, I feel, something entirely different."

Davis spoke up; first, his deep voice sounding calm and very much in control. "I know that we did not call the raid on Grand Terre. Let us look at that first. Just because we did not know of it does not mean it did not occur. I believe we are still on track. You will fight at the battle, and Dominique will be at your side, along with your men. Now that takes care of that problem. What we have to do is use all our heads and not panic. Grymes can keep an eye on the Governor, and I can still keep my ears and eyes open, as will Cisco and Marie. You two have to lay low and wait for our next move."

"You expect me to sit here and do nothing?"

"Just that. You have to get ready to meet with General Jackson, who should be coming to town sometime shortly. Until then, we can only make plans one day at a time. We will do our part, so you shall do yours."

"I agree," sounded Cisco with excitement in his tone of voice. Then with just a hint of seriousness, he added, "Don't you blow this. That means you have…"

Jean pulled on his mustache and forced a slight smile to tug at his lips. "I am aware of what you mean. Your colloquialism this time is one I am familiar with." He winked at Tori, trying to lift the mood in the small room.

Jean hated the idea but could see that to act without knowing exactly where he stood would be foolish. He could, he thought, keep writing his letters, and yes, he did have to prepare just how to approach Jackson and what to say to the man. In the end, everything would hinge on that meeting, a meeting that still had to be arranged. That in itself would be a difficult task. He had so many problems yet to solve and many plans to make.

All eyes were on him, and Jean knew that they were waiting for his answer. "I agree with you. We will stay put. Tori and I have much to work out here, and this quiet time may be just what we need to figure it all out. Until I get my rightful property back, one can say I have no other way to go. I must, it seems, place myself, my men, and all that will be in your capable hands once again. Let us hope that there are no other ugly surprises that you are unaware of."

The attorney's hand reached out and took hold of Jean's shoulder. "It is agreed then; we wait."

Grymes breathed easier, as did Davis.

Cisco looked at Marie, who, through slit eyes, watched each of them in turn. She felt great passion here in the room but no danger—nothing yet, at least, nothing that would indicate disaster.

Tori breathed a deep sigh; the primary issue had been that Jean would change his mind and not fight, that he would be so angry at the Americans that he would give up on offering his help. These thoughts had plagued her day and night, and out of fear of angering the man more, she had not pushed him. At last, she had her answer, and he had his; if given the opportunity, he would stand alongside Jackson.

Tori looked at Marie and smiled slightly. The woman had tried to tell her a few days ago that there was nothing to worry over. How she knew things, Tori did not understand, and why only certain things? How she wished the voodoo queen could have seen the forthcoming destruction of the pirate's home base. So much had been plundered and burned, some of which she dearly wished she could have saved. Still, what was, would be, and there was nothing left to do but concentrate on the future. Then another darker thought entered her mind. Was the reason for Jean's departure to Galveston because of his financial situation? Would he get back what the government had confiscated? He'd become a citizen, forgiven for his crimes, and hailed as a hero, so why leave? There was so much she wished, she knew, or did she? If Tori knew what the future held, could she keep the information to herself, she wondered? If she had known about the raid on Grand Terre, would she have kept quiet or told Jean? Maybe it was best not to ponder such qualms. It was best to face the days ahead and fight for what was right, not worry about what was wrong or could go wrong.

SEPTEMBER'S warmer days passed into October's gray and cold ones. The weeks had been filled with setting up a network of communication between Laffite, his lawyers, and friends. Livingston, who was not seen connected to Jean, had set up a way to get word to Dominique and the rest of Jean's men in jail.

With Cayetana's help, they kept a close tab on the Governor and Edward. It had become clear to all that Edward Duval was a driving force behind Claiborne's hate of the Laffites. He also cleverly stirred the Creoles and their high emotions and fierce loyalties away from the Americans every chance he got. Livingston held gatherings of citizens to counter these destructive activities, urging their allegiance to the United States. Grymes formed a committee whose job was to help the military authorities by suggesting means of defense. He could not sit on the committee himself but was able to place two close allies of Jean's, along with other well-respected citizens: Edward Livingston and Jean Blanque. Livingston also added Jean Destrehan to the committee and a few others he trusted. One American and many Creoles who were loyal to Laffite, and no one suspected a thing.

Meetings were held late at night at the blacksmith shop to keep Jean well informed. He was in contact with his men, who had escaped and made their way to a place known as Isle Derniere, and like those in jail, they had sworn they would fight alongside their Boss if they needed to. They may not like it, but they trusted their leader, and he had to have a plan that would get them back all they lost and then some. Their loyalty was strengthened with the promise of pardons to be gained and money to be made.

Cayetana had carefully and slowly started to work on her husband and his thoughts toward Laffite and the Baratarians. Undermining Edward was no easy task. Still, she persisted with patience and cunning. She also now had her hair done regularly by Marie Laveau. In this way, information was moved back and forth without anyone the wiser.

It was via the Cayetana-Marie network that Jean received two pieces of information in the middle of November. The first that the Governor had been informed by General Jackson, that fifteen to twenty thousand British had set sail from Ireland early in September. Their intended destination was thought to be Louisiana. The second piece of information, and far more critical, was that General Jackson himself was on his way to New Orleans and that Cayetana would let them know as soon as possible when he arrived. Two more weeks passed before that message came, and when at last, it arrived, Jean and Tori were more than ready. Still, caution was the caller of their actions. Jean knew Jackson had first to learn how desperate the situation was before he could approach the American with his offer.

Once again, the frustrated pirate found himself sitting and waiting for the right time. He trusted his contacts and laughed with Grymes often about his predicament. Just what would the General think if he realized that his military secretary, Edward Livingston, was, in fact, working for the very pirates he despised?

Nothing the General did went unreported to Jean and Tori. His first meeting with the Governor, and Mayor, was described in great detail within an hour of its completion. Mayor Girod, who spoke nothing but French, had to be told all that Jackson said through an interpreter. Girod was so grateful to the American General for coming to New Orleans that he had insisted he stay at a residence on Royal Street, a home unbeknown to either the General or the local politicians, that had been hand-picked by Jean, Davis, and

Livingston. So it was that the General's headquarters was set up in a most convenient location.

JEAN acted more like a caged lion, pacing continuously up and down the small space. "I take it that waiting is not one of your stronger points," laughed Tori, trying to lighten his spirit. But, instead, she saw only a dark scowl on his face. "Jean, if you don't sit down and stop your pacing, I swear to you, I'll sit on top of you and hold you down in one spot." Tori was thoroughly exasperated and meant what she said.

"Am I that much of a bear? Not that I am aware of how bears act, just that you have called me such many times in the past weeks." He sat down and looked at his love. "I assure you that my frustration is in no way directed at you. It's just that I feel so inadequate and out of control here."

"Jean, for God's sake, stop it. You are far from out of control, and as for inadequate, well, I would say that that is the understatement of the century. You have everything running just as you please, even hiding up here. You really do amaze me. Do you know that?"

Jean's lips finally curled upward as his face relaxed. He was smiling now and feeling somewhat better. He really did have things under control, and she had, like always, lifted his spirits. No one had ever been able to do that, to reach him and understand him the way she did.

"Jean, look, we know Jackson has been downriver for this past week."

"Over a week," he snapped back.

"Ok, a few more days longer. Give the man time, won't you? I mean, Ft. Philip is damn near the mouth of the river, and Ft. St Leon is closer, but it too needs to be set up just right."

Jean nodded his head in agreement. "I had told Livingston that they needed to secure those. It's a good location to keep any vessels out of the city. That bend is called the English Turn, how appropriate. One has to know how to navigate that stretch to sail up to our city. If Jackson learns the truth about that stretch, he will have no need to spend precious time viewing the Fort."

"See," Tori grinned, "you get it, his inspection of the forts and the river with Livingston and others is the reason why he has not yet called for you. I was as surprised as you to hear that Jackson had left the day after he arrived. I, too, was thinking he would send for you right away. History seems to be a bit more complicated than we thought; you and I both realize that. I am certain that it is unfolding as it should, though. This is but a delay caused by Jackson's duty to know the lay of the land and river."

"He is wise in what he is doing. Any man worth his weight would prepare as best he could. This General is doing nothing I myself would not do. Jackson, however, needs me, my men, and what we know."

"And he will have them. You need to trust me and the others. We know you will have your chance to help because we know you will be summoned. Take my word on this, will you?" She held her arms open in an invitation to embrace. Jean was about to go to her, to show his gratitude for her understanding of his impatience when Thiac called up to them that they had a visitor on his way.

NOT long after, Cisco entered the dimly lit room and smiled broadly at his close friends. "I hope you both know that I am having the time of my life playing 007. Do you have any idea what it took to get me here tonight, with what I have to tell you?

God, this is great, and I believe it's about to get even better. Got a drink around here?" He was grinning from ear to ear and looking around for the bottle of wine he knew they would have. "Not one word of what I have to say, will you get out of these parched lips," he joked.

Jean looked toward Tori. Now, he was the one with the exasperated expression. Tori realized that he would throttle Cisco if he did

397

not stop his antics, so she moved quickly between the two men and took Cisco by the arm, leading him to the small table and chairs. "Cisco, you idiot, you had best sit here and begin talking, or I'm afraid your James Bond days are in jeopardy of becoming extinct. You might say that right now, you are on the endangered list." Her eyebrow rose sharply as she gazed at her friend. Her silent warning did not go unnoticed.

Looking toward Jean and his thunderous glare, Cisco's smile faded. "Sorry, man. Sometimes I forget how difficult it must be for you, just sitting here waiting for news." He tried to look sincere and, pointing to the empty seat across from him, asked, "Will you join me?"

Jean inhaled deeply and, without speaking, walked to the chair. As he did so, Tori's friend continued with his crazy banter. "You know if I were you," said Cisco, "I would find myself enjoying these arrangements. Really Jean, you and your lady, have the perfect opportunity to…"

He got no further. Jean's temper snapped. His arm reached out and grabbed Cisco's shirtfront, pulling him across the table. Tori's reaction was to act without thinking, and she jumped toward the tabletop, placing her body between the two men.

It was over in seconds. As soon as her weight hit the table, it gave way, and before she realized what had happened, it crumbled and she had two men lying on top of her. Laffite's face was inches away from Tori's friend, who didn't seem worried at all that he was the cause of such a disaster. The table had collapsed and Jean's love had gone to the floor with them, was all he knew.

Laffite was about to reach out and grab the culprit when to his utter surprise, the younger man began to laugh. "Now, why'd you go and do a stupid thing like that?" Cisco spluttered the words, ignoring the glaring face of the man he had every right to fear.

Jean didn't hesitate to interrupt him. "Just whom are you asking that stupid question of? Me for wanting to wring your neck, or my lady here?"

With that, an outraged scream filled the room as Tori yelled at them both. "Get the fuck off me now! I can't breathe with either of you two assholes laying on top of me like this!"

Both men rolled off of her in different directions and ended up staring at her in stunned silence. It was like they had never heard a woman use such language before in their lives, let alone with such an angry tone of voice.

Cisco laughed first. Nothing it seemed, could dampen his high spirits. "I would say, Jean, my man, that she is well and truly pissed off."

Tori responded to this statement in a tone that showed she was not calming or forgiving. "I am more than pissed off. You two simpletons are acting more like immature boys than men."

"Pissed off?" Jean asked this with a slight smile tugging at his lips. "Now, there is an expression that has quite a ring to it, as I have often said. I gather, in this instance, Tori means she is furious with us? That she is in no need of a visit to the chamber pot?" Jean, too was now in a jovial mood. She was relieved to see that the men had found the whole event humorous and were not about to continue with their physical display, so she joined them and laughed. What else could she do?

Cisco sat up and reached for Tori's hand, pulling her to a sitting position. "Are you all right? No bones broken?"

"No bones broken, but I think my stunt woman days are short-lived if you get what I mean."

Jean always had difficulty following their conversations, especially when the two of them started talking like they were now. It might be considered English, but it was a jumble of words that had no meaning to his ears. He found himself quickly getting frustrated all over again. Looking toward Cisco, Jean's feelings showed and warned the younger man to pay attention.

Cisco was now ready to calm down and talk. "Look, you two, I came here tonight with information. Hand me that bottle, will you, Jean? The one that rolled over there, behind you. We don't need glasses. Just open the son of a bitch, and I'll start. I am parched."

Jean gave up. He knew that if he was going to get the news, it was going to have to be Cisco's way and the man loved drama.

"As I was saying before, your swan dive Tori."

"Damn it, Cisco, if you're going to talk, do so in English. And for another, swans don't dive!" snapped Jean.

"Oh, sorry there, man. I'll try harder to make it plain English. Well, as you know already, Livingston and his wife had Jackson to their home for dinner last night. The Governor and Cayetana were there, as were quite a few others. No Edward or Simone, though. She must have been royally pissed." He looked at Jean. "Whoops, sorry. I mean angry."

"I understand the meaning; go on."

"Well, today, Livingston had to write a letter for Jackson. It is on its way to Washington as we speak. As soon as Livingston could, he went to Grymes, with all the details of the letter and a message for you. Grymes came to Davis, who in turn told me, and here I am. See, I told you. It's like a Bond movie." He took the bottle from Jean and, putting it to his lips, took a long, slow drink.

Tori snatched the bottle out of his hands and held it out of his reach. "If you don't give me the message and stop hanging us out to dry, so help me, Cisco, I will thrash the daylights out of you."

"Okay, okay. Keep your pants on." He glanced at Jean and added, "Nothing personal, I assure you."

"I hope not, but what does, keeping her pants on, have to do with Livingston's message?"

"Nothing." Cisco and Tori were laughing now. "Look, I'll cut to the chase."

"To the what? There is going to be a chase?"

"Oh God, Jean. Just shut up and let him talk. Cisco, will you please just give us the God damn message."

"That is what I am trying to do. It's simple. The letter is asking for weapons and such. It explains how desperate the situation is here and how the General fears the worst. Livingston knows that the man's back is to the wall and that if the British were to arrive any time, well... the shit would hit the fan."

"I take it that what you are telling me is that Jackson requires my services, not that he is in need to relieve himself."

Cisco looked puzzled, and then as if a light went on, he chuckled. "I see, the shit part, it's not what you think, but let's move on and forget that for now. Tori will explain, I am sure. Anyway, he needs help. That's about the guts of it. Just like we told you. You, Jean Laffite, are about to save the day and supply all that the man needs."

Jean stood up and walked slowly to the far side of the room. He was thinking in silence. Cisco snatched back the wine bottle and took another long gulp. The gurgling sounds he made were enough to make Jean turn around to face them.

"I suggest you go easy there. We have to decide just how to go about this next step. You both know that in your time, it is said I meet with Jackson and make the arrangements and a deal. That may be well and true, but this is now, and we have to find a way for me to get to the man, and that won't be easy."

Cisco slapped the wooden floor with his hand as he coughed the wine that he'd swallowed the wrong way. Once he had control, he spoke. "Sorry to disappoint you, my friend. It's already been arranged. You meet him tonight." Jean's face went blank as what Cisco said sank in. "Look, it's like this. Livingston has known Jackson for years. They knew each other up in Washington. Hell, he and Jackson, it turns out, are Masons. Claiborne too, and a few others. Close-knit group and well, you know." He looked at Tori, "we didn't know this did we? Hell, even Davis had no idea. It kind of shocked us and gave us what we needed. Jackson trusts Livingston and listens to him if you get my drift?" He looked at Jean and saw him smile slightly.

Jean pulled on his goatee. "Another quaint term, but yes, I understand Cisco. You may proceed."

"He talked to Jackson after the letter was sent. Both men know that by the time it gets to Washington, it will be too late. Livingston talked with him, and the end result is that you and he, the General that is, will meet alone to talk. Jackson is not a fool. He knows that if meeting with hellish banditti, will get him men…"

Jean's eyes widened. "The hellish…"

"Oh, come on, you were told he does not like you or your men, at least for now. Anyway, he knows you have what they need, so meet you; he will." He took another swig from the bottle and then looked at it. "It's empty, got another? Jean, the man, does not hold you in any endearing light, that's for sure. He hates your guts, to put it mildly, thanks to our dear Governor and his everlasting letter-writing campaign. Egged on by our dear Edward, no doubt." Cisco had suddenly gotten very serious and looked away from Jean before continuing. "Two conditions stand for this meeting to come about. One, you had best present yourself as a gentleman. I suggest you change your clothes and two; Tori is to go with you."

Jean's face had gone from a smirk at the mention of his attire to horror at the mention of Tori joining him. "Under no circumstances is that going to happen."

"Which one?" asked Cisco, trying to sound concerned.

"You know just what the hell I'm referring to." His tone was deadly, matching his angry glare.

"You can threaten and storm all you want on this, Jean, but I'm here to tell you that this is the one time it is out of your hands. Tori will be going with you. The General is expecting you both." Cisco could see the look of thunder cover Jean's face altogether, and fearing his wrath, quickly placed the blame elsewhere. "Look, it was Davis's idea. Tori is needed as our insurance policy, so to speak. Grymes agreed and felt that one of us, who is fully aware of history, needs to be at this meeting with you. Besides, she will be an added insurance policy for Jackson too. He is just not going to go off into the backwaters with you, on your word alone. Hell, the man might think you are going to turn him over to the Red Coats. She has to go, so you can show him the stash; how else can he see that you have all the flints and powder he needs? Yep, he would definitely think you could be using the excursion into the bayous as a ploy to take him hostage, or worse."

Jean could see the picture clearly. It all made sense the way Cisco was describing it. The dark shadow that had engulfed him started to lift, and his expression softened into a friendlier expression. "You seem to have thought this all through. But, how in the hell does Tori fit in here? How can she be his insurance policy, I ask you? That is not clear to me."

"It's simple. Jackson will go with you if the one thing you love most is left behind with his men. It's insurance that nothing will happen to him." Cisco looked toward Tori and, knowing he had her on his side, looked back at Jean, who still had a questioning expression about him. "Jean, look, I don't know all the details about this. Davis and Grymes called all the shots and arranged it all with Livingston's help. There is no time to change anything. Just go along with this, all right?"

"Looks as if I have no choice in the matter, does it? I may not like it, but I do have enough wits about me to trust in the judgment of those, who I call my friends." He turned toward Tori and smiled. "Are you ready to do this?"

"Not right this second, but give me an hour to change and fix myself up a bit, and yes, I'm willing." She had tried to sound light-hearted about what was ahead of them. However, Tori avoided looking at him when answering his question for fear of letting him see the truth behind her eyes. She was excited and scared all at once. So much was riding on the outcome of the meeting that was only a short time away.

Jean nodded his head in agreement. "I suggest you change. Hell, how are you going to do that? I mean, change into what?"

Cisco put the empty bottle down. "A trade it is then. I happen to have all you need downstairs. I stopped in at your townhouse, and your housekeeper Bessy was very happy to help. I have outfits for you both. Sorry, Tori, yours is just simple and not as glamorous as I would have liked, but Davis said it was best if you dress down for this meeting. Jean will look his part, though. So how about it, another round for this thirsty friend?"

Tori looked at Cisco and wondered how he could remain so calm. After all, she was about to take Jean to meet Andrew Jackson himself. "Yes, that sounds good to me. I'll take a small drink, though, to calm my nerves. I mean, come on, you get it. Is it me? Am I the only one here who is feeling slightly, no, more like scared shitless? Sorry, Jean, I don't mean to swear, but Lord, this is crazy, and so much rides on the next few hours."

Tori looked back at Cisco and took the bottle out of his hands. "I changed my mind. Just go and get the outfits and let's get this over with. If I don't act now, I never will get the courage up. It's happening, really happening, and history is about to be made. One way or the other, we will keep the timeline as it played out; we must, not only for America but for America's future. Gentlemen, this is it; the day has come that we have waited for. I, for one, pray that all that is about to happen does as history played out and the books told. Cisco, fetch the outfits and tell Thiac one more bottle is needed. I'd take a valium; not invented yet, so a swig or two more will have to suffice. I am going to meet President Andrew Jackson and help him decide to trust you, Jean."

Cisco frowned and then added, "You know you can't let anything slip to the General; I mean, he can't know what you know. He is General Andrew Jackson and nothing more."

"Oh, he is way more than that Cisco; he is our hope, our destiny, and more, just as Jean Laffite is his."

"Well, if you put it that way, and I suppose you are right. Still, you have to keep your guard up and be careful with what you reveal. I have been told that Jackson is sharp as a whip and is a great judge of character. One slip, and all of it could go down the sink."

Jean laughed, "I have no intention of sinking. Like I have no intention of trying to understand you two a moment longer. Let's prepare for the meeting and pray that I am not tossed into jail alongside my men. Something I trust won't happen."

Cisco was serious when he responded. It was as if he understood the time for taking matters lightly was over. "If history is correct and we are right, that won't happen, and you Tori will see Dominique soon."

Tori giggled. "That will be one meeting I won't worry about. I miss the old sea dog. But meeting Jackson," she went serious in her tone of voice, "my God, some folks would jump at the chance both in this day and age and in the future. Let's get ready, Jean; we have to present ourselves and our case to the man who will save New Orleans if he listens and agrees to your terms."

"Of that, I have no doubt. After all, the man is not stupid or hell-bent on my destruction, unlike others in this city." Laffite looked at them both and winked at Tori. "I, just like Jackson, am smart enough to know that we need each other. My advantage is he needs me more than I need him right now. I will negotiate and win his support or my name is not Jean Laffite."

End of Book Four

Watch for the conclusion of the
Legends of NOLA series:

The Hidden Grave

Acknowledgements

I WISH TO thank my family, who visited New Orleans countless times over the years with me. Long before the internet was available, I had to do hours upon hours of research in and around the French Quarter. I want to thank all three of my children and offer my apology to them for all the times our family vacations involved plantations and battle sites. Somehow you endured the endless road trips with laughter and understanding.

I want to thank the Louisiana Historical Association and the Research Center on Charter Street. The personnel there never let me down or ceased to amaze me. One of my proudest moments came when they accepted a copy of my book for their archives.

The Destrehan Plantation was not open to the public when Daniel, my husband, and I first came upon it. They were battening down for an approaching hurricane when we pulled onto the grounds. Mr. Joseph Maddox listened to my husband's plea and was gracious enough to give us a personal tour and history of the place. We have since returned to visit Destrehan many times, and though our paths have never crossed with Mr. Maddox again, I wanted him to know that I did try my best to keep the historical facts correct as promised. From the shell of a neglected building all those years ago, now stands a proud and fine example of a historic plantation home. It is open for tours, and I highly recommend a visit.

To my friend, MaryChris Bradley, there are no words that can express my deep gratitude for all your help and wisdom. Without you, this book would still be sitting on my computer.

I would also like to thank the fine people I met at Lafitte's Blacksmith Shop, located on Bourbon Street. It was because they were always willing to talk about the building and its history that I was shown "the writing on the wall." May I suggest if you are ever in New Orleans, that you visit this bar, and be sure to tell them I sent you.

Ask to see the writing and the Lovers in Stone. I won't put a spoiler here; let us just say you will understand when you read the story. It is guaranteed to give you goose bumps.

Finally, with all my heart, thank you to Jean Laffite and Tori, for letting me tell their story and for never letting me give up. Together, we somehow always found a way to validate the historical events that unfolded in your epic adventure. I shall always miss your voices, your laughter, and you. It was hard saying good-bye, and it was not until I found myself typing Jean's good-bye that I could finally let go.

"Tommy's Song" by Goldillox, is available at: Spotify, Amazon, Google Play, eMusic, Simfy, Deezer, Rhapsody, X-Box Live, MixRadio, MUVE Music, and other music sites.

About the Author

D.S. Elliston currently lives in Florida. Most days will find her in her office, accompanied by her two cats who love to play in her numerous piles of notes. She admits she loves the long hours of compiling research material and historical facts for her projects.

Legends of NOLA is a multi-book saga. Her writing goal is to thoroughly entrance the reader to such a point, that they don't realize they are receiving a history lesson.

All her books are fiction based on fact and leave many wondering if the adventure they read actually happened or not.

Made in the USA
Monee, IL
10 December 2023

48788749R00233